Lindos Retribution

John Wilton

*For Karen,
Hope you enjoy it.
John xx*

ISBN: 978-1-326-62620-4

Copyright © 2016

All rights reserved, including the right to reproduce this book, or portions thereof in any form. No part of this text may be reproduced, transmitted, downloaded, decompiled, reverse engineered, or stored, in any form or introduced into any information storage and retrieval system, in any form or by any means, whether electronic or mechanical without the express written permission of the author.

This is a work of fiction. All names and characters are the product of the author's imagination and any resemblance to actual persons, living or dead, is entirely coincidental.

PublishNation

www.publishnation.co.uk

Acknowledgement

A big thank you to all my very good friends in Lindos, who gave me the idea for this story, and inspired and encouraged me to get on and write it, particularly Jack Koliais. Needless to say, this story is total fiction, but the magical village of Lindos, and its people, is just that – a magical paradise.

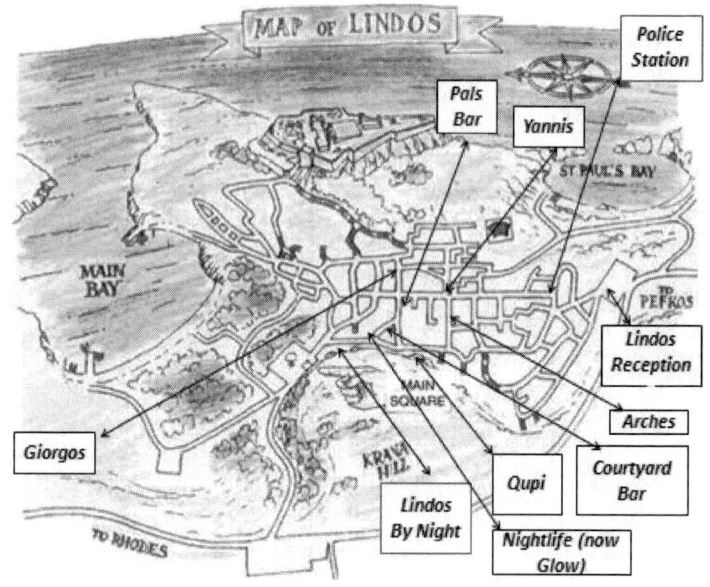

CONTENTS

Part One: Lindos 2004

    1 St. Paul's bay – weddings and a body   1

    2 June rain and an animated Russian conversation   4

    3 The victim   13

    4 The Courtyard Bar   22

    5 The 'busiest' ex-pat   30

Part Two: Secrets of the past

    6 Friends with everyone, friends with no one   40

    7 Old friends, comrades, lovers and killers   47

Part Three: Saturday

    8 An expert murder?   56

    9 A murder epidemic   61

    10 Two passports   68

    11 A busy Saturday afternoon and evening of interviews and interrogation   73

    12 The Lindos By Night Albanian barman   86

13	Chlamydia?	94
14	"Everyone is cheating, and no one likes each other, but reasons for murder?"	107
15	Deborah Harris and a different Carpenter	123
16	Saturday night outside Pals	133
17	Sunday Morning	143
18	Carol Hudson and Alan Bryant?	155
19	Deborah Harris, Dawn Parsons or who?	169
20	Tom Carpenter and Prague 1989	184

Part Four: Secrets of the past II

21	Prague 1989 – "One of you will die"	195
22	Moscow, early May 2004	200
23	Giorgos, Lindos June 2014	204

Part Five: Truth, retribution and mistaken identity

24	Radischev and Carpenter or Carpentar	209
25	A beginning in magical Prague and Vienna, an Amphitheatre ending in Lindos paradise	229

Part One: Lindos 2004

1

St. Paul's bay – weddings and a body

"Stop, stop the boat. There's a body, a body below in the water," Sue Thompson yelled as the little tourist filled Glass Bottom Boat glided sedately into picturesque St. Paul's bay.

For the past ten years Sue had been coming to work each summer on the Glass Bottom Boat that took tourists on trips for an hour from Lindos Pallas beach to a couple of the bays down the coast. As well as observing the underwater life through the boat's glass bottom the punters also got to swim off the boat in what had become known as Navarone bay on account of some scenes from the movie 'The Guns of Navarone' being shot there in the nineteen-sixties.

Sue was a blonde in her mid-thirties and originally from Cambridge in the U.K. Her regular summer activity on the boat from early May to mid-October kept her five foot five inch body tanned and trim. The constant jumping on and off the boat as it moored at various quays gave her legs a well-toned muscular look. Her personality was perfect for her summer job. She was outgoing and friendly to all the tourists she met, and not just those on the boat trips. Indeed, many returning holidaymakers, particularly families with young children, made a point of ensuring they took their annual Glass Bottom Boat trip specifically to see her.

The other bay the boat trip visited was St. Paul's, where the apostle of that name was said to have landed sheltering from a storm in AD51. On the edge of Lindos village it was a very beautiful setting with a small chapel that made Lindos one of the most popular places in the world for weddings. Some people claimed it was the second most popular. One way or another what was sure was that the wedding industry was a thriving and expanding one in Lindos, and the wedding parties with their many guests were a growing and key source of income for the bar and restaurant owners.

Lindos itself had been successfully fortified over the centuries by the Greeks, Romans, Byzantines, and The Knights of St. John during the period when they were defeated and expelled from Jerusalem, as well as by the Ottomans. Looming over the village with its white walled houses and apartments was the Acropolis, parts of which dated from the fourth century BC.

As the first Glass Bottom boatload of twelve tourists entered St. Paul's bay on that start of June Friday morning, they, and in particular Sue Thompson, made a scary discovery. The entrance to the bay was between two fairly high rock cliffs about thirty metres apart. When the boat entered the bay Sue took up her usual position at the bow, ensuring all was clear ahead as it moved slowly into the shallow bay, and making the boat owner at the helm, Michalis Kostas, aware of any swimmers in the water ahead. That morning she immediately noticed a large pool of dark liquid on the surface of the water about twenty metres ahead. Ignoring it for a moment, thinking it must be just some liquid that one of the other boats had inadvertently discharged into the bay, Sue moved back amongst the tourists in the centre of the boat by the glass floor panel ready to give her brief spiel about what could be seen on the sea bed in terms of fish, plants and the many different colours. After a further minute or so though, as the boat drifted further into the bay, the colours on the sea bed the tourist passengers and Sue observed were completely infused by the liquid, which it was now clear was a dark crimson. Realising it was blood, and a lot of blood, she gasped in horror. Then through a brief gap in the stream of blood she saw what appeared to be a body and let out a loud high pitched scream that was soon accompanied by a similar reaction from four of the women passengers who had been peering through the boat's glass panel at the sea bed.

The body was that of a man and had obviously been weighted down with something. It was lying face down on the sea bed a few metres below. The blood was coming from a wound in his neck and into the clear blue sea of the bay.

Sue's initial scream was followed by her shout to Michalis Kostas of, "Stop, stop the boat. There's a body, a body below in the water."

2

June rain and an animated Russian conversation

"Bloody rain, unbelievable, the fifth of June, this just doesn't happen here, never, never in June, maybe in early May some spots or for ten minutes, but not in June, not in Lindos." Tom was loudly voicing his exasperation for all to hear in Giorgos, and he had an audience of plenty of tourists who had been forced to savour their cappuccinos and eat their mid-morning breakfasts inside the café bar because of the unusual downpour. It was the torrential, vertical stair-rods sort of rain that arrives with a vengeance and the volume of a full scale symphony orchestra, overpowering holiday cappuccino conversations but only lasting for ten minutes or so. Nevertheless, just when the tourist season was getting into full swing in the little Rhodian village rain was not what the many bar, café and restaurant owners wanted to see.

Tom had been a regular summer visitor to Lindos for eight years and was five weeks into his 2004 summer visit having arrived in the first week of May. This visit was different though. Previously he had come two or three times throughout each summer for one or two weeks at a time. This year he was staying for six months. He'd rented a small apartment in the centre of the village for the very reasonable sum, so he thought, of three hundred euros a month. It wasn't exactly luxurious, more very basic typical Greek holiday island accommodation. A small lounge, a double bedroom, a small basic kitchen and a bathroom with a shower but no bath of course, was to be his living space for six months that summer. "Plan A," as he told anyone curious enough to ask just what he was doing there for the whole summer, was to, "write his novel in the mornings and go to the beach in the afternoons."

Although he had made a start on his 'great novel', Plan A had been adjusted a few times already due to an excessive intake of alcohol the previous evening and into the early hours of the morning in the many bars and the three nightclubs in the village – Nightlife, Qupi and Arches. Consequently, those mornings had been lost in an alcohol fuelled sleep haze from which he only surfaced around one or two o'clock in the afternoon for a very late breakfast, usually at Giorgos, This was one of those days, although he was late breakfasting slightly earlier than usual as it was only twelve-thirty.

The Englishman was fifty-eight and after many years telling his friends he was going to take a six month sabbatical from his job as a lecturer and write a novel on a Greek island he had finally taken the plunge. His son, Jim, and his daughter, Karen, were less than enthusiastic over their father's plan initially. For them both it was, "a classic airy-fairy academic dreamland," as Jim had put it, although at thirty-four and thirty-eight years old they had their own lives and had come to accept what their father wanted to do.

Tom's university head of department had been a little more understanding, not least because it was university policy for academics to be allowed to take a semester sabbatical after ten years employment and Tom had been there for eighteen. The aim of the policy was for individuals to undertake academic research and publish articles based on their findings. Tom, however, had deliberately developed a research project proposal and conveniently omitted to mention that his real intention was to write a novel.

His academic specialist area was Eastern Europe and the former Soviet Union, and he had been one of the few western academics in Prague in November 1989 at the time of the Czechoslovak 'Velvet Revolution'. It was during that time that he had experienced his last great romance, with not one but two Czech women, Dita and Jana. As usual he had made the wrong choice romantically in initially pursuing and having a relationship with Dita. By the end of 1989 though, and the culmination of the 'Velvet Revolution', he'd rapidly realised he was in fact in love with Jana. Consequently he ended his relationship with Dita, but at that time couldn't bring himself to tell her best friend, Jana, just how he felt about her. By chance over four years later he had met Jana in Prague and resolved to tell her the way he felt about her one night over dinner. By then, however, it was all too late. Before he could tell her how he felt she told him she was about to marry one of her close friends from the 1989 revolution student dissident movement, Jiří Kaluza.

Tom had met him a few times during the 'November days' of the revolution and for a number of reasons was always very suspicious of him. At times back then he'd actually thought he may have been a StB informer, a Czech Secret Police agent who had infiltrated the student dissident movement. For one thing he seemed to know an awful lot about what the StB and the Czechoslovak ruling communists at the time were up to, and usually very quickly after events occurred during those 'November days' in 1989. On a number of occasions it seemed like he was deliberately spreading false information and rumours in order to mislead people and create confusion. In fact, Tom carefully questioned Jana once about how he knew so much about the activities of the StB, and so quickly after events that had occurred, but she just dismissed it without showing any concern by simply pointing out that there were lots of rumours and information circulating throughout Prague at that time within the dissident movement.

In the end the Englishman just put his suspicions down to his jealousy of the seemingly close relationship between Jana and Kaluza, even though, in answer to one of his questions about Kaluza, Jana had once told him that Kaluza had asked quite a bit about Tom during that period, including about his relationship with Dita and where he was staying in Prague at the time. It wasn't exactly the safest time for foreigners to be staying in Prague, especially if they were staying with Czech nationals as Tom was, staying at Dita's apartment for the whole of that autumn of 1989. In some subsequent enquiries held by the new post-1989 Czechoslovak government following the revolution it was found that the student dissident movement had indeed been infiltrated by some StB agents and informers. Nevertheless, by the time Tom met her again over four years later Jana appeared blissfully happy that she was with Jiří Kaluza and was about to marry him, and despite his suspicions Tom had no evidence whatsoever that he was linked to the StB back in

1989. As a result he never really raised it in any direct way with Jana when they met over four years later.

It was that experience with Jana, as well as his shortcomings in terms of sustaining a meaningful relationship, that had put him off any sort of romantic involvement since. He had kept in touch with Jana through the odd email three or four times a year to exchange their news. She was now a happily married woman it seemed, living in Prague and she and Jiří had two young children, a boy and a girl. Jiří was now working for Price Waterhouse in Prague as an accountant. In his last email to her two months previously Tom had told Jana he was finally getting to do what he had wanted to do for many years and spend the summer in Lindos writing his novel, although as yet she hadn't replied.

He had been divorced for twenty-three years now, and although there had been some romantic entanglements between his divorce and his Prague disaster, nothing had survived the test of time. He still held some feelings for Jana, but had long given up on anything developing between them. Indeed, whenever he thought about it a small smile crept across his face, wondering if she'd even recognise him now ten years on. His height hadn't changed of course. He was just over six foot, but he was definitely wider and had gained a few pounds around his waist, around half a stone in weight at least. His fair hair was thinning and turning grey in places. Also, he'd grown a beard. Not one of those big bushy ones so popular with some Greek men, but nevertheless one that covered a fair part of the lower half of his face. This was also turning grey at the edges in sympathy with his hair. Anyway, it was all too late now to be hoping for, or pursuing, any long term relationship and he had consigned himself to being contented with a long summer in Lindos.

Giorgos always did a good daytime trade, particularly around lunchtime, and the customers were multinational. During the day the tourists came from Rhodes town on the day trip boats or on the multitude of coaches, and the little café bar got more than its fair share of custom then for drinks, coffees and basic lunches. Tom always reckoned it did the best English breakfast in Lindos, although no doubt many of the other cafes and bars would challenge his assessment. You could often hear French, German, Italian and increasingly Russian, as well as English, being spoken amongst the customers usually sat at the tables outside the café bar when there was no rain as they tucked into their lunches while watching the hordes of fellow passing tourists weaving their way through the narrow alleyways of the village. Inside the café it was usually bright and airy as the sunlight streamed in through the open doors and windows, reflecting off the white plastic tables and chairs and the white walls. Three televisions throughout showed endless repetitive British news and sport, evidence of the origin of most of Giorgos tourist and ex-pat clientele.

The little village of Lindos was a maze of narrow alleyways between white-washed houses and apartments. In the very centre the alleys were flanked by shops seemingly completely overstocked with souvenir t-shirts, bags, linen and the obligatory soft toy donkeys. Lindos was famous for its donkeys, or Lindos taxis, as many of the donkey owners referred to them, and there were lots of the Lindos taxis. At times they gave some of the alleys a very distinctive smell as they left their deposits. An endless stream of donkeys, and their owners, did a good trade ferrying the tourists from the main square down to the small scenic Pallas Beach or up to the ancient Acropolis above the village. Equally, the guy who had the hardly envious job of sweeping up the donkey shit as he followed them from the village square to Pallas beach or to the Acropolis was also seemingly constantly employed dealing with the endless stream. The village itself was off limits to cars or any other vehicles except the small trucks that squeezed through the narrow alleyways, often scraping the walls each side, in order to make deliveries to the bars, cafes and supermarkets. Some of the residents often joked that you could always tell if you had too much to drink the night before if you woke up with whitewash dust on your arms from bouncing off of some of the walls of the narrower alleys.

Along with the shops, houses and apartments there were a myriad of restaurants and bars in the village. Each of them had its own particular characteristic and its own characters that frequented, worked in, or owned them. Most of them relied on summer season workers for staff. Peculiarly a good many of those were Albanian. All of the staff in the restaurants and bars had the Greek way of friendly service. Instantly you felt you were their friend. No doubt because of that, and the charm of the village itself, people returned year after year for holidays, which was precisely what Tom had done for many years before.

As well as the younger Brits who came to work for the summer in the bars, cafes and restaurants there were a good number, thirty to forty maybe, older Brit ex-pats. Most of them had come to Lindos regularly in the past when they were younger to work for the summer, had stayed and now lived in the village or just outside all year round. Whenever Tom entered into conversation with these older ex-pats he always felt that with some of them there was a sort of competition between them as to who could go back furthest in their recollections of when they first came to Lindos and what it was like. Those ones were always fond of telling the world, and whoever would listen without being completely bored with their 'I know the place better than you' attitude, about what used to be the best bar or the place for the best parties back in the 'stone age'. Of course, nothing now ever compared to what it was like then, nothing was ever as good as when they first came. Tom found the Olympic event of 'I've been here a lot more years than you' between some of them mind-numbing.

They were a mixed bunch ranging from mid-thirties through to late fifties in age. Like many village dwellers back in the U.K. they were never short of gossip and opinion. In fact, most of them thrived on the gossip, usually about their so-called ex-pat friends who they were never slow to stick a knife into verbally behind their back. Tom soon learned that most of them were at least two-faced, and some even three or four-faced, so he never trusted them or confided in them. He'd learned to steer clear as much as possible. He always said a polite hello, but decided more than that wasn't worth it with some of them. He could weigh up people quite quickly and that is precisely what he'd done, especially those who were never slow to tell him how well they were doing in their business but had 'short arms and deep pockets' when it came to buying drinks. He had bought one particular ex-pat about five drinks over a period of a couple of weeks when they first met that May before he realised he was never offered one in return, although that particular guy was never slow in voicing what he knew about the village and the people in it. Obviously that never extended to knowledge of how to buy someone a drink in any of the bars.

Tom decided from experience that the worst gossip, the most two-faced and the person never slow to stick the knife verbally into the back of her so-called friends, was Carol Hudson. In fact, that was her maiden name which she continued to use even though a few years previously she had married a Greek guy in the village. Quite quickly the Englishman had become aware that she really was a nasty piece of work, never slow to poke her nose into other people's business and spread gossip, much of which he found very malicious. She was in her mid-thirties Tom reckoned and quite tall and slim, with shoulder length dark brown hair and what he would describe as narrowed piercing eyes. Originally she was from the West Country in the U.K., which he concluded accounted for her parochial vindictiveness exhibited during the few conversations he'd had with her. To call them conversations was probably a misuse of the word though, as they generally consisted of her relaying some malicious gossip about one particular ex-pat or other in the village with whom she professed to be, "good friends". All in all she had a very high and mighty approach to anyone and everyone she came into contact with, linked to an over-inflated opinion of herself it seemed. Although in the short time since his return to Lindos that particular summer Tom had heard quite a few stories and gossip suggesting that she wasn't alone in sharing and inflating that opinion of herself, and it wasn't only her Greek husband that was doing the 'inflating'. On the few occasions he'd unfortunately been cornered in conversation in a bar with a couple of the ex-pats they were definitely not slow in repeating gossip that Carol certainly, "put it about," as one of them so eloquently described her sexual activities. It seemed that over the past couple of years she'd had a string of affairs and slept with at least three of the ex-pats. Apparently her latest on-going fling was with the one who Tom had bought all those drinks for without getting one in return, the similarly named Tony Carpentar.

Carpentar was in his mid-forties and was one of the leaders in the Olympic event of 'I've been here a lot more years than you and know a lot more about the village than you'. Although he claimed to have first arrived in Lindos at least twenty years previously he had only returned three years previously to spend the whole summer working for himself as a handyman and general odd-job man. Tom had labelled him and one of his mates in the village, Alan Bryant, who also claimed to have been coming to Lindos for twenty years, as the 'tourist crashers'. Basically, each week he had noticed they would hit on a new group of tourists, single women or families, it didn't really matter to them, and in regaling to them all the supposed wonderful places in the village that they believed were best to eat and drink at, the two ex-pats would gladly accept the tourists' offers to buy them a drink. Then they would move on to the next group, do the same and continue their virtual free night out. Tom had seen them do this time and again, even in the relatively short time over the few weeks since he arrived. Now, according to the rumours, Carpentar was not only getting his drinks bought for him by the tourists but was also getting his 'after hour's refreshments' from Carol Hudson.

While he eagerly tucked into his badly needed two fried eggs on toast and coffee it wasn't British voices that Tom heard in Giorgos this particular June morning though, it was a very firm sounding Russian one. When he took a quick peek just around the corner from where he sat in the little café he saw that the voice was being directed at two very large, well built, muscular, shaven headed guys in shorts and white vests that exposed their almost completely covered in tattoos arms. They were being subjected to a seemingly quite animated conversation with a considerably thinner older looking third man who was much more soberly attired in a blue Ralph Lauren polo shirt and light beige chinos, and who was doing most of the talking. All three sported expensive looking sunglasses, even though their table around the corner from Tom's was inside the café bar. Tom didn't speak or understand much Russian, although from his academic research he could recognise a very few bits when he heard it. Even though he was speaking quite softly, and the noise in the busy café made it difficult to hear, it was clear from the more soberly dressed man's waving hands and general attitude that he didn't seem exactly pleased with the two shaved heads. What's more it didn't seem like tourist chat, and wasn't really that much of a conversation. The more soberly attired man was clearly their boss and he was firmly giving them a complete bollocking, after which they paid their bill and all left almost immediately.

Five minutes later, while the Englishman was finishing his eggs and idly pondering on just what the Russians' deliberations had been about, his curiosity was rudely interrupted by another one of the more gossipy ex-pats, Joan Mayweather, bursting into the bar and proclaiming loudly across the café to the owner, although clearly for everyone to hear, "They found a body at St. Paul's bay this morning, in the water on the sea bed, stabbed they say."

3

The victim

"Do we have any identification? Who found the body?" As Inspector Dimitris Karagoulis and his Sargent, Papadoulis, strode purposefully down the steep hill towards St. Paul's bay he wasted no time quizzing the local Lindos police officer, Tassos Samaras. Samaras was born and bred in the little Rhodian village, but in all his thirty years, the previous eight as a police officer, he'd never known a murder there.

"Yes, the woman who first saw the body from the boat, Sue Thompson, says he is an Englishman named Tony Carpentar," he began to tell the Inspector. "She knows him from the village and said he is some sort of handyman who does odd-jobs for people in the village. Apparently he has been to Lindos many times over the past twenty years, or so she believes. He was here for the whole summer over the last two years, and that is what he was doing this year. She thinks he was forty-five years old. She vaguely remembers a birthday celebration she saw him having with some friends in a bar in Lindos in October last year and someone from the party of English people with him telling her it was his forty-fifth birthday. Also, she said something about his name, but I didn't really understand what she meant, sir. It was something about it being unusual because it was spelt with an 'a'."

Unlike Samaras, who was taller and considerably slimmer, and who obviously made an effort to keep himself fit, Karagoulis was a short, stout, bald-headed man, in his early fifties, with a small dark moustache etched across the top lip of his round face. He was based in the main police station in Rhodes town. As soon as the local police had informed Rhodes of the discovery of the body he had rushed straight to St. Paul's bay, driven furiously over the forty minute journey by Papadoulis. A dead body found in one of the main tourist resorts on the island, and a possible murder, was not good news, and not just for the victim. It wasn't good at all for the main source of revenue and income on the island, the tourist industry.

Even in his open necked shirt, and although it was only early June and nowhere near as hot as it would get in high summer, Karagoulis was already beginning to sweat as he made his way down the steep hill into St. Paul's bay and the waiting body that had now been removed from the sea bed. Clearly overweight, no doubt from his love of far too much Greek Mythos beer and moussaka, he was puffing for breath while mopping his face with his white handkerchief as the three policemen reached the bottom of the hill. Pausing briefly in order to compose himself he told the other two officers, "Leave this to me for now, I will talk to the Thompson woman. You and Papadoulis take statements from the boat owner and the tourist passengers who were on the boat, Samaras. That will give the forensic team a bit of time and then we'll see what they've have initially turned up anything."

Sue Thompson was sitting on the small wall by the jetty to which the Glass Bottom boat was now moored. She was still quite white faced and shocked at what she had seen, and was intermittently sipping from a small bottle of water. Removing a small black notebook from his pocket and a pen Karagoulis approached her and identified himself, taking a seat alongside her on the low grey stone wall.

"My colleague tells me you were the first person on the boat to see the body and that you know the victim. You must be quite shocked. Are you feeling okay enough to answer a few questions?"

"Yes, it is a bit of a shock." She paused for a moment and then added," I am not sure quite what else I can tell you that I haven't already told your officer, but yes I am okay to answer a few questions."

"Was he a close friend of yours, did you know him very well? Officer Samaras said you told him he is an Englishman that works in the village."

"No, he wasn't a close friend. I knew him because I have been coming to Lindos and working here for the past ten years and he has been here during the last two summers, working in the village doing odd-jobs and as a sort of handyman. Our paths have crossed occasionally in bars in Lindos in the evenings sometimes, but really it was just a case of saying hello. I can't say I've ever really had a conversation with him."

"So, you don't really know much about him?" Karagoulis prompted her.

"Well, my friends and I always made a bit of a joke about him because he was a bit of a carpenter and somewhat pedantic about his name, as well as definitely a bit of a handyman in every sense of the word it seemed. I tried to explain to your officer about the name, but I'm not sure he really understood what I was trying to tell him. Anyway, Carpentar by name and carpenter by trade was the way he always introduced himself to people, and he always made a point of saying it was Carpentar with an 'a', which is actually an unusual spelling in England you see."

"Sorry?" the Inspector interrupted, with a confused frown across his still leaking sweaty forehead. "What do you mean, pedantic, and I also don't think I understand clearly the relevance of this thing about his name being spelt with an 'a'?"

"Oh, yes, sorry, it was just that apparently he always made such a point of it every time he introduced himself in the bars in the village, especially to tourists, that's what I mean by pedantic. It was a bit of a standing joke amongst some of the British ex-pats, and just fitted his general boring personality. He'd say, 'the name's Carpentar with an 'a'', as if anyone really would be that bothered about the way his surname was spelt. It wasn't like they were going to write to him or anything, Inspector, was it?"

"Err ... no probably not I suppose, but, I'm sorry I'm still not entirely clear what do you mean about this spelling and his name thing?" Karagoulis prompted her again.

"Well, usually Carpenter is spelt with 'er' as the last two letters, but his name, as he was fond of continuously pointed out, is spelt with 'ar' as the final two letters, which, as I said, is unusual in England."

"Right, now I understand, but also what did you mean when you said Mr Carpentar was definitely a bit of a handyman in every sense of the word?"

"Only the usual gossip you hear in the village among the British ex-pats all the time about almost everyone, especially the Brits themselves, Inspector."

"And what would that be concerning this Tony Carpentar?"

"Well, he was always fond of telling everyone how well he was doing and how well he'd done in the past. It seemed he'd been here, there, and everywhere in the world and he was never short of an opinion on anything and everything, and never slow to voice it to anyone who would listen. He loved a captive audience it seemed. One of his friends, another ex-pat, Alan Bryant, and him were well known among the British community for regaling people, some would say boring them, with their profound knowledge on any subject, and especially Lindos. They were particularly fond of sounding off to the weekly British tourists about the village, the best places to eat and drink, and how long they'd been coming here."

"It sounds like you didn't particularly like him, Miss Thompson." Karagoulis prompted her again, feeling that she had drawn back a bit and was having second thoughts about repeating village gossip to a police officer.

"Oh, I wouldn't go that far. As I said, I never really knew him that well. I only heard those sort of things from other Brits who are friends of mine in the village."

"So, do you think he made any real enemies in Lindos? Do you think there is anyone who would want to kill him?"

"I wouldn't know about that. I have no idea. I don't think anyone would want to kill him just because he was a little full of himself, as we English say. After all I don't think you would want to kill someone just because they are somewhat boring and a bit pompous would you? That's hardly a reason is it?"

"No, I doubt that was the reason, Miss Thompson," the Inspector agreed, still mopping his forehead with his now quite damp white handkerchief. "Can you recall when you last saw him?"

"Last night, and he was with a British woman who lives in the village, Carol Hudson, in a bar that quite a few of the Brit ex-pats drink in, The Courtyard. Most nights Alan Bryant and him are in there…err…were, now I suppose. I guess if you talk to the guy who owns it, Jack, Jack Constantino, he'll confirm it. He's Greek, from

Lindos, so I suppose he must have a Greek first name but everyone knows him as Jack, and a lot of people just refer to it as Jack's bar."

"Do you remember what time that would have been by any chance?" Karagoulis asked.

"It must have been around ten I guess."

"And this woman, Carol Hudson, what do you know about her, Miss Thompson?"

"Carol? Oh, she's been here quite a few years, although she's not really a friend either and I can't really say I know that much about her. She's from somewhere in the west of England I think and she came here to work as a tour rep originally. Like a few British women in the village she ended up staying and marrying a local Greek guy, Panos Koropoulis, who works in one of the restaurants. She works in a restaurant too, but not the same one. But you don't think she had anything to do with this surely? Like I said I don't know her that well, but I'm sure she's not the sort of person to murder someone."

Although wondering just who the sort of person to murder someone actually was, if there was such a 'sort', the Inspector ignored that comment and carried on with his probing, "And what was this Carol Hudson's relationship with Tony Carpentar?"

"Just friends or passing acquaintances, as we say in England, I think, like a lot of the Brit ex-pats. It's a small village and most of the Brits know one another from drinking in the bars and cafes. I don't really know either of them that well, so I couldn't tell you any more than that."

She took another sip from the bottle of water and then added, "Actually I'm feeling a bit tired now, I guess it's the shock and from sitting here in this hot sun. Do you have any more questions or would you mind if I went back to my apartment now? I need to lay down for a while I think."

"Yes, of course, I understand," Karagoulis reassured her. "Thank you, you have been very helpful. Officer Samaras will take some quick details from you about where you are living in Lindos and a contact phone number in case we need to talk to you again. Just one final thing, I don't suppose you know where Mr. Carpentar was living in the village?"

"No, not exactly, I think he had a small apartment or a room towards the top of the village, past Socrates bar and up towards the police station, but I couldn't be sure. Jack from the Courtyard bar may know. He knew him much better than me."

"Okay, I am sure we can check. Thank you for all your help."

With that the Inspector headed towards the place on the jetty where the body had been brought ashore and the forensic team had cordoned off the area. One of them, the pathologist Crisa Tsagroni, was kneeling by the body and turned her head round as she heard him approaching in order to greet the Inspector with an ironic, "Well this is a nice start to a sunny morning, Dimitris."

She was a petite, slim attractive woman in her early forties, with dyed blonde shoulder length hair, that was clearly showing its black roots, tied back from her face. The Inspector had known and worked with her for four years, ever since she first came to the island from Thessaloniki to take the pathologist job in Rhodes at about the same time as he arrived on the island transferred from Athens. He'd taken a shine to her and had something of a soft spot for her, even though he was married with two kids. She was divorced, and had been for ten years she'd once told him, with no kids. The banter between them when their paths crossed at work betrayed something more than their mutual occupational respect for each other. There was definitely something else between them.

"Yes, not exactly the way I was hoping to start my weekend. I assume there is not much doubt about the cause of death? Any rough idea how long he's been dead or how long the body has been in the water?" Karagoulis asked.

"I'll have to do full examination later of course, but yes initially there doesn't seem much doubt about the cause of death," she confirmed. "In terms of age I'd say he was in his mid-forties. From the amount of blood in the water and the body temperature I would guess that he's been dead no more than three to four hours, but I'll have a clearer idea tomorrow. There are signs of a blow to the head, so it looks like he was knocked unconscious before he was killed and dumped in the sea. One other thing I can tell you now, Dimitris, is that whoever did this knew exactly what they were doing and precisely where to plunge the knife for maximum instant effect.

From the wound I'd say it was a three centimetre wide blade that was plunged into the right-side Carotid artery in the neck and he would have bled out and died within a minute or two at the most."

"That suggests he was attacked somewhere else, in the village perhaps, brought here unconscious, stabbed and dumped in the water from the jetty," Karagoulis speculated. "That would mean at least two people involved in order to move his unconscious body, and I presume that sack tied to the rope that was around his waist is full of rocks to weigh the body down and ensure it sinks?"

"Yes, although even then the body would have floated a little way in the bay before it actually completely sunk. We'll do a full forensic examination on the rope and the sack as well and see if we can come up with anything on them that might help, although they look fairly standard stuff. I can't really tell you much more at the moment, so, unless there is anything else, Dimi, I better get on trying to see what else we can find from the jetty area and sorting out this English gentleman's final trip to Rhodes town and our laboratory for the autopsy."

While Karagoulis was telling her, "Okay, I'll come and see you tomorrow morning for a fuller report," and simultaneously allowing a slight comforting smile to creep across his lips that always appeared when she used the shortened version of his name, Sargent Papadoulis, approached him.

"Sir, one of the English tourists on the boat says that she's pretty sure that she saw the dead man in a bar last night in Lindos, The Courtyard Bar. She's staying in the village on holiday, and says he was with a dark haired woman, and according to her they were very friendly, very close. The woman was wrapped all over him and practically sitting on his lap on a seat in a booth in the corner of the bar. She says it was quite dimly lit but she's pretty sure it was him, although she doesn't know who the woman was."

"How else did she describe her, this woman?" Karagoulis asked quickly.

"She said that even though they were seated she could see that she was quite tall, and slim. Her hair was dark brown, she thinks, although again she said the corner they were in was quite dimly lit so her hair could have been lighter. She heard the woman speak briefly, asking the man to get her another drink, so she said she could tell that she was definitely English."

Karagoulis' immediate conclusion was, "That sounds like it could be the woman that Miss Thompson has just told me about seeing him with in the Courtyard bar last night, a friend of Carpentar's she said, a Carol Hudson. Seems they were very good friends. I think we need to go and talk to her, but first we should find out where Carpentar was living and have a look round it. See if there is anything unusual. Then we need to go and pay a visit to the Courtyard bar when it opens and have a word with the owner, Jack Constantino. See if we can get any more background information on Tom Carpentar and this Carol Hudson, and what seems like their relationship. Let's ask Samaras if he knows anything about the bar, he's the local."

Samaras had just finished taking contact details and where they were staying from the remaining boatload of tourists, and informing them they could go now, when the Inspector approached him and asked about the Courtyard Bar.

"It's a nice bar, very popular with the British tourists, and the owner, Jack Constantino, is a very good host. He's from Lindos, and his family has been here for generations. He spent some time in America when he was younger I think, but the Courtyard has been open for nearly ten years and we've never had any trouble there or with Jack. I can't imagine he has anything to do with this."

"No, probably not, it's just something one of the tourists from the boat told us about seeing the victim in that bar last night with a British woman," the Inspector reassured him. "Have you ever come across a British ex-pat woman called Carol Hudson? It seems she came here as a tour rep a few years ago and stayed, and is now married to a Greek guy in the village, Panos Koropoulis, according to the Thompson woman from the boat. She said Carol Hudson and the victim were just friends, but according to the woman tourist she saw them heavily entwined in one another in the Courtyard Bar and looking like a bit more than just friends."

"Can't say I've ever come across Carol Hudson or her husband," Samaras told him. "But a lot of British girls come here to work for the summer when they are eighteen, nineteen or twenty, and of course they meet a Greek guy here and convince themselves they are in love with them and that the Greek guy feels the same. The Greek guys have a different girl every summer though, and some of them every week. It's what's referred to here as the 'Shirley Valentine syndrome'. So, some of the British girls end up staying and living with or marrying the Greek guys, but some of the guys never change. You see them out in the clubs in the village at three or four in the morning, or later, after they've finished work in the bars and the restaurants. There are always groups of them, and most of the time their British wives and girlfriends are nowhere to be seen. They'll be at home in the village waiting for them, while their husband or boyfriend tells them he just needs a beer or two with the boys to unwind after work. For some of the guys though, it's never just with the boys. Old habits die hard, if you know what I mean, sir. Working in the bars and the restaurants are perfect places to meet the female tourists - British, Germans, Italians, Russians and others. The Greek girls would never put up with it. They know the place, Lindos, and some of the Greek men, too well. I've heard that a few of the British wives and girlfriends who live here get their own back though by putting it about and fucking other British ex-pat men who live and work here. Affairs and adultery amongst the British ex-pat community is rife if you believe all the gossip, although I think it's exaggerated myself. Although, apparently one particular British ex-pat woman is famous for it and has quite a reputation amongst the British community here, but I have never heard a name mentioned so I couldn't tell you who it is supposed to be."

Karagoulis stood listening to this intently, intermittently puffing out his cheeks at what he was hearing. As Samaras finished his somewhat graphic depiction of some of the relationships and life in the little Rhodian village he simply said, "Ok, that's very illuminating, Officer. We had better leave the rest of this here to the forensic team and head back to your station in the village to get some of the documentation on all this started. Can you find out where Carpentar was living? We need to check it over as soon as we can. Then I'll pay Mr. Constantino and his Courtyard Bar a visit for a little chat before it gets busy for the evening. What time does it open up?"

"Around six-thirty to seven usually," Samaras informed him.

4

The Courtyard Bar

Samaras had made a few calls to some of his contacts in the village that afternoon and after calling in a few favours had eventually located where Tony Carpentar had been staying. It was a typical small studio apartment off a courtyard in an old Lindian house towards the top of the village in the same street as the police station. The old Greek woman, who rented it out, along with three other studios in the house and courtyard, was very apprehensive and somewhat concerned when the police in the form of Samaras and Karagoulis turned up on her doorstep and introduced themselves. A look of horror came across her scraggy sun stained face when Samaras explained the reason for their visit. She instantly muttered something and made the sign of the cross across her chest.

Her answers to questions from Samaras and Karagoulis about Tony Carpentar were basic and pretty non-descript. She seemed much more concerned that the police might be interested in the way she collected her rent for the four apartments and what she actually declared to the Greek tax authorities, together with the fact that she had lost a tenant and would have to search for another one. Even though the two policemen constantly reassured her that the rent and tax issue was of no concern to them a permanent worried expression etched across her face. Whether it was her preoccupation with that, or actually the fact that she really didn't know him that well, she didn't have much to tell them about Tony Carpentar. Apparently he had only rented the apartment that summer having turned up in mid-April. He'd said he would be staying until the end of October. She thought he'd said that he'd rented a place the previous two summers in a house further down the village behind the Socrates bar.

As studio apartment was so small, it didn't take the two police officers more than twenty minutes to have an initial look round it. It was the usual old Lindian style room, with heavy dark wood basic furnishings and a small shower room off it at the back. In the corner was a two ring electric hob placed on the kitchen cupboards next to the sink. The place was pretty dingy and somewhat untidy, with clothes thrown on the double bed and over the back of the one chair. Karagoulis assumed it was just the usual guy's untidy apartment and having looked in the small chest of drawers and wardrobe, and around the place quickly generally, there didn't appear to be anything out of the ordinary.

"Okay, you had better get this place sealed off and get forensics to go over it thoroughly, although it doesn't look as though there is anything obvious here to help us," Karagoulis instructed Samaras.

The Lindos officer explained to the old woman owner what they needed to do, that a forensic team of two police officers would be turning up there immediately, and that under no circumstances was she to enter the room after Samaras and the Inspector left, and especially not try to clean it. She just seemed most concerned that she would not be able to immediately try and re-rent it out and consequently, would lose money. Samaras tried to reassure her that they would do what they had to do as quickly as possible and hopefully she would have her apartment back to rent out in three or four days. With that he made a call to the Lindos police station and another local officer turned up. Karagoulis left him and Samaras taping up the doorway to the studio apartment with yellow and black tape with 'crime scene, do not enter' written on it repeatedly, as he headed off to the Courtyard bar.

"Yes, they were sat over in the corner there in the booth. It's a quite dimly lit corner. He came in around nine-thirty I guess, and she showed up about fifteen minutes later. He was talking to a couple of foreign guys at the bar before she arrived. I thought I overheard them tell Tony they were from somewhere in Eastern Europe, although they didn't stay long and left just after Carol arrived. From what I could hear he was going on and on to the two guys about his favourite subject, Prague. Everyone knew he loved the place. Perhaps it was there that they were from? I don't really know, but they seemed to know the city. When Carol arrived she and Tony moved into one of the booths in the corner and the two guys left.

They were, to put it delicately, pretty friendly towards each other, if you know what I mean, but she only stayed for about an hour and was definitely gone by eleven. I remember that because that was when he came and sat at the bar, mentioned the time and ordered another beer. He drank that and was going to leave. That must have been between eleven-thirty and twelve. He said he was off to Arches, the club in the middle of the village, although he didn't actually leave straightaway and that is when it all kicked-off."

It was seven o'clock, early evening, and the Courtyard Bar had only just opened for the evening. It was still virtually empty, except for the tourist middle-aged couple enjoying an early evening cocktail in the fading sunlight at a table outside in the courtyard which gave the bar its name. Inside the bar was old style Lindian décor with its usual fair share of dark polished wood. The bar itself ran all along the length of the back wall, except for a few feet at the end where there was a doorway and narrow steps down to the toilets. At the opposite end was the music console, together with a larger and wider area with some tables and chairs and room for dancing, with stairs up to the open terrace. Jack Constantino was sat on a stool at the bar answering Karagoulis' questions on what the English woman tourist on the Glass Bottom Boat had told him earlier that day.

"Why do you think he mentioned the time, was he meeting someone later?" the Inspector asked.

"I've no idea, he never said. He just mumbled something like is that the time already, I think. Anyway, it wasn't the first time him and Carol have been in here being friendly to one another, and from what I've heard in the village it's not just in here that they were friendly, very friendly and close, if you know what I mean."

The Greek bar owner continued, emphasising the "very friendly and close" part of what he told Karagoulis, and simultaneously rolling his eyes and grinning. "I'm not sure what her Greek husband's reaction to all that would be, but it seems to be common knowledge in the village, especially amongst the Brit ex-pats."

Jack Constantino was a very convivial bar owner and host. Most of his customers were repeat ones who returned to Lindos, and particularly the Courtyard Bar, year after year and sometimes twice or three times a year. They spent a lot of time, and money, in his welcoming bar. It was particularly popular with families, not only because of its host but also because of the courtyard which made it perfect for them to sit outside the bar through the warm evening and still hear the music wafting through the bar's open doors. Some evenings there was live Greek music and dancing as Jack himself entertained the customers with his considerable various musical instrumental skills. He was a stocky, dark-haired, quite tall man in his early forties. Born and bred in Lindos he could relate many stories from his youth in the village in entertaining his customers. He'd also spent some time in America a few years before he married back in Lindos. Besides his bar, or maybe as well as is a better way of putting it, his passion was his music and he was a great fan of Cat Stevens, or Yusuf Islam as he now called himself. Jack would regularly entertain his customers with renditions on his guitar or bouzouki of the songs of his favourite musician.

The Courtyard Bar was also a popular late night watering hole for many of the Brit ex-pats, especially after the music stopped in all the Lindos bars at one a.m., as the local by-laws required. You could always get a late drink, sometimes a very late drink at three a.m. or later, in Jack's.

Registering Jack Constantino's earlier comment the Inspector prompted him with, "what do you mean it all kicked off?"

"It was just after Alan Bryant turned up, just before Tony was about to leave. One minute they were sat at the bar laughing and Alan was trying to persuade him to stay for another beer and the next Tony had him by the throat and they were shouting at one another. It caused quite a scene in the bar. We never have any fights here in the bar. Erik, my barman, who's a lot younger than me, tried to intervene but they started throwing punches at one another, not very effectively, and they fell off the bar stools as they wrestled each other to the floor. Erik and some of the other customers finally managed to separate them and after some more verbal abuse between them Tony stormed off still shouting at Alan as he left. Alan apologised to me and Erik, stayed for about twenty minutes and another beer and then he left as well."

"What were they arguing about?" Karagoulis asked.

"You had better talk to Erik. He was at that end of the bar serving another customer. I was at the other end of the bar serving. He's upstairs setting up the tables on the terrace. I'll get him."

Erik Hyka was a nineteen year old Albanian who was working in Lindos for his second summer. Two of his cousins also worked in bars in the village. As he emerged down the stairs with Jack Constantino he had a worried and concerned look on his face. Even though the bar owner had explained to him upstairs on the terrace precisely what the police wanted to talk to him about he wasn't exactly happy at being confronted by them. He had all the necessary papers and work permits. Jack had seen to that the previous year in the first summer he worked for him. Basically, he wouldn't employ anyone anyway who didn't have the necessary papers. Nevertheless, Erik was more than a little apprehensive.

"Did you hear much of what the two English guys were fighting about?" the Inspector asked him.

"It was over a woman. They were arguing over a woman. I didn't really hear how it started. I was busy serving some customers, an English couple, at that end of the bar where Tony and Alan were, and was just generally talking to them when the fight started. At first they were laughing and making some jokes quite loudly, about a woman I think, and then they just started fighting."

"What did you hear when they started fighting?" Karagoulis pressed him.

"It was Tony that was doing most of the shouting when the fighting started. He shouted at Alan something like, 'that's not fucking funny, you fucking keep away from her and stick to your own women', or something like that. I can't be sure and can't remember if that was exactly it, but it was something like that."

"Did you get any idea who the woman was that they started arguing about?"

"No, not really, only that at one point Tony was shouting 'isn't one fucking British woman here enough for you?' Most of the other customers were looking at them by then because you could hear them even over the music, and then Tony screamed at Alan, 'you've shagged most of the bloody Brit women in the village anyway, and probably even some of the donkeys and stray cats'. That's when

Alan threw a punch at him, but he ducked out of the way and the fight started. Some of the bar stools got knocked over and they both fell on the floor after Tony hit him in the face. I just jumped over the bar and tried to separate them, with the help of some of the other men customers in the bar. Once we managed to stop and separate them Tony stormed off still shouting at Alan as he left."

"What was he shouting then?"

"He just kept shouting over and over, 'you fucking keep away from her, she's with me", Erik added in response to the Inspector. "Then, as he reached one of the doors from the bar into the courtyard, he stopped, turned round, started pointing his finger at Alan and said quite slowly and much more calmly, 'or I'll fucking do you and you'll get seriously hurt, and I'll make sure a few husbands in the village know what you've been up to with a few of their wives'. It was quite nasty the way he said it. After Tony had left Alan ordered another beer and then he left about twenty minutes later."

"Did he say anything to either of you after Tony left? Did he say what it was about?" Karagoulis asked both of them.

"He just said sorry to me," Erik replied, and apologised to Jack. He said it was all a silly misunderstanding and tried to convince us that it was just because Tony was drunk. He wasn't though."

"He'd only had two beers," Jack added "After that Alan just sat quietly at the bar with his beer. He seemed okay, just a bit shook up I think. He wasn't cut on his face or anything, although I guess he might have had a bruise on his cheek, on the side of his face, the next day where Tony managed to land a punch. I don't think Alan actually managed to land a punch on Tony and, as Erik said, they both ended up wrestling one another on the floor. Alan had him in a headlock with his arm when we were trying to separate them."

"Have you seen Alan since?" the Inspector asked, directing his question specifically at Jack.

"No, but he usually comes in at least every couple of nights, often with Tony, and sometimes with some other Brit ex-pats or some British tourists, so I guess he may be in tonight"

"I've seen him," Erik interjected. "Well, I didn't actually see him, but I'm sure I heard him in the alley beside my flat later that night.

Well, I suppose it was almost early morning really. I finished work in the bar at around two and then went for a couple of beers in Qupi, the club in the alleyway behind the bar here. It was still dark when I got to bed. It must have been about four o'clock, but I couldn't sleep, as often happens after work. Anyway about half-an-hour later I guess I heard voices outside in the alley, a man and a woman's. They were arguing about something at first, but I couldn't hear what clearly. Then they stopped arguing and it sounded like they had become a lot nicer to one another, if you know what I mean. I heard him say 'pull your skirt up' and it sounded like they were shagging against the wall in the alley right under the window of my flat."

"How do you know it was Alan Bryant?"

"I heard his voice quite clearly because he was the one doing most of the shouting at first when they were arguing. He kept saying loudly three or four times, 'fuck him, you know you want to be with me'. He sounded a bit drunk and initially the woman only said, 'no, not now, not here'. But that was all I heard her say, and she spoke quite quietly. I guess she was worried someone in the apartments would hear them. There are quite a few tourist apartments along there. So, I couldn't say for certain who the woman was. She was definitely English though. I was really tired by then so must have just finally drifted off to sleep, and I certainly wasn't interested enough to get up and look through the shutters to see who it was. It was definitely Alan though, because I remember thinking that he couldn't have been that hurt by Tony in the fight."

"I don't suppose you have any idea where he is staying here? I think we'd better have a word with Mr. Bryant," Karagoulis said quite pointedly, adding, "and where is your flat here Mr. Hyka?"

"It's in the alley behind the bar here, just past Qupi nightclub on the right", the young barman told him. "I assumed Alan and the woman must have just left the club. I think he rents a room or a studio apartment for the summer somewhere up the top end of the village behind the Lindian House bar. That's what he told me one night if I remember right. He said he has been coming here for twenty years on one week or two week holidays, but this summer, like last summer, he was staying for five months from the start of May till the end of September."

"Thanks, you've both been very helpful. I'm sure it will not be difficult to locate him in a small village like this," Karagoulis told them. "Just a couple more things, do either of you know what Mr. Bryant is doing here for the whole summer? Is he working here? And what do you think Tony Carpentar meant by 'you've shagged most of the bloody Brit women in the village'?"

"No, I don't think he's working," Jack Constantino replied. "I think he's just here for the summer on an extended holiday. From what he's told me when we've talked in the bar he works in England through the winter and saves money to stay here through the whole summer. But your other question, there are obviously lots of rumours about affairs in the village, especially amongst the Brit ex-pats, but I couldn't really say exactly what he meant, and to be quite honest I find it is better as a bar owner here not to go repeating gossip. I guess you will have to ask Alan."

5

The 'busiest' ex-pat

As Dimitris Karagoulis made his way from the Courtyard Bar through the narrow white-walled alleyways of Lindos and back to the small police station towards the top of the village the many restaurants were just beginning to fill up with their evening tourist customers. It was approaching eight o'clock and the sun had gone down. It was still quite warm, although the slight breeze made it comfortable pleasant warmth. There were just three or four early evening drinkers in the bars he passed, the exception being Yannis bar in the centre of the village where all the outside tables and chairs in the bar's courtyard overlooking the small square were completely occupied and the place was buzzing with tourist chatter. It was the usual place for an early evening drink for tourists sat watching the world go by in the little Rhodian village before they moved on to one of the restaurants and their always good and tasty Moussaka's, Greek salads, Saganaki's and the like. The tragic events of earlier in the day at St. Paul's bay seemingly hadn't affected the tourist trade.

As Karagoulis entered the back office in the little police station Samaras was just finishing a phone conversation, while Papadoulis was staring at the screen of the one, fairly ancient looking computer and obviously trying to fill in some bureaucratic report forms about the murder.

Samaras instantly updated his Inspector with what he had found out. "I checked with the Rhodes local Labour Inspectorate office and Carol Hudson works at the Athenian restaurant, sir. I've also got an address for her from that, although it was last year so she may have moved. I've just spoken to the owner of the restaurant, Yiannis Katsouris, and he says she is working there tonight but last night was her night off. I told him not to mention to anyone, especially her, that I had called and that we would probably be in soon to talk to her concerning the murder at St. Pauls. He is a good friend of mine so I'm sure he will not tell her we will be coming in."

"Good, and we can manage without knowing where she is living at the moment," Karagoulis reassured him. We can get that when we speak to her, although given what we've heard so far about her and Mr. Carpentar, it is probably best not to do that at her home in case her husband is there. I'm sure she wouldn't want us to interview her in front of him."

"Also, according to the Lindos Town Hall Registry Office records for her marriage to Panos Koropoulis three years ago their address is the same one that the local Labour Inspectorate office in Rhodes has for her employment documents. She kept her own surname apparently, sir" Samaras continued.

"Okay, you had better come with me. It might be easier to get some time talking to this Hudson woman alone at her work if you know the owner well."

Karagoulis was a very experienced and skilled interrogator. He could be subtle and probing or brutally direct, and had learned expertly to weigh-up and read the person he was questioning, read their mannerisms and everything about them. He noticed every detail of their body language, the movement of their eyes and their head, as well as their facial expressions. Nothing passed him by, and he was fond of telling his officers that it was often what the suspects under interrogation didn't say, as much as what they did, that gave them away and revealed vital clues.

He had also developed a tendency to see everyone as guilty until proven innocent, not least due to the fact that he'd learned his trade as an officer in the worst areas of Athens, often dealing with some of the most notorious criminal gangs and the Greek mafia. However, he found himself transferred to Rhodes as a result of one particular investigation in the Greek capital that went spectacularly wrong. Although to this day he was adamant that he had done nothing wrong and was not responsible for the tragedy that had occurred, he had rubbed some of his superiors up the wrong way and dramatically burnt his bridges. He never spoke about it to anyone on Rhodes after he was transferred, even though his very good friend the pathologist, Crisa, had quizzed him about it on more than one occasion, even joking once that he must have done something really good to get a nice easy transfer to the sleepy island of Rhodes. In fact, he was presented with a stark choice at the time – leave the force or transfer to Rhodes. He opted for Rhodes, and after a relatively short period of adjustment over the first six months or so, had come to terms with the slower, more relaxed way of life and policing on the island. So much so that now, four years on, he much preferred his new easier life. Cases like the one he was now engaged on, murder, were extremely rare on the island, and certainly very much less of an occurrence than in Athens when he was working there.

The Athenian restaurant on the way to the small Pallas Beach was the usual three-storey or three tier Lindian restaurant with an inner ground floor and two open terraces up the wrought iron staircases. As the two police officers approached the stone arch entrance the young English lad in the doorway started to give them the usual spiel about how the restaurant had a wide and varied selection of traditional Greek dishes. Most of the restaurants in the village always had someone working on the door, or doorway, in order to try and entice or persuade the tourists to come into their establishments, and quite a few of them were young Brits working in Lindos for the season. Samaras couldn't avoid his usual slight smile whenever he heard one of them in an English accent talking to, or trying to talk to, passing tourists about traditional Greek dishes. On this occasion though, before the young English lad could get fully into his stride and rattle off something he no doubt said about a hundred times a night or more, Samaras interrupted him with, "Can you please tell your boss, Mr. Katsouris, that there are two police officers here to see him. He is expecting us."

Yiannis Katsouris was a tall upright man over six feet tall with thin greying hair and a small moustache that was also displaying his greying years. After Samaras introduced his boss the two policemen followed him up the first flight of wrought iron stairs. As they did so it was obvious that the constant walking up and down the stairs working in his restaurant had kept at bay for Katsouris the invading male Greek expanding stomach. He was slim, and for his age of approaching sixty seemingly very fit.

Reaching the top of the stairs he turned and pointed to a dark brown heavy wooden door saying, "You can use that small room to talk to Carol. I use it as an office. I'll go and get her." Turning specifically to face Samaras, he added, "As you told me, Tassos, I haven't told her you were coming or that you wanted to talk to her."

It was, indeed, a small room, no more than twelve metres square, with a small desk, three white plastic chairs and an old metal three draw filing cabinet jammed in one corner. The walls were completely bare and a very faded discoloured magnolia, except for one solitary small rather poor painting depicting what looked like Lindos bay hanging on the wall immediately behind the desk. When Carol Hudson arrived it was pretty cramped with the hthree of them in there, and not at all conducive to the habit Karagoulis had of pacing up and down while conducting an interrogation. Obviously though it was better and much more private than trying to talk to the English woman in the main restaurant area or the kitchen. Katsouris hovered in the open doorway for a moment, introduced the two policemen, and then left.

The Inspector went straight to the point. "We are investigating the death of Mr. Tony Carpentar. His body was found stabbed floating in St. Paul's bay this morning. I understand you were very good friends."

"Yes, I heard about it. In this village you hear about everything very quickly. It's very sad, but I'm not sure what it has to do with me or what you mean by very good friends? What gave you that idea?"

Her attitude was immediately very abrasive, and she shifted her position to sit up straight in the plastic chair with her arms folded across her body just below her chest. Karagoulis picked up her defensive attitude straightaway. It was clear to him immediately that she had something to hide and that the rumours he'd heard that day about her and Carpentar were almost certainly true. Although his feeling was that her defensiveness was more to do with her affair with the dead man than actually being involved in his murder. He decided quickly to be forthright and try and put her off-guard to see what her response would be.

"You seem a little agitated Miss Hudson. You do still use your maiden name, or should I call you by your married name?" He was letting her know that he was already aware of some of her personal background, and decided to plough on and be crystal clear about that. "I realise where you work may not be the ideal place to ask you about this, but I don't think you would want us to do this at your home would you?"

"No, no, I'm not agitated." She unfolded her arms and sat a little deeper in the chair, trying to appear calmer. "What do you mean by that? What makes you think I wouldn't want to do this at home?"

The Inspector wasn't going to let her off the hook so easily. "You were seen in a somewhat compromising situation, as it was described to us, with Mr Carpentar in the Courtyard Bar last night. In fact, two people have informed us of that, and we understand it was not the first time you and he have been, shall we say cosy, in there was it? Did you know that shortly after you left the bar last night he was involved in a fight with a Mr Alan Bryant? You know Mr Bryant very well too don't you?"

Karagoulis didn't really know how well or not she knew Alan Bryant, but he was fishing, clearly suggesting to her through his statement that he thought she was also having an affair with Bryant.

Her first response to that was another aggressive one. "It's none of your business what I do or do not get up to in my private life."

Karagoulis decided the best response to that was to become equally aggressive. "This is a murder enquiry Miss Hudson and what you were or were not up to with the victim makes it my business. Obstructing the police in a murder enquiry is a very serious charge. I'm sure you wouldn't want us to go down that route, would you?"

Her mood changed immediately. She leaned forward, rested her elbows on the desk and put her forehead in her hands. A couple of small tears started to trickle down her cheeks and her abrasive attitude evaporated like Ouzo vapour into air.

"What a mess, what a bloody mess," she started to say through her sobbing and sniffing. Samaras handed her a tissue from an open box on the desk, and after wiping her eyes and blowing her nose she confirmed what the two officers already knew.

"Okay, yes, I was having an affair with Tony, but I didn't bloody kill him. Yes I heard about the fight. Alan had tried it on with me a couple of times in the clubs here and he was always taunting Tony that he could get me away from him anytime he wanted."

"So, have you also slept with Alan Bryant? Are you having an affair with him too, Miss Hudson? Do you think Alan Bryant killed Tony Carpentar?"

Showing very little sympathy, the Inspector was determined to keep her off-guard. "After all, the fight they had in the Courtyard bar was over you so we've been told," which wasn't strictly true, as Karagoulis knew full well. Jack Constantino and Erik Hyka at the Courtyard Bar had both told him that they didn't know who the woman was that Alan and Tony had fought over. He was jumping to conclusions and trying his luck.

"Maybe it continued later and just got out of hand. People do stupid things when jealousy is involved. I guess that would apply to your husband, Panos, too though wouldn't it, Miss Hudson?" With that last comment he threw in another curve ball and her mind was racing all over the place, scrambled and unsure what question to answer first.

She plumped for dealing with the one that would cause her most problems at home. "My husband, no, Panos would never murder anyone, and I'm sure he had no idea about Tony and me. For God's sake, surely he doesn't have to know does he? I've been stupid."

Small tears were starting to trickle down her cheeks again as she added, "That would destroy my marriage and I certainly couldn't stay on in Lindos. You know how I would be treated here for this. Now Tony is dead surely Panos doesn't have to know about any of this does he?"

She was sobbing now quite uncontrollably, with her head in her hands and her shoulders shaking. Karagoulis was convinced it wasn't an act. Instead it appeared to be just an act of remorse for her marriage, although interestingly not one for Tony Carpentar's death. She was certainly a very selfish and self-centred woman.

"Yes, Mr. Carpentar being dead is very convenient for you I suppose," the Inspector taunted her again. "But how can you be sure your husband didn't know about your affair with him, and what about Alan Bryant? Do you have anything more to tell us about you and him? I ask you again, did you, or are you, having an affair with him too, Miss Hudson? Where were you between two and six a.m. this morning, and do you know where your husband was? We are going to have to speak to him you know. Where does he work? I think you would prefer us to interview him there rather than at your home."

She blew her nose into the tissue again and placed it carefully on the desk in front of her. Trying to compose herself she ran her hand through her hair sweeping it back off her face and gulped a couple of times before replying, "Panos works at Stefano's restaurant, but no, I am not having an affair with Alan Bryant. As I told you, he wanted me to and has tried it on a few times, but I've just kept turning him down. I don't think he liked it very much each time, but we are still friends, of sorts. He doesn't give up easily, Alan."

"It wasn't you having sex with him in the alley outside the nightclub, Qupi, about four o'clock last night then?" the Inspector interjected.

She looked a bit surprised as she replied, "No, of course not." The change in her voice betrayed her surprise and a somewhat incredulous indignation as elements of her previous abrasiveness returned. "I did go to Qupi," she continued, "and I did speak to Alan in there, but I only stayed for about half-an-hour and then I went home to bed by two o'clock. He told me about the fight, and I could see that he had a bruise on the side of his face. He said he wasn't going to Arches later as he often did, because Tony would be in there and he didn't want it all to start up again between them. I couldn't sleep after all that had gone on with Tony in Jack's bar and what he was saying to me, so I was still awake reading in bed when Panos came home just after three. I glanced at the clock when he came in. He said he'd been to LBN, Lindos by Night, for a beer with a couple of the guys he works with. It's a bar just along from Jack's, where some of the bar and restaurant workers go for a late drink after work."

In something of a change of focus and interest though, she added, "Are you sure it was Alan?"

"Sure what was Alan?" Karagoulis asked.

"Having sex in the alley by Qupi, are you sure it was him? I thought he told me in Qupi that he wasn't going to stay long because his face felt a bit swollen, so he was going to go home to bed soon."

"Well, one of the people we have interviewed told us they thought it was him, although they only heard what they thought was his voice and they never actually saw him. I'm not sure why that should concern you, Miss Hudson, if it wasn't you in the alley with him, but never mind that for now, how long just after three was it that your husband came home?"

Karagoulis pressed her, mindful that the pathologist, Crisa Tsagroni, had told him earlier that her initial estimate was that Tony Carpentar's body had been in the sea at St. Paul's bay for three to four hours before it was discovered just after nine that morning. If the pathologist's initial prognosis proved to be correct, and Carol Hudson was telling the truth, her husband would have been tucked up in his Lindian bed with her for a change when Tony Carpentar's body was dumped in the bay at St. Paul's, rather than her being tucked up in quite a few other men's beds in the village from what he'd heard so far. Of course, her husband could still have been involved in the actual murder, but it seemed unlikely unless he had an accomplice. Anyway, the Inspector would get a clearer picture of the timing of what went on, and the time of death, tomorrow from Crisa Tsagroni's autopsy report.

"Five past, five minutes after three," she snapped back at him. "I told you, I looked at the clock."

The Inspector decided to backtrack and ask what happened between her and Tony Carpentar earlier in the Courtyard bar.

"When you met Mr. Carpentar in the Courtyard bar last night what sort of mood was he in, what did he say in particular, what did you talk about? He seems to have been in a very agitated mood later with Alan Bryant."

"He was in a very good mood. For a couple of weeks he'd been trying to persuade me we should go away somewhere together, even if only for a weekend. He said he'd been talking to a couple of guys at the bar before I got there who said they lived in Prague. He wasn't sure if they were Czech, but he thought they were definitely Eastern European. In fact, he was still talking to them when I arrived and then we moved to the booth. He said he'd told them he'd been to Prague quite a few times and lived there for a short time, and I knew that because he was always going on about how it was a great and beautiful city, very romantic. So, he was full of it that night, going on about how wonderful Prague was and saying he wanted to take me there for a weekend soon. I told him that was impossible because of my husband. What was I supposed to tell Panos? This is a small village and if the both of us, me and Tom, disappeared for a weekend at the same time it would definitely be noticed and Panos was bound to be suspicious. Tongues wag here, amongst the Greeks and especially amongst the British ex-pats, even if a lot of the time there is no truth behind the rumours."

"Had you seen the guys he was talking to before?" the Inspector asked her.

"No, never, they were just tourists I guess, and they left almost as soon as I arrived. Jack didn't appear to know them particularly. He always seems to know most of his customers as most of the tourists are regulars. He usually gives the ones he knows a cheery goodbye. When those guys left though he didn't say anything I seem to remember."

She was much calmer now and Karagoulis decided there was little point in asking her anything more for the time being. He felt she'd probably told them all she knew and he'd already more or less decided it wasn't her that killed Carpentar. Glancing over at Samaras, who was leaning against one of the walls in the small room, he told her quite deliberately, "Well, I think it's time we had a word with Mr. Bryant, and unfortunately for you we will need to talk to your husband, probably tomorrow. I suppose that will give you some time to talk to him about all this. As I said before, this is a murder enquiry Miss Hudson and we have to interview everyone who could be implicated. Despite your opinion that your husband would never murder anyone, it would seem that he undoubtedly had a motive if he found out about you and the dead man."

She slumped back in the chair somewhat drained emotionally, gulped a little more and just gave a very slight nod of her head in acknowledgement of what the Inspector had said.

"So, we'll let you get on with your work here now, and you obviously have a busy and difficult night ahead of you at home. Goodnight Miss Hudson, we will probably need to talk to you again at some point, so don't go anywhere, don't leave the village until we say it is okay." With that Karagoulis motioned his head towards Samaras and the door, and quickly the two men left down the wrought iron stairs and out into the alley outside the restaurant.

Part Two: Secrets of the past

6

Friends with everyone, friends with no one

As Tom liked to put it, Dawn Parsons was friends with everyone and friends with no one. He had met her the previous summer on the first of his two one week holidays in Lindos that summer. When he returned in early May this year he found himself in her company quite a few times over the first few weeks, usually late at night or in the early hours of the morning in one of the bars or clubs. She said she was from Manchester, although her accent hardly betrayed that. It was quite refined 'Queen's English', posh at times, though there was definitely a north of England tinge to it with some words, but not necessarily Mancunian. She told him she had been living and working in restaurants and bars in Lindos for the past four years having decided to sell-up in England and pursue what she liked to refer to as, "living the dream in Lindos". In her mid-forties, shortish at around five foot four, she still retained what Tom considered a quite trim figure, no doubt the result of working up to ten hours a day on her feet as a waitress. Her shoulder length dark brown hair framed her somewhat chubby cheeked round face, which was still attractive when not suffering from the ravages of too much drink and a late night or early morning. It was one of those faces that always seemed to be about to break into a smile, and could certainly light up a room, except when she was angry, and then you really didn't want to be too near her face or any other part of her.

Each time Tom had bumped into her in one of the bars or clubs late at night after she'd finished work she was drinking like a fish, only quicker. Bacardi and coke was her favourite tipple, usually drunk at top speed. Maybe it was the late start – she never usually finished work until one a.m. – and she was making up for lost time, but the fizz had hardly gone off the top of the coke before the glass was half empty, sometimes completely empty. The numerous late nights and early mornings, plus the alcohol, were beginning to leave their calling cards through the increasingly dark supermarket sized bags often featuring beneath her brown eyes.

Dawn Parsons was not a person to suffer fools gladly, and was never slow in telling them. Tom had been on the rough end of her tongue on one particular occasion in the early morning after a long night's drinking when they were sat in the Arches club courtyard putting the world to rights. He had stupidly suggested that maybe she should not drink so quickly. The immediate scalpel like reply he suffered was a short, sharp, "Fuck-off! What's it got to do with you?" He never ventured that sort of advice again.

Despite that, he always felt there was some sort of connection between them, although he could never quite put his finger on just what it was, and indeed, whether it was just a connection on his side.

It was a strange kind of dance, a game, her and Tom played between them. Very seldom did she let her guard down and open up to him, and even when she did it was usually after she had a fair bit to drink. She had once told him, "She liked him very much and that no one made her laugh like he did." Although Tom reckoned many women thought that about him. They were, "friends, good friends," is what she also told him that particular night or early morning. It seemed she would go so far, and then draw back and go no further, like she was scared of exposing herself, or maybe her past, too much. She had never been married, but said she'd had a relationship for five years when she was twenty-one, but he'd become too possessive, so eventually she left him and had been on her own now for twenty years. She didn't have any kids.

Tom had never actually gone so far as to try it on with her. He had heard quite a few rumours in the village about her nocturnal relationships, not least with some of the ex-pat Brit married men. He dismissed most of them though as the usual village gossip. Although, as he told one of his visiting mates from the U.K, "A reliable source had told him that Dawn had definitely had a fling one night with Alan Bryant." Indeed, Tom had already heard one particular piece of ex-pat gossip that morning that suggested the fight between Alan Bryant and Tony Carpentar in the Courtyard Bar the night before was over Dawn rather than Carol Hudson, as most people seemed to believe. Maybe that was what had put him off going that extra yard and trying it on with her. "Bugger stirring his cold porridge," he told his visiting friend when relaying Bryant's supposed exploits with her to him, "especially given how much of numerous Goldilocks' honey shit has gone into his porridge in Lindos."

There was definitely more to Dawn Parson's past than she was letting on about. Some of the things she had told Tom, especially when she was savagely attacking the Bacardi bottle, just didn't fit. There were gaps, especially in the ten years before she came to Lindos. She said she had gone to university at eighteen and got a degree in computer science, but there was not a lot after that she had told him about, except for her five year relationship. Apparently, the guy involved worked for some security company. She had told him nothing though about the time between when she was twenty-six, and her relationship ended, and when she was forty-two and moved to Lindos four years previously. He'd asked a few times out of curiosity, but she'd always changed the subject. Where she worked during that period? He had no idea, except that he vaguely recalled her telling him one alcohol blurred night that she had lived in the West Country and then London. Gloucester, he thought, but he wasn't sure, the alcohol saw to that. Anyway, it was somewhere down that way, but his good friend Jack Daniels had clouded his memory far too much.

She was walking past Giorgos and saw Tom inside through the now re-opened doors on that particular June Friday morning just after the rain had stopped and the agitated Russians had left. She told him she was on her way to one of the little supermarkets in the centre of the village to get some cigarettes. She smoked like a chimney, one after the other when she was Bacardi-ing. She was always going to give it up, but never had the willpower to do so, and the cheap price of the cigarettes there didn't help. The same could be said for her alcohol intake, she often remarked.

"Can you order me a coffee, white no sugar please. I'll be back in a couple of minutes after I've got my fags," she shouted in to him.

When she got back Tom started to fill her in about the morning's events in St. Paul's bay, and then the agitated Russians she'd just missed. Strangely, although she knew Tony Carpentar she was much more interested in, and curious about, the agitated Russians.

"Are you sure they were Russians?" she interrupted him.

"Yes, definitely, can't mistake that language. I've been to Moscow quite a few times for work, remember. What about Tony's murder though? Aren't you shocked?"

"Yes, of course. Any gossip about what happened? Was the body in the water or on the beach? Any rumours about who might have done it? He had that fight in Jack's with Alan Bryant last night you know."

"Yes I heard, but do you think Alan might have killed him over that? I can't believe that, and anyway, I heard it was over a woman and that Tony started it."

Tom was probing. He had his suspicions about Dawn and Alan Bryant at different times, and he'd heard the gossip, but she wasn't responding to that.

"I don't know anything about the two of them and a woman, but no, of course I'm not suggesting Alan killed him," she replied in a somewhat agitated manner. "In any case, everyone knows about Tony and Carol Hudson, but I've never heard anything about her and Alan. Jesus, this place is getting a bit scary, what with this murder and the Russians."

"The Russians?" Tom was nonplussed. "Why are you so concerned and fixed on them?"

"No reason, just curious. In this place the smallest thing out of the ordinary seems like a major event." She was rapidly backtracking and playing down her interest in the Russians now.

Tom just couldn't relate to the way she had linked the two things, or even elevated one above the other – the wrong one, as he saw it. "The smallest thing...seems like a major event," she'd said. What, compared to a dead body found in the sea in St. Paul's bay? An odd way of looking at it, he thought. He knew from experience that she was pretty erratic and certainly at times a conundrum, especially after a few Bacardis. "A riddle wrapped in a mystery inside an enigma," he recalled was the way that Churchill had once described Russia? Given her current obsession with some agitated Russians in Giorgos he reckoned that description fitted Dawn Parsons perfectly. Although, comparing a verbal altercation between some Russians with a murdered body at St. Paul's bay was somewhat eccentric and bemusing even by her standards.

She wasn't letting it go though. She was like a Jack Russell terrier with its teeth deep into a cornered rabbit and she continued to shake it like a rag doll. In this case though it was Tom who was the cornered rabbit and she seemed determined not to let go until she got every last miniscule of information about the Russians out of him.

"What were they like these Russians? Do you think they were just angry tourists having a moan to the tour rep?"

"No, they definitely didn't seem like tourists." He tried to loosen her jaw-like grip on the subject by feeding her all he'd seen and heard. "It seemed to me that one of them was some sort of boss of the other two. He was quite smartly dressed and nowhere near as well-built as them. They were dressed like a couple of goons in their tight white vests, shorts and bulging muscles."

Her jaws were still firmly clamped around Tom's leg though, and showing no sign whatsoever of loosening. "Wonder what they're doing here? Did you understand any of their conversation?"

"Not really," he replied, "only that the boss man seemed pretty pissed off and angry with the two goons. From the very few bits of Russian I recall it sounded like they'd fucked up some job or other they were supposed to do for him. I caught the words 'Ne mozhete' and 'vy pravil'no', which I think in English is something like 'you' and 'nothing right', but I can't be completely sure, and at one point I thought I recognised the word 'brat', which means 'brother', but I couldn't really make a lot of sense of it to be honest."

A puzzled look engulfed her tired face, followed quickly by what he had come to recognise as her expression of apprehension. She bit the inside of her mouth, or at least appeared to be almost chewing it. It was usually a sign that she was thinking something over. He had seen her do it quite a few times before, usually when conversations between the two of them appeared to be approaching the subject of relationships, and especially when she was pissed. He had no idea why she was doing it now though over three Russians. So, he just decided to try again to move the conversation on and change the subject.

"Drink later after you finish work? Meet you in Jack's about half one?" he suggested.

"Err...yep, sure." She still seemed preoccupied in her mind with the Russians though. "Not Jack's though, not there tonight, and I need to see Deborah first so it may be nearer to two. Let's meet in LBN."

Like Jack's Courtyard bar you could always get a very late drink at LBN, the Lindos by Night bar. British ex-pat youngsters working in Lindos for the summer, other foreign workers and some of the Greek and Albanian bar and restaurant workers usually met up there after work around two for a drink often before decamping to one of the clubs in the village.

"Why don't you just text Deborah to meet us at LBN at one-thirty and then we can have a drink and all go clubbing if she fancies it?" Tom suggested.

Deborah Harris had also been living and working in Lindos for four years. Her and Dawn were good friends and appeared very close. Like Dawn Parsons though, whenever Tom had been drinking with her, or with the both of them, Deborah never really talked about her past, even when he probed and asked. Each of them just dismissed his questions most of the time with very vague answers or changed the subject completely.

All he knew about Deborah was that she was in her mid-fifties and had once told him she had a quite high-powered job and background in finance back in the U.K. before she quit it and decamped to Lindos. Just like Dawn she had visited the village and stayed there on holiday many times before she moved to live there, so she knew the place and quite a lot of the people very well. Maybe because of her previous employment and career, she never seemed short of a bob or two.

But even though Tom knew Deborah quite well and thought of her as a friend, a feeling he felt was reciprocated, Dawn wasn't having any his, "Let's all meet at LBN at one-thirty idea."

"No, I need to talk to Deborah briefly in private about something, Tom. Women stuff, you know, so let's make it at two at LBN," she told him.

He certainly didn't really know, but he did know from experience that trying to persuade Dawn otherwise once she had set her mind on something was pointless. "Alright, no problem, see you both at LBN at two, assuming Deborah wants to come out."

"Good, see you there. Now I had better get on, I've got some things to sort before I get ready for work," she told him as she gulped down the rest of her coffee, stubbed out the remnants of her fag and hurried off after giving him a quick kiss on the cheek.

"Hmm … just another bizarre Lindos day," he muttered to himself.

7

Old friends, comrades, lovers and killers.

"There are just a lot more Russian tourists here now. I don't know why you are getting so worried. Just bloody calm down, and be careful what you're saying anywhere. You never know who is listening. So they were Russians, it doesn't mean they were looking for us. Why would they be after all these years? It was almost twenty years ago for Christ's sake, Dawn, and it was a different world then. The 'Wall' was still up and the bloody Russians occupied half of Europe. Now they just invade it in their tourist hordes."

Deborah Harris was firmly trying to reassure Dawn Parsons over their first drink of the night after work. It was just coming up to one-thirty a.m. and the two women had agreed to meet in the Lindian Bar after Dawn's text that afternoon. The inner bar had a magnificent wooden Lindian carved ceiling, but they were sat in high-backed wicker chairs in the garden outside at the back of the bar. Four tables away the only other people in the bar, a group of two tourist couples, were chatting away in English over their final drinks of the evening. As it was gone one a.m. the music in the bar had stopped and most of the customers had left.

"It's just that Tom said it seemed like they were having an animated conversation in Giorgos and the better dressed one was giving the other two a right bollocking. From his limited Russian he reckons it sounded like the two men were being given shit by the other guy, who Tom said seemed like their boss, over something they should have done but fucked-up." Dawn was trying to justify her anxiety and was clearly still not totally reassured.

"What does that mean? Nothing, it means nothing, and it certainly doesn't mean they were looking for us. Why should they be? In four years since we left the agency no one has even remotely bothered us here with our new identities. What happened, what we did, is in the past. It belonged to a different world of twenty years ago. Back then people had to be killed. People on the other side, and who knows, people who played for both sides. We did what was necessary, sometimes what needed to be done. We did what we did for our country. It was the world we inhabited then. Yes, that meant disposing of Russian spies, but also even some of our own. The Russians did just the same. It was a dirty, bloody awful game, but we chose it, and we decided to get out when we did. We were good, bloody good, but the time was right to get out and start new lives after the fall of the Wall and the collapse of the Soviets. We talked it through remember, and the agency talked it through with us. That extensive de-brief and the new identities training over three months. It was our choice to come here to Lindos and start anew. We were told they could never guarantee we would always be completely safe forever, but the likelihood of anyone ever finding us is practically zero. You're just being paranoid again. You always do every time you hear a fucking Russian voice in the village. Well dear, you had better get used to it. There are going to be plenty more of them around here this summer and in future summers. They've got money now. Lots of money, and more and more of them are travelling and are into tourism. And let's face it the Greeks aren't going to turn them away are they, they want the money."

Deborah was leaning forward in her wicker chair now and almost whispering close to Dawn's face, although in a very firm manner. She gave her one more clear whispered reassurance as she leaned over even closer towards Dawn's chair.

"Look, I've told you before, not every Russian voice you hear in Lindos is ex-KGB or Russian Foreign Intelligence Service, SVR, or whatever they call themselves these days. In fact, I'm sure none of them are, not unless they happen to be here on holiday with their family. So stop worrying, they are not looking for us and they aren't here. Just because bloody Tom overhears an agitated Russian guy giving shit to a couple of what are probably his tour guides who fucked up doesn't mean they are KGB, or ex-KGB looking for us. As I said before, why should they be, and why now after all this time?

Now, let's go and meet him at LBN before he gets too pissed, and don't for Christ's sake mention the Russians or ask him about them again. He's not stupid. He'll start to get curious and wonder why you are so fixated on them. Just concentrate on your Bacardi glass girl. You're good at that."

Dawn Parsons still wasn't completely reassured by Deborah's comments. So much so that she blurted out one further bout of paranoia.

"But I'm sure someone followed me home last night after work."

Deborah Harris was not someone to mess with. Some of the people who worked with and for her in MI6 were never slow in describing her as a "right bastard," although her senior officer, her boss, often described her as a "brilliantly clever woman." She was always forthright and never liked to be doubted, something she had made quite clear right from the start when she was Dawn's boss and Staff Officer, and later her Station Head in Vienna. She was tall at around five feet ten, and even taller in the heels she loved to wear, even over the Lindos cobbles, giving her the air of a quite powerful individual. Slim, straight-backed, with shoulder length dark black hair, and always impeccably dressed, she cut an imposing figure. She had made many friends in Lindos over the last four years and worked some evenings as the front of house person at one of the village's best restaurants. Unlike Dawn, she was not the subject of endless gossip amongst the ex-pats in Lindos about her and men. She kept her distance, no doubt because of her past, again unlike Dawn.

Now she tried a slightly softer, even more reassuring approach to Dawn's latest concern.

"More paranoia, that's all that is. You heard all that stuff from bloody Tom and you're putting two and two together and making six. The alleys in Lindos are always full of people seemingly following each other. It's that kind of place. It's a small village, you know that. You can't go anywhere here without bumping into someone in the street or the alley, or seeing someone behind you walking in the same direction."

Dawn still wasn't leaving it at that though. She threw in one more question as Deborah was attempting to end their topic of conversation and move the pair of them on to Lindos By Night.

"What about your special Russian friend Ivan then, you heard from him lately?"

Now Deborah Harris abandoned her almost light-hearted reassurance and was angry.

"Look, you watch what you're saying woman!" she snapped back.

Although still whispering, Deborah's tone was raised and much more serious, exhibiting clear anger at her ex-colleague. It was the tone of the person she had been for over ten years before they both came to Lindos as new people; Dawn's superior officer.

"That was all in the past, eighteen years ago. You know what happened, and it's done with and has been for a long time," she added.

Although not public knowledge at the time, secret service agents from opposite sides of the 'Cold War' adversaries often came into contact with each other at various social functions in whichever city they were based. Deborah Harris and Dawn Parsons, although that was not their names back then, were both working in, and operating out of, the British Embassy in Vienna in the nineteen-eighties. Officially they held bureaucratic administrative positions, but in reality they operated as MI6 agents, linked to what was known as the 'Moscow Section' back at MI6 headquarters in London. During the period just after Mikhail Gorbachev came to power in the Soviet Union in 1985, at the time of the introduction of his glasnost and perestroika policies, the contacts between Soviet and British agents increased considerably. There appeared to be a clear change in attitude and policy by the Soviets, and MI6 instructed its agents that any indication of such a change should be reciprocated.

When she was formally introduced to him in January 1986 at an Austrian Ministry of Culture drinks reception to commemorate the two hundred and thirtieth anniversary of Mozart's birth Deborah was already fully aware that Ivan Radischev was head of the KGB section based in Vienna and Prague. She immediately found him striking and somewhat handsome with his swept back jet black hair. He was as tall as her, even though she was wearing four inch high heels, and his stature was upright, almost overpowering. She had been highly trained to play the diplomatic game and not give away too much information about herself or especially her work, even her supposedly mundane administrative position in the British Embassy. On this occasion though, she found herself succumbing to the Russian's charm a little too easily for her liking, and ultimately far too easily for Dawn's. He either also knew how to play the diplomatic game exceedingly well, and somewhat better than her, or else he really was attracted to her, and he, in turn, was simultaneously becoming increasingly attractive to her. So much so that she slipped quickly into smiling, nodding in agreement to his comments in perfect English, and even chuckling slightly at his little jokes. Throughout the evening Dawn constantly warned her to be careful, but by the end of it Deborah found herself doing something that was totally against all she had learned as an MI6 agent. Rather than initially establishing some verbal or general communications contact, as would have been usual, she convinced herself that in line with the new MI6 edict that any apparent Soviet contact or approach should be reciprocated it would okay to meet him straightaway. At that time, of course, she was telling herself that it was strictly professional MI6 business. They agreed to meet on the coming weekend on Sunday afternoon for coffee. Knowing it would be too dangerous, and far too public, to meet in Vienna, she suggested they meet at three in a café in the main square in Baden, a spa town twenty-five kilometres south of the Austrian capital, and he agreed.

By the next weekend after their first meeting in Baden they had embarked on a torrid affair, almost ripping each other's clothes off in the lift of the Hotel Sauerhof in that town, where it is claimed Beethoven finished his Ninth Symphony, based on Schiller's poem 'Ode to Joy'. It was, indeed, a joyous, but crazy, dangerous and out of character time for Deborah. She was definitely experiencing her own personal 'glasnost' as far as Russians were concerned. Early on in their relationship the two of them agreed very formal clear and firm ground rules. They agreed not to ask each other anything about their work or discuss any subject that might infringe on secret or classified information outside of the information that the two organisations had agreed and suggested could be exchanged. For three months though they spent endless afternoons and evenings entwined in various hotel rooms, exploring every part of each other's body in hot, steamy sex. The English woman was insatiable, and Ivan Radischev was never one to disappoint her. It was a miracle that their liaison was never discovered by either of their organisations, and it was only when the Russian was required to spend much more time in Prague because of his position that things eventually cooled off between them as it became increasingly difficult to meet. As she told Dawn six months later after the affair had run its course, "It was the best sex I have ever had. I never knew the Russians could be such good lovers, and there was definitely nothing about it that could be described as 'Cold War'. You know I have always loved the Russian language; well this was certainly the best linguistic 'tongue' I have ever experienced. He 'spoke' to me in places I never knew existed." As she said it back then a slight mischievous satisfied smile spread across her lips. It was a mood, and a side of her, that Dawn had never seen before in her superior officer.

The two women hadn't spoken about it since, but now eighteen years later Dawn was questioning whether Radischev had been in touch with Deborah since the pair of them had left MI6 and decamped to Lindos, and their new identities.

"I get the occasional email from him. He got demoted over that Prague fiasco in November 1989, and when Gorbachev lost power and the Soviet Union broke up he was put on trial for crimes against the State and the people, like a lot of ex-KGB agents. He was sentenced to fifteen years I heard. I have no idea how he got my new email address, but you know as well as I do there are leaks everywhere in the Agency. He probably still has some contacts there and maybe called in some favours. I don't know, but anyway I replied and asked, but he then replied saying he still had some contacts and had got it through them, although he didn't actually say it was someone in the Agency. Whoever it was I am sure they weren't in MI6, who knows, but I can't imagine that is anything to worry about. He wanted to see me, but I told him no, which he seemed to accept without any problem. He just wrote back again saying okay, but let's keep in touch. The last email I had from him was a couple of weeks ago asking how I was and some general pleasantries, like he assumed I had immersed myself socially in the British ex-pat community here, if there was one. Again, I never told him where I was, so he must have got that from his contacts too. I just wrote that the social life was quite good and there were quite a few Brit ex-pats here, but I never mentioned you, of course, and nor had he."

"So, like I said before, Dawn," and her voice hardened once again from the slightly softer tone she had adopted in explaining her contact with Ivan Radischev, "that's all in the past now, and he said he's working for a private security company in Moscow. I heard it's a bit of a 'Wild West' city there now, so I guess he has plenty of work."

"He definitely didn't ask about me then?" Dawn sought further reassurance.

"No, I told you, he doesn't know you're here. After what you did in Vienna in 1988 I don't think you'd be very popular with him and his ex-KGB comrades, do you?"

"I did what I had to do, you know that." Now it was Dawn's turn to adopt a stern face and firm tone. "I was in a tight spot when he attacked me in the flat. The kitchen knife was the nearest thing I could grab when he had the cord around my neck trying to strangle me. Of course, with all the thawing of relations between us and the Russians that was going on at that that time the Vienna Section Commander in the Embassy and you weren't going to be happy, but what else was I supposed to do? My cover was blown and all in all the Section did a good job cleaning my flat up, getting rid of the body, and getting me back to London straightaway."

"Well, when the agent you killed went missing somehow the Russians knew immediately it was you who killed him," Deborah reminded her. "Maybe they had a contact in our Embassy, a double agent, or maybe they just put two and two together and came up with the right result. They obviously knew the agent you killed was shadowing you. Perhaps he wasn't working alone that night. They usually operated in pairs, you know that, so maybe there was a lookout outside the flat while he came in. He obviously didn't expect you to be there. Anyway, I heard that Ivan and his reform communist comrades inside the KGB were pretty pissed off with you. That time was a key period for them. They were desperately trying to win the ideological battle supporting Gorbachev's reforms inside the Soviet

Communist Party and the KGB. There they were trying to convince some of their wavering former hard-line comrades that the 'Cold War' was over and you go and kill one of their agents. I heard at the time that the guy you killed was the brother of one of Ivan's top officers, and also the nephew of one of the key KGB officers he was trying to persuade to support Gorbachev and his reforms."

"For Christ's sake, Deborah, I told you and I told the Service then, it was him or me. I didn't know he was following me. I don't know how he got into my flat, and when he attacked me I even had no idea he was a Russian agent. With a cord tightening around my neck I wasn't about to enquire who or what he was, and the ideological struggles inside the Soviet Communist Party was the last thing on my fucking mind, believe me!"

Now she was raising her voice, but fortunately the only other people, the two tourist couples, who had been in the Lindian House garden had left. Nevertheless, Deborah reminded her where they were and told her forcibly, "Lower your voice and calm down, Dawn."

"Okay, but look, as I said at the time, I thought he was a stalker and was going to sexually attack me. If you ask me it was all a set-up by your friend Ivan's hard-line opponents inside the KGB. They wanted an incident, any incident, to point to and say, 'see, the Cold War isn't over'. So, as it turned out I gave them one to save my own skin. Sorry about that, Deborah, and I'm really sorry if it upset your bloody marvellous Russian lover and his grand plans. Anyway you're not my boss anymore, remember. We decided to get out when we had the chance, when the Cold War ended and the Soviet Union collapsed and everything changed. They didn't need agents like us anymore. We were being replaced by more and more technology and electronic surveillance, and I certainly didn't want to go to bloody sleepy Cheltenham and boring GCHQ. I didn't quite see myself eventually ending up as a genteel old lady in the Cotswolds, and I certainly couldn't see you like that either."

"You're not wrong there girl. I wasn't going back to the UK to sitting behind some desk trawling through endless electronic surveillance reports either, and it definitely all went pear shaped when they started using fucking psychologists and their reports, and when the bloody politicians and lawyers started getting more and more involved. We did the right thing getting out when we did. Then there were the people we were supposed to be fighting against. You knew where you were with the Russians and the KGB, but these days al-Qaeda and that lot are a different kettle of fish, completely splintered, unstable and with no real central focus in terms of control. Give me an easy life in the sun here any time, Dawn, and a couple of hours a night stood outside a restaurant trying to persuade tourists to come in and have dinner, rather than all that shit. That's all gone, another life for both of us, so stop worrying about non-existent Russians here, relax and enjoy your new life."

Dawn was still not totally convinced though, and tried to suggest one more course of action for reassurance. "Maybe I should call my contact at The River House, just to see if they've picked up anything from Moscow that we should be concerned about? After all, they gave us that emergency number and the instructions were to contact them if there was anything suspicious that we were concerned about."

The 'River House' was how MI6 headquarters in London was referred to by people who worked in, and operated out of it.

Deborah just glared sternly in her face saying, "Don't, like they are going to tell you anyway, don't fucking ask them anything. Don't trust them. They'll fuck you over, and the both of us, if it's in their interests to do so anyway. You know that just as much as I do. Who knows what sort of shady deals they may have going on and with who. It was the nature of the job, remember. Everyone watched everyone, and no one trusted anyone, especially the people you worked with in the agency. Just bloody leave it, it's nothing. I've had enough of this shit now, let's go."

In one movement Deborah was stooping down to pick up her handbag from alongside her chair, rising from it, and with a short, "Come on," urged her friend and former colleague to do the same so they could go and meet Tom at LBN.

Part Three: Saturday

8

An expert murder?

Having returned to Rhodes town late the previous evening, before driving back to Lindos on Saturday morning the Karagoulis called in on Crisa Tsagroni at her laboratory to see what more she could tell him from the autopsy. It was approaching nine-thirty when he entered her lab. Although he had experienced many such rooms the antiseptic smell always made him queasy, something that the pathologist knew full well and never missed a chance to gently tease him about.

"Good morning, Dimi. Hope the place is nice and clean enough for you," was how she greeted him as he came through the examination room swing doors.

"Yes, thank you, Crisa, very clean I'm sure and good morning to you too. Don't you people have any nice Rhodes' lemons smelling air spray you can use to remove this awful sickly smell?" was his somewhat sharp response.

"No we don't have any of that, but I always rely on a nice expensive Armani perfume to make sure that I don't smell of the antiseptic cleaner. You could always buy me some more if you want, Dimi. I can give you the name of it," she taunted him with a broad grin across her olive tanned face as she removed her green examination gown.

"Yes, I'm sure you'd like that, but maybe I'll just stretch to a can of lemon air spray for you. In the meantime, what have you got for me on the victim please?"

"As I told you yesterday, he was stabbed in the neck with what looks like a knife with a three centimetre wide blade and that punctured his right Carotid artery, which would have killed him almost immediately; a minute of consciousness maybe two at most usually. Judging by the bump and cut on his head though he was obviously knocked out first, which suggests he could have been taken to St. Paul's bay unconscious before he was killed. In any case, if not he would have been unconscious within thirty seconds after being stabbed and would have bled out very soon after, a matter of seconds. Judging by the amount of blood in the water when the body was found I guess he was killed there and quickly disposed of in the bay. It was a clinical stabbing, Dimi. Whoever did it knew exactly what they were doing, precisely where to stab him in the neck to kill him quickly. As I said yesterday, it looks like he'd been dead for three to four hours when the body was found, so the time of death would be between five and six in the early hours of Friday morning. I don't suppose there was anyone hanging around St. Paul's at that time of the morning to witness what happened, unless there were any early morning fishermen there? Any luck with finding the murder weapon?"

"No, nothing yet, we've got a team of officers searching all around the bay but there is a lot of rough grassy areas and ground so the knife could have been dumped anywhere. Also, the killers could have taken it with them or even tossed it into the sea in the bay, I guess. No, we've not turned up any witnesses who were down at there at that time. Not even any fishermen."

"Given that the killer knew exactly where to stab the victim for maximum effect, I would guess that he or she would have their own knife rather than one recently acquired," the pathologist suggested. "So, I think you are very unlikely to find it in the bay or around St. Paul's, Dimi," she added as she proceeded to wash and scrub her hands having removed the latex gloves.

"You're probably right, Crisa. But everything we've heard and discovered so far points to some kind of love triangle, or even four people involved, and a crime of jealousy in the village, rather than a professional killer. Sounds like we need to do some deeper background checks on the people we've been talking to and suspect of being involved to see if any of them have a history of violence or even some medical background. Someone with that would know exactly where to plunge the knife then?"

"Yes, I guess so. As well as the bump and cut on his head from a heavy object there is some bruising to his back and his neck, Dimi. Caused by a punch or a series of punches I'd guess. It seems likely that he was attacked and struck from behind to his back, neck and head as there is no bruising on his hands or arms, which suggests he was taken by surprise and didn't have any chance to fight back. It also looks like he was gagged with gaffatape, presumably after he was knocked out. There are some traces of adhesive around his mouth."

"Anything on the rope and the sack with the rocks?" Karagoulis asked her.

"Nothing, the sack is just a regular one you can buy at any hardware depot, and so is the rope. I would guess that the rocks are from the area around St. Paul's bay, although we will do a check and compare them if you want?"

"I doubt that will be necessary, and anyway I can't see that would help us much, Crisa."

"So, jealousy and a love triangle," you think, Dimi? In a little village like Lindos, really?" she asked, with something of an incredulous tone in her voice.

"It certainly all points to a 'crime of passion' from what we've heard so far and been told by witnesses who saw him and a woman in a bar in the village the night before. But, as you said Crisa, this doesn't look like the work of an inexperienced amateur, and certainly not someone operating alone. He's quite a well-built guy, a little overweight even, and it would certainly have taken two people to get him down into St. Paul's bay and dump him in the sea."

"Figuring that out is your area of expertise. I've done my bit and I'll have my full autopsy report to you later today. I'm sure you'll work out who the killer was, I have every faith in your investigative powers and methods of interrogation, Inspector." Another bright white smile stretched across her lips as she glanced up at him and added a little flirtatiously, "After all, I know you're good at it. When we first met it only took you ten minutes to figure out that I was divorced and on my own."

Glancing sideways at her he returned her smile and replied, "Unfortunately, I am not on my own, as you know, Crisa, but I do, of course appreciate your faith in my powers of investigation. Getting back to Mr. Carpentar, was there anything of interest in his pockets?"

"Just some loose change, a twenty Euro note and a key, presumably to his flat in Lindos. They are here." She handed him a sealed plastic bag containing them.

"No mobile phone?"

"No sign of one. Perhaps the killers took it or maybe he never had one, unless it's at his apartment?"

"We never found one there. We can check with the mobile network providers." Karagoulis said. "Okay, I better get off to Lindos, I've got a few more people to talk to. Hopefully what they tell me will help. Thanks, Crisa, I'll look forward to your report." He couldn't resist responding to her earlier flirtatious comment, adding, "It's always good to see you, even in these circumstances and with this smell."

"Wait, Dimi, there are just a few more things you should know before you go. He had a high amount of alcohol in his blood stream. He was obviously quite drunk when he was attacked, which may also account for why he didn't fight back. And did you notice his tattoo yesterday at St. Pauls? It is only small so you may have missed it."

"Can't say I did, where is it and what is it?"

"It's on the inside of his lower right forearm, and that's the thing. It just says the number 89. It has an apostrophe before it, but I've no idea what it means. Any ideas, you're the detective?" .

"Not got a clue, Crisa. Maybe some of the people we talk to in the village will know, anything else?"

Well, besides the tattoo Mr. Carpentar had something else on his body, or rather in part of it. He had a little visitor. A little present that he would have passed on to anyone he slept with and was probably passed on to him by someone. He had a sexually transmitted disease, Dimi, chlamydia. Of course, if he passed it on it can take one to three weeks for the symptoms to occur, and in some cases even months."

"That's interesting, not sure how it relates to his murder, but it makes the love triangle and jealousy angle even more relevant. And.it means I definitely need to go back and talk to someone in Lindos I've already interviewed. Thanks once more, Crisa."

"You're welcome. I always save the best till last." She couldn't resist adding, "And don't forget that perfume you promised me."

9

A murder epidemic

Dimitris Karagoulis had just parked in the car park at what was known as Lindos Reception following his forty-five minute drive from Crisa Tsagroni's laboratory in Rhodes when his mobile rang.

"We've got another body in Lindos, sir, another murder," Tassos Samaras voice came down the phone before he could even say hello.

"For fuck's sake, this is Lindos not fucking Chicago," was the Inspector's immediate response. "This certainly isn't going to help the tourist trade. Where is it?"

"The rubbish collectors found the body this morning in one of the large rubbish bins in one of the back alleys towards the top of the village. It's a woman, sir, and I'd say from the look of her she's not Greek. Crisa Tsagroni and her team are on their way. She said you left her about three-quarters of an hour ago. I guess you're in Lindos by now?"

"I've just parked by Lindos Reception."

"You're close by then," Samaras told him. "As you come down the hill take the first alleyway to the left. The rubbish bin and the body are about a hundred metres along there on a patch of rough ground. We've cordoned off the area. The woman has been stabbed in the throat, sir. It looks very similar to yesterday's murder, and Crisa Tsagroni said to tell you thanks for ruining her Saturday beach afternoon."

"Yes, yes, very good, Samaras, I'll be with you in a minute," and Karagoulis strode off in the already hot June sun down the hill towards the village and the second murder victim.

Forty minutes later the pathologist arrived from Rhodes, but not in the best of moods, giving the Inspector a verbal barrage..

"What's going on, Dimi? Do you think I'm underworked or something? Two bodies in two days in Lindos, it's unheard of, even across the whole island. The only tragedies that ever happen here are if some poor soul jumps off the Acropolis, or if someone slips on some donkey shit and breaks a leg or something. Not content with ruining my Friday, now you're ruining my Saturday afternoon at the beach."

"Well I'm not exactly happy about it, Crisa. Like you said, it's unheard of here. From what Samaras tells me though, it's a similar murder, with a stabbing in the throat just like the one yesterday. Only this time it's a woman, but again not a Greek it seems."

"At least the killers are consistent, although they could have made it a bit more interesting and given us a bit of a variation, Dimi," the pathologist joked, trying to lighten her attitude.

"I think you will find they have, Crisa. It looks like this time they came from behind with some sort of cord around her throat at first, instead of the blow to the head on yesterday's victim. There are some bruises on her upper arms, probably where one of them held her while the other strangled her and then finished her off by the stabbing to the side of the neck. It's a bit messy, to say the least."

It was, indeed, a bit messy. Areas of the large stone-slabbed untidy alley were covered in bright crimson, already dry, pools of blood.

"Carotid artery again, Dimi?" Crisa Tsagroni asked.

"You're the expert. That's what we get you out here and pay you for on a Saturday morning, but that's my guess and again, that there were at least two people who attacked her."

"Okay, let's have a look at her then and see if your powers of deduction are as good as you think they are, Inspector."

As Karagoulis paced a few steps up and down the alley and fiddled with his wedding ring, twisting it around his finger, as he often did quite noticeably when he spoke with Crisa Tsagroni, the pathologist put on her latex gloves, unzipped the body bag the victim had been placed in and quickly confirmed his prognosis.

"Yes, stabbed in the Carotid artery and you're right, there are bruises on her arms and marks from some sort of cord around her neck. From the large pools of dried blood over there near the wall it looks like she was killed here. The bleeding would have started quickly after she was stabbed. Like yesterday's victim she would have died almost instantly. Seems like whoever did this again knew exactly what to do to effectively kill someone quickly, which, like you said, suggests it was the same people. Presumably they then dumped her in the large rubbish bin over there judging by the trail of blood. Any sign of the cord? I don't suppose you've found the murder weapon, a large knife I'd guess from the wound, similar to yesterday's with a three centimetre wide blade."

"No, no sign of the cord or the murder weapon as yet. We're searching all the rubbish bins here and the alleys, but nothing yet and I'll be surprised if we find anything. It's definitely looking very much like the same killers as yesterday, and again something of a professional job. Leaving no murder weapon or the cord suggests they knew exactly what they were about, although dumping her in the bin and all the blood about here suggests it was a bit of a spur of the moment decision to kill her here, unlike yesterday when the victim was clearly taken to St. Paul's bay before he was murdered. A preliminary quick estimate on how long she's been dead, Crisa?"

"I'd say between four and six hours. I'd put the time of death at between four-thirty and six-thirty this morning. Again, just an educated guess, and I would put her in her mid-forties in terms of age. That's about all I can tell you now, Dimi. I will have a clearer idea and more for you, hopefully, tomorrow morning, or later today if you prefer me to call you? Otherwise you'll have me working on Sunday too and I will get to see you in my nice smelling laboratory two days running."

With a slight tilt of her head and a grin spreading across her mischievous lips she added, "I don't suppose you'll bring that perfume you promised me with you?"

"That's right, Crisa, I don't think so. I am a little too busy at the moment dealing with what is becoming a murder epidemic to go shopping for perfume this afternoon, and anyway I don't actually recall promising it to you. Besides that, we need to get something resolved quickly on this and catch the murderers before it starts panicking the tourists and affecting that trade. So, give me a call later today please with anything else you've got."

"Okay, Dimi, of course, right let's get this one back to Rhodes," she told him with her more professional face back on, although she couldn't resist a cheeky, "please, Dimi, no more of these tomorrow. It is Sunday you know and everyone deserves at least one day of rest."

"Sure, I'll see what I can do, although it seems to be a little out of my control right now,. Speak later," he replied as he set off down the alley to where Samaras was organising two other officers searching the area and adjoining alleys.

"Any identification?" he asked Samaras.

"Nothing on her, sir, not even a handbag. She doesn't look Greek to me, and I have some vague notion that I've seen her in the village over the past couple of years so I don't think she's a tourist. She's got a tattoo of a rose on her upper left arm so that may help identify her."

As he spoke, Samaras slightly distorted the cheek on one side of his sun-grazed long face.

"What's up, why the grimace" Karagoulis asked? "You don't like tattoos?"

"No, I woke up with a slight toothache this morning and I think there is some bread stuck between my teeth. I was just trying to suck it out."

"Oh, well maybe you will get time eventually to get to the dentist, but probably not till at least Monday if this murder a day keeps up. In the meantime get a photo of the victim taken before Crisa Tsagroni takes the body off to Rhodes, though not the side of the neck where she was stabbed, and try a few of the bars and restaurants in the village to see if anyone knows her. Start with Jack Constantino at the Courtyard Bar, he seems to know most people living and working in the village, including most of the foreign workers if she isn't Greek."

As he issued his instruction Karagoulis rubbed his hand across his bald head, feeling the already hot sun upon it, and saying, "I need to get my hat from my car, otherwise I'm going to have a sore head later to match your sore tooth."

"I doubt if we will get any witnesses or anyone who may have heard anything in this part of the village, sir, although we'll knock on all the apartment and villa doors and see," Samaras suggested. "It's a back alleyway and not many people use it. Although Qupi is only a hundred metres or so along here most people don't come this way to get to it. They tend to go up the steps by Jack Constantino's Courtyard Bar."

"Ah, yes, the night club, the young guy who works in Jack Constantino's bar mentioned that. Maybe someone coming out of there saw or heard something, although tracking them down is not going to be easy I guess."

The alleyway was quite narrow, only between two and three metres wide, dusty, and with uneven under foot large stone slabs alternating with rough strips of equally uneven concrete. There were some black marks on the whitewashed walls along each side, evidence of the struggle the small vehicles collecting the rubbish from the large bins experienced early each morning or late at night. The body had been placed in one of the rubbish bins on a patch of rough scrubland between two buildings. It had obviously been occupied by a building of some sort many years before, but that had since been demolished and the ground left to overgrow.

Just as Karagoulis was about to set off back to his car to collect his hat one of Samaras' colleagues called him and Samaras over to where he was taking a statement from the Lindos rubbish collector who found the body.

"This is the man who found the body, sir, Panagiotis Frantzakis. He says he knows the dead woman. Her name is Dawn Parsons and he says she's English."

"How do you know her, Mr Frantzakis?" Karagoulis asked.

"From the village, she works in the Village House restaurant. She's been working and living here for three or four years now I think, in different bars and restaurants. I've seen her in the bars and clubs regularly after work. She liked to drink, a lot sometimes, and I've seen her drunk a lot of times."

"What time this morning did you find the body?"

"About half-past eight, just as me and Nikos over there, who does this round of rubbish collection with me, were collecting from the last few rubbish bins on our way to the dump. We always do this alleyway last as it's on the way." As he answered Karagoulis the rubbish collector pointed over to his colleague five metres away giving a statement to another officer.

"And did you see or pass anyone along the alley before you got to these two bins?" the Inspector added.

"No one, hardly anyone who doesn't live along here comes this way, especially tourists. It's mainly locals who use it, but we didn't see anyone. We don't usually see anyone.."

"I don't suppose you have any idea where this woman lived in the village?" Karagoulis asked.

"Not really, although I've seen her a few times eating breakfast and having coffee outside Café Melia in the square by the Amphitheatre, so I assumed she lived somewhere near there."

"Okay, thank you Mr Frantzakis. The officer will take your address and contact details in case we want to speak to you again. Just one more thing though, where were you between four and seven o'clock this morning?"

"At home, getting a little sleep before I started on my round collecting the rubbish."

"Alone?" Karagoulis pressed him.

"No, with my wife, I also work in Anthony's restaurant in the village in the evening so I try and grab a few hours' sleep before I start work on this. But I saw the dead woman last night about two o'clock in Lindos by Night. I went in there for a quick beer with Albi after I finished at Anthony's, before I went home to get some sleep."

"Albi?" the Inspector interrupted.

"He is my friend of many years and is a barman there. He's Albanian. This dead woman was in there drinking with another English woman who has been here for three or four years, Deborah Harris. They are, were I suppose now, good friends. They were with a man, who was also English, but I don't know him."

"And what do you know about Deborah Harris, Mr Frantzakis, apart from the fact that she was good friends with Dawn Parsons?"

"Not very much, as I said, they have both been living here for about the same length of time. They seemed to be very good friends and when I saw them they were always drinking together, although it always looked to me like Dawn drank much more than Deborah. As I said, I saw her drunk quite a few times but I never ever saw Deborah drunk. She works in Symposio restaurant sometimes in the centre of the village, as front of house I think you call it, three or four times a week depending on how busy they are."

"How did the three of them, the two women and the man, seem?" the Inspector asked. Were they friendly or was there any arguing?"

"Arguments? No, not at all, in fact quite the opposite. They were at the other end of the bar, the inside bar downstairs from the one with the view of the Acropolis, and they were laughing and joking quite loudly between them, and with Albi, who I think knows the two women quite well."

"Thank you again, Mr Frantzakis. You have been very helpful. We will not detain you any further. As I said before, if you give the other officer your contact details, I am sure you will want to get home to get some more sleep."

As Frantzakis walked over to give one of the other police officers his details Karagoulis turned away with Samaras saying, "I think we had better go and see this Albi guy later to see if he can tell us anymore, like who the English man that Dawn Parsons and Deborah Harris were drinking with was, and then we'll need to go and see Deborah Harris. I hope you haven't got a nice Saturday night planned, or are hoping to get that tooth of yours looked at any time soon, Samaras, because it looks like we are going to be interviewing a lot of people about these murders this afternoon and evening. After what I heard about his little fight in the Courtyard Bar with our murder victim from yesterday it's time we had a word with Alan Bryant, and then another word with Carol Hudson is called for, particularly to ask if she has any extra little sexually transmitted visitors. Crisa Tsagroni told me this morning that Tony Carpentar had chlamydia."

Samaras smiled at his Inspector, offering him an ironic, "A busy Lindos Saturday night then, sir."

10

Two passports

As the Inspector and Samaras came through the door into the small office at the back of the little Lindos Police Station Karagoulis decided the most urgent matter at that time was to put some food into his stomach. He had only managed to grab a quick cup of coffee before he left his home in Rhodes that morning before going to Crisa Tsagroni's lab. Papadoulis was his chosen errand boy.

"See if you can get some rolls and some coffee in the village, Sargent, while Samaras and I try and find out where Alan Bryant resides and where Dawn Parsons lived. Then we can go and have a look at her place to see what, if anything, we can find, before we go and see Mr. Bryant."

"Café Melia in the square by the Amphitheatre will be the nearest, and they do the best filled rolls," Samaras suggested.

While Papadoulis went off to get their lunch, the Inspector started to put together on the large white board the names of all the people they had come across so far linked to the two murders, together with the names of the two victims, what they already knew about them and the method of their killing. He referred to it as the 'Incident Board', as he instructed Samaras to make some phone calls to his local contacts in the village to try and find out if any of them knew where Alan Bryant was living.

In such a small place as Lindos, where everyone seemed to know everyone and their business, it took less than fifteen minutes before Samaras was able to come up with what they needed. Just as Papadoulis came through the door into the office carrying a bag full of filled rolls and three coffees in a cardboard tray from Café Melia Samaras announced, "One of my contacts tells me that as far as he knows Alan Bryant lives in a small studio apartment at the top of the village, near the Atmosphere bar on the way to Lindos Reception. He told me exactly where, but he also said that on most Saturday afternoons Bryant is usually found down on Pallas beach by Skala restaurant or in it drinking."

"Good, Samaras, but I think we should have a look at Dawn Parsons' place first before we talk to Bryant. Any luck on that?"

"The rubbish collector guy who found the body said she worked at the Village House restaurant and I guess that if she has been here for three or four years, as he thought, she would have registered at the Labour Inspectorate office in Rhodes to get her work papers. That will have her address, or at least one of her past addresses even if she's moved, but they will not be open until Monday morning, sir."

"I think we can use our authority to get round that problem. I know a couple of people there, quite high up in the bureaucracy. I'll give them a call after we've had our lunch. I'm sure they'll be able to help, or if not we'll have to get some heavier, more important high-up police influence to bear on them. We can't wait till Monday, we need that information today."

A couple of short and firm phone calls after their lunch and Karagoulis had just what he needed. Dawn Parsons had lived in a small apartment just off the square by the Amphitheatre, as the guy who found her body, Panagiotis Frantzakis, suggested.

In fact, it was little more than a room rather than an apartment, with a typical Greek combined toilet and shower room at the back. It was in a courtyard shared with four other so-called apartments, behind a high stone wall and large wooden double doors. The two policemen had to knock twice using the large, somewhat rusted, circular ring knocker on one of the outer wooden doors before the owner of the apartments slowly opened it. He was an elderly, tall, grey haired man with glasses and something of a stoop in his stature that caused his upper body attire of a white vest to droop around his shoulders like a billowing sail on one of the sailing boats in Lindos bay. He looked a little disorientated, like he had just begun his afternoon nap and had been woken up by the unexpected thud of the door knocker. His bemusement was added to when Karagoulis identified himself, along with the accompanying Officer Samaras. Showing him his police badge, he asked if he was the owner and whether Dawn Parsons lived there. In response he identified himself as Kostas Sarikakis, the owner, confirmed that she did, but told Karagoulis that he thought she wasn't in at the moment. At that point the Inspector informed him quite bluntly and in an official manner that she had been murdered, and that they needed to have a look at her apartment. The old man was visibly shocked, but after a few seconds managed a brief reply of, "Yes, yes, of course, this way," and with that let the two policemen into the courtyard directing them to the second dark wooden door on the right-hand side of a row of three.

"I need to get my spare key to let you in," he told Karagoulis. A minute or so later he returned and let them into the apartment. As the old man turned the key in the lock Karagoulis turned to Samaras and observed, "She must have had the key to this on her when she was murdered, but we never found anything, not even a handbag. That means she probably did have a handbag with her and the killers must have taken it."

"Maybe it was robbery, sir?" Samaras commented.

"Maybe or maybe they took it because they wanted it to look like that." As he made that observation the Inspector turned his head back to peer through the open doorway and focus on the interior of the apartment. He was immediately stunned. "Has anyone been in here, has there been a break-in, a burglary, Mr. Sarikakis?" he asked, as he observed piles of clothes on the floor and over the bed. Two of the draws in a small three draw chest had been left half open, and a large number of shoes and some handbags had seemingly just been thrown on the floor into a corner. Underneath the pile of clothes the bed was unmade, even though it only consisted of a top sheet which had been screwed up and thrown to one side. Virtually every surface in the room was covered, either with clothes or remnants of fast food packaging, including two empty pizza boxes.

"No, no break-in and no one has been in here, I'm sure. I live across the courtyard and I would have heard or seen them," Sarikakis replied. "This is the way she lived. I had to come in here a week ago to look at the toilet because she complained it wasn't working properly. It was just the same then. One of the most untidy tenants I have ever had."

"Okay, well we need to have a look around in here, so we will let you know when we are finished, probably in about half-an-hour I think, although some other officers and forensic people will also be here shortly to take some of this stuff away and seal off the apartment. No one can come in here after that, not even you, until we say so."

Sarikakis nodded his head in acknowledgement and headed back across the courtyard towards his own apartment.

As he left Karagoulis told Samaras, "You take that side of the bed, including that chest of drawers, and I'll make a start going through the clothes on this side and on the bed, and going through these three handbags on the floor over here. What a bloody mess. Anyone would definitely have thought the place had been ransacked."

The Inspector started on the handbags, but apart from a couple of empty cigarette packets and a screwed up five euro note, he found nothing. He was checking if any of the four pairs of jeans slung across the back of a chair had anything in the pockets when Samaras, who had been working silently through the clothes on his side of the room and had now started on the chest of drawers said, "Sir, there's something taped to the bottom of one of these drawers, the one that was unopened. There's nothing interesting in the draw, just some jewellery, quite cheap looking and just thrown in, but there is a brown envelope taped to the underside of it."

Karagoulis removed the envelope and opened it, noticing there was nothing written on it, not even a name or address. "A British passport, presumably hers, driving licence, what looks like a birth certificate," he commented as he began removing the contents, adding, "seems like an odd place to keep your personal documents, even if you are concerned about losing them if someone breaks in to rob the place."

As he put those to one side on top of the chest of drawers he reached back into the envelope and drew out another smaller brown envelope, opened it and said in surprise, "Another British passport." After checking in the first one that it was actually Dawn Parsons' passport, he flicked quickly through the pages of the second one to the back, raised an eyebrow and asked rhetorically, "So, Samaras, just who do you think Jacki Walker is?"

He didn't wait for an answer as he showed the photograph to Samaras. "It's definitely Dawn Parsons, but she has short blonde hair. Her date of birth is the same though as in that other passport. So, why did she have two passports, and the one for Jacki Walker issue date is 1995, but the Dawn Parsons one was issued in 2000. And Jacki is an odd first name, or at least a not usual one or one I've come across before as English names go. I guess it's short for Jacqueline, but that can't be her proper name or it would have to be the one in the passport, so it must be Jacki. Who the bloody hell was Dawn Parsons or Jacki Walker then?"

The Inspector was thinking out loud, and raising more and more questions in his mind about Dawn Parsons' murder.

"I'm beginning to think there is more to this Lindos murder epidemic than meets the eye, Samaras. Why, and who, would murder a woman who wasn't who she seemed or claimed to be, and why would the same person or people apparently murder an Englishman who was living and working here for the summer? What's the connection? Are they murders of passion, jealousy and revenge, or something else? Alan Bryant and Carol Hudson definitely had connections to Tony Carpentar, so both of them, or either of them, could have been involved in his murder, or even Carol Hudson's husband, Panos Koropoulis, but what do they all know about Dawn Parsons, or even Jacki Walker, I wonder? Let's leave the rest of this mess in here to the forensic team and go and see Alan Bryant on Pallas Beach and see if he can tell us anything about all of this, and then we need to go back and see Carol Hudson, and her husband. I don't think we'll mention Jacki Walker to any of them just yet though."

11

A busy Saturday afternoon and evening of interviews and interrogation

As the hot early afternoon sun bounced off the white walls and the two policemen made their way through the narrow alleys of the village and down the hill to Pallas Beach Karagoulis' mobile rang. They were halfway down the path of the steep hill as he stopped and sheltered in the shade under some trees by a couple of wrought iron benches in order to answer it.

"Hello, Crisa, I wasn't exactly expecting to get a call from you this soon, although as you know I am always pleased to hear your voice."

"Yes, yes, and I'm always pleased to hear yours too, Dimi."

This time though she wasn't about to enter into their pleasant little game of back and forth banter and flirting. It was a hot Saturday afternoon and she still wasn't best pleased at being stuck in her lab working. The beach and the clear blue sea beckoned.

Ignoring the Inspector's flippant attempt at flattery, she continued, "Anyway, I thought you'd like to know some of the things I've found so far about the latest victim in your little murder epidemic, Dimi, not least that Dawn Parsons had the same little visitor as the first victim."

"Chlamydia, that's interesting, Crisa. Useful to know before we interview some of the people we are going to see now and later today."

"As I thought, the marks around her neck and the bruises on her arms suggest she'd been strangled from behind. That would have rendered her unconscious, but it's unlikely that killed her. As I said earlier, the knife in the Carotid artery would have done that instantly," she continued. "I'll finish a more complete autopsy later today and send you a full report. I would like to get to the beach sometime today, Dimi, but I thought you'd like to know straightaway that the victims had something in common, other than the way they were killed."

"Thanks, and any better idea of time of death?" he asked.

"My estimate at the murder scene was about right, between four-thirty and six-thirty this morning, and as I also said, I'd put her age as mid-forties."

"Good estimate, Crisa, she was forty-six according to her passport, well both of them we just found in her apartment."

"Two passports, really Dimi, seems like you have got a real mystery on your hands after all then?"

"Yes, but that's not common knowledge at the moment, and I think we'll keep it that way for a while and see first what we can come up with from talking to a few of the characters involved in all this," he told her.

"Okay, but before you do that there are another couple of things you might want to know right away, Dimi, and I must say that's a very entertaining and interesting little village you've got there, especially the British ex-pats living in it."

"A little too entertaining and interesting for my liking at the moment," he interrupted, adding, "But what do you mean?"

"She had sex recently, in the last twenty-four to thirty-six hours, including anal sex, and from the bruising around her buttocks I'd say it wasn't consensual."

"Jesus, can this get any messier and complex? Rape, are you sure, Crisa?"

"The bruising on her buttocks is older than the ones on her arms. I'd say approximately twenty-four hours older, so it wouldn't have been done by whoever killed her. It seems everybody is at it in Lindos, at least amongst the Brits, and busy passing chlamydia on to one another maybe? Also, she had quite a lot of alcohol in her system, so she was almost certainly drunk when she was attacked, Dimi."

"Christ, maybe we should do a medical test on the entire Lindos population, although I don't think I have the power to do that exactly. Seems like maybe Tony Carpentar and her were very friendly. I never figured that. I assumed the fight Alan Bryant had with him the night he was killed was over Carol Hudson. Perhaps it was over Dawn Parsons? Time we had a little word with Alan Bryant I think. We are on our way to see him now down at Pallas Beach, although I don't think I can get him to agree to a medical examination," the Inspector joked, adding, "Carol Hudson's reaction to all this might tell us more. Is it possible, Crisa, that whoever raped her then murdered her the next night? Is there any way of checking or proving that it was the same person?"

"Unlikely, Dimi, unless we can trace anyone else's DNA on her clothes from the night she was murdered and match it to what we have from her having sex the night before. We'll do some checks, but it's a long shot. All I can tell you at the moment is that it definitely looks as though she was forced, but it could have been anything up to thirty-six hours before she was murdered, so the two things may not be connected."

Thanks again, Crisa, I owe you that small bottle of perfume for sure now. Enjoy the rest of your weekend."

"You definitely do, Dimi. I'll send you that full autopsy report later. Try not to disturb my Sunday with any more murders please."

With that she hung up and Karagoulis turned to Samaras asking, "What part of the beach is this Skala Restaurant on that Bryant is supposed to frequent on a Saturday afternoon?"

"It's the far end, sir, by the jetty. You can see the sign, there," and he raised his right hand and pointed. Despite a warning from Samaras about how shiny and slippery the flagstones on the path down to Pallas beach was from the constant to and fro of the Lindos donkey 'taxis', not to mention the occasional donkey shit, the Inspector twice almost lost his footing before finally making it to the bottom of the hill.

The picturesque small Pallas beach was packed with tourists, many of whom were taking advantage of the warm, clear, blue water in the bay. Skala was the last restaurant at the end of the small Beach. It had a quite long covered veranda that led in the centre down three steps to the narrowest part of the beach. At the farthest end was another terrace, uncovered, but with numerous large white parasols providing some shade from the hot sun above tables and chairs that looked out directly to the long jetty from which day-trip boats to Rhodes Town and the Glass Bottom Boat departed. On that particular Saturday mid-afternoon Skala was still quite busy, with groups of people dotted on a dozen or so tables finishing their long Greek lunches. As Karagoulis and Samaras approached the restaurant along the wooden slatted walkway at the back of the beach they could hear a group of quite loud English voices that belonged to four men sat at a table at the far end of the covered veranda. There were a number of Greek Mythos beer bottles on the table, mostly empty, but one in front of each of the men still in use and being consumed. They were clearly enjoying themselves.

The two policemen climbed the three steps and approached the table at which the four men were seated. Although he had no idea what he looked like, Karagoulis immediately guessed that one of them was Alan Bryant. That one was sat facing the beach and the sea, and was holding forth quite loudly to his companions and pontificating on the merits or otherwise of women in general.

"Mr. Bryant?" Karagoulis interrupted, producing and showing the group of men his police credentials as he spoke. "Inspector Karagoulis, Rhodes police, I'd like a word with you please about the murder of Tony Carpentar. I believe you knew him? I would have said a friend, but judging by that bruise on the side of your face, and from what we have been told, I gather that may not have been the case recently? You had a bit of a falling out, I understand."

Bryant was a quite tall man at just under six foot. He was by no means slim though. His chubby face betrayed the early forties extra weight he carried around his midriff, which was clearly visible from the pot-belly drooping over his swim shorts, exposed by the fact that he wasn't wearing anything on the top part of his sun-tanned body. He sported that pushed up at the front and brushed back hair style that gave off a suggestion of sophistication, but in his case singularly failed to deliver.

"Yes, I knew him, but I'd say we were acquaintances rather than friends. He was here for the whole summer, I am here for the summer, and like me, he has been here in Lindos lots of times before, so he told me. I don't know anything about his murder though, so…"

To Karagoulis his whole demeanour and body language was immediately aggressive and dismissive. As he answered the Inspector he only briefly glanced sideways at him and then immediately leaned forward to face the beach and the other three men at the table, picking up his beer bottle and taking a swig as he finished talking. Before he could say anything more though, if he indeed intended to, Karagoulis interrupted, simply saying, "I think it would be better if we had this conversation up at the police station, Mr. Bryant, rather than here in public, don't you?"

"I don't know about that. Are you arresting me or something?" His attitude had quickly softened somewhat.

"No, I'm not arresting you, Mr. Bryant. I just think we need to have a little chat up at the station. There are a number of things I want to ask you about, that I am sure you can help us with in our enquiries, and believe me I don't think you would want to discuss them here. I am not in the habit of conducting police investigations on a beach or even in a beachside restaurant. Anyway, you haven't got anything to be worried about have you?"

"No, nothing, why should I have, but okay, I'll get my t-shirt and bag from the sun-bed on the beach there. I still don't see what I can tell you about the murder though. It's got nothing to do with me." As he spoke he pointed to a sun-lounger just a few yards in front of the Skala veranda, got up from his chair, and went to collect his stuff.

Within fifteen minutes the two police officers and Alan Bryant were walking through the small courtyard in front of Lindos police station, through the front reception area, down a short corridor and into the cool of the air-conditioned, white walled, sparsely furnished interrogation room towards the back of the building. Bryant sat on a plastic chair at the metal table, but Karagoulis and Samaras both preferred to stand, the Inspector hovering by the other side of the table and the local officer leaning against the wall by the door. As soon as he sat down Bryant's aggressiveness returned as he blurted out, "So, why do you think I had anything to do with Tony Carpentar's murder? I didn't know him that well, just had the odd beer with him. It's a small village. We were both here for the whole summer. Of course our paths would cross..."

"Well, you knew him well enough for him to give you that nasty bruise on the side of your face in the Courtyard bar the night he was murdered, didn't you? It was over Carol Hudson wasn't it?" Karagoulis interrupted and was doing a bit of fishing as he started to pace back and forth across the room. Quickly turning and aggressively looming over Bryant he stared straight into his face adding, "She was having an affair with Tony Carpentar and you were jealous, weren't you? The night of the fight Mr. Carpentar was heard shouting at you as he left the bar that you should keep away from her, but you didn't, did you? You were heard in the alley way with her near the Qupi night club around four a.m. that night."

Bryant sat back in the chair saying, "Yes, okay, we did have a fight in Courtyard, well, more of a scuffle really, although he did catch me on the side of my face. But you know all that, and yes I was in the alley along from Qupi later that night with a woman, but it wasn't Carol Hudson. The scuffle in Courtyard was over Carol, but it wasn't her I was in the alley with. I was just winding Tony up about Carol, saying she obviously fancied me, that I could go with her anytime I wanted for a shag, and that she'd shagged half the village ex-pats anyway. He was already quite pissed, told me to keep away from her, and that they were going away together for a weekend in Prague soon. He was always going on about how great that place was to anyone who would listen. I told him that was bollocks and that she would never be able to get away from the village with him, her husband would kill her."

"Or kill Tony Carpentar?" Samaras asked.

"I don't know about that," Bryant continued. "I don't know him at all. Whenever I've seen him in the bars and clubs after he's finished work he's with his Greek friends. That's what most of the Greek guys do here. You don't see them out in the village at night with their wives very often. I guess that suited Carol."

"So, who was this woman you were in the alley with later that night, Mr. Bryant, if it wasn't her?" It was Karagoulis' turn again to press him.

Bryant hesitated for a few seconds, rubbed the side of his face where the bruise was and answered, "Dawn Parsons, it was Dawn Parsons. She works in the Village House Restaurant. She was in Qupi that night. Carol was also in there, but only for about half-an-hour or so. After she left I got talking to Dawn. We've sort of sparred around bantering, and flirting I suppose you'd call it, for a few weeks now. We had a few drinks and one thing led to another. We were going back to my place, but she suddenly said she couldn't do it and had changed her mind. She started going on about some other guy she'd met and that she didn't want to fuck that up by having sex with me because she knew it would get round the village. She never said who it was, and I reckoned she had just got cold feet and was bullshitting, making it all up, so I started shouting at her to forget about him. Anyway, one thing eventually led to another and it all happened there and then in the alley. Afterwards she said she'd kill me if I told anyone and that it was just a one off."

"Have you seen this woman, Dawn Parsons, since? Did you happen to see her last night?" Karagoulis asked.

"I was out drinking last night and yes, I saw her briefly up at Lindos by Night late on, must have been after two, but she was with in the bottom bar with Deborah Harris and another guy that I don't know. She gave me a bit of a sideways glance as I came in. It didn't seem very welcoming so I never went over or spoke to her, just got a beer and went up to the top bar. You don't approach Dawn if she gives you a certain look. I've learned that about her from experience, believe me. She can be moody, especially when she's had a drink, and that look meant 'don't come near me'. But why do you want to know whether I saw her last night? What's that, and her, got to do with this and Tony's murder?"

Karagoulis ignored his question, preferring to keep him in the dark about Dawn Parsons' murder for the time being, and asking, "Where did you go after that?"

"We, a couple of the guys I was on the beach with today who are Brit ex-pats who live here, went to Nightlife, the club by Jack's Courtyard bar."

"And what time were you there till?"

Bryant hesitated for a moment and brushed his hand through his hair before replying, "Blimey, we had a few drinks and were on shots at one point. So I was pretty drunk, we all were, but I guess it must have been gone five in the morning because the place was emptying and it was starting to get light. We went to Bar Code, next to Nightlife, for some food. It was definitely daylight when we left there, it must have been gone six."

"And the guys you were with can confirm this, Mr. Bryant?"

"Yep, I guess so, although they were pretty drunk too. I'm not sure any of us can be exact about the time, although I'm sure they can confirm it was daylight, and the staff at Bar Code would definitely remember us. Why are you so interested in where I was last night though, I thought Tony Carpentar was murdered the night before? Anyway, I'd be grateful if you didn't ask Dawn about Thursday night in the alley outside Qupi though, she swore me to secrecy, and as I said, she said she'd kill me if I told anyone. She's not a woman to mess with. She's got quite a temper on her."

The Inspector stopped pacing back and forth and again loomed over Bryant across the table, once more fixing a stare on him and telling him, "Her temper is not something you should worry about, Mr. Bryant. We will not be asking her about that. She was murdered last night, stabbed, in the alley not far from where you had sex with her the night before if you are to be believed."

"Shit! What? How? Why? What the fuck?" Bryant was visibly shocked and slumped forward a little to rest his forearms on the table. "What's going on in this bloody village? First Tony Carpentar and now Dawn, it makes no sense. Do you know what happened? You surely don't think I had anything to do with that murder either, do you? "

Karagoulis was observing every part of his reaction closely as he replied, "That's just it, Mr. Bryant, it was just along the alley from Qupi, obviously quite near where you and her were the previous night, or rather early morning, having sex."

The blood was clearly draining from Alan Bryant's face as even his sun-tan was fading a little. His earlier cockiness had vanished completely and he was increasingly looking worried as the Inspector continued, forcibly verbally spelling out his predicament while again looming over him across the table.

"It seems to me that we can link your movements over the two nights to both the victims, and you obviously had some motive in terms of Tony Carpentar's murder. Revenge was it, after your scuffle that night in the Courtyard bar, anger and frustration after a few drinks maybe? You lost your temper and decided to get your own back on him, and perhaps the whole thing just got out of hand? Then there's also your, what shall we call it, liaison perhaps, with Dawn Parsons. She didn't consent the night before though did she, Mr. Bryant? You forced her to have sex, didn't you? We call that rape. The autopsy has already revealed that, and it wasn't very pleasant was it? You'd well and truly lost your temper by then, hadn't you? The bruising on her body illustrated that."

Bryant was vigorously shaking his head and looking stunned as he replied, "No, I told you I had nothing to do with either of the murders. I was in Nightlife and Bar Code last night until the early hours of this morning, and there are three guys who can corroborate that because I was with them all that time. And I didn't have to force Dawn into doing anything. She was changing her mind all the time, but in the end she wanted it as much as me."

"You would say that, wouldn't you, but that's certainly not what the evidence of her autopsy suggests by any means. Of course, if she were still alive we might well be charging you now with rape, Mr. Bryant, but her being dead makes that not really possible. Convenient for you, don't you think? As for your alibi, you did say you and your friends were all quite drunk, so maybe their memories will not be quite as clear as yours? Perhaps you weren't really quite as drunk as they were and slipped away for a time to murder Dawn Parsons?"

Karagoulis softened his approach slightly in order to try and draw more out of the Englishman as he went on, "Perhaps you were just a little drunk, confused, worried about what you'd done the previous evening and that Dawn would claim you raped her, maybe report you to us, so again you panicked and in a mixture of your confusion and anger had a moment of madness and killed her."

Pacing once more slowly back and forth across the office and rubbing the top of his bald head with his left palm the Inspector concluded his prognosis with, "Maybe you did try to reason with her, maybe that's what happened, suggested to her that she wanted it as much as you the night before, as you said, but she didn't accept that did she, and after an argument you lost control, lost your temper again, just as you did with Tony, and you killed her. Is that what happened, Alan?"

Once more he was slumped back in the plastic chair, but before he could even attempt to answer or offer a denial Samaras intervened with, "Nightlife is usually pretty packed between four and six in the morning, with everyone wanting some food in their alcohol filled stomachs. It would have been relatively easy for you to slip out for half-an-hour or so without your friends even noticing, wouldn't it?"

The two policemen were operating in tandem now, and not pausing for any reply from Bryant Karagoulis followed up Samaras' intervention with, "Yes, perhaps you had arranged to meet Dawn Parsons and did just slip out of Nightlife, but she was still angry about the previous night and what had happened and wasn't having any of it, so, as I said, you just lost your temper again. Is that what happened, Mr. Bryant? You met up with her, lost your temper, tried to strangle her and ended up stabbing her in the neck, just as you had Tony Carpentar?"

"No way, of course not, there is no way I left Nightlife and I'm sure my friends will confirm I was with them the whole evening and through the night into the early morning. There must have been at least twenty other people who saw me in Nightlife and later in Bar Code. What is this, Inspector? Are you so desperate you are just trying to pin these murders on the first person you can think of? Yes, I knew both of them, one of them intimately recently, but I never bloody killed them, and as I said before, I never raped Dawn. And I certainly never lost my temper with either of them."

"You threw the first punch in the Courtyard bar that night, Mr. Bryant. We have witnesses to that, and someone who heard you shouting and arguing with Dawn Parsons in the alley before you and her had sex. What would you call that? I'd call it losing your temper, wouldn't you?" Karagoulis pressed him, adopting a much harder attitude again.

"Okay, maybe I did lose my temper briefly on both occasions, but I didn't murder them, either of them, and like I've told you a few times now I had an alibi for the night Dawn was killed, plus how was I supposed to be murdering Tony when that night I was shagging Dawn in the alley by Qupi?"

"Well, unfortunately we can't ask Dawn Parsons about that can we?" Samaras said pointedly.

"I'm not saying any more about all this without a lawyer. I think I've said enough already and clearly I've got nothing more to tell you because it has got nothing to do with me. So, unless you are going to charge me I would like to leave now." Bryant was getting up out of the chair and adopting his aggressive tone once again.

"Just a couple more questions before we let you go," Karagoulis told him. "Ever had anything to do with the medical profession in your background, any medical training?"

"I trained as a male nurse twenty years ago, but I gave up that profession ten years ago. What's that got to do with all this?"

"So, you'd know about various organs of the body then? The Inspector probed further.

"Yes, of course, some of them anyway, but I still don't see what that has to do with any of this."

"Oh, just background," the Inspector informed him cagily, quickly adding while Bryant was still confused over why he'd asked the previous question, "and what about sexually transmitted diseases, any of those recently?"

"What? What the fuck has that got to do with all this? Is this a bloody joke?"

"Just answer the question please, Mr. Bryant. We have our reasons, and I should remind you that this is a double murder enquiry, and it is certainly no joke, so I should take our questions very seriously if I were you," Karagoulis again firmly told him.

"No, nothing, as far as I know, although I haven't exactly been rushing to the doctors in this village to find out, Inspector, not that it's any of your business anyway."

Karagoulis walked away from him towards the other side of the room where Samaras was still leaning against the bare wall, waited a few seconds, leaving Bryant to stew in his own bewilderment, before informing him, "Both Tony Carpentar and Dawn Parsons had chlamydia. How do you suppose they both got that? Could it be that Tony had been there before you, as I think you Brits say, Alan? Perhaps he was the guy she meant when she wanted to stop that night in the alley by Qupi when you raped her?"

He was calling him by his Christian name again now, not without a certain amount of patronising irony, and clearly trying to see if Bryant angered quickly and easily. But apart from repeating, "I never raped her," he just sat slumped in the chair and said nothing more in response.

Now it was Karagoulis' turn to lean against one of the walls of the room as he continued with yet more probing and prompting "Maybe that's what got you angry with both of them, that and Tony's affair with Carol Hudson. You tried it on quite a few times with Carol didn't you? She told us as much. Quite competitive in that respect you and Tony obviously. It seems you have quite a reputation amongst the Brit ex-pats in Lindos, don't you. What was it Carpentar shouted at you in the Courtyard bar the night of your fight? 'You've shagged most of the bloody Brit women in the village anyway, and probably even some of the donkeys and stray cats.' Wasn't that it? What did he mean by that, Alan? I bet that got you really annoyed didn't it? Something like that being broadcast in public, and the Courtyard was pretty busy that night too. That must have really pissed you off, that and the blow to your face."

"No way, that's all bullshit. I have no idea, and couldn't really care less, whether Tony had been with Dawn. I didn't ask her, and I've no idea if he was the guy she was on about that night. There are always plenty of rumours about that sort of thing amongst the Brit ex-pats in this place, and Tony was one of the worst of them. But if you believed them all, especially the ones when people have had a few drinks and like to gossip, then everybody would be shagging everybody here. And yes, even including the bloody donkeys! All I know is that Tony had been with Carol quite a bit. I don't know if her husband knew about it, but Tony was always going on about getting away with her, usually to Prague because he fucking loved the place and would bore anyone to death about it if you let him. He was besotted with her if you ask me, and besotted with bloody Prague because he'd lived there a while apparently. So, unless you have any more questions, Inspector, or are going to charge me with anything, I'm leaving now."

With that he stood up and headed towards the door of the interrogation room. As he did so Karagoulis informed him, "No doubt we will want to speak to you again, Mr. Bryant. We will also want to interview the friends you said you were with on Friday night. Before you go give Officer Samaras here their names please, and where they are living here."

12

The Lindos By Night Albanian barman

Albi, the Albanian barman at Lindos by Night, had the sort of personality that wouldn't have been out of place in London's East End. He was indeed a cheeky chappie, even down to his five-foot four inch stature. He owned the inside bottom bar at LBN, not literally, but in every other sense. He ran it from top to bottom, making sure it would always be a good place to be if you were a customer, and many of his customers were regular tourist Lindos returners who made a point of going to see Albi. Very few of them bothered to learn his other name. To them, and most people, he was just Albi. He certainly knew how to make his customers comfortable in the bar. He was sharp, street-smart, and cleverer than your average barman, even though he didn't always give that appearance. Coming to Lindos seven years before at the age of twenty-one, he'd stayed and quickly taught himself not only Greek, but also English and Italian. He knew most of the British ex-pats, many of whom used the bar regularly, and most of the people in Lindos, Greeks and Brit ex-pats, knew Albi.

When Karagoulis pushed his way through the swing doors and into the long narrow bar at LBN at just after six o'clock Albi was busy cleaning and setting up the bar for the evening's trade. As he introduced himself as a Police Inspector from Rhodes the Albanian's first reaction was, "You want to see my papers and work permit? I assume that's why you're here?"

Seating his growing weary body on one of the bar stools, Karagoulis informed him, "No, it's a bit more serious than that, it's about Dawn Parsons and Deborah Harris. I understand they were in here last night and that you know them well?"

"They were in here drinking for about an hour yes, from about two o'clock last night, but I only know them from their drinking in here, so I don't know if you'd call that knowing them well. I heard about Dawn's murder though," the barman replied.

"News certainly travels fast in this village, doesn't it, Albi They were drinking with a man I believe? Do you know him and where they were going after they left here?"

"Well, like you said, Inspector, it's a village. I don't really know the man they were with though. He's been in here drinking with Dawn a few times over the past couple of weeks, and a couple of times on his own. She just introduced him as Tom, so I don't know his second name. I had a couple of conversations with him in the bar on the nights when he was here alone and we weren't busy, but I never bothered to ask his full name, why would I? And I thought I overheard Dawn say something about going to Arches, the club just up the alley from Yannis bar."

"What did you talk to him about on the nights when he was here alone?"

"Just general stuff mostly, Inspector, you know, football mainly. Although there was one night when it seemed like he'd had quite a bit to drink and he was going on about Dawn. Something about how unpredictable and unreliable she was, and that you never really knew where you stood with her, was the way he put it. He seemed a bit pissed off with her, saying stuff like that, and that she blew hot and cold with him."

"What do you think he meant by that?"

"Not sure, but I did notice that when they were here he always seemed to be the one buying the drinks, so I thought maybe he meant that, although to be fair he was never slow to buy anyone a drink. I just told him to stop being so nice."

"And what did you mean by that, Albi?"

"Just that, Inspector, he should stop being so quick to buy her, or anyone, drinks."

"Was he angry at her then?"

"No, it didn't seem like that, just a bit frustrated and confused I think, and as I said before, a bit drunk."

"Interesting, thanks," Karagoulis told him, and then changed the subject, asking, "Were you busy in the bar last night?"

"It was Friday night, always a busy night. I've never figured out why it should be any different from any other night, but for some reason it always is. Some of the usual Brit ex-pats were in. They tend to have a good drink and night out on a Friday. It's a British tradition I guess. There were some tourists, mostly British, including a group of six young women, a couple of Germans, and a couple of Russian guys. At least, that's what I think they were."

"No one unusual then?" the Inspector added.

"Not really, all pretty normal for a Friday night."

"And the two women, Dawn and Deborah, and this, Tom, what was their mood like?"

"Good, very good, we were laughing and joking and drinking shots, although the conversation got quite serious at one point when we talked about what happened to Tony Carpentar at St. Paul's."

"So, did you, Dawn and Deborah know him quite well then?"

"Only from him drinking in here too," the barman replied. "He seemed to get on quite well with Dawn, but no so much with Deborah, I thought."

"Why was that?" Karagoulis pressed him.

"I don't really know. It was just a feeling I always got every time I saw the three of them together. Deborah always seemed a bit stand-offish with him. Maybe I'm wrong, it was just a feeling and nothing I could point to."

"Do you know Alan Bryant too? I heard he drinks in here as well."

"Yes, he does, often with Tony Carpentar, or he did, I suppose I should say now. They seemed to get on well as drinking mates, although I heard about the fight in Jack's the other night."

"What about with Dawn Parsons and Deborah Harris? How did he get on with them do you think?" Karagoulis asked.

"Not sure about with Deborah, she was always a bit careful with him as well I thought. He seemed to get on well with Dawn though, although she always gave the appearance of getting on well with most people, especially the men Brit ex-pats."

"Did you ever see him lose his temper here in the bar?"

"Most of the time he was fine, just enjoying his drinks and the company, although one time a few weeks ago he did flare up at one of the young Greek guys, Aggelos, who sometimes works in the bar here," Albi informed the Inspector.

"Why was that, what happened?" Karagoulis asked.

"Alan was trying to chat up a couple of much younger Austrian women. It was clear they weren't really interested in him. He was much too old for them. They were probably in their mid-twenties. Anyway, Aggelos was working behind the bar here that night and they were much more interested in him. He's only twenty. He was chatting to them over the bar and suddenly Alan, who'd had a fair bit to drink, started shouting at him telling him to 'fuck-off and do his job. Aggelos and the two women just started laughing, which seemed to make Alan even angrier. After he started to threaten Aggelos, the other British ex-pat guys he was with told him to calm down and eventually got him out of the bar. It was all very unpleasant. He saw Aggelos in here a couple of nights later and I thought he'd apologise, but he just acted like nothing had happened. He seemed to completely block it out of his memory. Maybe he was too drunk to remember, or too embarrassed to apologise, or too pig-headed perhaps."

"So, Mr. Bryant has a short temper then?" Karagoulis was fishing, but the barman wasn't adding anything more other than, "I don't know about that. It was just that one time I saw him lose his temper. The rest of the time he's been fine."

Karagoulis decided there was nothing more to learn from the barman about Alan Bryant's temper, telling him again, "Thanks, you've been helpful."

"There is one other thing about Dawn's murder I think you should know though, Inspector," the barman added just as Karagoulis was about to leave. "Erlind, who works here, thinks he heard it happening. Well, he heard some shouting and a scream, but didn't think it was anything serious, obviously wrongly."

"What! You should have told me this immediately. Where is he now? Why hasn't he reported what he heard to us? I obviously need to talk to him," the agitated Inspector asked.

"He works on the door here and as a waiter. He was in a rather difficult situation when he heard the scream. He can explain that to you, Inspector. I'd rather not get involved. He's in the top bar. I'll go and get him."

Erlind was another Albanian and Albi's cousin. It was only his second season working at Lindos by Night. He was six years younger than his cousin, taller by a good six inches, slim and good looking. He always tried to give off the impression of being a real cool guy and was very popular with the younger female clientele at LBN, as what he was about to tell Karagoulis demonstrated. Albi filled him in about the reason for the Inspector's visit as the two Albanians descended the wrought iron staircase from the outside top bar. After Karagoulis introduced himself he went directly to the point.

"You heard Dawn Parsons being murdered but you never did anything or even bothered to contact us after about what you heard? Is that right?"

"I wouldn't say I heard her being murdered, at least I didn't think it was someone being murdered when I heard what I heard," Erlind protested. "I heard a sort of muffled scream and some voices in the alley. They sounded foreign, I mean not Greek or English, but I couldn't be sure as they were not very clear either."

"Where was this and where were you?" Karagoulis interrupted.

"That's the tricky bit, Inspector. I was in one of the tourist apartments in the alley near where Dawn's body was found, according to what Albi told me."

"You were with a tourist in her apartment? I assume it was a girl?"

"Yep, it was a girl, but it wasn't her apartment. She was here with her parents on holiday for two weeks. She left today with them to go home to England."

"So, it was her parent's apartment? Where were they and what time was this when you heard the scream and the voices?"

Albi, who already knew the full story, was grinning, but Erlind was squirming under the Inspector's assumption and questions.

"I'm not completely sure about the time. I'd guess it was around four-thirty, but no it wasn't her parent's apartment. We could hardly go there, if you know what I mean, Inspector, and I share an apartment with Albi, and as he'd gone back there earlier when we finished in the bar here I couldn't really take her there."

Karagoulis was confused and a puzzled look stretched across his weary face. He'd had a hard couple of days. Trying to solve the murders and catch the killers was getting more and more complicated by the minute with all the entangled relationships in Lindos. His patience was now wearing thin, evident by his change in tone with the young Albanian doorman.

Levering himself up from the bar stool he told him, "Look young man, this is a serious business. There have been two murders in two days. So, stop pissing around worrying about the delicacies and confidentialities of your sex life. Just tell me clearly how you came to be in this apartment that you say wasn't where the girl you were with was staying and what you fucking know now, or I will charge you with wasting police time."

Erlind was visibly shocked at the Inspector's aggressive change in character.

"It's…it's…err…it's what some of us guys who work in the bars and restaurants here do, Inspector," he stuttered nervously.

Karagoulis interrupted him, again with an aggressive edge to his voice displaying his mounting impatience. "I bloody know that young man. I was a young Greek guy myself once, so getting off with the young women tourists, and some not so young, is what guys, Greeks and Albanians, do here and in all the holiday resorts."

"Yes, but that's not what I meant," the Albanian responded. "You see, we use the empty holiday apartments. If an apartment has not been occupied by the tourists in a particular week, but some are arriving for the coming week, some of the local girls and women who clean the apartments will do that the day before the tourists arrive, instead of on the morning of their arrival. When they are finished cleaning they leave the keys to the apartments in the door outside and the door unlocked. There are some girls who regularly do that so they don't have to get up so early the following morning, or they don't have so many apartments to clean on the morning that the tourists arrive. It's easy to check out which ones are empty for that one night with the key in the door. So, that's where we go with any of the female tourists we meet if we can't go back to where they are staying. For instance, most of the flights from Britain arrive on Wednesdays and Saturdays, so Tuesday night and Friday night there are always some tourist apartments empty with the key in the door. Of course, you have to be careful and make sure you leave the place, well the bedroom, tidy after, and also make sure you leave by around six in the morning well before the tourists arrive. I know one young Greek guy who works in a bar here who fell asleep with the English girl he was with, eventually anyway, and they were still in the apartment when they heard the tourists arrive through the door at ten in the morning. Seems they'd only come from Rhodes town having had three days of their holiday there. Luckily it was a villa and the girl and the Greek guy had to quickly climb out of the bedroom window after they heard the tourists downstairs. All a bit of a game really, Inspector, I suppose."

"Very enterprising, so that's why you were reluctant to inform us of this before?" the policeman interjected.

"Yes, plus I just thought the scream I heard was some girls who'd had a few drinks, were pissed, had come out of Qupi and fallen over in the alley, and that maybe the voices I heard were just some foreign tourists with them, not Greeks or Brits if you know what I mean. It was only when Albi told me late this afternoon about Dawn Parsons being murdered that I thought maybe what I heard had something to do with it, so I was, really was, going to come and report it tomorrow morning, Inspector, because I have to work here tonight until around two or three in the morning."

"So, any idea of the language and nationality the people you heard, and how many of them would you say?" Karagoulis asked in a more measured and relaxed tone.

"Like I said, I couldn't really say for certain what nationality they were, or even for certain they weren't British. It was very muffled and I only heard them very briefly after the scream. I think there were two people, but again I couldn't be sure."

"Was it an apartment opposite the patch of rough ground along there in that alleyway that you were in? Karagoulis asked.

"Yes, that's right. We left there pretty soon after. There's not much lighting along there and we didn't hang around in case anyone saw us leave, so we didn't really see anything or even stop to look around. After all I didn't think what I heard was anything unusual. People are always shouting and screaming when they come out of the clubs drunk, especially some of the British hen and stag parties."

The Inspector handed him his card telling him, "If you think of anything else contact me on this number or come to the police station. It's a pity you didn't report this sooner, then we could have also spoken to the girl you were with before she left Lindos in case she heard or remembered something you didn't. I will refrain from asking how old she was."

Erlind volunteered the information anyway. "She was seventeen, but I really don't think she would have liked her parents to know what she'd been up to if you had interviewed her about this, Inspector"

"I should imagine not, definitely not," Karagoulis agreed as he headed towards the swing doors and down the flight of stairs to the alleyway below.

13

Chlamydia?

As he left Lindos by Night Karagoulis called Samaras, telling him, "Meet me at the Athenian Restaurant in ten minutes, we need to have another little chat with Carol Hudson. You had better give your friend the owner a call and warn him that we're coming. We'll need to use his office again. I don't imagine they'll be that busy yet, it's still early. Then we need to go and interview her husband."

Carol Hudson was hardly pleased to see the two police officers again, although this time she was much less abrasive, telling them straightaway as she entered the small office, "I'm not sure what more I can tell you, but I'll obviously help if I can."

"That's a nasty bruise you have on the side of your face, Miss Hudson," Karagoulis observed as she sat down on the white plastic chair by the desk.

"I walked into a door, just wasn't looking where I was going," she told him.

"A door, that must have been painful? Are you sure? It wouldn't have been a blow from your husband by any chance? Is he usually a violent man?" The Inspector recognised an opportunity when he saw it and was instantly probing to see if she would give anything away.

"No, Panos isn't a violent man, and it wasn't him. I told you it was a door." She was insistent.

"But I assume he's heard about you and Tony Carpentar then? That must have produced quite an argument between you? Is that when he hit you? Does he lose his temper easily, Miss Hudson?"

"How many times do I have to tell you, it was a door. Panos didn't hit me, and no he doesn't lose his temper easily, and he didn't this time either." She was managing to remain calm and despite the Inspector's continued questions about it still showed none of the aggressive response that she had initially exhibited in the previous interview.

"I told him, but he said he knew, he'd known for a while, everyone did in the village. He said it was common knowledge, but the Greeks in the village didn't like that sort of thing at all. Family is family, and marriage is sacrosanct for them. Wives don't cheat on their husbands as far as most of the village is concerned. It made him look a fool. That's what he said, and yes he was shouting and screaming at me when he said it, but he said he was more angry with that bastard Carpentar, as he put it, because he had been telling everyone in Lindos who would listen that I was going away with him, leaving Panos. That was what he'd heard from one of his Greek friends that he works with. Panos said that Tony was always shouting his fucking mouth off around the village about what he'd done and what he was going to do, and couldn't keep anything to himself."

As was his way, Karagoulis was now pacing back and forth across the small office, occasionally turning to face the English woman and approach where she was sitting. "So, your husband was bloody angry with Tony Carpentar you say, angry enough to kill him maybe? Jealousy is a powerful thing, and especially when honour is involved in a small traditional village community like this, isn't it Samaras? And I think you would agree wouldn't you, Miss Hudson?" He was deliberately bringing his local police officer colleague into the interrogation to confirm his comment and put more pressure on her.

Samaras just nodded his head in agreement and contributed a very short, "Yes, it is, sir," but apart from that he remained silent, leaning against one of the office walls opposite where Carol Hudson sat. Karagoulis was prompting and probing, but Carol Hudson wasn't agreeing. She shifted her position slightly in the chair, her hands were clasped in front of her resting in her lap, but her thumbs were twitching and tapping together betraying her obvious anxiety.

"Panos never killed Tony. He wouldn't. Yes, he was bloody angry, why wouldn't he be, and yes he said he'd confront him and tell him to stay away from me, but he's not like that, he's not a violent man. Anyway, if the rumours I've heard about when Tony was killed are true Panos must have been at home in bed with me at the time. I heard it was in the early hours of the morning."

"Maybe," Karagoulis interjected, but he wasn't giving up that easily. "Maybe he was at home with you, but equally he could have had accomplices that murdered Tony Carpentar for him and dumped his body at St. Paul's while he was home with you. That would give him a nice alibi wouldn't it, Miss Hudson? As you said, feelings run high amongst the Greeks in the village about adultery and honour, especially among the men, so I'm sure there would have been friends of his prepared to help him."

Carol Hudson was starting to look confused and a frown came across her face, like it was slowly dawning on her that what Karagoulis was suggesting could have happened. He was successfully putting doubts in her mind. The only hesitant defensive response on behalf of her husband that she could come up with was, "But he was at LBN before that with some of his friends he works with, they could confirm that."

"Yes, they could indeed, Miss Hudson, but then maybe they would wouldn't they if they were involved. He didn't have to be there for the actual murder. He could quite easily have arranged for it to be done for him. Friendships and family are strong amongst Greek men, especially in a small village community like this, and even more so where a man's honour is concerned over his wife and his marriage. We obviously need to go and talk to you husband now at his work, at Stefano's Restaurant I think you told us before."

"Yes, he'll be there now," she confirmed, adding as if she was now trying to convince herself as much as the police officers, "but I'm certain he had nothing to do with this."

Ignoring her comment, Karagoulis told her instead, "Just one more thing that maybe you can shed some light on before we go, Miss Hudson. Have you ever had any sexually transmitted diseases, like chlamydia for instance?"

"What? Why are you asking me that? I don't see what a question like that has got to do with any of this, or that it's any of your business."

She sat upright in the chair, and rather than make any eye contact with the Inspector standing to one side of her, stared straight ahead across the small desk at the blank discoloured magnolia wall as she made her indignant response.

"If you could just answer my question please, Miss Hudson. It will assist our enquiries I can assure you," Karagoulis pressed her.

She hesitated and sat staring blankly ahead for around half-a-minute while Karagoulis and Samaras remained silent, but exchanged glances. Still choosing not to make any eye contact with either of them, she eventually said, "Erm...okay, yes. The doctor in the village told me I had it two weeks ago. I've managed to not tell Panos about it though. Don't ask me how, because I'm not going into that. I completely refuse to explain that, but how did you find out? It's supposed to be subject to doctor and patient confidentiality, that's why even Panos doesn't know."

"We didn't know, but the preliminary autopsy found that Tony Carpentar had it. Presumably, from what you've just told us, your husband hasn't got it?"

"Not at the moment, no, as far as I know, although the doctor told me I'd have to tell him soon as he could have it. He said it can take three to four weeks for it to be passed on and develop in a man. I had no idea Tony had it though. He never told me, and I never told him I did."

"I expect you got it from Tony Carpentar, or maybe he got it from you. Although the autopsy on her also confirmed that Dawn Parsons had it, so maybe Tony Carpentar got it from her?" Karagoulis was standing across the desk and staring into her face as he made that remark, looking carefully for any reaction from her.

She dismissed his suggestion instantly, with a raised voice. "Dawn Parsons? What makes you think Tony could have got it from her? Of course he didn't. He wouldn't go near her. She was always drunk. I heard rumours about her and another British ex-pat man, but never anything about Tony and her. He was totally involved with me, he even told me as much the night he was murdered when he was trying to persuade me to go to Prague with him for a weekend. He said he was in love with me."

Her anger had returned now as a result of Karagoulis' suggestion, and her raised voice portrayed it clearly. Her aggressive, almost indignant, tone had resurfaced, but Karagoulis sensed she was uneasy and uncomfortable at the mention of Dawn Parsons and wasn't letting her off the hook. He was pacing back and forth in the little office once more, only this time a little more slowly.

Eventually he paused after a minute or so to turn to face her again, leaning over her as she sat at the desk, and deliberately trying to provoke in a calculating manner as he told her, "I think that perhaps you killed Dawn in a jealous rage. You found out about her and Tom Carpentar didn't you? Maybe you're lying and you even found out about the two of them and the chlamydia. She was drunk, you had an argument over Tony and you lost control? Is that what happened, Miss Hudson? Just where were you between four and seven on Saturday morning?"

"At home in bed sleeping, that's ridiculous," she responded, still displaying her anger, this time over being accused.

"Alone?" Samaras asked.

"Yes, alone, Panos was out drinking. I met him in Arches after we both finished work. He was there with a couple of the guys he works with and I went there after work with one of the Greek girls who works here as a waitress. I didn't stay as long as Panos though. I was tired and it was busy and pretty packed, so I left around three-thirty. We didn't get there until gone one. Panos came in to Arches with the guys about half-past one I guess. When I was leaving he said he'd stay for one more drink with the guys, but I must have gone off to sleep straightaway because I never heard him come in."

"So, you don't really have anyone who can confirm where you were between four and seven?" Karagoulis pressed her.

"Panos told me this morning that he came home just after four, so I guess he can confirm where I was then, but you can ask him when you see him."

For some reason she was obviously worried about the Inspector's suspicions and was shifting uneasily in her chair. Her discomfort had made her more conciliatory though in trying to answer the questions, and without prompting she added, "I saw Dawn in Arches though. She was with Deborah Harris and another guy that I don't know. I presume he was English by the way they were chatting and laughing between the three of them."

"Did you speak to her?" Karagoulis asked.

"No, she was at the other end of the bar, but I could see them talking away and laughing. She looked pretty drunk though, which is not that unusual for her, or maybe I should say wasn't that unusual for her."

"What time was that?" Now Samaras joined the questioning again, which startled her slightly and she turned her head to answer,

"They came into the club about half-an-hour before I left, so I guess it must have been about three o'clock. They were still there when I left. I thought there were a couple of other guys with them at one point, or at least who knew them, because they were stood at the end of the bar where I was with Panos and one of them was pointing over at the three of them, Dawn, Deborah and this other English guy, but strangely they never actually went over to talk to them. I didn't actually see Dawn acknowledge them though, so maybe she didn't really know them. Perhaps they'd eaten in the Village House restaurant before, where she worked, and they recognised her from there. One of them seemed to get quite agitated at one point though, and was raising his voice and waving his arms around, until the guy with him calmed him down. I thought they had an argument and were going to have a fight between them there and then in Arches, but I've no idea what it was about."

"Do you know them?"

"No, I've never seen them in Lindos before," she replied. "They weren't Greeks or English though and they were a couple of well-built guys. Panos said he thought they were Russian. He guessed from their accent I think, because one of them asked him in broken English if he could get to the bar where we were stood to get served. Anyway, you can ask him when you see him."

"Yes, and we will want to know where he was between four and seven as well, as it seems both of you don't have anyone to corroborate where you were at a time when Dawn Parsons was murdered."

"As I told you before, Inspector, I was at home in bed sleeping, and no doubt Panos can tell you the names of the guys he was with from work until four in Arches, and then he was at home in bed with me."

"But we only have his word for when he actually came home don't we, Miss Hudson. You said yourself that as you were sleeping you didn't hear him come home." Karagoulis was challenging her again, and once more trying to plant some doubt in her mind, but she wasn't responding in the way he'd hoped.

"That makes no sense whatsoever." She was raising her voice again. "That's bloody stupid! Why on earth would Panos kill Dawn Parsons? What reason would he have for that?"

"Who knows, Miss Hudson," the Inspector replied, equally forcibly. "Who knows what happens in this village? From what we've already learned over the past two days there seems to have been any amount of strange things going on, and should I say, strange liaisons forming. Maybe your husband had his own little indiscretion that you had no idea about? What is it you English say? What's sauce for the goose is sauce for the gander? I think it's time we went and had a little talk with this husband of yours now, and maybe we can get some answers to some of these riddles."

Intentionally leaving that thought hanging in the air, and in her head, Karagoulis added quickly, "Thank you again for your time. We will let you get back to work now, but if necessary we'll talk to you again."

She slumped back in the white plastic chair, looked visibly stunned and just mumbled to herself, "Panos and Dawn Parsons, no way, that's not possible," as the two policemen made their way through the door of the small office and out of the restaurant, Karagoulis offering a brief, "Thank you," once more to Samaras' friend the owner as they did so.

As they reached the street the Inspector told his officer, "I'll go and talk to her husband at the restaurant where he works. You go and see if you can find the owner of this Arches Club. Talk to him, and the staff he had working there last night, and see if any of them saw what time Dawn Parsons left the club and when the people she was with left. We need to know if they all left together. See if any of the staff recall when Carol Hudson left and when her husband left. When you've done that go and talk to Alan Bryant's drinking buddies from last night, see if what they tell you matches his story and backs up his alibi."

As Karagoulis made his way through the narrow Lindos alleys it was approaching eight o'clock on a busy summer season Saturday night in the little village. The tourists were out in force making their way to the multitude of restaurants and bars and he was attempting with some difficulty to slowly weave his way between them. It was still warm and during the day the hot summer sun had heated up the narrow streets. According to the large sign giving the time and the temperature on the wall by the Symposio Restaurant it was still twenty-seven degrees. Stopping briefly to remove his jacket in an attempt to cool down he was rudely reminded by a rumbling in his stomach that he hadn't eaten since the rather small roll that his Sargent had got for him at lunchtime from Café Melia. He decided he could spare a few minutes to stop and buy a savoury crepe from one of the many kiosks selling them.

Feeling a little fuller, and his not inconsiderable stomach having stopped rumbling, he arrived outside Stefano's Restaurant in the square by the Amphitheatre. It was an Italian restaurant, one of the very few non-Greek restaurants in Lindos. There was a young, blonde, attractive looking girl on the door of the restaurant doing the 'meet and greet'. From her accent as she greeted him with a pleasant, "Good evening," closely followed by, "we have a good menu of Italian food, would you like a table for one?" Karagoulis guessed she was from Eastern Europe or more probably one of the Baltic States.

He immediately put her straight. "No thank you, I'm sure the food is very good, but I'm a police officer, Inspector Dimitris Karagoulis, and I'd like to see the owner please."

The restaurant was already quite full as she led him through the open inner courtyard and between some of the diners at the tables to a door to the kitchen in the corner, telling him, "If you just wait here I'll get him."

Half a minute later the owner appeared through the door and introduced himself as Angelo Mazzotti, followed by, "What can I do for you, Inspector?"

"You have a Panos Koropoulis working here I understand. I need to have a word with him, in private if that is okay please. We believe Mr. Koropoulis may be able to help us with our investigation into two murders in Lindos over the past twenty-four hours. Is there somewhere less public that I can talk with him?"

"Yes, of course, Inspector, you can use my office upstairs. I'll show you, and then I'll fetch Panos. He is serving on the terrace upstairs."

The room was another small one with similar bare furnishings as the one in the Athenian Restaurant Karagoulis had just left. Panos Koropoulis was a tall, very slim guy in his mid-thirties with slicked back dark black hair and a long thin face. As soon as he entered the little office Karagoulis couldn't help noticing he had a grazed and bruised right hand.

After introducing himself, inviting Koropoulis to take a seat, and explaining he was investigating the murders, the Inspector asked, "How did you hurt your hand? Was it from hitting your wife by any chance? I've just seen her and she has a nasty bruise on the side of her face. Did you do that in anger, Mr. Koropoulis? Do you often lose your temper, lose it easily?"

"No, she walked into a door, but yes I did hurt my hand in anger. I punched the wall while she was telling me about Tony Carpentar and her. I'd heard rumours about them from my friends in the village, but this murder business has made it even more public. Everyone is talking about it. It's humiliating for me, and when she started to tell me I got angry. But I would never hit her, or any woman. I took my anger and frustration out on the wall, but as you can see I obviously came off worse."

Karagoulis saw his chance and immediately interrupted. "Not hit any woman, does that mean you would hit a man? Or maybe even kill him, or get someone to kill him for you, some of your friends in the village maybe?"

"No, I didn't kill Tony Carpentar, and I didn't get any of my friends to do it for me either. Carol said that she told you I was home in bed with her by just after three that night, and before that I was with some guys from work. They can confirm that."

Karagoulis wasn't completely convinced. "Well, if they were involved, and did it for you, they would say that wouldn't they, Mr. Koropoulis. You'd give one another an alibi then, wouldn't you? What about Dawn Parsons? How well did you know her?"

Koropoulis looked confused. "Dawn Parsons? I hardly knew her at all. I just saw her around the village, mostly late at night in the clubs, and often quite drunk. I barely ever even said hello to her, just a nodded acknowledgement mostly. Carol introduced me to her a few years ago after she first arrived to live here. Of course, I heard about her murder. It's a village, news and gossip travels fast, as I found out over Carol and Tony Carpentar. But I had nothing to do with that either. Why would you think I had?"

"Ever had the sexually transmitted disease chlamydia, Mr. Koropoulis?" Karagoulis was trying to unsettle him with a change of direction in his questioning. Before the waiter could respond he continued with, "I don't think she's told you yet but your wife has it. She confirmed that when I interviewed her again this evening, and according to the autopsy reports Tony Carpentar and Dawn Parsons had it when they were murdered. Quite a little village community sex foursome we have here, wouldn't you say?"

Koropoulis looked stunned. He sat frowning, looking puzzled and staring at the blank whitewashed wall across the desk in front of him for about a minute.

"Well, Mr. Koropoulis, do you have anything to say about that. No comments at all?" Karagoulis pushed him.

"I...err... I," he started to answer but took a gulp and hesitated trying to compose himself before continuing, "I had no idea. Carol never told me, but the other two having it has nothing to do with me. As far as I know I haven't got it, so if you are suggesting there was something going on between me and Dawn Parsons on the basis of that you are very, very wrong, Inspector, I can assure you, completely wrong. I suppose it's pretty obvious how Carol and Carpentar got it, but I don't see how Dawn fits into that, unless of course some of the rumours about her and Carpentar were true."

"Rumours?" the Inspector was doing his usual pacing back and forth across the small office and fishing for any further information.

"There were always lots of rumours about Dawn and various British ex-pat men in the village, some about her and married men, as well as her and single men. She liked to party in the clubs and bars after she had finished work, and she liked to drink, as I said. I guess that made her an easy target for the gossips in the village, especially amongst the ex-pat British community. It was usually the women amongst them, some of them who were her friends supposedly, who had the worst things to say and most liked to spread the rumours. Carol told me that once, although I suppose that now it seems she was just covering herself. Anyway, I never took much notice of the rumours about Dawn and I can't say I ever saw her getting too friendly with any man in any of the clubs and bars, if you know what I mean. I did see her having coffee outside Giorgos with the same guy a few times recently though. Also, she was in Arches with Deborah Harris and him on Friday night. I think he's English, but I don't know him."

"So, you were in Arches on Friday night when Dawn Parsons was there. What time was that?" Karagoulis interrupted him, intent on checking if his story matched that of his wife's.

"I went there after work with the same guys I was with the night before. We got there about one-thirty I guess. I think Dawn, Deborah and the guy they were with came in around three. I was with Carol then, as well as the guys from work and a Greek girl from the restaurant where Carol works. Carol will confirm that. She was tired and left about three-thirty. I had one more drink with the guys and got home just after four. Dawn was still there when I left, and was getting pretty drunk as far as I could see. Deborah and the guy were also still there with her."

"Yes, your wife told me earlier that she was in Arches with you that night, and that Dawn was there with Deborah Harris and another guy. What she told me about the times seems to match up with your recollections, although the time of Dawn Parsons' death is believed to be between four and seven that morning. Obviously from what you and your wife have told me it couldn't have been before four o'clock as you said she was still in the club at that time drinking, and presumably the staff at Arches and this Deborah Harris can confirm that. So, until we know what time she left Arches, and have a witness to that effect, we can only assume she was murdered sometime between four and seven that morning. Of course, you say you were at home in bed just after four Mr. Koropoulis, although again we only have your word for that as your wife told us she was very tired, went straight to sleep and never heard you come home. So, she would really have no idea of the time that you actually came home, would she?"

Karagoulis stopped pacing back and forth and turned to face Koropoulis directly as he made that last statement. He was intent on provoking a reaction from him, and emphasising the weakness in his alibi, but Koropoulis didn't budge in his protestation of innocence.

"Are you seriously accusing me of killing Dawn Parsons, Inspector? And just why would I do that, that's crazy, like I said, I barely knew her. What are you thinking? Presumably that we were having some wild, crazy affair, presumably in the belief that I was trying to pay Carol back for what I'd heard about her and that bastard Carpentar. That's absolute rubbish, and I'm sure you have no evidence whatsoever for that, not least because none exists and it's not true. I don't think for one minute that you'll find anyone that might suggest it was, with the possible exception of a few of the gossipy British ex-pats of course."

He was losing his composure and growing angry, but before he could go on Karagoulis interrupted him again, asking, "Talking of ex-pats, Mr. Koropoulis, what do you know about Alan Bryant?"

That only increased his anger. "That bastard, he's another one. Thinks he's God's gift to women. He must think I'm really stupid. I know he's been trying to get Carol into bed for weeks. Everyone knows that's what the fight in Jack's bar on Thursday night was about. Apart from that, him trying to get into Carol's knickers, and seeing him and his mates around drinking in the bars and clubs in the village, I don't know him at all, and I can't say I particularly want to, Inspector. He's a prat!"

"Do you think he would kill someone? Like Tony Carpentar, for instance?" Karagoulis was trying to prompt him to go even further in his character assassination.

"I have no idea, although I did hear from one of the Albanian guys who works in one of the bars here he has a quick temper, especially when it comes to arguments about women, or if he can't get his own way over them."

"Your wife said something about some Russians, or she said you thought they were Russians, pointing over at Dawn Parsons in

Arches on Friday night?" Not getting any further with that line of questioning, the Inspector changed tack again.

"There were two well-built guys by us at the bar, but I didn't see them pointing over at Dawn. I only noticed them when they wanted to get past us to the bar. One of them put his hand on my shoulder and said something in broken English that I didn't really hear clearly, but from the way he was pointing towards the bar I assumed he wanted me to move aside so he could get served. His accent sounded Russian to me, but I couldn't be sure, it could have been anywhere in Eastern Europe I suppose. They seemed to be having a bit of an argument between them briefly just after that, but I couldn't tell you what that was about. Like I said though, I never saw them pointing specifically at Dawn, and anyway Carol is always imagining things like that and is prone to a bit of exaggeration sometimes, Inspector. Arches was crowded, so if they were pointing then they could have been pointing at anybody. Why are you interested in them? Do you think they had anything to do with Dawn's murder?"

"It was just something your wife mentioned, probably nothing to do with any of this at all. So, unless you have anything else you would like to tell me, Mr. Koropoulis, I'll let you get back to work. I expect the restaurant is busy now, being a Saturday night, and your boss will want you back waiting on the tables. If we need to talk to you again we know where to find you."

Panos Koropoulis nodded, and with a somewhat relieved look across his face made his way out of the office and back to his work, while the Inspector made his way down the stone steps to the now busy restaurant courtyard where he bid a brief, "Thank you," to the owner and left.

14

"Everyone is cheating, and no one likes each other, but reasons for murder?"

By the time Karagoulis got back to Lindos Police Station it was coming up to nine o'clock on Saturday evening. He arrived in the rear office to find Sargent Papadoulis tussling with the ancient computer and the inconsistencies of the Lindos internet connection.

As the Inspector headed towards the kettle to make a coffee the Sargent informed him in his thick throaty voice that belied his thirty-six years that, "It took an age because of the bloody useless internet connection in this back of beyond place, but I finally managed to do some background checks on Tony Carpentar and Dawn Parsons."

"Anything interesting?" the Inspector asked.

"Not really, nothing odd in relation to their financial backgrounds and bank accounts, except that Dawn Parsons was in receipt of a monthly payment from a pension company in England. I managed to check the company on the internet, when the connection worked. It looks like a public service pension, but I would have thought she was still a bit young to be getting that. Also, the only background stuff on her I could find is very thin, almost non-existent in fact. I turned up very little about her relating to the time before she came to live in Lindos. There's nothing at all unusual or out of the ordinary in Carpentar's background, although to be honest, sir, there's not a lot I could find on him either. It does appear that both of them had Greek mobiles, or at least sims. I managed to track down their Greek mobile providers by trawling through most of the companies, although we still haven't found their phones."

"I suspect they may have been tossed in the sea by whoever murdered them. I doubt we'll ever find them," Karagoulis suggested. "Anything stand out in their call records?"

"Over the three days before he was murdered Tony Carpentar made quite a few calls to what I tracked down as Carol Hudson's number, but I guess we already know what was going on there. Dawn Parsons doesn't seem to have made many calls generally, although she did make one to a Deborah Harris yesterday at two-thirty in the afternoon. I checked the employment office records in Rhodes and Miss Harris works at Symposio Restaurant, which apparently is in the centre of the village."

"Yes, Sargent, Carol Hudson and her husband told me that they saw Dawn in Arches on Friday night with this Deborah Harris and another English guy that they didn't know, plus the Albanian barman at LBN said the three of them were in there drinking before that. Once Samaras gets back and tells us what he's found out from the owner and staff at Arches I think we need to go and have a word with Deborah Harris to see what else she can tell us about Dawn's activities on Friday night, and just who the English guy is that the two of them were drinking with. Meanwhile, Sargent, let's get some of this stuff up on the Incident Board and see if we can make any sense of it. As far as I can see everyone involved, including a number of the British ex-pats here, seem to have been cheating on each other, and behind their backs no one really likes each other, despite the appearance of being friends. Whether that is a motive for murder is another matter, of course. In my experience, in murder investigations like this you can usually identify a normal level of events and incidents that occurred, but alongside them a very weird, unusual and extraordinary level of things going on. We've had far too many unusual events going on here in such a little village like Lindos. There has to be some connections and some reasons behind them, some motive or maybe motives."

As Karagoulis stood sipping his coffee and intermittently rubbing the forefinger of his left-hand up and down his nose deep in thought in front of the Incident Board fixed on one of the office walls, Papadoulis added, "Just one other thing, sir, I did a general search of Rhodes police records for anything on the two victims and Tony

Carpentar reported his passport stolen from his rucksack in Rhodes town four weeks ago. It's the only thing that showed up for either of them."

"Just his passport, no money, credit cards, mobile phone maybe, nothing else?" Karagoulis asked as he turned away from the white board and wandered slowly across the room towards the small office window.

"Well, he didn't report anything else," the Sargent confirmed.

"Sounds like just the usual tourist robbery in Rhodes Town, but it's unusual for other things not to be taken. We'll stick it on the board just in case, but can't really see at the moment if, or how, it could be connected. What about the crime scene for Dawn Parsons' murder, have we turned up anything there?"

"Nothing, sir, no sign of a weapon, just the bloody mess of the pools of dried blood, and so far none of the people who live along that alleyway, or any of the tourists staying in apartments along there, have told us they heard anything."

As he placed his now empty mug down on the desk and headed back across the room towards the Incident Board Karagoulis said, "Well, according to Crisa Tsagroni the murderer's method of stabbing an artery in the neck would have killed her almost immediately, just like with Tony Carpentar apparently, so it's unlikely she would have been able to cry out or that anyone would have heard anything."

Standing in front of the white board he continued, "Right, let's see what we've got then shall we, Sargent. The two victims are both British, in their forties, been working and living in Lindos for the past three or four years, but there is no clear connection between them, unless we count them both having the same sexually transmitted disease and seemingly both being murdered in a similar way. Given the way they were both killed, the murderer, or murderers, would have to have had a knife with them, which suggests both murders were planned in advance. You don't go wandering around Lindos in the early hours of the morning carrying a probably quite large bladed knife on the off chance you're going to run into someone you don't like or have a grudge against, like jealousy perhaps, do you? Even in this place, where quite a few people actually do appear to dislike one another behind their back, from what we've heard over the past two days, that seems unlikely."

"It does seem like the two murders are connected though, sir, don't you think?" Papadoulis suggested.

"At this point I don't know, Sargent, and couldn't say for sure, although I must say it looks like it as it is a hell of a coincidence if they aren't," Karagoulis replied.

He was tapping the end of the black felt tip marker on the board underneath the names of Tony Carpentar and Dawn Parsons written on it as he went on, "So, did these two have sex together? No one has suggested they were that close, although again, from what I've heard over the past two days in this place who knows. We know Dawn Parsons had sex with Alan Bryant in the early hours of Friday morning, and that Tony Carpentar and her were both drunk when they were murdered, or at least had a good amount of alcohol in their bloodstream. We don't have their mobiles, but they don't seem to have been communicating with each other, at least in that way, according to their phone records. There is nothing odd in their financial records, except maybe for this pension payment to Parsons each month, although that could simply have been a pension she contributed to when she was working in England before and simply took the monthly payment early instead of when she is, or rather would have been, older. We know Carpentar was having an affair with Carol Hudson, and that there were plenty of rumours about Dawn and ex-pat British men in the village, although the only one we definitely know about is her sexual liaison with Alan Bryant the night before she was murdered."

Papadoulis remained silent, stroking the side of his long, thin suntanned face with the palm of his left hand while his Inspector was thinking aloud. As the Sargent then moved it to rub his palm across his close cut dark black hair in what looked like bewilderment, Karagoulis took a sideways step to shift a little to stand in front of the part of the board marked 'Suspects'. He continued, "So, Sargent, just who out of these people is our murderer, or murderers?"

"Well, sir, from what we know it seems almost certain that two people committed both the murders. It needed two people to get Carpentar down to St. Paul's after he was knocked unconscious, and from the marks on her arms and neck Dawn Parsons was attacked from behind and held while someone else stabbed her in the neck."

"So, we have two murderers," Karagoulis agreed. "That means two out of these three could have done it together, but which two? Or is there something we're missing here? Alan Bryant had a fight with Tony Carpentar the night he was murdered, and although they were supposedly friends there was obviously some tension, competition and bad feeling between them over women, particularly Carol Hudson. Bryant has a medical background, so he may have had knowledge of just where was the most effective place to kill someone quickly, with the knife in the artery in the neck. On the other hand, the night Tony Carpentar was killed he says he was having sex with Dawn Parsons in the alley by Qupi. One of the guys working in Jack's Courtyard Bar said he heard him, and there's no real reason to believe he's lying to protect Bryant, although he could have just mistaken his voice for someone else. He thinks it was about four-thirty that morning. Bryant could still have murdered Tony Carpentar after that I suppose, but he would have needed help. When Dawn Parsons was being murdered he claims to have been with two other Brit ex-pat guys drinking and eating in Nightlife and Bar Code. Samaras is going to check that with them after he's seen the people at Arches. We will see what they have to say and if Bryant's alibi stands up. So, our abrasive, and seemingly short-tempered, friend Mr. Bryant had some motive for Tony Carpentar's murder at least, although he would have needed help from someone. Maybe from one of his drinking buddies that he says will give him an alibi for Dawn's murder? Perhaps Tony had upset one of them in the past too?"

The Inspector was going round in circles in terms of his reasoning and rubbing his nose again as Papadoulis started to make himself some coffee, asking his boss if he wanted another, feeling it could be a long Saturday night. Karagoulis told him, "Yes, and make it strong please," while now pointing at Carol Hudson's name on the Incident Board.

"Then we have the delightful Carol Hudson," he said ironically. "We know she was having an affair with Carpentar, and she hardly seems to be what you might call a woman of virtue. On the contrary, in fact she seems a rather nasty piece of work. Not only was she cheating on her husband, but somehow, somewhere, she contracted a sexually transmitted disease from someone that she may well have passed on to him, but decided not to tell him. Could she really have killed both Tony Carpentar and Dawn Parsons though, and why, what motive did she have? She definitely couldn't have done it alone."

He stopped talking for a moment and stood staring at the board, while simultaneously scratching the back of his bald head and gently shaking it from side to side. It wasn't clear to Papadoulis and Samaras though whether the shaking of his head was an indication that he didn't think Carol Hudson was the murderer or whether he was just exhibiting his total disgust at her actions towards her husband.

"Of course," he eventually continued, "as I said before, we know that the two victims also had chlamydia, so maybe they were having an affair as well. What if the fight in the Courtyard bar was over Dawn Parsons and not Carol Hudson? Maybe Carpentar was actually sleeping with her as well as having the affair with Hudson and Bryant found out, wanted to sleep with Dawn Parsons himself, and taunted Carpentar that he could if he wanted. We know that he had sex with her on the night Carpentar was murdered. So, maybe Carol Hudson found out about Dawn and Carpentar, perhaps Alan Bryant told her to get back at Carpentar, and she killed them both in acts of rage, revenge and jealousy?"

Even he didn't seem to really believe his own conjecture and once again he was shaking his head as he went on, "But I don't see how that was possible as it's certain that two people were needed to carry out both murders, and for sure to dispose of Carpentar's body in St. Pauls bay, and who would she possibly get to help her?"

"Maybe Carol Hudson had help from Alan Bryant? Perhaps he was her accomplice?" Papadoulis interjected, trying to help out his Inspector. "What if, in fact, they were having an affair that they managed to keep it hidden in the village? We've heard from a few people that Bryant was always goading Carpentar that he could have Carol anytime he wanted and take her away from him. You said that even her husband told you that Bryant was always chasing her, Inspector. What if, in fact, he already had been successful? What if most of that, his goading of Carpentar, was all a bluff just to cover up the fact that Bryant and Hudson were already having it off?"

"Well, that's one possibility, I suppose, Sargent," Karagoulis agreed circumspectly. Bryant would easily have been strong enough to restrain a drunken Dawn Parsons, and to help get Carpentar's body into the water in St. Paul's bay, but does that mean Hudson would have to have done the stabbing in the neck, at least of Dawn Parsons?"

"Jealousy does strange things to people, sir, especially women. It could have happened that way, couldn't it?" The Sargent wasn't giving up on his theory easily, and now it was his turn to rub his chin, though in his case with the palm of his right hand.

"Yes, it could have done, happened that way" the Inspector agreed, "but I still think we are missing something here. There has got to be a more plausible scenario."

Still not entirely convinced that his theory was wrong, Papadoulis shrugged his shoulders and walked over to pour himself yet another coffee. At that point Samaras appeared through the office door.

"A coffee for me too please, Sargent. I need to lubricate my throat after all that talking to the staff at Arches and Alan Bryant's drinking partners," were his first words.

Well, anything interesting, Samaras?" Karagoulis wasn't about to wait for him to lubricate his throat with the coffee. He was getting increasingly frustrated at not being able to see any clear connection and motives between the suspects and the murders, and he wanted any information that could help him to do that immediately.

"I spoke to the owner at Arches and he let me talk to two of the bar staff, as well as one of the guys who works on the door, who were working last night and the night before," Samaras started to tell the Inspector as Papadoulis handed him his coffee. After taking a quick sip, he continued, "The guy on the door remembered Carol Hudson leaving last night. He's Greek and said he knows her through her husband, Panos. Everyone knows everyone in this village, sir. He confirmed it was around three-thirty, because it was just before he started his fifteen minute break at that time. He said her husband left just before four, just after he got back from his break. Deborah Harris and the English guy she was with left just after he reckons, but Dawn

Parsons definitely didn't leave with them. He was adamant about that. He doesn't know the English guy they came in with and were drinking with, but he said he's seen him around the village over the past month or so. He thought it was gone four-thirty when Dawn left, just before the incident on the door."

"What incident?" the Inspector interrupted, "and what do you mean 'on the door'?"

"Arches has a door sound lock system, sir. As it's in the centre of the village, and because of the ban on music here after one o'clock at night, they have two doors with a compartment between them. As the customers come in the outer door is opened by one guy outside. Once they are all in the compartment between the two doors and the outer door is closed the inner door is opened by another guy inside the club and they are let in. It prevents the noise from the music in the club from getting out and disturbing the residents in the village."

"Okay, so what happened last night with the door, this incident you mentioned?" Karagoulis was getting even more impatient.

"The guy I spoke to was operating the inside door and he said it actually happened just after Dawn Parsons left. Apparently, he let her and a couple of other people out, but just after he'd closed the inside door, and as the guy outside was opening his door to let Dawn and the two people out of the compartment, two guys, well-built guys he said, came charging over to where he was standing and tried to pull the inside door open themselves. But he had his hand firmly on the door handle and his foot and body wedged firmly against it as he tried to tell them in English that he couldn't open the inside door yet because the guy outside had opened the outer door and was letting people out."

"Was Dawn Parsons with those other two people she was leaving with then, in their company during the evening?" Karagoulis asked.

"I asked him that, sir, but he said he was pretty sure she didn't know them. Apparently, there was a bit of a scuffle then inside the club by the inner door and the two guys got quite angry until some of the other Arches staff appeared and they calmed down. He doesn't think they understood English or what he was trying to tell them about the door system and the sound lock. They were shouting at him, but it wasn't in Greek or English and he didn't recognise the language."

"So, did he think those two guys had anything to do with Dawn, were with her?" the Inspector asked.

"He said he didn't think so. He couldn't say for sure, but thought they weren't, as they didn't actually initially go to leave with her, just tried to a few seconds after. He couldn't be certain but he thought they might actually have been the same two guys who were in Arches the night before, on Thursday night, that he saw talking with Tony Carpentar at one point. He said Carpentar was pretty drunk and seemed bloody angry when he came in that night, but he didn't stop long. He thought he left about two-thirty. "

"What about those two guys he was talking to then, did they arrive and leave with Carpentar? If not, what time did they leave?" Karagoulis asked.

"He said they definitely didn't come into the club with Carpentar, and he left on his own. He doesn't know what time the two guys left though. He thinks it must have been when he was on his first break, which was just after two-thirty that night, as he doesn't remember them leaving later."

"Hmm … probably nothing to do with Dawn Parsons or Carpentar's murder, I guess," was Karagoulis' assessment of what Samaras had reported as the Inspector once again rubbed his chin in bemusement. "The door incident was maybe just a couple of foreign tourists who'd had too much to drink and just wanted to get out quickly most likely. Apart from that though, we don't have much information on Carpentar's movements between then and when he was killed in the early hours of Friday morning. What about Alan Bryant's friends? What did they tell you about Friday night, and his alibi?"

"Well, that was interesting, sir. I eventually tracked the two of them down at Jack's Courtyard Bar. At first they both seemed to clearly confirm that what Bryant told us about his movements on Friday night was correct. Both the guys agreed it was daylight when they were in Bar Code. They said they were pretty sure it was around five when they left Nightlife, because it was closing and that's about the time it does. When I pressed them a bit more about being in Bar

Code though they were a lot less certain or clear about confirming anything in there. They said they were all pretty drunk by then, including Alan. I asked if they were all in each other's company the whole night. Initially they said they were, although one of them then said he vaguely remembers Alan disappearing into the toilet in Bar Code at one point for what seemed like quite a while, but he really had no idea exactly how long. He said it was all a bit hazy because of the alcohol. Apparently, when Bryant eventually reappeared he said he'd been sick in the toilet, but his friend told me, somewhat jokingly, that he never actually went to check that. I suppose we could check with the owner to see if any of his cleaners saw anything that looked like someone had been sick."

"Sounds like you're volunteering to check then, Samaras," Papadoulis joked.

The Inspector gave his Sargent a stern sideways glance as he began once again prowling back and forth across the office in an agitated manner. "Mmm...maybe it will actually come to that, Sargent, checking at some point if people have been sick in a toilet. What if he was not actually that drunk, and was simply putting on an act, making out he was drunk so he could disappear for a while and murder Dawn Parsons, or help someone else murder her? Did his friends have any idea at all what time it was that he disappeared, Samaras?"

"No chance, sir. I asked them that and they said they had no idea of the exact time, or even any very vague idea. All they could confirm, as I said, was that it must have been after five o'clock because that's when Nightlife closes, and it was closing as they left."

Karagoulis picked up his almost empty, no longer very hot, mug of coffee from the desk and walked over to once again stand and gaze at the Incident Board. "So, we know that Dawn Parsons wasn't killed until after four-thirty because that's when the guy on the door at Arches said she left there, and Crisa Tsagroni puts the time of death at between four-thirty and six-thirty. Meanwhile, Alan Bryant disappeared for a while from his two friend's company in Bar Code at some time after five. We know that he had a fight with the first victim, Tony Carpentar, in the Courtyard Bar the night he was murdered. He also admitted that he has a medical background and trained as a male nurse, so he could possibly know exactly where to stab someone to kill them instantly. Although he could hardly have restrained Dawn Parsons and stabbed her in the neck at the same time, so someone else must have helped him and held her arms."

Placing his empty coffee mug on the desk, the Inspector returned to stand in front of the Incident Board. Once again tapping the end of the board marker on the white board, this time at Alan Bryant's name, he continued, now with a little more conviction in his voice, "It would seem that Mr. Bryant is our prime suspect. Perhaps your theory about him and Carol Hudson is right after all, Papadoulis, although do we think that she would have been strong enough to do that Sargent, hold Dawn Parsons arms while he stabbed her? She would only have needed to have held her arms for a few seconds though while he stabbed her, especially if they took Dawn by surprise and Bryant knew exactly where in her neck to plunge the knife."

Karagoulis was clearly trying to convince himself that his scenario was correct, and Papadoulis wasn't slow to back him up and attempt to provide more support for what was, after all, initially his theory.

"Hudson's quite tall and Dawn was quite drunk by all accounts, sir, so she probably wouldn't have needed to be that strong and Parsons probably wasn't in much of a fit state to put up much resistance. Plus, as Crisa Tsagroni said, it would have all been over in a matter of seconds."

Karagoulis was now pointing at Dawn Parsons' name on the Incident Board as he continued, "Yes, that's true, Sargent, and Bryant's alibi for the night Dawn Parsons was murdered definitely has a bit of a hole in it, the period he was supposedly being sick in the Bar Code toilet. I wonder why he didn't mention that when we interviewed him earlier? Maybe he thought his friends wouldn't remember it as they were drunk, unlike him, who maybe was only pretending to be drunk? He had a motive for Carpentar's murder, anger after their fight and competition over women. He would have needed an accomplice for that murder too, but maybe one of his British ex-pat Friday night drinking friends helped him on the

Thursday night, although if that was the case why wouldn't he back up Bryant's alibi for the Friday night a hundred percent?"

"But there were two of them out drinking with Bryant on Friday night, sir. So, if one of them, the one who wasn't his accomplice for Carpentar's murder, remembered him disappearing in Bar Code for a while, the other one, who was his accomplice in murdering Carpentar, could hardly contradict him could he," Samaras pointed out.

"That's possible I suppose," Karagoulis agreed. "What's the motive for him killing Dawn Parsons though? Unless she was going to claim that he raped her in the alley by Qupi on the Thursday night and he simply panicked. Crisa Tsagroni said the bruising on her body around her arse suggests that the sex definitely wasn't consensual. Having disposed of Carpentar the night before maybe he just thought one more murder wouldn't make much difference. What if Bryant and Hudson were the murderers, but for different reasons? Hudson because Bryant had found out that Tony Carpentar and Dawn Parsons were having an affair, perhaps Carpentar boasted to him about it and taunted him, and then Bryant told Carol Hudson. She was angry and wanted revenge, but Tony was already dead, so she took her revenge out on Dawn. And Bryant helped her because he saw it as a way to silence Dawn Parsons and stop any possible rape allegations over the night before, although I'm certain he wouldn't have told Carol Hudson that was the reason, of course. So, Alan Bryant seems to be the common denominator in all this. He could have murdered Carpentar on Thursday night with perhaps one of his Friday night ex-pat drinking buddies as his accomplice, and then on Friday night killed Dawn Parsons with Carol Hudson's help, while he was supposedly being sick in the Bar Code toilet, but with her unaware of his part in the murder of her lover, Carpentar, or of his rape of Dawn Parsons. And, as you suggested earlier, Papadoulis, perhaps Bryant and Hudson were having their own little very discreet affair all along.

I think we need to talk to Mr. Bryant again, as well as his two drinking friends again also, to check in particular where they both claim to have been on Thursday evening and in the early hours of Friday morning when Tony Carpentar was killed. If we can connect

Alan Bryant in any way to Carol Hudson and a relationship or an affair, now or in the past, he is our prime suspect even more. Perhaps we need to ask his two ex-pat drinking friends a little about him and Carol Hudson. He doesn't seem the sort of man who would be able to easily keep anything to himself that was going on between them, so maybe he couldn't resist boasting to his mates?"

Just as Karagoulis was beginning to think that he had a plausible line of enquiry at last, as well as viable motives, and his frustration and irritation was beginning to subside, Samaras reminded him of another element in the various love and infidelity triangles. "What about Carol Hudson's husband though, sir, Panos Koropoulis? He had the clearest motive of all of them to murder Tony Carpentar surely? In this small Greek village I am certain he wouldn't have had any trouble at all finding one of his male friends, or more than one of them, to help him avenge his honour. It's a pretty strong thing here when those sort of things go on over a man's wife. Yes he had an alibi on both nights it seems, but he could easily have got Carpentar's murder done for him, sir, as you've said before."

"What about Dawn Parsons' murder then, Samaras? What was his motive for killing her?" Papadoulis was unconvinced by Samaras' counter scenario and was quick to let him know.

"Maybe Carol Hudson's husband was playing his own little game and paying her back for her infidelities?" Samaras responded. He wasn't letting go of his theory that easily. "Perhaps he was also having an affair with Dawn Parsons which no one knew about, and he heard about her and Alan Bryant the night before from someone in the village, was angry at being cheated on twice, by Dawn and his wife, and killed her in a rage or got the same person to kill her for him too? What if we are looking in the wrong direction at all this, sir? What if it wasn't Carol Hudson who was the source of the chlamydia, what if it was her husband who contracted it from Dawn Parsons and it was him who passed it on to his wife, who then infected Tony during their affair?"

Samaras was clutching at straws a little and Karagoulis let him know in no uncertain terms, not least because he was somewhat annoyed. Having thought he'd found clear motives and plausible situations implicating Carol Hudson and Alan Bryant as the killers,

Samaras was raising doubts and challenging that with his alternative theory about Hudson's husband being the killer.

"That seems bloody unlikely, Samaras. From what we've seen and heard in this village so far, and from what you've told us about the place, even you would admit that with all the gossip that goes on they would have had to have been very clever and discrete to keep something like that quiet. An affair between Dawn Parsons and Panos Koropoulis, really, we've uncovered absolutely nothing at all, and heard and been told nothing, that suggests that."

Samaras decided to sip his coffee and remain silent, not least because he did, indeed, have nothing to back up his theory. Although he was thinking at the time it was also true that in all their investigations they had actually not heard anything either, or been told anything, to suggest that Carol Hudson and Alan Bryant were having an affair, as per the Inspector and Papadoulis' prognosis. He determined though that it was probably best to keep that observation to himself for the moment.

Even so, Karagoulis still didn't appear completely convinced of his and Papadoulis' theory. He stood in front of the Incident Board once again, muttering to himself and scratching the back of his head again in puzzlement. He kept going over and over what they actually knew, rather than what the three of them had just been speculating about. He paced across the office, back and forth three times while the other two policemen remained silent staring at his deliberations one moment and then back at the Incident Board looking for clues to help their Inspector out of his anguish. Halfway across the office for the third time he stopped, glared once again at the white board, and said much more loudly with some irritation as he pointed again at the board, "And what about this second passport that we found in Dawn Parsons' apartment in the name of Jacki Walker? What's that got to do with all this, if anything? Did she have two lives, two personalities? Maybe she was involved in some things she shouldn't have been? Did you manage to turn up anything more on that, Sargent, and the unknown Jacki Walker?"

"I contacted the UK police and they spoke to their UK Passport Office contacts, but all they came back with is mostly what we already know from the passport itself," Papadoulis informed the

Inspector. "They confirmed that a passport with that number was issued in 1995 to a Miss Jacki Walker, so it's not a fake. I asked if that was the full name and they said it was the full name given on the application, and spelt exactly like that, which they agreed was a little unusual.. The address that they said was on the passport application might be of some interest though, sir. It was in a place called Corbridge, which, according to the UK police, is a village in Northumberland about fifteen miles from Newcastle."

"I don't follow, what's so interesting about some village near Newcastle in the UK and Jacki Walker," Karagoulis interrupted. But before his Sargent could answer, Samaras started to do it for him. "I'm sure someone we've interviewed - Alan Bryant maybe, or Deborah Harris, sir - said Dawn Parsons was from Manchester."

"Yes, that's the address on the application for the other passport apparently, the one in Dawn's name that was issued in 2000," Papadoulis confirmed.

This time rubbing his stubby fingered hand across his chin the Inspector proclaimed, "So, why did Dawn Parsons, or Jacki Walker, or whoever she really was, have two passports, and why say she was from two different parts of the UK? What's all this got to do with her murder or Tony Carpentar's for that matter, if they are connected? Well, we don't know who Jacki Walker is, but maybe there is someone else involved in all this, as I said before, that we are just not identifying, not picking up on, someone we're not seeing?"

Pointing to the names of Carol Hudson, Alan Bryant and Panos Koropoulis on the board, he added, "Perhaps Hudson and Bryant being our murderers is correct, but on the other hand, if we can't connect these three, then maybe there's someone else involved that we haven't spoken to or found yet? Or maybe the two murders aren't connected after all? Perhaps it's just a coincidence?"

Now Karagoulis was going round in circles once again, while the two other officers remained silent, knowing better than to interrupt their superior officer's train of thought, not least because neither of them could really add much to his deliberations. All three of them stood in silence in front of the board for about a minute, Samaras and Papadoulis intermittently sipping the remains of their coffee.

Eventually Karagoulis continued, "Wait a minute, what about this other English guy that we keep hearing about?"

As he added the words 'Englishman friend of Dawn Parsons', followed by a question mark, to the board, he went on, "The Albanian barman at Lindos by Night said he was drinking there with her and Deborah Harris the night Dawn was killed, and Carol Hudson and her husband both said they saw him with the two women in Arches later that night. Her husband also told me that he saw Dawn with him having coffee outside Giorgos café bar a few times in the past few weeks. We need to find this mysterious Englishman that nobody seems to know the name of soon. I guess Deborah Harris should be able to help us with that. So, it's time we went and had a word with her I think, rather than going round in circles with this here anymore. Symposio restaurant is where she works according to the Rhodes employment office records, you said, Papadoulis?"

"Yes, sir, that's right," the Sargent confirmed.

Glancing at his watch, the Inspector said, "Well, it's almost ten-thirty, let's go and see if she working tonight, Samaras. If she is, she should be almost finished by now. While we're doing that, Papadoulis, see if you can find out anything more about her in Rhodes residence and employment records, and any other background you can dig up from the UK. If she's been here in Lindos a few years there must be something on her here. Hopefully she will also be able to point us in the direction of Dawn Parsons' Englishman friend and tell us just exactly who he is. Then we can try and find him on a Saturday night in the village and talk to him. We also need to get Bryant back in here and see if we can get anything out of him to back up our theory about him and Carol Hudson, and talk to his Friday night drinking buddies once more. That can all wait until tomorrow morning though, until after we've spoken to Deborah Harris and see what she's got to tell us."

15

Deborah Harris and a different Carpenter

As the two police officers climbed the few small stone steps at the front of the Symposio restaurant the bright green digital sign on the wall outside showed it was still a warm twenty-five degrees and twenty minutes before eleven o'clock. They had made their way from the police station at the top of the village down the slightly sloping narrow alleyway and through the large number of tourist bar-hoppers, periodically having to stop to let groups of late evening drinkers come through the crowds in the opposite direction, much to Karagoulis' growing annoyance. Despite the murders over the two previous nights, Lindos was now packed. The serious tourist drinkers had taken over occupation of the village and its numerous bars.

Having heard them enter the old stone building of the restaurant a tall woman with shoulder length dark black hair turned around to ask them, "Would you like a table inside here or upstairs on the roof terrace gentlemen?"

"Neither, thank you," Karagoulis put her straight immediately, adding, "Miss Harris is it? We are police officers, Inspector Karagoulis and Officer Samaras, investigating the murders of Tony Carpentar and Dawn Parsons. We understand you were good friends with Dawn and were out drinking with her the night she was murdered?"

Although she was, indeed, good friends with Dawn Parsons, Deborah Harris exhibited very little emotion in her response, instead giving off a very 'matter of fact' impression, no doubt a result of her previous MI6 training. "Yes, I'm Deborah Harris, and yes I was out with Dawn that night, but I left her in a club about four o'clock, in

Arches, terrible business, terrible. Have you any idea who did it yet?"

As she motioned to the two police officers that they could sit at a small table in the corner of the pleasant traditional Lindos restaurant, Karagoulis ignored her question and instead asked again, "And you were good friends?" adding this time before she could answer, "did she ever mention anything to you about anyone she may have fallen out with in the village, anyone who may have wanted to kill her?"

"Yes, Inspector, Dawn and I were friends, but I'm not sure you would say we were good friends. I met her here just after I arrived four years ago. We both came to live here at about the same time."

"You didn't know her before that then?" the Inspector added. "What about her background, her past, did she ever tell you anything about that? What about any family?"

"I never really knew much about her, or her past, before she came to live here." Deborah Harris was well trained in being able to tell a convincing sounding lie and in ensuring her body language backed that up.

"We were just drinking buddies really. She said she was from Manchester originally I think. I gathered that she had never been married though, and had no kids. And, to answer your other question, she certainly never said anything to me about thinking there was anyone here in the village who would want to kill her. She could definitely be abrasive, and sometimes easily fell out with some people here in the village, but not enough for it to come to murder I'm sure."

"What about her relationships, Miss Harris? Did she ever tell you about them, about any in the village?" Samaras asked.

Deborah let out a little chuckle as she threw her head back slightly, and a small smile crept across her face as she told them, "Oh, there were plenty of rumours about Dawn in that respect. They used to drive her mad, especially the ones about her and British expat married men here. She never told me anything that suggested any of them were true though. In fact, she was always very vociferous and adamant that none of them were bloody true. They were her exact words usually, or sometimes even stronger, if you know what I mean, Inspector."

"Yes, I think I get your gist. So, no relationships, not even casual ones then?" Karagoulis pushed her.

"No, Inspector, not that I know of. Of course, they may have been happening, and there may have been some truth in any one of the rumours, but I never saw it or believed any of them. Dawn got more and more angry whenever she heard them and always completely denied them. She did appear to be quite friendly with one man here recently, but it seemed to me that it was only a friendship. He's English and here for the summer, writing a book he says. I gather they knew each other from the past two summers here when he was on holiday. Basically, they were drinking partners on a few nights this year and I think that's all there was to it. I've been out drinking with them both on some nights after work. He was out drinking with the both of us the night Dawn was murdered, but he left Arches at the same time as I did, around four. Dawn stayed for another drink. She'd already had quite a few by then, of course, as was usual for her some nights. Once she was out partying, she was out, if you know what I mean, and she wouldn't let up until it was daylight and the sun was coming up. She liked a drink. She worked hard and played hard did Dawn."

"What's his name, this English guy?" Samaras asked.

"Tom, Tom Carpenter. He says he's been to Lindos quite a few times before over the years on holiday for a week or two at a time, but this time he's here for the whole summer, like I said, writing a book. I do remember meeting him here last year at some point, although Dawn remembered him much more than I did. She said she knew him from two years ago."

The two police officers gave each other a quick sideways glance, and briefly hesitated before Samaras gave way to his senior officer who asked, "Is he related to Tony Carpentar? Maybe he can help us with some more information about both murders?"

"No, he's not, or maybe I should say he wasn't, Inspector. Their surnames are, were, spelt differently. Tom's is Carpenter with an e, t-e-r, while Tony's was Carpentar with an a, t-a-r. Tony was always making a point of how his name was spelt a little differently to the usual way it's spelt in Britain. They were about the same age though and similar looking, although Tom has a beard."

"Do you know anything more about this Tom Carpenter then," Karagoulis pressed her. "Do you think he is the sort of man who would kill someone, a crime of passion, perhaps? You said he was very friendly with Dawn, and from what we've been told Tony Carpentar was also a bit of a ladies man around the village. Maybe Tony was having an affair with Dawn that no one knew about and this guy Tom Carpenter found out, was jealous, and murdered them both?"

"Dawn and Tony Carpentar, I don't think so, Inspector. That's like 'chalk and cheese', as we say in Britain. They knew each other here obviously, it's a small village, but I'd be amazed if there was anything going on between Dawn and Tony. I never saw them even so much as drinking together, only just a nodding 'hello' to each other occasionally, as I did, whenever I was out with her and we saw Tony. Like I said, it's a small village, it would be very difficult, if not impossible, to hide something like that going on in this place. Someone would be bound to see them and then the gossip would start. That's the way it is here." Pointing to Samaras she added, "I expect your officer here knows, and can confirm, that. And anyway, most of the time Dawn made it quite clear whenever we saw him in any of the bars or clubs that she couldn't stand the man. 'Full of bullshit', she always said, one of her favourite phrases in summing someone up."

Samaras just nodded slightly in agreement over her comment about it being impossible to hide any relationship in the village and Karagoulis continued, "So, you don't really know much about this Tom Carpenter then?"

"Not really, he was more of a friend of Dawn's than mine. I only met him a couple of times I think, when I was out drinking with Dawn, as I said before."

Karagoulis hesitated and paused from asking his questions as a couple of diners from the top terrace of the restaurant made their way down the narrow circular wrought iron staircase and Deborah Harris told him, "Excuse me a moment, Inspector," and she got up from the table to ask them if they had enjoyed their meal.

Once she had done her job, and bid the diners goodnight, Karagoulis asked, "What about Tony Carpentar, how well did you know him?"

"Again, not much really, Inspector, I've seen him around in the village for the past few years. I heard he's been here over a few summers and did some work as a handyman. Turned his hand to anything, one of the ex-pat Brits told me. Of course, there was the usual village gossip among the ex-pats."

"Gossip?" Karagoulis prompted her, knowing full well what she meant.

"There was always gossip about him and some of the British ex-pat women in the village, Inspector, including one particular married woman. Dawn and I always chuckled when we heard someone say that he could 'turn his hand to anything'. They meant it in terms of his handyman work, but we always put a different meaning to it from what we'd heard and saw it somewhat differently." Deborah expanded her comment a little, but again her previous training stopped her giving too much away.

"You mean Carol Hudson, Miss Harris?" The Inspector prompted her again, this time leaning forward with his elbows resting on the crisp white tablecloth of the restaurant dining table.

Deborah was too experienced to be drawn by that though, and just answered with another matter-of-fact, "If you say so, Inspector. You have obviously heard as much as I have about that, maybe more."

"What about Carol Hudson's husband then, Miss Harris, Panos Koropoulis, do you know him at all? Have you ever seen him lose his temper?"

"Yes, I know Panos, and of course I know Carol, but again I only know them in passing in the village. I'm not friends with them. We always say hello though, and that's about all. No, I've never seen him lose his temper, but then I've not really been in his company, or even drinking in the same bars that often. I can't really help you there."

"Did you ever think he was good friends with Dawn, ever have any reason to think they were even more than good friends perhaps, Miss Harris? Samaras was searching for something that might help support his theory about Carol Hudson's husband and Dawn Parsons having a secret affair, as he suggested earlier in the police station.

"Panos and Dawn, that's even more unlikely than what the Inspector here suggested before about Dawn and Tony Carpentar." She let out another little chuckle as she finished.

Karagoulis switched back to Carol Hudson, asking, "You said you only know Carol Hudson in passing in the village, but what about her, Miss Harris, have you ever seen her lose her temper, in a bar perhaps?"

"Not really, like I said, I only know her to say hello in passing in the village. Although, thinking about it, there was the one time I saw her have a right go at another woman in Giorgos bar one day. It was another ex-pat, Joan Mayweather. She is one of the biggest gossips in the village and I think Carol must have heard her saying something to someone about her. There is always a lot of gossip in the village about Carol and one man or other, and I guess she must have overheard Joan on this occasion. Anyway, she let her have it with both barrels, and they had a real stand-up row right by the tables and chairs outside Giorgos. I just sat there having a mid-morning coffee when it all kicked-off. Very entertaining, Inspector, and never a dull moment in this place, although I guess that's not really the right thing to say given the events of the last few nights. Anyway, at one point I did actually think Carol was going to hit her, but she just grabbed her arm, held it for a minute or so wagging and pointing her finger at her in a threatening way while she gave Joan a real mouthful, including some real industrial language, and then pushed her away. Joan stumbled a bit and did actually fall over, but although she was crying and visibly shocked she didn't seem to be seriously hurt, and eventually she just got up, brushed herself off and went off up the alley."

"So, Miss Hudson has a bit of a temper then. What about Alan Bryant, what can you tell us about him? Ever see him and Carol together looking like more than friends?" Karagoulis was fishing for anything, even more gossip, but the response he got was a return to cagey.

"I expect you know as well as I do that he had a fight with Tony in Jack's bar the night Tony was murdered, Inspector. I'm pretty sure you must know what it was about, Carol I assume. Although no, I've never seen Alan and Carol together looking like more than friends, as you put it. They are friends, of course, I'm sure. I've seen them out in some of the bars with some of the ex-pats here, but nothing more as far as I could see. Alan does have a certain reputation in the village concerning women, as they say, but that's all I've heard and that's all I know, and what's more that's all I'm prepared to say. I can't help you there either."

"Did you know he had sex with Dawn the night before she was murdered, the night Tony was killed, the night of Tony and Alan's fight?" Karagoulis watched closely for her reaction as he told her.

For once she lost her calm composure a little and genuinely looked surprised. "Dawn and Alan, are you sure? That doesn't seem at all likely, Inspector. No, no, I'm sure Dawn wouldn't have. In fact, she was always going on about how Alan Bryant would shag anything that had a pulse. I remember her once saying that she thought even the donkeys weren't safe when he was around."

"Well Dawn can hardly confirm it, but the autopsy showed she had sex sometime in the previous thirty-six hours. It also found she had a lot of alcohol in her bloodstream. Alan Bryant though seemed only too happy to tell us about it." Karagoulis was exaggerating somewhat about Alan Bryant's eagerness to tell them in order to try and provoke a further reaction from her and see what else she might tell them.

Deborah was shaking her head from side to side in disbelief. "Really, no, I don't believe him. No, he's just the sort to make something like that up, especially if he knows Dawn can't deny it now. Maybe he was just protecting someone else, another woman in the village perhaps?"

"Yes, perhaps, Miss Harris, although he did actually tell us about it, and that it was in the alley just along from the Qupi nightclub, before we informed him of Dawn's murder. So, at that point, if he didn't know she was dead, he would surely have believed that if it wasn't her then she would deny it if we asked her. We would then know he was lying about it, wouldn't we? Unless of course, he already knew she was dead because he was involved in her murder? That logic would fit with what you're telling us, Miss Harris, don't you think? So, are you suggesting that Alan was involved in Dawn's murder then? Do you know anything else about it that you're not telling us?"

She retreated back to her former life and non-committal comments. "I have no idea, Inspector, and I am definitely not suggesting that. All I am saying is that I would be very surprised if Dawn did actually have sex with him. I find it very hard to believe and very unlikely."

Karagoulis decided it was best not to tell her at that time that it looked like the sex wasn't exactly consensual on Dawn Parsons' part.

"Okay, so were you in Qupi the night Dawn supposedly ended up with Alan Bryant having sex in the alley, the night Carpentar was murdered?" Samaras once again threw in a question.

"No, I went straight home after work. I was tired and we'd had a busy night in here, so I was home by twelve o'clock. I never saw Dawn that night."

At that point Karagoulis decided he wasn't going to get any more out of her about Tony Carpentar or Alan Bryant, even if she knew anything more, so he switched back to Dawn's Englishman friend. "What about this Tom Carpenter? Do you have any idea where he is staying here, where we can find him? We obviously want to talk to him soon."

"He said he is living in one of the apartments in the street behind Yannis bar, the one that goes down towards the Italian restaurant and Café Melia in the square by the Amphitheatre. But I doubt if you'll find him there at this time on a Saturday night," Deborah added. "He'll be out drinking in some of the bars in the village."

"Any idea which ones?" the Inspector asked.

"You could try Jack's or Pals just down the alley from it. They are two of his regular drinking haunts, I think. That's where I've seen him mostly so far this summer. Those two and the Lindos by Night bar, but he usually only goes there late on, after one a.m. Ask Jack or any of the bar staff in Pals, they'll know him and should be able to point him out to you if he's there. Sometimes he sits outside Pals drinking."

"Okay, thanks, that's helpful, we'll let you get on with your job now and go and see if we can find him," Karagoulis told her.

"I'm sure you'll find him in one of the bars, or someone who has seen him tonight, Inspector. I can't really see how he's your murderer though, but I hope you find the bastard who did it soon. Dawn had her faults, but there's no way she deserved that." For the first time Deborah Harris was actually exhibiting some emotion about the murder of her friend.

As he got up from the table and took a couple of steps towards the restaurant open doorway Karagoulis suddenly spun round on his heels and asked, "Just one other thing you may be able to help us with before we leave, Miss Harris? Have you ever met a woman called Jacki Walker? Her first name, J-a-c-k-i, is spelt a little differently from the usual way in England I think?"

Deborah Harris gave nothing away. The only thing her facial expression betrayed was her MI6 training. Her face depicted all the frowned bewilderment of an infant seeing the first image of itself as she told the two policemen with another slight shake of her head, "Jacki Walker, no I don't know anyone by that name. Why? Is it someone in the village? I think that sort of spelling of her first name is common in the north-east of England, but no I've never met anyone of that name."

"Oh, no reason, just something that popped up in our investigation that I thought you may be able to help us with. Never mind, it's not important." Karagoulis wasn't totally convinced by her answer, but he decided to play it down for now and not make a big thing of it until he had anything more on the mysterious Jacki Walker, alias Dawn Parsons. "We'll get off now and see if we can find this Tom Carpenter guy. Thanks again for your help, Miss Harris," he told her.

"Before you go there was another thing I've just remembered, Inspector. I don't know if it helps or not but Sandra, who works here as a waitress, told me she saw Dawn in Nikos' pizza place by Yannis bar the night she was murdered."

"Is she working here tonight?" Karagoulis asked.

"Yes, upstairs on the terrace, I'll get her." With that Deborah Harris made her way up the wrought iron circular staircase and emerged back down barely a minute later followed by an attractive, shoulder length blonde curly haired woman in her mid-thirties, introducing her to the two police officers as Sandra Weston.

"We understand that you saw Dawn Parsons the night she was murdered? Miss Weston. "What time was that?" the Inspector asked.

"It must have been about five in the morning, I guess. I left Nightlife just as it was closing which was just before five, and went to Nikos for pizza. She was in there getting some pizza."

"Did you speak to her and did she leave before you? Was she alone or with anyone? Did you notice which way she went after she left?" Karagoulis was firing off a volley of questions to the English waitress.

"She was already in there when I arrived, so she got served before me and then left. She said hello, but I only really know her in passing, so to speak, and through Deborah. She wasn't with anyone as far as I could see. She left on her own and headed up the alley towards Arches. I don't know if she went in there though, and it was probably closing then anyway. I never looked up the alley when she left, I was too busy trying to get some pizza."

"Did you happen to notice anyone leave just after her, Miss Weston? Anyone you think was following her?"

"Not really, there were quite a few people in Nikos, there usually is at that time as the clubs are closing, as well as a couple of guys sitting on the wall by Yannis eating chips and gyros. They had left by the time I got my slice of pizza. I guess they just finished their food and left, but I never saw them go or in which direction they went. I just remember thinking as I came around the corner and into Nikos that they were a couple of well-built guys. It looked like they worked out. Sorry, but I can't really tell you anymore, Inspector."

"Thank you, Miss Weston, that's helpful in trying to pin down Dawn's movements that night, and it helps in determining just when she was murdered, which was obviously after five a.m. on Saturday morning from what you've just told us." Karagoulis turned to Deborah Harris and once again thanked her for her help, adding, "I think we will go and find this other Carpenter guy that you told us about now and see what he can tell us."

16

Saturday night outside Pals

As the two policemen left the Symposio restaurant it was just gone eleven o'clock. By that time the Lindos Saturday night was in full swing and the busy bars were blaring out their various forms of pop music. Even though Samaras had heard some rumours that afternoon of concern over the two murders amongst the bar and restaurant owners, and how it might affect trade if it caused panic amongst the tourists, nothing to that affect was remotely evident and the centre of the village was as busy as usual.

It was only about thirty metres or so to their first 'port of call' in search of the mysterious Tom Carpenter, Pals Bar. Pals was situated on the corner of the main alleyway through the village and the alley running at ninety degrees to it going up to Jack Constantino's Courtyard Bar. It was a very small, but very popular bar, with two sets of double folding doors on each side through which the drinking clientele spilled out onto the alleys on the two sides. Outside on one side were some more comfortable padded benches and seats, and around the corner were some more usual small tables and stools. Its clientele varied, mostly tourists, but some Greek and Brit ex-pat regulars from time to time, and they tended to be middle-aged or even older. It was very popular with British couples on holiday, and many of its regular tourist customers, who returned to the little village year after year, were of the opinion that Pals played the best music in Lindos.

That particular Saturday night it was just as packed inside as usual, so much so that a quite large number of people were standing, as well as sitting, outside in groups of four or five. The two policemen had no idea just which of the many customers might be Tom Carpenter, not least because half a dozen of them wore the beard they had been told he had. Karagoulis told Samaras to wait outside while he fought his way through the packed small bar to the counter to try and ask one of the two young guys serving if they knew the Englishman and if he was in there that night.

"Tom, yep, he's outside there sat on one of the stools, on his own I think," one of the bar staff told the Inspector, pointing to the doorway directly opposite the bar. "He's wearing a dark blue polo shirt and some white shorts, and he's got a beard. You can't miss him."

Karagoulis squeezed his way back through the packed customers in the bar and out through the open doors. As he emerged, Samaras, who was leaning against the whitewashed wall next to the Crepe shop opposite, was on his mobile. "Ok, well I can't help it can I, I'm just going to be late," he was saying in a disconcerted way into his phone. "I have no idea what time, as soon as I can I guess. I'll bring some pizza, just warm the bed up for me and I'll get there as soon as possible. I've got to go now, bye."

"Who was that, Officer?" the inspector enquired, with a mischievous grin spreading across his face, knowing full well that Samaras wasn't married.

"Just a friend I promised to take out to dinner tonight, sir, but that was before all this stuff kicked off."

"Nice is she, and you must be good friends if you're asking her to warm the bed up for you, Officer?" Karagoulis' grin was getting wider.

"It's called a life, sir," Samaras told him, returning his grin, and with just a hint of a suggestion in his tone of voice that Karagoulis didn't really have one in that respect.

Turning away to face Pals, Karagoulis spotted a man wearing a dark blue polo shirt and white shorts sitting on a stool at a small table opposite and nursing a small beer. Indicating to Samaras that was their man, the two policemen took the few steps across the alley and the Inspector enquired, "Tom Carpenter?" Before the man could answer he added, "Inspector Dimitris Karagoulis, and this is Officer Samaras. We are investigating the murders of Tony Carpentar and Dawn Parsons, and we'd like to ask you a few questions."

"Yes, I'm Tom Carpenter, Inspector," he confirmed, adding immediately, "but I don't know how I can help. Of course I will if I can. Bloody awful thing to happen, and in such a lovely place as this, I knew Dawn from last year, and the year before, when I was here on holiday, but I didn't really know Tony Carpentar."

As the two policemen sat down on a couple of very low, rickety stools at the small table, and Karagoulis perched a little awkwardly and precariously on his, he said, "You know you bear a resemblance to him, Mr. Carpenter. You could be related. I expect people have told you that though, except for the beard of course."

"A few people have mentioned that to me here, but like I said, I didn't really know him that well, Inspector, and we weren't related. Our names are spelt differently."

"Yes, I know that," the Inspector informed him, "Deborah Harris explained it to us."

"We only ever had a few conversations, usually over a beer in one or other of the bars in the village," Carpenter continued. "Like me he'd spent some time in Prague and loved the place, so that's basically what we talked about a few times. Also like me, by coincidence he'd had an affair with a Czech woman there, years ago he said. Apart from the first time I met him though, when we talked a lot about Prague, they were mostly short conversations because, and I hope you don't think this was a reason for me to murder him, but he was always somewhat slow in putting his hand in his pocket, if you know what I mean. So, I quickly learned from experience and stopped buying him a drink whenever I bumped into him in a bar or a club here."

Karagoulis chose to ignore that and instead asked, "I understand you are here for the whole summer, writing a book, and that you have been here quite a few times before on holiday. What exactly is your background?"

The Englishman took a sip of his beer before answering, "Yes, I've always wanted to take a whole summer off and write a novel, so this summer that's what I'm doing. I work at a university in England, so I guess you would say I'm an academic really, although I don't really think of myself as one."

"Why's that?" the Inspector asked.

"Oh, I don't really buy into all that academic stuff associated with universities and some of the arseholes I have to work with, other Professors I mean. Full of their own self-importance if you ask me."

"Do they annoy you easily then, Mr. Carpenter, and do people in general annoy you easily, make you lose your temper easily perhaps?"

"What? No, not people in general, and no I definitely don't usually get annoyed easily. It's just people full of their own blown-up self-importance that pisses me off."

Carpenter was shifting a little uneasily on the rickety stool as Karagoulis asked, "What about Dawn Parsons? You said you knew her from the past two years?"

"We were just drinking partners really. She certainly liked a drink, Bacardi. We just met up a few times for a drink after she finished work, usually around one a.m., and sometimes we went to the clubs after LBN or Jack's Courtyard bar, to Nightlife, Qupi or Arches. Sometimes all three, and often it would be daylight and the early hours of the morning before we left there."

"Did you ever sleep with her, Mr. Carpenter?" Karagoulis went straight to the point, leaning forward on his stool and adding, "Did you know she had a sexually transmitted disease? Have you ever had chlamydia?"

A surprised and startled look came over Carpenter's face, but he quickly and firmly replied, "No, and no, Inspector. I never had sex with her, if that's what you mean, and I've never had chlamydia or any sexually transmitted disease, thank you."

"You were in Arches with her and Deborah Harris the night she was murdered weren't you? Do you remember what time you left?" Karagoulis was checking what Deborah Harris had told him.

"Around four I think, I left at the same time as Deborah."

"And where did you go after that?"

"Home, back to my flat and to bed. Dawn stayed in Arches. She always had to have just one more drink. She tried to persuade me to stay for one more, but I'd had enough and was knackered."

"So, no one can verify where you were when she was murdered then, Mr. Carpenter?" Karagoulis pressed him.

"No, Inspector, I was in my bed in my flat, alone. I never got lucky that night, or any other night as far as Dawn was concerned, before you ask."

"What about the night before, Thursday night, the night Tony Carpentar was murdered? Where were you between five and six on Friday morning, Mr. Carpenter?"

"In my flat in bed alone again, pretty sad life I have here don't you think, Inspector?"

"So, no one can verify where you were when Tony Carpentar was murdered either?"

"No, I guess not, but like I said before, him not putting his hand in his pocket to buy me a drink after I'd bought him a few is hardly a motive for murder is it?"

"As you say, Mr. Carpenter, hardly, but if you thought Dawn and him were having an affair though, then jealousy can be a powerful motive, can't it?"

The Englishman allowed a slight wry smile to creep across his lips. "Tony Carpentar and Dawn, I'd find that very hard to believe, and I don't do jealousy. It's a waste of energy and emotion. If people are going to do the dirty on you then they are going to do it, and there's not much you can do about it. I know from experience believe me, but Dawn and Tony, nope I wasn't jealous over them. That rather assumes I was interested in Dawn as more than just a friend, Inspector, and anyway I'm sure there was nothing to be jealous about. If there was anything between them they must have been bloody good at keeping it hidden because I never saw anything, and I never heard anything like that about them from anyone here in the village. All I ever heard was about Tony and Carol Hudson. Everyone in the village knew about that, even her Greek husband I reckon."

Karagoulis decided to change approach a little and be less accusing. "What about when you and Deborah were with Dawn on Friday night, did she seem agitated or worried about anything? "What sort of mood was she in? Did you by any chance get any impression someone may have been watching her when you were in Lindos by Night or Arches?"

"Her mood usually depended on how many Bacardis she'd had, Inspector. She seemed fine on Friday night. She could have a bit of a temper on her at times, and she could certainly look after herself."

"What do you mean by that, Mr. Carpenter? Did you ever see her lose her temper with anyone?" Karagoulis pressed him again.

"Well, there was the time one night a few weeks ago in Qupi that she had an 'in your face' argument with Carol Hudson. I really thought she was going to hit her."

"What was it about, about Tony Carpentar by any chance?"

"I don't really know, Inspector. I came back from the toilet and Dawn had her by the hair and was screaming at her telling her to 'just fuck-off'. I asked her after it all quietened down, but Dawn just said it was nothing, so I never pushed it. You didn't with Dawn. If she wanted to tell you she would, but mostly she only told you what she wanted you to know and you certainly didn't want to push it too much and end up really on her bad side. I don't know just how much truth there is in it, but I did hear that a customer, a guy, got stroppy one night in a restaurant she was working in here and she stabbed him in the thigh with a fork. Like I said though, I don't know how true that is, but I certainly was never going to ask her."

"So, as I asked, was she in a mood or agitated over anything on Friday night, Mr Carpenter?"

"Not really, as I said she was doing what she does, or did, best, getting pissed. If anything she seemed really relaxed, but I guess that was the Bacardi. She was much more agitated in Giorgos on Friday afternoon."

"Over the discovery of Tony Carpentar's body at St. Paul's? So, perhaps there was something going on between them after all?" Karagoulis asked, immediately jumping to the conclusion that his conjecture, and Papadoulis' theory, earlier in the police station was correct. Maybe the argument between Dawn and Carol in Qupi that Tom Carpenter had just told him about was over both their relationships with Tony, he thought. His brain was racing way ahead, drawing a connection and conclusions he was desperate to find, but Tom Carpenter's answer didn't really fit or help his supposition.

"Not much about that really, she seemed much more interested in the argument I told her about that three Russians had in Giorgos just before she arrived. It wasn't really an argument as such, more a case of one of them bollocking the other two. I thought he must have been their tourist agency boss and they'd obviously done something, or not done something, in their job that he wasn't best pleased about."

"Why was she interested in that do you think? Did she speak to them?"

"I've no idea, Inspector. They'd left by the time she arrived, so no, she never spoke to them. I expect she was just curious. People in this place get curious about even the smallest thing out of the ordinary, and from what I knew of her, Dawn was no different. There are a lot more Russians here this year though. I guess the Rhodes Tourist Agency must have had a big advertising push there."

Ignoring the Russian diversion, Karagoulis asked, "Have you any idea who might have wanted to kill Dawn then?"

"No, no idea at all, Inspector. As I said, I didn't really know her that well, only to go drinking with, and Dawn never really gave much away about herself, even when she was drunk."

Karagoulis glanced across at Samaras as Tom Carpenter added, "If there's nothing more you want to ask I told Jack I'd look in his place for a beer tonight, so I'd like to get off up there if it's ok with you?"

"Just one more thing, Mr. Carpenter, before you go, what about Alan Bryant? How well do you know him? Did you ever see him and Dawn together, being more than just friends, if you know what I mean?"

"Obviously I've seen him around. I understand he's been coming here for years, and I thought he was a good mate of Tony's, although I heard about the fight in Jack's the other night, the night Tony was murdered. I probably know him even less than I knew Tony though, hardly had a conversation with him, just a nodding 'hello' in bars in the village occasionally. I saw him and Dawn chatting and drinking together a few times in the clubs, but usually in the company of other people as well, and they never gave the impression of being more than just friends, as you put it. I can't really tell you much more than that about him though, or about him and Dawn."

"Okay, thanks, we'll let you get off for your beer in Jack's now. We may need to speak to you again. From what you said you're here for the whole summer, so I guess you will not be going anywhere soon. Deborah Harris told us you're living in one of the apartments in the street behind Yannis bar, the one that goes down towards the Italian restaurant and Café Melia?"

"Yes, that's where I call home here, Inspector, the second door on the right as you come round the corner from Yannis, but I'm not sure there's much more I can tell you." With that he gulped down the last dregs of his beer and wandered off up the alley towards Jack Constantino's Courtyard Bar. As he did so, Karagoulis glanced at his watch and told Samaras, "I think that's enough for tonight. It's nearly midnight and even policemen have to stop sometime. So, unless your urgently wanting to dash off to that bed of yours, and your woman friend warming it up for you, I suggest we go and have a beer, just one, maybe in this Giorgos bar that keeps popping up in our investigations."

"Okay, sir, but just one," Samaras agreed. Pointing thirty metres in the opposite direction down the alley from Pals Bar and the Courtyard Bar, he added, "Giorgos is just there."

Giorgos was still busy, even at that time of night, mainly with older couples and families; a different sort of clientele tourists from the more raucous ones packing the small Pals Bar and spilling out into the alley. Within half-an-hour of finding two stools at the bar the two policemen had finished their small beers and Samaras was anxiously raising himself from his stool intending to leave for the comfort of his woman and warmed-up bed. As he did so though, Karagoulis suggested, "One more before you go?"

"Thank you, sir, but no, I should get off to see my friend, if that's ok?"

"Sure," the Inspector told him, "I'll have one more though and then crash out in the cell in the police station. No point in driving back to Rhodes. I want to get on early in the morning and try to get to the bottom of this."

The bar was thinning out now. Three of the tables outside were still occupied with couples, but no one was left inside, either seated at the white tables or on the white plastic stools at the bar. The waitress, who Samaras said was Slovak, stood in the doorway to the bar aimlessly looking down the alley and then checking if any of the couples still at the tables wanted any more drinks. No doubt she was anxious to finish work and get off to one of the clubs with her friends. The bar owner was cleaning up behind the bar directly in front of where Karagoulis was perched somewhat awkwardly again on a stool, his weight precariously activating the pneumatic effect of it. As the owner turned around the Inspector asked, "I hear Dawn Parsons was a regular daytime coffee customer of yours?"

"Yes, Dawn was a regular. Bloody awful business, the murders, I didn't really know her that well though, just as a customer." The owner obviously knew the now departed Samaras as a police officer in the village, and from overhearing some of their earlier conversation he guessed that Karagoulis was his superior officer from Rhodes.

"I heard there was a bit of an argument here on Friday lunchtime? Was she involved?" Karagoulis knew that according to Tom Carpenter the argument happened before Dawn Parsons arrived at Giorgos, but he wanted to check what he'd said.

"No, Dawn wasn't involved. She wasn't even here. It was all over by the time she arrived. She was with Tom Carpenter, well, he was here and she joined him. The argument was between three Russians, although it wasn't much of an argument really, more of a disagreement it seemed to me. Big guys they were, the two of them in vests and shorts, so you could see they were well built, but the guy doing most of the talking and finger jabbing was much better dressed, and very thin. So thin, that at one point I thought he must be ill. He looked as if he could do with a good moussaka or two. You could see he was their boss and was giving them a real telling off. I've no idea what it was about though; I only overheard a very small part of it as I went to serve Tom."

"Have you seen them in here before or since?" the Inspector asked.

"No, never seen them before, or since. Martina there, our waitress, she said she saw two of them, the well-built ones, last night kicking off with one of the guys on the door in Arches. They were having a right go at him over something, she said. You can ask her if you like, but she was sure they were the same guys."

"Thanks, but the guy from Arches already told us about that. What about Dawn and this Tom Carpenter though?" Karagoulis asked. Did they seem like more than just good friends to you?"

"Not really, Tom's only been here a few weeks so far this year and they've had coffee in here around lunchtime a few times. They never seemed like more than just friends to me. They were also in here on a couple of nights for one drink after Dawn finished work, after one o'clock usually, before they went off to the clubs. I guess they were just drinking friends. I couldn't say more. Tom's been coming here for quite a few years, so we know him quite well. He often comes in for a late cooked breakfast if he's been out drinking the night before. That's what he was here for yesterday when Dawn turned up."

Karagoulis finished his second small beer, said, "Goodnight," to the owner, and on his way out had a quick word with the waitress, Martina, who was still stood in the doorway, to see if she could tell him any more about the door incident in Arches. Basically, she just confirmed what he already knew. Then he made his way slowly through the still busy Lindos alleyways and past the noisy packed bars to the police station and his welcoming cell bed.

17

Sunday Morning

He had grabbed just over five hours intermittent sleep on the less than comfortable police station cell bed when the warm early morning Lindos sun began streaming through the small barred cell window at seven o'clock. His brain had refused to shut down and he'd spent most of the night tossing and turning while struggling to find the key to unlock the mystery of just who the killer or killers were. Once the sun had made the cell even more uncomfortable Karagoulis decided, after laying there for another fifteen minutes, that the best thing to do was to get up, make some coffee, and try and get on with piecing together the murder puzzle.

He quickly updated the Incident Board, adding Tom Carpenter's name and some brief background about tenuous links to Dawn Parsons and Tony Carpentar. Clutching his mug of thick black coffee he was sat staring at the board when Samaras arrived just after eight o'clock with some freshly baked croissants from Café Melia. "I thought you might like some of these for breakfast, sir, and I also brought you a razor and some shaving foam."

"Thanks, I didn't think you'd be in here quite so early this morning, Officer, especially after you told me you had someone waiting for you in your bed last night. I bet your bed was somewhat more comfortable than the cell bed here, with or without someone to share it. Papadoulis left a note for me when I got back here last night saying he'll be back from Rhodes just after eight this morning, so he should be here soon too. Hope you've got enough croissants there for all of us?"

Just as Samaras was confirming there were plenty for all of them the Sargent arrived. As Papadoulis went to pour himself a coffee Karagoulis quickly brought him up to speed on what they'd learned from talking to Tom Carpenter the night before. The Sargent then updated the Inspector on his previous evening's activity and investigations.

"I had another look further back at Dawn Parsons' and Tony Carpentar's Greek mobile phone records, sir, but there was nothing more there than we already knew. There were quite a few calls between Carpentar and Carol Hudson, and a few more between Dawn and Deborah Harris. I had a look at both their laptops, but there wasn't really anything that stood out on them, not unless you count Tony Carpentar's screensaver photo. A very nice one of what I recognised as the Charles Bridge in Prague."

"Yes, Tom Carpenter told us last night that Tony was a bit obsessed with that city," Karagoulis said.

"There was one thing that may be interesting though on Dawn Parsons' laptop, sir. She had obviously backed up all the phone numbers in her contacts list on her mobile, but when I cross-checked them there were a few extra in the laptop contact list that weren't in her mobile contact list, nine altogether. I checked them out and five of them were Greek mobile numbers just registered to individuals. The other four were UK numbers. I checked with the UK police and they came back late last night saying that three of those, all mobile numbers, were registered to UK individuals, none of whose names I recognised. The UK police said they had nothing in their records on those individuals. The other one was a UK landline number, but the UK police told me that they couldn't give me any information on that one. I asked them why, whether it was because they didn't have anything, but they were very evasive and just said they couldn't tell me anything more on it because they had nothing. Then an hour later, just as I got back to Rhodes around one o'clock, I got a very strange and official sounding call on my mobile. The guy, with a very upper class sounding British accent, wouldn't even tell me who he was, just that he was calling from London, and that the landline number I asked the UK police about was classified. He wanted to know why I was asking about it, and even though I told him it was connected to a murder enquiry, he just repeated it was classified and that they couldn't help. All a bit mysterious, sir, don't you think, any ideas?"

Karagoulis stopped munching on his croissant and started to rub the back of his neck. He was clearly getting more and more annoyed and obviously decided to vent his frustration on the local police officer and his little station.

"For Christ's sake put that useless aircon on, Samaras, will you. It's already getting bloody hot in here and as useless as it is maybe that will at least help a little. I can't think with it getting so bloody warm in here. That's just one more ingredient to add to the bloody mystery then, Papadoulis. Maybe it has something to do with all this, but maybe not."

As he finished speaking he wrote on the board under Dawn Parsons' name the words 'Jacki Walker two passports', and 'mysterious phone number'. Asking his Sargent what the number was, he added it, plus the word 'classified' and a question mark.

Pointing to the Incident Board he continued, "We also found out from Dawn Parsons' English friend, Tom Carpenter, last night that her and Carol Hudson had an argument and almost came to blows in Qupi a few weeks ago, although he says he doesn't know what it was about because he was in the toilet when it started."

Adding to the board the words 'Dawn Parsons and Carol Hudson argument in Qupi', and a question mark, Karagoulis couldn't resist commenting, "It seems toilets are increasingly figuring in this investigation, what with Alan Bryant supposedly being sick in Bar Code's toilets the night Dawn was murdered and Mr Carpenter being in the Qupi toilet when she was having her altercation with Carol Hudson."

He stepped back a couple of paces and was fiddling with the top of the board pen as he said rhetorically, "So, who out of this lot is our murderer, or more likely, murderers, and why? Why did they kill Tony Carpentar and Dawn Parsons, assuming it was the same people? What is the connection between the two victims, besides the fact that they were both British ex-pats living and working in Lindos, and both had a sexually transmitted disease? Who would want to kill both of them?"

He put the pen down on the desk and was now wandering slowly across the room rubbing his chin with his right hand and muttering random comments related to his own questions while the other two policemen munched on their croissants and stared at him in equal bewilderment. "From what we've consistently been told they don't appear to have been lovers, or if they were they kept it really well hidden, which would have been difficult, if not impossible, in a small village like this, as plenty of people have told us. Although, nothing has been quite what it seems with this case, and with these two murders. In this place it seems that a lot of people, British ex-pats, were having affairs and then stabbing each other in the back with the gossip, if we believe the gossip. Or maybe that should be stabbing each other in the neck in two cases."

With that he turned to face both Samaras and Papadoulis, asking, "On that point, no sign of any murder weapons, I suppose, or any further clues at the crime scenes?"

"No, sir, and nothing new at the crime scenes either, sir," his Sargent confirmed.

The Inspector strode across the room more purposefully, indicating just how much his frustration and agitation over not being able to see any connection between the two murders was growing. Standing directly in front of the Incident Board once again he added, "Somebody out of this lot of characters is not telling us something." He hesitated and stared at the board in silence for around a minute, while his two officers also remained silent, knowing better than to disturb his train of thought.

"Maybe we are just looking in the wrong place, looking at all this the wrong way," he eventually continued. "We've been trying to connect the two victims. Perhaps we should be looking more closely at the connections between some of these other people, the possible murderers. Maybe that will lead us to the connection between the two victims?"

"You mean between Carol Hudson and Alan Bryant, sir, and that they were having an affair, as I suggested yesterday?" Papadoulis interrupted.

"Well, yes, I was actually thinking of a few people on the board here, including those two, Sargent. From what we've been told from a number of sources they do both have a reputation in the village that they'd shag anything that moves or draws breath, but we've also been told nothing by anyone that connects them. Once again, in a little place like this surely someone would have seen or heard something if it had been going on."

Papadoulis sensed that his theory was beginning to gain at least some plausibility and moved across to stand alongside his Inspector in front of the Incident Board as Karagoulis continued, "I'm certain Alan Bryant would have liked to, and no doubt probably tried it on with Carol Hudson at some point. Everyone seems to assume that was what the fight was about between him and Tony Carpentar in the Courtyard Bar, but we've come across nothing, found absolutely nothing, that suggests they were having an affair. Despite that, Sargent, maybe your little theory about them is correct and we need to investigate it a little more with those two and get them both in here together this morning. Let's throw some accusations at them and see what turns up, see what their reactions are.

Before we do that though, we should check out Bryant's alibi for Friday night at the time of Dawn Parsons' murder a little more. We need to go and talk to the owner of Bar Code to see if any of his cleaners reported any mess in the toilets from Friday night from Bryant supposedly throwing up in there. Not a great job and line of enquiry I'm afraid, Samaras, but as a local I guess you will know him from the village and where to find him on a Sunday morning, so it's best if you do it rather than Papadoulis or me. Once you've done that you can go and invite Mr Bryant to visit our little station here again. Be firm though Officer, don't give him any option, he seems like an arrogant bastard and I guess he will not be in much of a good mood this early on a Sunday morning, especially if he was out drinking last night. So, he may try and refuse. If he does, tell him it would be in his best interests if he came and that we are getting Carol Hudson in at the same time as him. His reaction should be interesting, and that should persuade him. Before you see him call me and let me know what you found out from the Bar Code owner about his toilets. It will be useful to know before we question Bryant again whether the contents of his stomach were deposited in the toilets, and if that part of his alibi, when he went missing for some time, stands up.

While he's doing that Papadoulis you can go and also invite Carol Hudson to join us here at the station for another interview. Tell her we are getting Alan Bryant in at the same time for another interview and see what her reaction is too. Don't take no for an answer, Sargent.

While you two are doing that I'll use that razor and shaving foam and jump in that shower you have in the back of the station here to freshen up before you get back with our guests. A cold shower, I think, as it's already getting bloody hot and it might wake me up and get the deduction part of my brain working. Once we've seen Bryant and Hudson this morning we should go and see Deborah Harris again, unless we get a confession out of them, of course, which I doubt. Did you turn up anything more on her background, Sargent? Anything on before she came to Lindos?"

"Very little, sir, and virtually nothing on her in UK records according to the British police. It is mostly the sort of information you would get from a passport application. It's a bit strange, like she had no life before she came to Lindos, or at least nothing out of the ordinary. In a way it is very similar to the very little we found on Dawn Parsons, very ordinary and nothing unusual. Still, perhaps it is not so strange at all and that's why they both ended up here, because their lives in the UK were so mundane."

"Yes, perhaps that's the case, Sargent," Karagoulis agreed. "Nevertheless, I think there are a few more questions Deborah Harris needs to answer about Dawn Parsons while she has been here in Lindos, and maybe even about the mysterious Jacki Walker. I think we need to be a little more forceful with her. Do we have an address for where she's living, and, on a different point, do you have any towels here by any chance?"

"Yes, sir, there are some towels in the storeroom next to the toilet and shower, and Deborah Harris lives in a villa in one of the alleyways opposite the small supermarket on the way to Pallas Beach. It's the alleyway on the left just before you get to the health spa place. The name of the villa is Afroditi. There's a ceramic plaque on the wall with the name on it, you can't miss it," Samaras told him.

"I've still got a hunch that we should be looking in another direction," the Inspector repeated. "Maybe we should be looking more closely at the relationship between Dawn Parsons and Deborah Harris. There is something we are missing there I'm sure, something Ms Harris is not telling us. They were supposed to have been best mates and yet, according to her, she knew very little about Dawn's past. Also, there is the question of the two Englishmen with the similar sounding name, the murdered Tony Carpentar and Dawn Parsons' friend, Tom Carpenter. Could there be any connection there I wonder, other than their supposed love of the city of Prague, and from what we've been told by Tom Carpenter, its women. Maybe they had more of a connection than Mr Carpenter is telling us? It's time to stop pissing around with these people I think."

"Yes, sir, I think it is," Samaras agreed. "Not least because I heard in Café Melia this morning while I was getting the croissants that some of the bar and restaurant owners in the village are getting more than a bit concerned over all this business. It seems they are concerned it might affect the tourist trade if it's not resolved soon."

Karagoulis picked up the razor and the shaving foam and told the two officers, "Precisely, the longer this goes on the worse it's going to look for us. Nevertheless, it's only just before nine now, so I guess we had better give Bryant and Hudson another half-an-hour or so to wake up. You can put some more coffee on in the meantime, Samaras, for when I'm done showering."

Just as the Inspector was issuing his instructions and heading towards the small storeroom to collect some towels for his shave and shower Samaras' mobile rang. Within a minute of answering it he told the caller, "Right, hang on a moment," and shouted through to Karagoulis in the storeroom, "Sir, it's the forensic team at Tony Carpentar's apartment. There are somethings you should know."

As the Inspector came back into the room Samaras was finishing the call with, "Okay, let us have your report as soon as possible."

"What is it?" an even more impatient Karagoulis asked.

"The forensic team just found what they reckon is a kilo of cocaine in Tony Carpentar's apartment. They said it was hidden in an air vent in the shower room. They are pretty sure it's coke."

"Oh great, another fucking piece in the puzzle, drugs." The Inspector's Sunday morning, lack of sleep mood, wasn't improving. "So, maybe Carpentar was murdered over drugs? Any sign or indication, any inkling that he was involved in that sort of thing in the village, Samaras, or even any sign of that at all in the village, drugs and drug dealers?"

"Nothing, sir, we've picked up stories of the odd tourist, usually the younger ones, and cannabis, but nothing serious, and nothing as heavy as coke. It has to have been brought in by someone from outside the village, foreigners, maybe people we don't usually see here and not the usual and regular tourists. The forensic team also said they found a couple of odd things in Dawn Parsons' apartment that they think we may be interested in," Samaras added.

"Drugs?" Karagoulis interrupted. "That would tie the two of them together nicely, maybe that's the link we've been looking for?"

"No, sir, I'm afraid not, they found a Russian dictionary and a hand-written note inside it. The numbers zero five, a hyphen, zero five, a hyphen, and zero four were written on it, with the word 'out' and another word in what they say looks like Russian, but they don't have anyone who can confirm that on the team here in Lindos or translate it if it is. I told them to send one of the team over here with it and the dictionary straightaway."

I'll jump in the shower, you get that coffee on, Samaras, and by the time I look more civilised and presentable hopefully this mysterious piece of paper and Russian dictionary will have arrived and we can set about trying to decipher it. We will also need to get it checked for fingerprints, Papadoulis, just in case Tony Carpentar's show up on it by any chance. Plus, when we get Hudson and Bryant in here this morning I think we should ask them about Tony's little drugs stash and see how they react, see what they knew."

Karagoulis had showered and shaved and was sat at the desk with his fresh mug of coffee when one of the forensic team arrived with the hand-written note and Russian dictionary. The note had been placed in a plastic bag to protect it for later forensic examination and for fingerprints, but through it the words 'Радищев' and 'out' were clearly visible to the Inspector as he was handed it, plus '05-05-04'.

Samaras and Papadoulis peered over his shoulder and both shook their head, but the policeman from the forensic team told them, "One of the guys on the team reckons he can recognise some Russian letters, some similarity with Greek he says, and he thinks it's something like 'Radileb', but he couldn't be sure."

"'Radileb', 'out', 04-04-05, what the bloody hell does that mean?" Karagoulis exclaimed while simultaneously scratching the back of his bald head. A drugs code and Russian contact perhaps? One minute this case seems to get more straightforward, either it is a crime of passion or a couple of revenge killings over drugs and a deal that went wrong, and the next minute it is just a muddle and a puzzle again. You two get off and see the Bar Code owner and get Bryant and Hudson in here. I'll do some digging on this note and try some of my contacts in Athens to see if any of them knows Russian and what to make of this code."

Just as the two officers were about to leave the police station Papadoulis stopped in the office doorway, saying, "Sorry, sir, there was something else I discovered in my background searches that I forgot to tell you. I'm not sure how important or relevant it is to the investigation, but I'm sure you'll want to hear it too, Samaras. Carol Hudson's husband is not Greek, he's Lebanese by birth. When I ran a background check on him it came up that he moved to Rhodes with his family when he was eleven years old, and for some reason, which I could find no trace of, they changed the family name to Koropoulis soon after they arrived, and he took the name Panos."

"I had no idea. Ever since I've known him I always assumed he was Greek by birth. I'm sure he told me at some point that he was born in Rhodes," Samaras commented.

"I checked, sir," Papadoulis continued, "and any person who is ethnically Greek born outside Greece may become a Greek citizen through naturalisation, providing they can prove a parent or grandparent was born as a national of Greece, and provide the necessary birth and marriage certificates. I guess that's what his family did."

"Interesting, Sargent, but like you said I'm not really sure how, if at all, that has anything to do with the case, but while you two get off I'll add it to the Incident Board."

A few minutes later Karagoulis was doing just that when his mobile phone rang. Answering it a female voice asked him, "Is that Inspector Dimitris Karagoulis?" Confirming it was, he was told, "I have Police Lieutenant General, Mr. Giorgos Katsouris, in Athens for you, sir. Hold the line please, I will put you through."

Karagoulis knew immediately that this must be something serious for the Chief of the Hellenic Police in Athens to be calling him at around nine-thirty on a Sunday morning. He didn't have to wait long to find out exactly how serious.

"Good morning Inspector Karagoulis, Lieutenant General Katsouris here," came down the phone in a very serious, officially sounding voice.

"Good morning, sir," he somewhat nervously replied.

"I understand one of your officers made an enquiry to the British police concerning a particular UK phone number," the Chief of Police asked.

"Yes, sir, that's correct, it's in connection with a murder investigation we are in the middle of here in Lindos, two murders unfortunately," Karagoulis confirmed.

"It is a listed classified number, Inspector. You and your officers will not pursue any further enquiries in respect of that number. Do I make myself clear?"

"Yes, sir, of course, completely clear, sir," Karagoulis knew better than to think about asking why or hesitating before voicing his agreement, even if he certainly wasn't clear just what 'listed classified' meant exactly.

"Good, I trust you will find your murderers soon, Inspector, goodbye," the Police Chief told him, and with that the phone went dead.

"What the bloody hell, stranger and stranger, what a fucking puzzle, what the fuck was that about?" Karagoulis muttered in the empty room. He was still shaking his head at that strange twist in the investigation as he made the first of two calls to his contacts in Athens about the Russian word on the piece of paper in the dictionary in Dawn Parsons' apartment. Neither of the calls yielded anything though as his contacts were unable to enlighten him immediately on its meaning. Russian letters aren't the easiest of things to describe over the phone one of his contacts pointed out on his second call, suggesting instead he fax a copy to him or email him a photograph of the piece of paper, and he would try to get back to the Inspector on Monday morning.

Karagoulis was staring intently at the Incident Board again, hoping for some inspiration and further clues as to who the murderer or murderers were, when his mobile rang again. He could see from the call display that this time it was Samaras, reporting back already on his meeting with the owner of Bar Code.

Displaying his frustration over what had just occurred in the previous calls he had received and made, the Inspector never bothered with even a "hello", but just settled for an abrupt, "Well?" followed immediately by a curt, "that was quick."

"I bumped into the Bar Code owner straightaway sat outside the Red Rose Bar having coffee, sir. He said the cleaner never said anything to him about anyone having been sick in the toilet on Friday night. I asked him to check, so he called her and asked her directly, but he said she was certain that no one was sick in any of the toilets. He said she was pretty reliable, so it must be right."

"So, Mr Bryant lied to his drinking buddies about that then. They said he was gone for quite a while, long enough to murder Dawn Parsons perhaps?" Karagoulis was thinking aloud down the phone to Samaras.

"Maybe he got a message from her wanting to meet some time in the early hours of Friday morning while he was with his mates in Bar Code," he continued. "What if she wanted to confront him over what had happened the night before in the alley by Qupi? Perhaps she told him she believed that he'd raped her. Crisa Tsagroni said the bruising on the lower part of her body certainly indicated that. We have already been told that she was pretty drunk in Arches and later in the pizza place at around five that morning. What if she did then meet Bryant, confronted him over what she believed was rape, they argued, it got out of hand and he killed her? We need to check her phone records again to see if there was any message that evening from her to Bryant, or to any number not in her contacts list that we haven't traced. It would help if we could locate her bloody mobile phone, but I'm guessing the murderers took that though."

"It's only about a hundred metres up the steps and along the alley from Bar Code to where Dawn Parsons was murdered, sir. He could easily have arranged to meet her along there, although he'd need an accomplice, and he'd also need to have slipped out of Bar Code without his drinking mates seeing him, unless of course they were both in it with him and they actually were his accomplices. The toilets are at the back of Bar Code and there is only one entrance and exit. It would be very difficult for him to have got out of there without them seeing him, unless they went with him and the sick in the toilet story is a complete fabrication by all three of them? Although I don't really get that, sir, why bother to make up a story like that, why not just say they were altogether all night and not bother to say Bryant disappeared for some time?" Samaras continued to pour cold water on his Inspector's theory by adding, "And then there is the murder weapon, sir, the knife. Where would he, or even all three of them, have got hold of that at such short notice if he really was responding to an angry phone message from her wanting to meet him?"

"Yes, you're right, Samaras, that doesn't really add up and it seems her murder was much more premeditated. So, perhaps, as Papadoulis reckoned, it was Carol Hudson who was Bryant's accomplice in murdering Dawn, and her husband is covering for her in saying he was at home in bed with her from after four on Saturday morning. Or maybe that is just what he told her and he came home much later, and was up to something he didn't want her to know about. After all, she told me she was asleep when he came home that night and had no idea really what time he actually got home, only from what he told her. Either way, whether it was Bryant and one or both of his drinking buddies, or whether it was him and Carol Hudson, there a gap in his alibi about being sick in Bar Code toilet. So, let's get Bryant and Hudson into the station as soon as possible and try and get the truth about just what they were actually up to that night."

18

Carol Hudson and Alan Bryant?

Around forty minutes later Samaras arrived back at the station and guided Alan Bryant into the interrogation room, where Karagoulis was already waiting for him with Papadoulis and a rather twitchy Carol Hudson, who was sat in front of the small desk. Bryant and Hudson exchanged a quick sideways glance and a nod of the head acknowledgement, but never spoke, as the Inspector placed a chair alongside her at the desk for him.

Alan Bryant exclaimed aggressively as he sat down, "What the fuck is this about now? I told you all I know yesterday, and what's Carol doing here? We've got nothing to do with the murders!"

Not prepared to put up again with Alan Bryant's obvious belligerence the Inspector spun round on his heels from his slow walk across the room and responded with, "So, you speak as a couple then do you, Mr Bryant? You speak for Miss Hudson as well do you? That's interesting, how do you presume to know why she is here, and indeed, that she has nothing to do with the murders, as you put it?"

Clearly shaken out of his hostility by that interpretation of his questions, Bryant lowered his tone, and his voice betraying his discomfort he replied, "No, of course not…of course we are not a couple…I…err…don't know where you got that idea from. It's just that I know I had nothing to do with it, and from what I know about Carol I am sure she had nothing to do with all this either."

The Inspector uttered only a soft, "Hmm," then stepped back a pace and leaned against the white-washed office wall, raising his eyes and nodding his head very slightly in the direction of Samaras, who was also leaning against the opposite wall and on cue said, "how is your stomach now, Mr Bryant? Has it recovered?"

"Now what are you on about?" Bryant responded, his tone displaying some mounting aggression once more.

"Your stomach, one of your drinking friends said you told him you had an upset stomach on Friday night, or should I say early Saturday morning, while you were out drinking. When I interviewed him yesterday he told me you disappeared into the toilet in Bar Code for some time, and when you returned you said you had been sick."

Samaras had moved away from the wall as he spoke and was now standing beside the small desk above Alan Bryant as he continued, "But, you see according to the owner of Bar Code, his cleaner said there was no sign of anyone being sick in the toilets when she came to clean them on Saturday lunchtime, Mr Bryant. Odd that, unless of course you cleaned it all up yourself, I suppose, although you also told us previously that you were quite drunk, so I can't imagine you would have been in any fit state to do that, can you?"

Samaras was taunting him and checking for a reaction. But he said nothing, instead it was Carol Hudson who reacted by giving a quick glance sideways at him sat in the chair next to her, and then returned to her fixed stare ahead at the blank white wall.

Seeing her reaction, Karagoulis took his turn and switched the questioning to Carol Hudson. As he moved across from leaning against the wall to perching on the corner the desk in front of her he asked, "What about you then, Miss Hudson. Did he not tell you his excuse for slipping out of Bar Code to meet you that night was that he had thrown-up in the toilet? It was you that he slipped away to meet wasn't it? You weren't at home in bed at all at around four that morning when your husband says he got home was you? He lied for you, didn't he? Or was he just so drunk he couldn't remember and maybe thought he needed an alibi himself?"

Alan Bryant started to try and get up out of his chair, saying, "This is..." But before he could get any further Samaras placed a firm hand on his shoulder, telling him, "I think you should sit down Mr Bryant. We aren't finished with you two yet by any means, and I'm sure you wouldn't want to leave before we get to the bottom of this would you?"

Karagoulis quickly added, "According to the pathologist report there was substantial bruising on Dawn Parsons' arms caused by someone restraining her while another person stabbed her in the neck. So, it seems at least two people were involved in murdering her."

"And you think it was us two, that's crazy, why would we do that?" Carol Hudson interrupted.

Karagoulis deliberately ignored her protestations. Determined to repeat the accusation he'd made to Alan Bryant in their previous interview the day before, in order now to observe how Carol Hudson's reacted, he continued, "There was also substantial bruising around her lower body and her buttocks. That bruising was older though, around twenty-four hours older according to the pathologist. As I suggested to you yesterday, that was caused by you restraining her and raping her in the alleyway by Qupi the night before, wasn't it, Mr Bryant. You forced her to have anal sex didn't you?"

Carol Hudson looked horrified, and immediately turned, leapt to her feet and began to hit out at Bryant while loudly exclaiming, "What! You fucking, fucking bastard, you fucking piece of shit!"

Papadoulis, who had remained silent throughout standing in one corner, now moved quickly to grab hold of Carol Hudson's forearms. Firmly restraining her he told her, "I think you had better calm down and sit back down, Miss Hudson. There is a little more you might want to hear."

She was starting to weep and two small tears were dribbling down each side of her face as Samaras handed her a tissue. Bryant, in the meantime, had flinched away from her attempted blows. He moved his chair slightly away from her, but said nothing.

Karagoulis was not relenting though. "Judging by your reaction, Miss Hudson, I take it that there is something the both of you have not been telling us. You have been having an affair, haven't you? It would be better for the both of you if you told us the truth now please."

The Inspector was standing over the two of them once more as he continued, "It's obvious from your reaction that you didn't know about that little episode between Alan here and Dawn Parsons did you, Miss Hudson, and you certainly don't appear very happy about it? I suppose you also didn't know that Dawn Parsons had the same little visitor as you and Tony Carpentar, chlamydia, did you? How do you suppose she got that? Maybe it was her who gave it to Tony, who then gave it to you? Or maybe Alan here gave it to her after he got it from you? Of course, we don't actually know if Alan has it, do we, Mr Bryant? He refused to say when we asked him about it yesterday, or to be accurate, he denied having it. Quite a little puzzle isn't it, and all a bit of a surprise to you I expect Carol?"

The Inspector was using her first name and trying, at least, to adopt a more 'good cop' sympathetic tone. She just sat mopping away the tears from her cheeks, with a numb look on her face and not reacting any further to any of his suggestions. So, he pushed her a little more, "Was that what you had the argument with Dawn about in Qupi a few weeks ago, Carol, the chlamydia? Or was it just over Tony or Alan here? We were told it almost came to blows, and that at one point Dawn had you by the hair. That must have been very embarrassing for you."

Carol Hudson was continuing to wipe away her tears, but before she could answer, Alan Bryant finally proclaimed forcefully, "I'll tell you again, I don't have fucking chlamydia. I told you before I never forced Dawn or raped her. She wanted it just as much as me. I knew she did, she just didn't want to say so."

"But that is why you killed her isn't it, Mr Bryant?" Karagoulis responded, "Because you thought she was going to report you for rape, or at least tell someone about it, and eventually that would get back to Carol here. I'm guessing that was the gist of a phone message you got from Dawn sometime around five on Saturday morning, wasn't it, and that's when you arranged to meet her with Carol here, and then kill her. That's what happened wasn't it, Mr Bryant?"

Bryant and Carol Hudson were both trying to loudly proclaim their innocence with an almost harmonious chorus of, "No, no, that's not what happened at all." Alan Bryant added an indignant, "That's complete bullshit, what phone message? I never got any phone message from Dawn at any time that night or in the early hours of the morning. You can check my phone if you want, and I'm sure if you check Dawn's that will show she didn't send me any message or call me."

Before either of them could say any more though, Karagoulis pressed on putting to them his belief about what happened, as he now leaned right across the desk and stared intently into Alan Bryant's face. "You killed Tony Carpentar because of jealousy over him and Carol didn't you Mr Bryant, and then you got Carol here to help you dispose of Dawn in case she claimed you had raped her. Although you couldn't tell Carol that was the reason, could you? Of course you couldn't, as that would completely ruin your relationship. So, you made up some story about Dawn and Tony Carpentar, about her trying to take him away from Carol weeks before, and that's what your argument with her was about in Qupi wasn't it Miss Hudson? That fictional story you fabricated about Dawn and Tony having a relationship also helped you get Carol here away from him didn't it, Mr Bryant, something you had been trying to do for months according to Carol's husband."

Bryant and Hudson both sat in silence staring ahead at the blank wall for about a minute. The three police officers waited, exchanging knowing glances about remaining silent. Eventually Alan Bryant looked sideways at Carol, and turning back towards Karagoulis admitted, "Okay, I wasn't sick in the toilet, and yes I did meet up with Carol that night after I slipped out of Bar Code, but it wasn't to then meet up with Dawn, and I didn't murder her, or Tony either. Sure I had that fight with him on Thursday night in Jack's, and sometimes we had our differences, and usually over women, but I wouldn't have murdered him over them. Okay, I had been trying it on with Carol for weeks, and yes, Inspector, we have been having an affair. It started about three weeks ago and Carol had been trying to finish her relationship with Tony ever since."

"But he wouldn't take no for an answer," Carol Hudson interjected. "He just wouldn't let it go, and then he kept coming up with these crazy plans about the two of us going away to Prague for a weekend. He thought that would make everything alright between us. That's what he was going on about again in Jack's bar on Thursday night. I only met him to tell him again that we had to stop, but he wouldn't listen. I never told him about Alan and me though."

"That's why I slipped out of Bar Code, and made up the story about being sick in the toilet." Now it was Alan Bryant's turn again to explain their actions in the early hours of Saturday morning. "As I said, I did meet up with Carol, but it definitely wasn't so we could murder Dawn. I wanted to warn Carol about Tony and drugs in case you asked her about them. I knew you would find them in his place eventually and that he was dealing in them, but I didn't think she knew anything about it. He told me once that he was sure she didn't know."

"That was what the argument with Dawn in Qupi was over," Carol interjected again. "She said she knew that Tony was dealing heavily in drugs with some people from outside the village, and wanted to warn me. But I didn't believe her, and told her so in no uncertain terms. I told her to stop spreading malicious rumours. She'd had a few drinks, as was often the way with Dawn, and I thought she was just shooting her mouth off. She was never slow to spread gossip, and I just thought it was something to do with her fancying Tony."

She paused briefly, reached for another tissue from the small box that Samaras had placed in front of her on the desk, wiped away the remains of her tears and blew her nose. Before she could go on Karagoulis asked, "Did you ever see any evidence of that? Ever see them together in what looked like a more than friendly way?"

"Dawn and Tony, no, Inspector, not at all, never, but that didn't necessarily mean she didn't fancy him," she answered. "I always got the impression she didn't like me really. I assumed it was just jealousy and that she was just making up the stuff about the drugs to put me off him. But what I said to her about not spreading malicious rumours seemed to tip her over the edge. She started shouting loudly that everybody in the village knew that, 'I wasn't little Miss Perfect', but then she said 'drugs were a whole different ball-game that I hadn't a clue about'. By then she was screaming at me that, 'the world Tony inhabited most of the time was a whole different world to the perfect little one that I believed I lived in'. I told her to calm down and stop spreading malicious gossip, and that people were starting to look over at us. She was screaming so loud that she could even be heard over the music by some of the people around us. But that seemed to only make her even angrier, and the next thing I knew she grabbed my hair and told me not to be so 'fucking stupid'. She said she knew about those things and about the people Tony was dealing with, and that a stupid bitch like me had no fucking idea. Then, just as her friend the English guy came back from the toilet, she let go of my hair and said that unlike me she knew from her past how to take care of herself."

"What did she mean by that?" Karagoulis asked.

"I've absolutely no idea. Once that English guy she was always hanging around with and drinking with came back from the toilet it all calmed down. I left soon after and she never mentioned any of it to me again, not that I really spoke to her very much after that, or even before really."

"What about you, Mr Bryant, you said you knew Tony was dealing in drugs, any idea who the people he was dealing with were? According to Dawn Parsons, they were from outside the village then? " Now it was Samaras' turn to ask a question.

"No idea, I only know because he asked me if I wanted any at one point. Before you ask, I said no. I don't use that shit, alcohol is bad enough for me. So, yes, I did slip out of Bar Code to meet Carol, and okay I wasn't sick in the toilet, but it really was just to warn her about the drugs and Tony." Bryant was now repeating himself, trying to emphasise in doing so that he was telling the truth at last, as he went on, "Like I said, he'd told me that she didn't know anything about his drug dealing. Just in case he was lying though, I wanted to check that she really didn't have any, but that if she did, tell her to get rid of it straightaway."

"So, it turns out that you were so concerned about that because the two of you were having an affair after all." Sargent Papadoulis eagerly intervened as he tilted his head slightly to one side and glanced across at Karagoulis, eager to connect Bryant and Carol Hudson, and justify his theory about the murders; that, in fact, they were the murderers they were looking for.

It wasn't Alan Bryant who answered him though. Before he could say anything a still tearful Carol Hudson said, "Yes, I have been having an affair with Alan for the past three weeks."

Turning again towards Alan Bryant and wiping away more tears, her venom emerged through a few sobs, "After what you've just told me about him and Dawn though, Inspector, I obviously should have known better than to trust this piece of donkey shit. Everyone says even the donkeys aren't safe with him around. Now I know what they mean."

Bryant tried to divert the conversation away from him and donkeys by adding, "That was what really caused the fight between me and Tony on Thursday night in Jack's, Inspector. There was a bit more to it than I told you yesterday. I was goading him about how I could get Carol away from him if I wanted. I already had, but I wasn't about to tell him that as Carol didn't want me to. She said she would break it off with him, and was trying to, but he wouldn't let go. In the end I just lost it because he kept going on and on about the two guys he'd been talking to in the bar earlier and how they knew Prague, and that he was definitely going to take Carol there. It was the way he was talking about her. He was so sure of himself about it, but I knew different. I just kept saying three or four times that I knew she would never go to Prague with him because, I told him, I reckoned she was more interested in me. But he just told me to 'fuck off and stop dreaming'. That was when I snapped and the fight started."

As he handed Carol Hudson yet another tissue out of the box, somewhat relieved to be getting to some of the truth of what had been going on at last, Karagoulis realised he still wasn't any nearer to solving the murders. Although he couldn't resist a sarcastic, "Well, I'm sure your husband will be relieved to hear that you have learned the error of your ways, Miss Hudson, at least over Mr. Bryant here. When we interviewed you before why did you deny so strongly that you and Alan were having an affair? "

She looked up at him with yet more tears still running down her cheeks and between sobs replied, "Because of Tony. I panicked and thought that you might try and connect it to his murder, but I didn't kill him, and even though, from what you've just told me, I now think he is a real piece of shit, I don't believe Alan killed him either, Inspector."

Shifting awkwardly in his chair, desperate to get out of there and put an end to his growing discomfort, Alan Bryant asked, "Is that all, Inspector? Can we go now?"

"Just a couple of more questions, one to you both and then one just for you, Miss Hudson," Karagoulis replied. "Do either of you know a woman called Jacki Walker, or have you ever heard of her in the village?"

Carol Hudson shook her head, while Alan Bryant said a firm, "No, never heard of her, why?"

"Just a name we've come across in our enquiries. It's probably not important," the Inspector told them.

"Maybe she has something to do with the dealers Tony was involved with over the drugs, Inspector. They killed him, don't you think?" Alan Bryant couldn't resist his usual superior 'know-it-all' approach that had swiftly returned.

"Well, we don't know that do we, Mr Bryant, so we can't be as sure about that as you seem to be. Is there something more that you are holding back on about the drugs, something else that you haven't told us that makes you so certain that was reason Tony Carpentar was murdered? After all, we've learned a few things here this morning that you've been holding back and didn't tell us previously, like your relationship with Carol here." Karagoulis was holding out the palm of his hand in the direction of Carol Hudson as his voice betrayed yet again his annoyance and frustration with Alan Bryant's attitude and how long it had taken to get to the truth.

"No, nothing, there's nothing more to tell you, that's all of it, and unless you've got any more questions-" Before he could say any more Karagoulis had decided he'd had enough now of Bryant's once more returned arrogance and proceeded to spell out his situation to him in the clearest possible terms.

"You don't seem to realise you are a prime suspect in two murders, Mr Bryant. I will decide when we have finished our questions and when you can leave. You had a motive for Tony Carpentar's murder with your argument and fight with him over Miss Hudson, and now, at last, you admit you were having an affair with her behind your supposed good friend's back. With your rape of Dawn Parsons you had a clear motive for her murder in order to cover that up if you thought she was going to expose that and damage your relationship with Carol, as well as the possibility of you facing prosecution over it-"

Alan Bryant attempted to interrupt, saying, "Alleged rape and we've told you-"

An increasingly angry Karagoulis wasn't letting him finish though, going on as he loomed over the seated pair from behind them with, "You went missing from Bar Code on the night Dawn was murdered and then lied about being sick in the toilet, and now you say you met up with Carol that night to warn her about Tony's drug dealings. How are we to know just what to believe from either of you two, after all you also both denied previously that you were having an affair? That's a lot of lies you've concocted between the two of you over the past couple of days, don't you think, Mr Bryant. I don't think you realise the seriousness of your situation. When you add all that up, put it all together, it doesn't look good. I think you should bear that in mind and take your situation, both of you, a bit more seriously."

Alan Bryant looked somewhat shaken by the ferocity of Karagoulis' points as the Inspector glared down at him once more. Staring straight ahead towards the blank interrogation room wall he took a deep breath and simply said, "I wish to leave now, if you don't mind. I think that if you wish to see me again, and have any further questions, it will have to be with a solicitor present acting on my behalf, Inspector." Half turning towards Carol Hudson he said to her, "I don't know about you, but I'm leaving now."

Karagoulis chose to ignore his comment to her, and instead just added, "Okay, thank you, we will be in touch with you if we need to see you again. You can go, Mr Bryant. Officer Samaras will show you out. Just one more question to you, Miss Hudson, alone please, if you don't mind."

After Bryant had left the office with Samaras, Karagoulis took the chair in which Alan Bryant had been sat, placed it on the opposite side of the desk to Carol Hudson and sat down on it with an audible sigh. Looking her squarely in the face across the desk, he asked, "Did you know your husband is not Greek, Miss Hudson? He's Lebanese, isn't he?"

"Yes, of course I know. I know all about his family history and his name change. He told me before we got married, of course, but what has that got to do with your investigation. His papers are perfectly in order."

"We know that, we checked," Karagoulis told her, "and probably nothing, it probably has nothing to do with our investigation. I just wanted to find out if you knew. It seems that quite a few people in this village have secrets and I just wondered if that was another one of them." As he got up from his chair he added, "That's all for now, Sargent Papadoulis here will show you out."

A few minutes later, mugs of coffee once more in their hands, the three police officers were back in the main office again standing in front of the now very full Incident Board. "So, what do you think, sir? Are Hudson and Bryant our killers, as I suggested?" Papadoulis couldn't resist reminding his superior officer.

"I just don't see Hudson as a killer, Sargent. She's definitely not a nice piece of work given all she's been up to in this village, and from the way she tried to attack Bryant just now she's definitely got a temper, not to mention being somewhat of a hypocrite. She sleeps with Carpentar, sleeps with Bryant, all while she's married, and then she calls Bryant a piece of shit for cheating on her with Dawn Parsons. Incredible hypocrisy and amazing double standards, but that doesn't make her a killer necessarily, or one of our killers. Unless she was strong enough to restrain Dawn Parsons, which from the account of their confrontation in Qupi she wasn't, she would have to have been the one plunging the knife into her neck while Alan Bryant held her arms from behind. Perhaps I'm wrong, but I just don't see it, Papadoulis. Bryant, yes, maybe, I could see that arrogant shit with his temper doing it, and with his medical background he would possibly know exactly where to plunge the knife in the neck for maximum effect and kill her almost instantly, as Crisa Tsagroni told us. Although, again, this looks more and more like it was premeditated, and I just can't see Bryant sending a message or calling Hudson in the early hours of Saturday morning and telling her to bring a knife, can you? So, maybe we are back to Bryant and one, or both, of his ex-pat drinking buddies being our murderers. That would fit for both murders, Tony Carpentar and Dawn Parsons, and maybe there is a link somewhere between Bryant, his two mates, and the drugs. Bryant is definitely the sort of person that makes my skin crawl, Sargent, but that's hardly a reason to charge him with murder, unfortunately."

In his usual manner Karagoulis had paced across the room and back twice as he spoke, and now stopped to stroke his chin with the palm of his right hand as he briefly hesitated and then added, "I think we should get some search warrants for Bryant's place and those of his two friends' as soon as possible. You can sort that with Rhodes, Papadoulis."

Yet again the Inspector stood gazing at the Incident Board, while his Sargent went over to the telephone to call about arranging the search warrants. While Karagoulis had been taking his shower earlier Samaras had added to the Incident Board all that they had found out that morning from the forensic team about the cocaine, the mysterious note and the Russian dictionary. He had also added a section headed 'Russians', with the various incidents involving them over the past three days beneath it.

Eventually, after a couple of more minutes silence, Karagoulis rubbed both hands down the side of his face to meet under his chin and reached for the blue marker pen. As he removed the top of the pen he managed to get some of the blue marker ink on the thumb of his right hand. After pausing to spit on his thumb and attempt to rub the ink off he carefully and somewhat deliberately drew a line between the names Dawn Parsons and Tony Carpentar, adding a question mark between them under the line followed by the word 'drugs'.

"So, we are back to just what is the connection between these two, the two victims?" he said, as he turned away from the board and walked across the room, all the while clicking the top of the marker pen on and off. "Are we looking at crimes of passion here, or murders connected to the drugs, or maybe something else that we just aren't seeing?"

Samaras was now perched on the corner of the small office desk. Before he could think of contributing anything in answer to the Inspector's questions though, Karagoulis exclaimed, "Wait a minute," and strode purposefully back towards the Incident Board. As he reached it he added, "What about these bloody Russians? Russians are popping up everywhere in this investigation, like a bad smell. Tom Carpenter said there were some having an argument in Giorgos the morning after Tony Carpentar was murdered. What if they were the same two guys that Jack Constantino told us Carpentar was talking to in his bar the night before? He said he thought they were from Eastern Europe, so they could just as easily have been Russian. Then there were the two, again maybe the same two, who caused the incident in Arches with the guy on the door the night Dawn Parsons was murdered. He said they were a couple of well-built guys who definitely weren't shouting at him in English or Greek, and the woman who works at Symposio, Sandra Weston, said she noticed a couple of well-built guys who looked like they worked out sat outside the pizza place when she saw Dawn Parsons just after five the morning she was murdered. Maybe it's the drugs and the Russians that is the connection? What if Carpentar and Parsons were both involved in the drugs business, and Carpentar, or both of them, owed the Russians money?"

Karagoulis was walking back and forth across the office in an increasingly agitated way once again as he brainstormed all this about the Russians in machine-gun fashion to Samaras, who couldn't get a word of response in, not that the Inspector really wanted one. He was simply thinking aloud.

"Tom Carpenter said that he thought the guy doing most of the heated talking and pointing in Giorgos on Friday morning, giving the other two a bollocking was the way he put it, was their boss, maybe a tour company boss, he thought. What, though, if he was giving them a bollocking because they hadn't got the money for drugs they'd supplied to him out of Tony Carpentar?"

Now Samaras decided he could speak as he thought he should challenge the Inspector's logic.

"Although, if he owed them money it wouldn't make much sense to kill him as they wouldn't get paid, would they, sir?"

"That's true, Samaras but maybe the two 'heavies' had inadvertently overstepped the mark and had actually killed him. Crisa Tsagroni said he had been knocked unconscious before he was murdered and dumped in St. Paul's bay. Perhaps they got disturbed, or they thought they heard someone coming at St. Paul's as he was coming round, and they panicked and killed him? So, the boss-man was pissed off with them because they'd fucked-up, and he knew he wouldn't get his money now. You reckoned that the coke had to have been brought in by someone from outside the village, foreigners you said. So, maybe that is really why Carpentar was murdered?"

"That does sound plausible, sir," Samaras agreed. "What about Dawn Parsons though, how is her murder connected.

"Perhaps somehow she was mixed up in it all as well," Karagoulis added. "What if it wasn't the case that she and Tony Carpentar were having an affair, but instead they had a nice little business deal going on between them supplying coke in Lindos? Carol Hudson said her argument with Dawn in Qupi was because she tried to tell her Carpentar was heavily involved in drug dealing. Of course, Carol says she didn't believe her, but how would Dawn Parsons know that it was true, unless she was in it with him maybe, and she was just warning Hudson off. And perhaps the second passport we found in the name of Jacki Walker has something to do with Dawn Parsons' and Tony Carpentar's little drugs business? Also, there's the Russian dictionary and the piece of paper in it from Dawn Parson's apartment. What did that mean? What if the word 'Radileb', or whatever it translates to from the Russian, and 'out 05-05-04' on the paper, are some kind of code connected to the drugs and the Russian dealers?"

Now Karagoulis looked across at the name Deborah Harris written on the Incident Board, and underneath it written the words 'friend and drinking partner of Dawn Parsons', but nothing else. "Hmm ... we don't seem to know much about Miss Harris do we, or even that much more about her friend Dawn?" he said. "Let's investigate this drugs and Russians theory a bit more. Let's go and see Deborah Harris again now, Samaras, and find out just how much of a friend of Dawn's she was, and how much she really knew about her, especially in respect of drugs and Russians. When we interviewed her last night I just got the impression that she knows a lot more about her friend Dawn than she was saying. I guess she should be up and about by now."

19

Deborah Harris, Dawn Parsons or who?

Deborah Harris had been sat for the best part of an hour in the kitchen of her villa on Sunday morning going over and over in her mind the events of the past few days in Lindos, trying to decide what was the best course of action in her situation. She hadn't slept very well and had woken intermittently throughout the night tussling with the same problem. Eventually she reached for her mobile and from memory tapped in a UK number that wasn't in her phone's contacts list.

As soon as it stopped ringing and there was a click of her call being answered, before the person at the other end of the line could speak she slowly and clearly said, "I'd like to cancel the Greek salad delivery," after which she immediately hung-up.

One minute late her phone rang. Before she said anything a very formal correct sounding English voice said down the phone, "You have a problem?"

In an equally serious and deliberate tone she replied cryptically, "Yes, a parish religious representative has been killed."

"We know," the voice replied. "There was an enquiry from the Greek police to the UK police about this number and we blocked it. It has been taken care of. What do you know?"

"That's just it, I don't," she replied. "I don't know much at all really." She decided not to mention the call she had received the previous evening from her former Russian lover wanting to meet her. He was insistent, and she was definitely tempted, but eventually, after some hesitation as he continued to try to persuade her, she declined. That call had also caused her to suffer from sporadic insomnia throughout Saturday night. She reckoned that to mention it now though would open up too much of a web of intrigue - or a can of worms, or maybe both, she wasn't sure which metaphor best described it - leading back to the liaison they had in Vienna in 1986. So, instead she just told the MI6 voice down the phone, "I think the local police suspect it is a crime of passion. There appears to be a lot of affairs going on here amongst the ex-pats."

"Yes, that's what we heard," the voice confirmed. "That's what our sources tell us, which is why we believe there isn't any cause for you to be concerned at all. From what we also learned your former colleague was a lot less careful than you in terms of alcohol and liaisons while she's been in Lindos. We'll keep you apprised of any developments, should there be any, but we don't believe you need to worry. Remember, don't use any landlines if you find out anything more and need to call us again. Use this phone and keep it with you at all times, if we get anything more we think you should know we'll call you on this phone immediately."

With that the phone went dead and 'the voice' hung up. She sat pondering just how her former employers knew so much about her and Dawn's activities in Lindos, and was definitely worried by that revelation. Within a few minutes though she concluded that what she had just been told, and the accompanying reassurance, was probably correct. Anyway, she was sure that thinking it over would be much easier and calmer up on the terrace of her villa looking out over beautiful Lindos bay with a nice cool soft drink and a couple of late breakfast croissants.

It was approaching noon and the hot midday sun was causing Karagoulis to mop his brow with a handkerchief again as he approached Deborah Harris' villa with Samaras. As they came down the slope of the alleyway approaching it the Inspector could see her sat under a sunshade on the raised villa terrace sipping a drink and surveying the impressive panoramic view. Rather than use the large brass doorknocker on the wooden door he called out. "Miss Harris, can we have another word please?"

She turned in her seat with a bit of a start, but as soon as she recognised who it was responded with, "Yes, Inspector, I'll let you in."

She led the two policemen up a flight of stone steps alongside one of the villa's walls in the cooler inner courtyard and on to the terrace. As she showed them to the table and chairs beneath the sunshade Karagoulis commented, "It's quite a view you have here, very nice."

"Yes, Inspector, I love it. It's so peaceful and Lindos bay is spectacular with the clear blue water, the beaches and the cliffs each side. I like to call it paradise."

"Yes, I suppose it is, although the last couple of days and nights in Lindos can hardly contribute to calling it paradise can they, Miss Harris? That's what we came to see you about. I have a few more questions, if you don't mind."

Before he could start his questions, she replied with, "Of course, but what am I thinking, would you both like a drink, a cold one or some coffee?"

"Water will be fine for both of us, thank you," Karagoulis responded, without even thinking to ask Samaras, who in any case nodded his head in agreement.

While she went down the steps to her kitchen to fetch the water the Inspector instructed Samaras that he would do most of the questioning and that the officer should be careful what he gave away in information should he feel the need to intervene. "You can ask her about the drugs, but remember, Samaras, question everything, learn something, but answer nothing," he added.

"Sounds like a detective's creed, sir," Samaras commented.

"No, officer, it is Euripides, but it could well be I suppose. Wise advice in this situation, when I have a hunch Deborah Harris is not exactly all she appears to be or telling us quite all she knows."

"Euripides, sir?" the officer queried.

"He was an ancient Greek tragedian playwright, Samaras. It's a form of drama based on human suffering. Very apt for the situation in Lindos over the last few days, don't you think?" Karagoulis liked to think of himself as a very educated man, and was never slow to try and demonstrate it.

"I suppose so, if you say so, sir. Euripides, hmm, I'll have to look him up."

As Samaras was repeating the Greek playwright's name Deborah Harris came up the stairs and back onto the terrace with two bottles of water and two glasses. "Euripides, Inspector, don't tell me he's involved in your investigation?"

"No, Miss Harris, of course not, but you've heard of him?"

"Yes, I studied Ancient Greek in my dim and distant past. Very interesting, which is why I love Greece so much I suppose, that and this view," as she spoke and sat down at the white wrought iron table she waved her right arm towards the view of the bay.

"So, you're quite well educated then?" Karagoulis asked.

"Well you could say that, a first in PPE at Cambridge, Inspector, politics, philosophy and economics."

Aware that their background searches on her had turned up nothing on that Karagoulis decided to probe a little deeper before he got to the questions he originally came to ask. "Seems a little odd I must say to have such qualifications and be living in a place like Lindos? Why is that?"

"Like I said, look at the view, Inspector. I'm living in paradise, why would I want to be living or working anywhere else?"

"Yes, I can certainly see what you mean. What about before though? Were you living in England? You must have had a good job there given your qualifications."

"I lived in Windsor, near London, and I worked in finance for a bank in the city. I am from there originally. I suppose you could say it was a very good job, yes, but just over four years ago I decided I'd had enough and wanted to live abroad. I came to the conclusion I could afford to, even before I got my little job here at Symposio. I had been to Lindos quite a few times before on holidays for a week or two, so I decided what better place could there be to live? Except for the events of the last few days, of course, that has certainly been true. I've never regretted it." She hesitated and took a sip of her drink before adding, "But I don't see what my background, my past, can possibly have to do with your investigation, Inspector."

Throughout all this Samaras sat on the opposite side of the round table silently observing Deborah Harris' response to his Inspector's questions, as instructed, and making notes in his black police pocketbook. The impression going through his mind was that her background story was all a little too neat, almost rehearsed, which prompted very brief circumspect eye contact with Karagoulis at one point. The two men were communicating without speaking and it was obvious to each of them that they were drawing the same conclusion.

"No, no, nothing at all really," the Inspector responded. "Being a policeman I'm just naturally curious I suppose, particularly about you being here with such eminent educational qualifications. Is it those that made you and Tom Carpenter such good friends then, with him being a Professor?" Karagoulis was probing in order to see just how friendly she really was with him.

"I've never really thought about it like that at all, Inspector, but Tom and I are hardly such good friends, as you put it. I only know him through Dawn. She was much more of a friend with him than I am. Mostly I only ended up drinking with him and Dawn after work, and all I know about him is what I told you last night at Symposio."

"Anyway, it seems there's more to you than meets the eye, Miss Harris. I believe that's the phrase you Brits use, isn't it? With your educational qualifications I mean. You're hardly someone I'd expect to find working as a 'front of house' person in a Lindos restaurant, are you?" Karagoulis was still fishing for anything more he could find out about her background, but her training in her previous life meant he was having very little success.

"Yes, that's the right phrase, Inspector, but I told you why. Look at that." Again she pointed to the view from her terrace over the sun-drenched and clear blue sea of Lindos bay, adding with a little growing irritation, "But you said you had some more questions for me, and as I said, I'm sure they weren't just about my education and personal history."

"Yes, well, to use the same English phrase as I did a minute ago, it seems there was more to your friend Dawn Parsons than meets the eye too, wasn't there, Miss Harris?"

Deborah Harris' facial expression gave away absolutely nothing as she responded with, "Was there, Inspector, I wouldn't know. As I thought I told you last night I didn't really know that much about Dawn's background. She kept most of that to herself. So, what do you mean?"

Before he answered her question Karagoulis decided to change tack and see how she reacted. "Who do you think killed Dawn, Miss Harris?"

"Err...I have absolutely no idea, Inspector." This time she was just a little startled. "That's a strange question to throw at me out of the blue. Why should I know? I suppose I just assumed from what you were suggesting last night at Symposio that it could have been sexual and related to a casual affair in the village here. Or, of course, I suppose it could have been an attempted robbery while she was drunk that went wrong, or even a male tourist trying it on for sex."

"Yes, well I did tell you about the incident with Alan Bryant in the alleyway by Qupi on Thursday evening, or I should say the early hours of Friday morning. Lindos is hardly a place with a history of sexual assaults by tourists though, as you no doubt know, or even robberies on the street. Officer Samaras here can confirm that I'm sure."

"That's right, sir, it's very safe, usually," Samaras took his cue and intervened. "Some nights there can be a lot of drunken people in the village, what with the stag and hen parties from the weddings, but we don't usually have any trouble. They are just here to enjoy themselves."

"That's true I guess. That's another reason I like it here, no trouble, usually, as you say, officer. But, you never said, Inspector, what did you mean there was more to Dawn than meets the eye?" She was curious and keen to find out what Karagoulis knew, especially given her telephone conversation earlier with London.

"For a start she had two passports. We found two in her apartment, one in the name of Dawn Parsons issued in the year 2000, just before she came here I guess, and one issued five years earlier in the name of Jacki Walker. The address on the application for that one was a place called Corbridge in Northumberland in the UK. Are you still sure you don't know any Jacki Walker, Miss Harris?"

Karagoulis leaned across the table looking at her straight in the eye as she replied, "As I told you last night, no I don't know any Jacki Walker, and I certainly didn't know Dawn had two passports. Anyway, she told me she was from Manchester. Are you sure the second passport was for her?"

Outwardly she was very calm and relaxed looking as she responded, although inside her head a voice was screaming fucking stupid cow, why the fuck did she keep that? Destroy all past personal documents we were told. And why the bloody hell didn't the agency get it from her? We were supposed to hand in anything we didn't destroy. Someone obviously fucked up.

As those thoughts were racing through her brain Karagoulis decided to blatantly ignore the order from the Hellenic Chief of Police in Athens and handed her a piece of paper with a UK phone number on it, saying, "Yes, both passports were definitely for her, but what about this phone number? Do you recognise it by any chance? It was in Dawn's phone contact list on her laptop, but we haven't had any luck tracing it."

Deborah Harris recognised it immediately. It was the number she had called that morning, less than an hour before, but again her expression and voice betrayed nothing as she simply said, "No idea, Inspector, it's not familiar to me. From the international code it's obviously a UK number, but I don't recognise it. Was there no name with it?"

"No, nothing at all," Karagoulis confirmed, as he took back the piece of paper and sat back in his chair. "According to her phone records Dawn called you on Friday afternoon. What was that about?"

"She wanted to know if I wanted to meet her and Tom Carpenter for a drink on Friday night after we finished work, and that's what we did."

"That was all, nothing else. She didn't seem concerned about anything?"

Being economical with the truth yet again, she told him, "Yes, that was all, and no she didn't seem concerned about anything. Far from it, she just wanted to meet for a drink and a Friday night out. We often went out on Friday's after work, and anyway she said it was Tom's suggestion that we go out and meet at LBN."

"What about what she did for a job before she came here? Did she ever tell you anything about that?"

"Office work, I think, somewhere in the West Country in England, Gloucester springs to mind, but I couldn't be certain." Once again she was being deliberately vague.

Ignoring the nearby glass Karagoulis took a swig of water straight from the small bottle before he asked, "Do you happen to know if it was in the public sector at all? From our check on her finances and bank account it seems she was in receipt of a monthly payment from a public service pension company, but she seems a bit young to have been drawing a pension."

Deborah Harris knew full well what that was. She was in receipt of one herself every month from the organisation set up as a public service pension provider by the agency, MI6. Once more though, she played it very cagily. "Again, I can't be sure, Inspector, but I seem to vaguely remember that when I asked her once about her financial situation, and being able to come and live in Lindos, she said she had taken her pension early, including a lump sum payment. I have no idea about the figures though. I didn't ask her, but yes, I suppose she was a bit young to be drawing a pension. Anyway, I think that was what she told me."

The Inspector was rubbing his chin with his right hand as he made eye contact with Samaras, which was his signal for him to stop scribbling notes and intervene. "Did Dawn ever mention anything about drugs to you at all, Miss Harris? Did you ever get any impression she was mixed up in anything connected with drug dealing, especially with any Russians?"

The introduction of questions referring to Russians caused her much more concern, but she decided the best tactic was to try and steer the questions on to the drugs element. Ignoring the Russians part of the question, she turned slightly in her chair towards Samaras and responded with, "Drugs, in Lindos, really? Are you serious? No, Dawn never mentioned anything about drugs to me, and I certainly never got any impression she was mixed up in anything like that. Where did you get that idea from?"

Watching her response carefully, which he did get the impression was one of genuine surprise, Karagoulis took over again from Samaras, telling her, "Dawn had a blazing row with Carol Hudson in Qupi a few weeks ago trying to warn her off Tony Carpentar and saying he was involved in drugs and drug dealing. We found cocaine stashed in his apartment, what looks like around a kilo. We think it might be linked to some Russians who have been popping up in the village in quite a few places over the past few days making a general nuisance of themselves, mostly a couple of well-built guys, but sometimes three of them. We think they could have been Tony's suppliers and he owed them money, which is why they killed him maybe? As Dawn seemed to know so much about Tony and drugs in the row she had with Carol, it seems likely that she was involved in some way, wouldn't you think?"

Alarm bells were really ringing in her head now as she leaned forward and picked up her glass to take a final swig of the now not so cold drink in order to buy some time to mull over in her brain what she had just been told. From that she was now beginning to suspect that her former-lover, Ivan Radischev, wasn't in Lindos just to try and reignite their relationship, despite what he'd told her in their phone conversation the previous evening. He obviously wasn't alone, so if he was there just to see her why would he need to bring along a couple of other guys with him? With her previous training it took her only seconds to put two and two together and come up with what she thought was four maybe. She was wondering now if she knew exactly why Dawn had been murdered, and she was kicking herself for not telling the agency in London about her call from Radischev. One thing was certain, she was sure that Dawn's murder wasn't about drugs, as Karagoulis was suggesting, or even over some sordid sexual affair. She was now seriously beginning to wonder if it could have been about revenge for Dawn killing one of Radischev's men in Vienna in 1988.

As she sat inwardly digesting that, detecting her hesitation Karagoulis prompted her for a response. "Miss Harris...your friend Dawn, drugs, Tony Carpentar and some Russians, is there anything you can tell us, anything you know about all that at all?"

She was pretty convinced Dawn was murdered by the Russians now, if not by Radischev then certainly by his men, or his comrades as he would no doubt refer to them. But, Tony Carpenter, why the bloody hell would they murder him? Maybe that was over drugs after all and it wasn't the Russians who killed him? Before she could answer Karagoulis' question though, Samaras threw another ingredient into the mix, another Russian one.

"Do you know if Dawn spoke Russian, Miss Harris?" he asked.

Now she was even more stunned. This was getting a little too close to home, home being her past, a little too close for comfort. "Err...Russian?" she began, "why do you ask that, I...err...don't think so, although I don't really know. She never said, it never came up, and I never ever heard her speaking it." She was deliberately trying to give the impression of being confused and vague.

"Do you," Karagoulis followed up.

"Do I what?"

"Speak Russian?" the Inspector added.

"Me, no, why should I?" She was desperately trying to maintain her composure through what was now a growing web of lies and half-truths. Given her previous employment and past life, her Russian was excellent.

"Oh, I just thought that maybe with your educational background there was a chance you might do," the Inspector explained as he raised his eyebrows and tilted his head slightly to one side, giving off a suggestion that he was not exactly completely convinced by her answer. Handing her another piece of paper he asked, "I don't suppose you know what this means then? We found this in a Russian dictionary in Dawn's place. We thought it might be some code connected to the drugs."

She knew exactly what it meant. Why wouldn't she? 'Радищев' was the Russian for Radischev, and the word 'out' and the numbers '04-05-04' were simply the date he was released from a Russian prison. Although what was going through her head was, why the fucking hell did that stupid prat need to leave that around, surely she could have remembered a simple bloody date," she just responded to Karagoulis with a blank look and a simple, "No idea, Inspector. Doesn't mean anything to me, you think it's connected to the drugs then?"

Although the Inspector was answering her question, Deborah's mind was wandering into a minefield of questions that were increasing her concern about her own current situation, in particular how Dawn came to know exactly when Ivan Radischev was going to be released and why would she want to know that? She could only have found out through someone in the agency back in London, which meant that she must have been in touch with them. Yet despite her concern over the Russians arguing in Giorgos on Friday morning that Tom Carpenter had told her about, which she had relayed to Deborah in their conversation in the Lindian House on Friday evening, Dawn never saw any reason to tell her former MI6 colleague and boss about being in touch with the agency.

"Yes, we think it could be something connected to the drugs, and Tony Carpentar and his Russian suppliers. You didn't answer my question just now about that though. So, did Dawn ever mention anything to you about Tony and drugs?" Karagoulis asked her. Noticing a somewhat vacant look on her face, as though her mind was elsewhere, he added, "Miss Harris…?"

She hadn't really been listening, however, and instead had been too focused on thinking about her concern over why her friend Dawn was so interested in Ivan Radischev's release from a Russian prison.

"Sorry, Inspector, did Dawn ever mention what?" she asked.

"Tony Carpentar and drugs, did she ever mention anything to you about him and drugs, or even Russians and drugs?"

"No, as I told you before, Inspector, she never mentioned anything about any of that. As far as I could see she couldn't stand Tony. She was always going on about how he was full of bullshit and that you couldn't believe a word he said most of the time. Not that I think she was in his company much at all. I think it was just what she had often overheard him spouting forth on, as she liked to put it, in various bars, especially in Jack's late at night. She even set him up one night in Socrates bar and got Tom to catch him out. The bar was packed and that was really embarrassing for Tony. He had quite an argument with Tom over it that night. He liked the sound of his own voice and an audience, did Tony. Everyone knew that. Anyway, given what she always said about him I couldn't ever see Dawn being in some drugs thing with him, no way."

"Hmm…so, Tom Carpenter had an argument with Tony in Socrates." Karagoulis had got up from his chair as he spoke and was starting to pace back and forth the short distance across the terrace while rubbing the back of his neck with his left hand. "Funny that he never mentioned that when we spoke to him last night outside Pals," he went on. "He just said he'd had a few conversations with Tony about Prague as they both loved the place. He did say that he'd taken a dislike to Tony because he never bought him a drink, despite Tom buying him quite a few when he first met him. What was the argument over?"

"Yes, Tom wasn't exactly Tony's biggest fan, Inspector," she confirmed. "Anyway, it was over Prague, Prague in November 1989, was what it was about. Dawn said she'd had enough of Tony's bullshit and she got Tom to engage Tony in conversation about it in front of us and the people who he was with. Alan Bryant was one of them and Carol was there, of course."

"Carol Hudson?" Karagoulis interrupted.

"Yes, and Tony wasn't very happy at all about being shown up as a bullshitter in front of her, believe me. I think that is mostly why he got so angry. At one point I thought it was going to come to blows between him and Tom."

"So, what precisely was the argument about?" This time it was Samaras who prompted her.

"Dawn was the one who instigated it really. She'd had a few drinks. We were stood at the bar next to Tony, Alan and Carol, although not actually talking to them. In fact, I think Carol had her back to us. Her and Dawn weren't exactly best friends at that time, or most times really. But as usual Tony was talking so loudly most of the bar could hear him, even over the music. And believe me, Inspector, the music is always loud in Socrates, so you can imagine what Tony was like. Dawn just flipped and at first was just going to tell him to shut the fuck up, as she put it. Tom calmed her down though, and that was when she made the bet with him."

"What bet?" Karagoulis asked.

"She said she'd buy Tom a double Jameson and coke if he could expose Tony as a bullshitter there and then. So, he said it would be 'a piece of cake', and he did. I remember that Dawn was smiling broadly as Tom leaned over Carol's shoulder and said to Tony that he'd seen the tattoo on his arm, the one that said eighty-nine, and asked him what it meant. Tom knew what it was because Dawn had already told him. Anyway, Tony started to say it was to commemorate the Velvet Revolution of 1989 in Prague, at which point Tom asked him if he was there, adding that it must have been an exciting time if he was. Dawn knew that Tom had been there then, because he'd told her a lot of stories about it that she passed on to me. So, Tony started to tell one of his stories about it, but Tom interrupted him and asked if he'd actually been on the demonstration on the 17th November 1989? Again, Tom had told Dawn previously about being on that demonstration with a good friend of his who was Czech, and that he was actually beaten up by the police when the demonstrators were attacked. He said it was generally acknowledged as the incident and the date that the revolution really started.

Anyway, Tony said yes, of course he was on the demonstration. Then Tom started firing a load of questions at him about it, like was he at the start, where did it start from and what route did the march take, what was the initial reason the demonstration was organised and who by, what happened after the demonstration, and a few more. Basically, Tony couldn't answer any of them. He mumbled something about how the communist regime fell after the march and mentioned Vaclav Havel, but really he had very little idea about how to answer Tom's questions. That was when Tom answered all his own questions, telling Tony quite loudly that he was full of bullshit, and that he may have been to Prague at some point, but he certainly wasn't there in November 1989 or on the demonstration because Tom was, and if Tony had been there he would have been able to answer Tom's questions. I remember clearly his exact words to Dawn as he turned away from Tony, and his little group of Carol and Alan, back towards her and me, 'Same bullshit as fucking usual. That good enough for you, you owe me a Jameson and coke, a double I think you said.'

That really pissed Tony off, being embarrassed and exposed like that, and there were quite a few of the Brit ex-pats in the bar then. Dawn was almost roaring with laughter of course, as she tried to get Tom's double Jameson and coke. She had that nasty streak in her. Tony started poking Tom on the shoulder, jabbing him with his forefinger, as he kept saying you're a fucking liar, you're wrong, what the fuck do you know? That was when Tom turned and grabbed his arm and Alan and Carol intervened and pushed Tony away from the bar and towards the exit doors."

"When was that?" Samaras asked.

"Phew...I'm sure it was on another Friday night. It was the first or second week of the season I think. So, it must have been about three weeks ago, I guess, although I couldn't be sure."

Karagoulis had sat back down at the table under the sunshade out of the hot sun and was now mopping his forehead with his handkerchief as he startled Deborah Harris a little with his direct question. "Do you think Tom Carpenter would have murdered Tony over that then?"

"Kill someone because they bullshit? Blimey, Inspector, if that was the case at least half the Brit ex-pats in Lindos would be dead. A murderer, no, I can't say I really know Tom that well, but he doesn't strike me as someone who could kill anyone, not even such a bullshitter as Tony Carpentar."

"But, tell me, was Tom always in the habit of doing things like that to please Dawn, playing games for her? It seems he obviously liked her quite a lot from what you've just told us."

"I don't know about playing games for her, Inspector, but yes, I think he liked her a lot. As I'm sure I told you before, they were good drinking buddies, and they seemed to be on the same wavelength, if you know what I mean. When it came to having a good night out and drinking, and sometimes, to be honest, being a little crazy, yes they were definitely on the same wavelength."

"Tom Carpenter, a little crazy, but he seemed like quite a serious academic when we spoke to him."

"That's as maybe, Inspector, but as I said, he was a different person when he'd had a good drink, just like Dawn, which is why they got on so well, I suppose. Don't get me wrong, I don't mean crazy like he would kill someone though, just crazy in terms of having a good time, a good night out."

"Is that the only reason he got on so well with her do you think, Miss Harris? Was there something more?" As he asked that Karagoulis was once again leaning across the table looking her in the face intently.

"Okay, well I can't be sure, but there was something Dawn said about Tom the next time I saw her after that incident that night in Socrates. I can't remember exactly what it was that made me think something more had happened later that night between the two of them, but she kept going on about how great it was that Tom made Tony look such a twat, as she put it. That was one of her favourite words when it came to insults. I went home to bed after Socrates, but she told me the next night that she and Tom had gone to Nightlife and then Arches, and that she'd had a great night that she didn't want to end. I think that's the way she put it. As I said, I can't be sure, but I just had a feeling something more had happened between them that night. I never asked her and she never said, and neither did Tom, of course. I may be wrong, who knows."

"It seems we need to go and have another chat with Mr Carpenter after what you've just told us, Miss Harris. Do you know exactly where he is staying here by any chance, although I suspect that at this time he'll be on one of the beaches?"

"I doubt it, Inspector. At this time, just coming up to twelve o'clock, he'll still be in bed, or just getting up, after a late night and early morning in one of the clubs. He may already be in Giorgos having breakfast if he is up. If not, his apartment is in the alley behind Yannis bar, down to the left of the 404 bar and round the corner. There's no number, but it's the second door on the right as you go down the alley. It opens into a courtyard and his place is the one to the left. I think there is a number on that door, number one I think. I went there with Dawn for a lunchtime coffee earlier in the season, nothing else, in case you're wondering, Inspector."

As he got up from his chair, Karagoulis said, "Thank you again, Miss Harris, and for the water. You've been most helpful. We may need to see you again, of course, but that will be all for now."

Not quite as helpful as you may think or I could have been, Deborah Harris thought, as she showed the two policemen down the stone staircase and out into the alleyway

20

Tom Carpenter and Prague 1989

As Karagoulis and Samaras left Deborah Harris' villa and reached the end of the short alley running from directly outside her place they ran into a heaving, sweating tide of humanity and donkeys in the main narrow route between the Pallas beach and Lindos Main Square. It was twelve o'clock and the tourist boats had arrived from Rhodes bringing their hordes of Lindos day-trippers. Even though many of the tourists were making their way up from the jetty and the beach to the little village and its shops, bars and cafes on foot there were still a good many who were giving the donkey owners their trade riding up on the 'Lindos taxis' for five euros a donkey.

"Oh, I lost track of the time and forgot about this, sir," Samaras explained as they shuffled along at a snail's pace behind the tourists and donkeys in the narrow alleyway. "In a few metres though, we can cut through by the church. I expect most of these tourists will be heading for the Main Square initially. The donkeys certainly will."

Samaras was right and within a minute they were able to go to the left and head on through the rest of the village towards Tom Carpenter's apartment. The rest of the narrow white walled alleyways were still busy, however, with other day-trip tourists who had arrived on the coaches from Rhodes a little earlier than those who had preferred the more leisurely sea route, and they were now slowly perusing the small shops with their multitude of Lindos souvenirs. Within another few minutes they had reached the little square by Yannis' bar with its thick trunked tree surrounded by a low white wall just in front of Bar 404. There was more space in which to avoid the tourists, so Karagoulis told Samaras, "Hang on a minute I need to call Papadoulis to get him to do something while we go and see Tom Carpenter."

Samaras sat on the wall while the Inspector made his call as discreetly as he could in the alleyway alongside Bar 404, telling the Sargent they were about to go and re-interview Tom Carpenter and to run a background check on him, if he hadn't already done so. "Call me if anything at all unusual comes up, or if you find anything at all that you think I should know about while we're with him. We'll head back to the station after we've seen him and pick up some rolls for lunch on the way from that café we got some from before. It's just around the corner from Tom Carpenter's flat I think."

Papadoulis started to say, "Tuna salad rolls would be...", but before he could enlarge on his preference Karagoulis hung up.

A few seconds later the two policemen were standing outside what Deborah Harris had informed them was the door to the courtyard in which was Tom Carpenter's apartment.

Just as Karagoulis raised his hand to bang on the door with his clenched fist having not observed any door-knocker, Samaras reached across him and pulled a little wooden grommet with a string attached. The door opened into a small courtyard. Just inside the door was a single quite high step and on the left hand side there were some wrought iron stairs with railings that went up to what the policemen assumed was another apartment. Directly in front of them were some double doors with the number two on them, but as they reached the part of the courtyard where the stairs began a similar pair of glass fronted double doors with wrought iron protection came into view. They had the small number one on them. There was no knocker or bell so this time Karagoulis did manage to actually bang on the door with his clenched fist. A croaky male voice from inside said, "Just a minute." Half-a-minute or so later they heard a key turn in the lock on the inside of one of the doors and it swung open.

A bleary-eyed Tom Carpenter, wearing only swim shorts, and who had clearly only just woken up, greeted them with, "Oh, it's you Inspector, what time is it?"

"Just gone twelve o'clock, Mr Carpenter, we'd like another word with you please. We have a few more questions," Karagoulis informed him, adding, "It's a bit warm out here in this enclosed courtyard in the midday sun, do you mind if we come in?"

"Err...sure, Inspector, come in." He held the door open and stepped back out of the doorway into the small lounge of the flat adding, "Sorry I've only just woken up. Another Lindos late night or more like early morning really. Take a seat, please."

Karagoulis and Samaras sat down on a beige coloured, quite uncomfortable looking couch with wooden arms at each end that was situated against the wall to the right of the apartment doors. As they did so Tom opened the double windows in the lounge and the outside wooden shutters that covered them to let in some badly needed fresh air, after which he headed across to sit on an old looking upright dark wooden chair alongside the small table in the corner of the room.

"What more can I tell you, Inspector?" he asked as he sat down, followed by, "I'm not sure I can tell you much more than I have already though."

"You told us last night that your initial conversations with Tony Carpentar were mostly about Prague, but you never spoke to him much after that, something to do with him not buying you a drink in return for ones that you bought him," Karagoulis explained.

"Yes, but as I told you, Inspector, that's hardly a reason to kill him, is it?"

"No, of course not, but you didn't tell us you had an argument about Prague with him in Socrates bar about three weeks ago did you, Mr. Carpenter? We heard it nearly came to blows. You seem to have forgotten to mention that last night."

"I didn't think it was all that relevant or important. I can't see how it would make any sense thinking it might be connected to his murder. It was just a bit of a joke really." Tom looked confused over the fact that Karagoulis should think it was important.

"It might not make sense to you, but it might make some sense to us, if at some point it relates to some other incident we uncover in our investigation," Karagoulis told him. "So, what happened?"

"It was Dawn's idea, she goaded me into it. He was next to us, me, Dawn and Deborah Harris, at the bar in Socrates. He was with Carol Hudson and Alan Bryant and was spouting off and pontificating about something in that loud way of his, like he always did. Even though it was gone one o'clock the music was still playing, but he was almost shouting, so much so that you could even hear him above the music. I think at one point Deborah asked him quite politely to keep it down a bit as we couldn't even hear ourselves in our conversation next to them. Deborah was always much more diplomatic than Dawn, although it didn't make much difference. He was going on and on about something to do with Prague and the revolution in 1989. I knew what he was saying wasn't right, so I just said quietly to Dawn and Deborah at one point that what he was saying was 'a load of bollocks'. Dawn had had a few Bacardis by then, quite quickly. She always drank quickly. Anyway, she said she'd buy me a drink, a double, if I was so sure he was wrong and pulled him up on what he was going on about. Embarrassed him over the bullshit he was spouting, as she put it. Although I think the way she said it was, 'expose the twat'. So, that's what I did. I asked him some questions about the demonstration on the 17th of November 1989 that really kick started the revolution, and that he was claiming to have been on. Dawn knew that I'd actually been there at that time, and on that demonstration, because I'd told her previously. Well, of course Tony couldn't answer any of my questions, and if he had been there he would certainly have been able to. Probably not very diplomatically, I told him he was full of bullshit, as usual. Meanwhile, Dawn was pissing herself laughing. He got very angry, started jabbing me with his finger and I grabbed his arm. Alan and Carol pulled him away and got him out of the place."

Karagoulis moved forward to sit on the edge of the couch, saying as he did so, "That all sounds a bit unpleasant."

"I suppose so, but an argument over what happened in Prague in 1989 and exposing his bullshitting over it, is hardly a reason for me to kill him, Inspector. It was just Dawn having a bit of fun when she was pissed, which wasn't unusual for her. She liked to wind people up, or goad other people into winding them up."

"Maybe so," Karagoulis commented as he scratched the side of his head, "but you had an argument with one of the murder victims that nearly came to blows. You embarrassed and obviously humiliated him in front of quite a lot of people in Socrates, many of them Brit ex-pats living here, so we've been told. And, Mr

Carpenter, you appear to have been very close to the other murder victim, Dawn Parsons, so much so that she wants you to embarrass Tony and you gladly do it."

"It was for a drink, a sort of a bet, that's all. What are you trying to imply?"

"I'm not implying anything," Karagoulis told him. "I'm just stating the facts of the situation as we've been told them, including I might remind you, by yourself, and when you look at them like that it doesn't look very good for you, does it?"

The Inspector then threw in a question deliberately designed to see the way Tom reacted, and just how angry he became.

"Did you have some sort of brief sexual relationship with Dawn Parsons? Some people in Lindos think you did, Mr Carpenter, and have told us that."

"What? I told you..." he began, but Karagoulis didn't let him finish.

"Maybe you found out about her involvement with Tony Carpentar, and some drug dealing he was involved in with some Russians, and you were jealous, argued with him, it got out of hand and you killed him. Maybe Dawn was just playing you off against one another that night in Socrates."

"That's rubbish, Inspector, a complete fabrication. I don't know who these 'people in Lindos' are who you say think I had a sexual relationship with Dawn, but they're wrong I can assure you. I told you last night I never slept with her." He was growing angry and shaking his head from side to side in disbelief at Karagoulis' theory as he reached over for the small bottle of water on the table and took a swig.

"Hang on, what drugs, what Russians?" he asked as he placed the bottle back on the table.

"We found a kilo of cocaine in Tony Carpentar's flat and we found a piece of paper with a note on it in Dawn's place that seems to be some sort of code connected with the Russian drug dealers," Samaras told him.

"Dawn did seem more than a little obsessed with those Russians that I saw arguing in Giorgos on Friday morning. She kept asking me about them that morning, but I told you that, Inspector. I can't believe she was mixed up with anything to do with drugs and some Russians though, and she loathed Tony. I'm sure about that, not least from her actions in Socrates that night. Her only drug was Bacardi, believe me. So, if it was Cubans then maybe, for the Havana Club, but not Russians." A slight ironic smile crept across his lips as he went on, "She was always venomous about Russians whenever they came up in conversation, like when I told her about my experience in Prague in 1989. I wasn't exactly over fond of them myself, and we seemed to have that in common."

Karagoulis got up from his position perched on the uncomfortable couch, put both hands into the small of his back and tried to straighten up and stretch it as he walked over to the open window for some fresh air and the warm sun.

"Yes, you mentioned Prague and 1989 before. Despite what you say, I still think these murders have something to do with drugs and Russians, and that Dawn and Tony had some connection with them. Tell me more about you and Prague though." Karagoulis was fishing for anything now, any background information that might incriminate Tom Carpenter. He decided to let him talk as much as possible and see what emerged.

"As I said before, I was there then, during the time of the 'Velvet Revolution', as it was called," the Englishman started. "I was doing some research for my academic work all across East and Central Europe and I got caught up in everything when it all kicked-off that autumn of 1989 in Prague. In the end I lived there for the best part of three months. I met a couple of women who I liked. I will not bore you with the whole story of my relationships with them, but, yes, I was on the demonstration with one of them on 17th November."

"That must have been interesting times, and a little dangerous maybe?" Karagoulis asked as he turned to face into the room with his back resting against the wall under the open window.

"Yep, it was, very dangerous, believe me, Inspector. I got entangled with the Czech Secret Police at one point. It was a bit dodgy, if you know what I mean, being a foreigner in Prague at that time, and a western foreigner at that. The bloody Russians were everywhere too, the KGB I mean. They didn't like or trust the Czechs. That was obvious, and the Czechs certainly didn't like them.

Anyway, after the revolution and the fall of the communist regime it emerged that the KGB had a plot to discredit the dissidents over a fake incident on the demonstration on 17th November. The idea was then to eventually replace the old hard-line Czechoslovak communist leadership with a reform communist leadership, similar to Gorbachev in the Soviet Union.

Of course I didn't know about all that at the time, but I even got taken to meet with one of the reform communists at one point during that time, at the request of him and the people he represented actually. That was really scary because I was sure that the woman academic from the university who arranged it and me were being followed on the way to the meeting. Then when we left the meeting in the guy's apartment block on the edge of the city she actually pointed out the man across the street that had been following us. The reform communists contacted me through the Czech woman I was with on the 17th November demonstration, Jana, and her friend, the university academic. Jana was involved in the student dissident movement, and another friend of hers, a guy called Jiří Kaluza, who subsequently became her husband a few years later, was quite high up in the student dissident leadership. I met him a few times and he seemed to know quite a lot about what was going on, what the Russians and the KGB were up to. I never really took to him to be honest and always thought he was a bit dodgy."

He wasn't exactly sure just where this was going, and what it even remotely had to do with the investigation, but Karagoulis decided to let Tom Carpenter go on, briefly asking, "In what way?" Meanwhile Samaras sat on the uncomfortable couch looking a little bemused over his Inspector's line of questioning.

"He just seemed to know a bit too much about what the Russians were up to in Prague for my liking, and he kept asking a lot of questions about what I was doing in Prague, to me and apparently to Jana," Tom continued. "I must admit that at one point during the autumn of 1989 I thought he might be an agent for the Czech Secret Police who had infiltrated the student dissident movement. In the end I just put it down to my jealousy as he seemed to be very close to Jana. She seemed to idolise him. He did ask a lot about me though, and not just directly to me and Jana, but also to another one of her friends I found out later. It almost felt like he was reporting back to someone on me at one point. Just paranoia though, I guess.

Anyway, the reform communist guy that I met wanted me to feed some information to the western media and press about their reform plans in order to take some heat off them from the west. As I said, it was all a bit scary really, and yep interesting and dangerous," Tom finished saying.

He sat back in the chair and took another swig from the bottle of water as Karagoulis asked, "So what happened, what went wrong?" Meanwhile Samaras was looking over at his Inspector with a furrowed brow, increasingly exasperated with this line of questioning.

Tom screwed the top back on the bottle of water, and leaning forward in his chair with his elbows resting on his knees he continued, "In the end it all went pear shaped, as we say in England. It all went wrong. The Czech Secret Police fucked up, the Russians too, and the whole system collapsed and came tumbling down. The so-called 'Velvet Revolution', that's what happened, Inspector. After that, of course, it all really went wrong for the Russians, especially some of those high up in the old communist regime, including in the military and the KGB. I heard some time afterwards that the high ranking KGB officer who was in charge and organised the whole plot and operation in Prague around the supposed incident on the 17th November demonstration ended up in a Russian prison. Apparently, he was put on trial in Moscow a couple of years later, after the fall of the Soviet Union. Radischev, his name was."

"Radischev," Karagoulis exclaimed to Samaras, and frantically reached into his trouser pocket for the clear plastic forensic bag containing the piece of paper from Dawn Parson's Russian dictionary. Striding quickly away from the open window and over towards Tom Carpenter, Karagoulis thrust the bag with the piece of paper in front of his face. Pointing to the word 'Радищев' written on the paper, he asked, "Is that what this says?"

"Yes, why?" the Englishman asked.

"Maybe it is just a coincidence. After all there's no reason to think it's the same person, but it does seem a hell of a coincidence.

We found the paper in a Russian dictionary in Dawn Parsons' apartment. Do you know if she spoke Russian?"

"No idea, but why would Dawn have that? When she asked me about Prague and what it was like to be there in 1989 during the revolution, and I told her what I've just told you about Radischev, the KGB and the Russians, she did seem really, really interested, but how can this be connected to her murder, Inspector? I assumed all that was just something she was generally interested in, you know, sort of curious historically, if you like. Although I do recall that there was one night when she got very drunk, I mean very, very drunk, even for Dawn, and we were sat on the wall outside Niko's pizza place in the early hours of the morning eating pizza, and she started going on about how I had no idea about the Russians and the KGB. She said her and Deborah could tell me a few things about those bastards, as she put it, which I would be horrified to hear and make me squirm."

"What do you think she meant by that?" Samaras asked, as he now got up off the couch and went over to the open window, casting a glance to his Inspector on the way and raising his eyebrows.

"I've absolutely no idea. As I said, she was drunk, very drunk, I doubt if she even remembered it the next day. She often never remembered most of what she said when she was drunk, and I never asked her about it or mentioned it again."

"What about Deborah Harris? Did you ask her about it or tell her what Dawn had told you, tell her Dawn had mentioned her name in connection with the Russians?" Karagoulis asked.

"No, I never did. I just put it down to the Bacardi in Dawn talking. She always had plenty to say when she'd had a drink. But I still can't figure out why she would have a piece of paper with Radischev's name written on it, Inspector, and why in Russian?"

"Well, that's what we don't know, and until you just told us we didn't know it was his name did we. We assumed it was something to do with drugs and a code," Samaras answered this time.

"You're missing the point officers. That's not a code. It's a date. The fourth of May two thousand and four, just about a month ago, and that's why she has also written on it the word 'out'," Tom explained. "From what I heard from my academic contacts, and read in my work and research, Radischev was sentenced to fifteen years in what the Russians call a corrective labour colony by the new regime in Russia after the fall of the Soviet Union. As I told you before, it happened to a lot of the high-ranking KGB officers after the communist regime collapsed and Yeltsin took over. There were a lot of people in the new government with a few old scores to settle, if you know what I mean. Anyway, that was in nineteen-ninety-two, if I remember correctly. My guess would be that he's been a good boy while in prison, or perhaps someone has pulled some strings for him with President Putin, and he's had his sentence reduced on the pretext of good behaviour. So, he's been released three years early, on the fourth of May, a month ago. After all, Inspector, Putin is a former head of the KGB you know, so it wouldn't be that improbable would it, and highly likely that Radischev still had some friends in high places in Putin's new regime. But how the hell did Dawn know his release date, if that is the case, and why would she have been so interested in it?"

"Jacki Walker, Mr Carpenter, does that name mean anything to you?"

"Who...Jacki Walker?" Tom again looked bemused at what seemed to him a change of direction in Karagoulis' questions. His head was still a little muzzy from his Saturday night out and the drink, plus from what he'd just heard and learned from the policemen's questions. "Jacki who, never heard of her, should I have?" he added.

"We found a second passport in that name in Dawn's apartment, and it's definitely her. She never mentioned anything about having another name and another passport to you then, even when she was very drunk at any time?"

"No, never, Inspector, it seems there was a lot more to Dawn than any of us knew."

"That may be so, although there may be one possible exception to that, Mr. Carpenter. One person who may know a lot more about Dawn Parsons than they have been telling us, given what you say Dawn told you about her and Deborah Harris and Russians. I think we need to go back and ask Miss Harris some more questions about that now. Before we go though, one more thing, did you ever meet this guy Radischev while you were in Prague in 1989? If not, have you ever seen a photograph of him or know what he looks like?"

"Sorry, Inspector, no idea, never met him and I've never even seen a photograph of him. I wouldn't have a clue what he looks like. High ranking KGB officers hardly went round freely having their photo taken at that time, except by other intelligence agencies I'm guessing."

"Okay, you might want to splash some water on your face and run a comb through your hair, Mr Carpenter, as well as putting on a t-shirt."

"Why, what for, are you arresting me?"

"No, not at the moment, but I think it would be very helpful if you were to come to Deborah Harris' villa with us now while we ask her about what you've just told us. I can't quite work out how all this fits together yet, how it connects to the murders, but I just have a feeling that somehow it does. So, I think we need to ask Miss Harris a few more questions, specifically about what it was that her and Dawn knew about the Russians. I'd prefer it if you didn't mention Radischev to her or what you know about him from Prague in 1989, Mr. Carpenter. Leave that to us please. Once we've brought him up, and asked her a few questions about him, feel free to say what you know, but not until then please. So, if you wouldn't mind getting dressed. Try and be as quick as possible please, Mr Carpenter."

Part Four: Secrets of the past II

21

Prague 1989 – "One of you will die"

"You will select one of your best agents to carry out our plan on the demonstration next week, on 17th November. They need to be completely trustworthy and carry out the operation to the minutest detail. My personal reputation and standing within the party and the organisation depends on this succeeding. One little breach of security about our plot and I will ensure that there will be dire consequences for those responsible. The agent you choose will fake their death from a beating by the Czech Secret Police on the demonstration. After the Czech police stop the march in Národni, halfway up that street, and keep the demonstrators penned in for an hour, they will attack them near the arches and the passageway. Your man must be near the front of the march and he will supposedly die from a beating in the passageway. One section of six State Security police officers from the StB will pick him out and confront him as the demonstrators are attacked. They will snatch your agent from the demonstrators. Unfortunately he will have to take some beating to make it look real. We will make sure that enough people see his body being removed later after the demonstration has broken up, as well as ensuring that the news of his supposed death gets out in the Czechoslovak State media and to western journalists. As you obviously are aware, Musil, the demonstration is supposed to be about commemorating the fiftieth anniversary of the student demonstration against the Nazis on which a student was killed by them. So, having one of your men posing as a student who is supposedly killed will have great significance and completely discredit the existing hard-line Czechoslovak communist leadership, as well as the dissidents, who will no doubt report it erroneously to the western media. Then we will be able to replace the hard-line leadership with a more reform minded Gorbachev-type set of communist leaders more to our liking."

Ivan Radischev was forcibly issuing his instructions in Tomas Musil's office in the StB Czechoslovak Secret Police headquarters in Prague. Musil knew better than to listen anything other than very attentively. Radischev was a top KGB officer, based in the Soviet Embassy in Vienna, and had been sent to Prague in late October 1989 in order to orchestrate the Soviet plan to replace the hard-line Czechoslovak Communist leadership with a 'Czech Gorbachev' reform communist. The Soviets believed this would secure the continuation of the communist, and ultimately Soviet, control in Czechoslovakia. As the Chairman of the Czechoslovak Communist Government Committee for State Security Musil understood very well the consequences for him of not making sure the KGB plan was carried out to the letter successfully. Radischev was firmly ramming that point home to him.

Musil was a tall, straight-backed, slim, dark haired man. He had a long thin face with a small moustache barely covering his top lip below a sharp beak of a nose and narrow small eyes. His face displayed his serious approach to not only his position in the StB, but to his life in general. He had risen through the StB ranks over twenty years after being recruited whilst a student at Charles University in Prague following the crushing of the 'Prague Spring' reforms in 1968 and the subsequent period in Czechoslovakia referred to as that of 'normalisation'. Every action he undertook in his career was carefully considered and designed to further his own position, often at the expense of others, whom he was never slow to denounce to his superiors and expose their aberrations. He was ruthless and determined, as well as a total believer in the communist cause.

Radischev was even more ruthless and determined, if that were possible. He had reached the higher echelons of the KGB through his single-minded pursuit of what he believed to be the communist cause, and his aspiration towards the military and political leadership of the party. Although at first dubious about Gorbachev and his reforms introduced in 1986, he was now a devout disciple and was determined to ensure the survival of not only the communist cause, but also the Soviet Union itself through the implementation of Gorbachev's ideas. Those plans also included what should be done in the six so-called Soviet satellite states in East and Central Europe – Czechoslovakia, Hungary, Bulgaria, Romania, Poland and East Germany. He was acutely aware of Gorbachev's wish to be seen in the western world to have 'clean hands' in respect of what happened in those states in the late nineteen-eighties.

Despite that Radischev also exhibited the all too familiar superior Russian attitude and trait of disdain towards not only Czechs and Slovaks, but also nationals in the other five satellite states. This was particularly true in respect of the State security services in all the six states. As far as he was concerned they were unreliable and often incompetent. Consequently, they needed to be guided firmly by their Russian comrade superiors, who oversaw all their actions and activities. This was especially the case at this time of great threat to the survival of what Radischev, along with the Soviet political leadership, liked to describe as the 'socialist commonwealth'.

Like Musil, he was a tall, straight-backed slim man, betraying his military training and background, although with a much fitter and toned body than the Czech. His attitude of superiority and determination loomed over Musil, ensuring that he fully understood that failure of any part of the proposed operation would have dire consequences for him. He wasn't prepared to leave anything to what he considered the general incompetence of the Czechoslovak StB, adding, "I've looked at the files of the agents you have undercover in the leadership of the student dissident movement and I've decided there are two possibilities for the faked death, a Jiří Kaluza and a Martin Šmid. Šmid is the best choice, but you need to get both of them in your office to brief them about this because Kaluza needs to be on the demonstration near the front of the march also, so that he can help lead the students into the trap."

"Right, of course, sir," Musil confirmed.

"Wait, Musil, there's more, especially about Kaluza," Radischev added. "It seems that as usual you and your agents haven't really been on the ball on this. Kaluza is very friendly, shall we say, with a Czech woman, Jana Sukova. Our Russian agents say that she, in turn, is much too friendly with westerners and foreigners. She spends far too much time in their company for her own good, particularly an English university lecturer. It seems she has been spending a lot of time with this man, far too much time for our liking."

Radischev's tone was now clearly an even more forthright and aggressive one as he continued, "So, although Šmid is clearly the one for the job of being the dead student, when you get them both in for the briefing you need to find out more from Kaluza about his relationship with this Sukova woman, and also what he knows about her English academic friend, particularly what he's actually fucking doing here. Got it, Musil? You understand? We can't have any fuck-ups on this, or all our balls will be on the line, starting with yours." Now the Russian had stopped pacing back and forth across Musil's office and was leaning over him pointing his index finger at him in an aggressive manner.

"Absolutely, sir," the Czech confirmed, completely understanding Radischev's not very veiled threat.

"You need to make it clear to Kaluza that he should be much more careful about just who his friends are." Again Radischev forcibly rammed home his point with a jabbing finger into Musil's left shoulder. "Because of this Kaluza would be too much of a risk. He's much too well known by Sukova and her English friend to be able to 'play dead' on the demonstration. Find out what you can about his relationship with the woman, and about the English academic, but make it clear to Kaluza to be careful, and make it very clear to him that this is all classified information." Raising his voice he added, "Under no circumstances is he to tell anyone about this operation, or even hint at it in any way, and particularly not to the Sukova woman."

The Russian strode a couple of paces away from Musil's desk, turned again to face him, and said once again forcibly, "You will report directly to me and only me on all of this. Get the two agents in straightaway. The demonstration is only a week away and I want a full report from you verbally on your meeting with them immediately after you've seen them. Don't put anything in writing under any circumstances. I want to know their responses and reaction, especially Kaluza's. I hope I've made myself clear, Musil, and, of course, we have never had this meeting and conversation. I'm sure you clearly understand what I'm saying, don't fuck this up!"

"Certainly, sir, very clear, I understand totally. I will get the two of them in tomorrow morning and report to you by tomorrow afternoon."

"Right, I look forward to that," the Russian told him with a slight mixture of disdain and sarcasm in his voice. With that he turned and headed towards the Czech's office door without even the hint of any of the pleasantries of "goodbye" or "good day".

22

Moscow, early May 2004

The wind was swirling between the nearby grey blocks of Moscow flats as the small door to the Butyrka Prison clanked open at six-thirty and a tall, grey haired, very skinny man, in a dark suit that may have once fitted him perfectly but was now clearly too big for him, stepped through it and into the cloudy, polluted early morning air. His face was drawn and pale, and although it was an overcast gloomy morning he was struggling to adjust his eyes to the light. Simultaneously the rear door to a large black Zil limousine parked nearby swung open and a well-built man in a short black zipped leather jacket stepped out of the car and walked across the prison forecourt to greet the released prisoner. There was no sign of a smile of recognition or even a word of greeting from either man. Their mood was as dark and chilly as that Moscow early morning. A brief perfunctory handshake was the initial exchange between them before the man from the limousine took the small old battered leather bag from the released prisoner and held open the rear door to the limousine for him.

"We will take you to the apartment first, sir, and after you have had a chance to freshen up your friends from 'the Comrades of '89' have arranged a small drinks reception and some food for you," the man from the limousine informed the ex-prisoner as he settled into the rear plush black leather seat next to him.

Clearly not in the best of health from his time in the Moscow prison, and before that in the FGUIK-14 corrective labour colony in Yavas, Mordovia, the man simply replied wearily, "Thank you, but I hope you also have some information for me."

"We do indeed, Comrade Radischev. In the end we had to apply a little gentle persuasion and pressure on him by threatening to leak to the Czech media his role as an agent in 1989 for those useless shits the Czech Secret Police, but Kaluza eventually came back with the information that we wanted. He got what we needed from the woman Sukova, who is now his wife. He has a high-powered, well paid job and a prominent position with the American accountancy company Price Waterhouse in Prague, so he obviously didn't want to put that in jeopardy through stories about his past. He saw sense eventually, sir."

Radischev just stared impassively out of the car window as it sped through the chilly Moscow streets and, betraying his growing impatience over too much background information, simply firmly said, "And?"

"Apparently, his wife is still in touch with the Englishman from time to time, sir. According to Kaluza, the last she heard he was going to be in a village on the island of Rhodes in Greece for the whole summer from the middle of this month, a place called Lindos. One of our comrades on the island tracked him down and managed to relieve him of his passport a few days ago. The passport was only issued two years ago so the photograph is a recent one, so we should be able to identify him easily."

"What about my other instruction, comrade, what have you got for me on that?"

As you ordered, sir, we managed to find out where your woman friend from British MI6 in Vienna is living now. Our source inside the British Secret Service found out that by a strange coincidence she is living in that same village, Lindos, on Rhodes. Apparently she left MI6 four years ago and now has a completely new life and identity. Her new name is Deborah Harris. From what we've found out from our various contacts on Rhodes it seems there is quite a British ex-pat community in this village of Lindos. We even got her new email address and have been sending her sporadic emails, supposedly from you, trying to carefully probe for any information on the ex-pat community there and in particular Sukova's Englishman friend, although we haven't referred to him or asked about him directly of course. We're pretty sure he's still there though, and it seems he's there for all this summer, as Kaluza told us. We've got his passport, so he can hardly go anywhere quickly, sir."

"Good, it's time to settle some scores then," Radischev replied. "Those fucking Czechs and that fucking investigating commission that the shit-bags in the new post-communist government set up, exposing our November 1989 plot, cost me twelve years of my life in those hell holes, as well as my career. Them, and that drunken bum Yeltsin, caused the collapse of our beloved Soviet socialist commonwealth.

The ones I really want to get and settle up with first though are the ones who blabbed and gave away all our plans. Fucking Kaluza obviously told that woman of his, Sukova, and she must have blabbed to her English academic friend. That's obviously why what we had planned for the demonstration all went fucking wrong. Kaluza and the English guy were both trying hard to get into her knickers at the time and you can bet Kaluza would have told her anything to do that, probably to impress her about how important he was and get one up on the Englishman. It's quite a list I've got, but I think we should start with the Englishman on Rhodes, and who knows, maybe it'll give me a chance to get reacquainted with my good friend from Vienna, Elizabeth, although you say her name is Deborah now? First things first though, some good Russian food for a change and some vodka with the comrades I think. Thankfully there are still some of the old guard communists around in the 'Comrades of '89'."

"Yes, sir, there are still twenty-five of us left from the party who were in Prague and Vienna in 1989, and the organisation is still actively preserving the Soviet ideals, although these days we are mainly based around Moscow. Like you, all the comrades believe Comrade Putin will eventually lead us back to the glorious Soviet Union and its true communist ideals, and Russia will be great in the world once again. As the Slavophiles said in the past, sir, it is Russia that is the light that will lead the world to true freedom, peace and communal contentment in life. As I've heard you repeat many times, sir, their belief is that the key to the way forward for the world and its people is in the Russian soil and the Russian soul, 'sobornost'. One of the comrades in the organisation, Vladimir Dobrovski, says his brother and him were in your unit in Vienna in 1986, sir. He will be at the reception and is anxious to meet you and help you in any way. He really wants to travel to Rhodes with you to help settle your score with the Englishman, and then later with the others, he says."

"Dobrovski, yes he was with me in Vienna, but I remember that some bastard murdered his brother, stabbed him," Radischev confirmed. He was tracking a woman at the time who was a British agent and we were pretty sure it was her who killed him. Even though we thought we knew her she was taken out of Vienna immediately by the British, probably back to London, so we never got her. I'll be happy to take him along to Rhodes with me as soon as possible, and I'll need one other comrade as well."

23

Giorgos, Lindos June 2014

"No, Dobrovski, you've already fucked up once. I know he was your brother, but I don't want you doing anything more that might draw attention to us. If you start following her around, and trying to check if it is her for certain, then who knows what that might lead to. Someone might start getting suspicious, not least her. Anyway, I've got some unfinished business here myself and I don't want anything to interfere with that, or cause me problems with that, do you understand? We will be here a couple of days more while I deal with that, and while we're here for the rest of the time we keep a low profile, got it?"

Ivan Radischev was quietly, but firmly, emphasising his superior position and orders to his two comrades, Dobrovski and Sokolov, in Giorgos café bar while they sheltered from an early June rain shower with some Friday mid-morning coffees.

"Yes, sir, of course," Dobrovski acquiesced, but couldn't resist tentatively enquiring, "what do you mean we fucked-up, sir, we checked what you wanted to know didn't we?"

"His phone, you threw his bloody phone in the sea, when I told you to get it for me." As he spoke Radischev turned his body sideways to his right on the purple cushioned bench seat they shared at the white plastic table and glared directly into Dobrovski face from only inches away in order to stress his anger.

"Sorry, sir, that was my fault," Sokolov intervened in order to try and save his colleague from Radischev's anger. "I checked his pockets and found his phone while he was unconscious. As I was going through his phone contacts list though, before we killed him and threw the body off the cliff into the bay, it rang suddenly. He seemed to twitch a little and I thought he was going to come round, so I panicked and dropped it, and it fell of the cliff into the sea. But we never threw it into the sea, sir, and before I dropped it I did manage to see that there was definitely no number for the Sukova woman in his contacts list, not even any number under her married name of Kaluza."

"You're sure it was him though, even though he never had her number? I suppose there is no reason why he should still have it, I guess. It was almost fifteen years ago, and she's married now. Why would he keep it? Was there anything else in his pockets confirming it was him?" Radischev was seeking further confirmation that the man they had murdered definitely was the one he wanted to take his revenge on for what had happened in November 1989; one of the people he blamed most of all for his plan going wrong, and his subsequent imprisonment and loss of career.

"Nothing, sir, but we are sure it was him," Dobrovski confirmed. "It was the same man as the one in the photo from the passport that Sokolov got from our comrade in Rhodes town, the one he stole from his rucksack a few weeks ago. Plus, he had a tattoo on his arm of the number '89, sir, which I guess related to Prague that year."

"You're right, I guess it all points to it definitely being him," Radischev was calming down and becoming convinced they had got their man, and that, at least in one case, he'd got his retribution.

But, thinking he'd hopefully convinced his boss that Sokolov and him hadn't 'fucked up', Dobrovski returned to his previous request. "I obviously understand your point about not drawing attention to ourselves, sir, but I am absolutely sure it is her, the bitch who killed my brother. I know it's a hell of a coincidence that she's here, but she was working in the British Secret Service at the time with that woman friend of yours who is also living here now, Deborah Harris as she now calls herself. What if they both got new identities and moved here?"

Radischev had turned away to face Sokolov sat opposite him while he listened to his comrade's plea. He impassively took a sip of his coffee as Dobrovski continued, "I was outside her flat in Vienna, sir, working with my brother as a look-out when he went into the bitch's place. I was on the operation with him, so I know what she looked like from the photos we were given, but we didn't think she was in the flat at the time. The intelligence we had was that she was away from Vienna in London that weekend. But she was there and she killed him. I waited and waited for half-an-hour outside, but he never came back out. I tried to call his mobile, but there was nothing. It never even rang, it was dead. The bitch must have taken it and removed the sim card. I knew something had gone wrong. Eventually a large black car drew up. Four men went inside and two of them came back out straightaway. She was with them. The three of them got in the car and it sped off. Fifteen minutes later a white van pulled up, two more men went inside with a large wooden crate and an hour later they came out with it, loaded it into the back of the van and drove off. I knew it was my brother. I knew it was him in the crate, but I couldn't do anything about it. And I know it was that English bitch who killed him and that she is here now. I'm sure I've seen her here. I am sure it was her who went past this café yesterday at lunchtime while Sokolov and I were sat outside having some lunch. Just like you wanted revenge on the English guy over what happened in Prague in 1989, sir, I want revenge for my brother on the bitch that killed him in Vienna in 1988. Surely you can understand that. I may never get another chance, and I'm certain it's her."

Radischev continued to stare dispassionately past Sokolov at the row of bottles on the shelves on the white back wall behind the bar along one side of the café. He remained silent for around half a minute after Dobrovski had finished, continuing to stare at the wall. Eventually he said, "No, we can't risk it. I fully understand your need for revenge, Dobrovski, but there are bigger things at play here as far as the 'Comrades of '89' are concerned. There are so few of us left at the moment and we can't risk you, or all three of us, getting caught here. It looks like so far we've managed to get away with killing the Englishman without any suspicion, but if we start going on a killing spree in a little place like this someone is bound to spot something. It's too risky. We'll stick to our original plan, act like tourists, and spend another couple of nights here in the Memories hotel. It's out of the village, so we should be able to keep a low profile and not arouse any suspicion. In any case why should anyone suspect Russian tourists, there are plenty around here in places like Lindos now. You and Sokolov can spend a couple of days around the pool at the hotel getting yourselves a tan while I arrange to meet my woman friend from Vienna, Deborah Harris as she now calls herself. I have to figure out first though just how to contact her carefully, and more directly, other than by her email address that the comrades got from our source in the British Secret Service. I really need her mobile phone number. I want to see her, but whatever happens with her we'll leave for Athens late on Sunday afternoon, and then Moscow from there Sunday evening or first thing Monday morning, depending on flights from Athens. You check and book those, Sokolov."

After Sokolov said, "Okay, sir, of course, I'll get straight online and check flights," Dobrovski decided to try one more time, but he barely managed a, "but, sir-" before Radischev said firmly, "You will do nothing, right, Dobrovski, you got that, even if he was your brother? You understand!" Without waiting for a reply, he added, "Right, the rain seems to have stopped, so let's get out of here and head back to the hotel."

Even though Radischev was speaking in Russian it was said loudly enough to cause a few people on nearby tables to look over, and one to even peer around one of the corners in the little café.

Just over twenty-four hours later, however, Radischev was again raising his voice to Dobrovski as he burst into the Lindos Memories hotel room that he shared with Sokolov.

"You fucking killed her, didn't you, you couldn't bloody leave it could you, you fucking idiot!" Radischev was displaying his extreme anger while simultaneously trying to keep his voice down to a level that would not carry to the adjacent hotel rooms. Without allowing his Russian comrade to confirm or deny it, he continued, "I've just been in the hotel reception and two British women tourists were going on about how awful it was that there had been another murder in the village." He repeated, "You fucking idiot! One murder, yep who knows, maybe that's just over some argument or involves tourists, but two murders in twenty-four hours is bound to raise suspicion of anyone who doesn't appear to be genuine tourists, like us. And I bet you did it the same way didn't you?"

Dobrovski, who had been lying on his single bed as Radischev towered over him venting his anger, now raised himself and stood facing his superior. "I needed to avenge my brother, sir, and yes it was a knife in the neck, the same as the other one, but I still don't see how anyone is going to connect it to us. She was drunk, very drunk. She didn't know what hit her. The knife in the neck meant the bitch died instantly. We followed her after she left the club, Arches, and then the pizza place. But no one saw us, I'm sure. We did it in one of the alleys at the back of the village and at that time early in the morning there was no one around. Then we dumped her body in one of the garbage bins, where she belongs."

"You bloody idiots! Not only do you go ahead and murder her when I specifically ordered you not to, but you do it in the same way as the first murder. Two murders in a little village like this and both of them carried out in the same way. Didn't you think that would arouse suspicion? A little out of the ordinary, don't you think comrades? The Greek police are not that stupid. They will already be looking for connections between the two. Fucking stupid!" Radischev's anger wasn't abating.

Desperately trying to appease his superior, Dobrovski said, "But we got her phone, sir, and your woman friend's mobile number is in it, under the name Deborah Harris. I thought you would be pleased about that."

Dobrovski removed the mobile phone from the bedside cabinet draw and handed it to Radischev, who calmed down only slightly as he responded with an emphatic question to Sokolov. "Did you book the flights?"

"Yes, sir, tomorrow late afternoon at five-fifteen from Rhodes to Athens, with a connecting flight to Moscow at eight-thirty that night. So, we don't have to stay over in Athens. I thought that would be better as we will not have to hang around in Greece any longer than needed," Sokolov replied.

"Yes, that's best," Radischev agreed, as he moved towards the door of the hotel room and added, "I have some business here to attend to this afternoon and tomorrow before we leave. You two keep a low profile, around the pool, or on the beach if you want. This time do as I tell you and act like tourists for fuck's sake!"

Part Five: Truth, retribution and mistaken identity

24

Radischev and Carpenter or Carpentar

"Back so soon, Inspector," was how Deborah Harris greeted Karagoulis and Samaras as she opened the door to her villa, followed by "Oh, hello, Tom, have you been roped in to help the investigation too?"

"The Inspector just wanted me to come with them while he asks you a few more questions about Dawn's murder," the Englishman explained. "I'm not quite sure why, but here I am."

"Well, it's always good to see you anyway, you know that. Come in all of you, and let's go back up on the terrace, if that's ok with you, Inspector?"

"That'll be fine," was Karagoulis' somewhat sharp reply. He was clearly growing sick of being sent around in circles by some of the people he had interviewed in Lindos. He was growing increasingly annoyed, and was in no mood now to be lied to or told half-truths any longer.

As the four of them sat around the white circular wrought iron table under the sunshade he got straight to the point. "Dawn told Tom here one night that you both could tell him some stories about the Russians that would make him squirm. What do you think she meant by that, Miss Harris?"

"Absolutely no idea," as she replied, in a very matter of fact, way she was frowning and shaking her head slowly from side to side. She attempted to deflect the question with, "One night, you say, Tom? Had she had a few Bacardis by any chance?"

"Well, yes, it was the early hours of the morning actually and we had been drinking, but…"

Before Tom could finish Deborah jumped in with, "There you are then, Inspector. Dawn was always saying crazy things after she'd had a few drinks, or more than a few, if you know what I mean. It usually got worse the more she had, crazier and crazier sometimes. I expect that was one of those times. She liked to stir people up did Dawn, and she was very good and very convincing at it most of the time. I heard her say some really unbelievable things about people sometimes, but I just got used to her Bacardi-talk I guess."

She was running down her so-called friend's character a little too much for Karagoulis' liking and he was watching her closely, as well as occasionally checking out Tom's reaction, which was one of a surprised look spreading across his face. Deborah Harris was very well practiced at giving away nothing from her expressions and body language though, unless she wanted to convey some deliberate impression, and the Inspector was picking up nothing unusual. Glancing briefly across at Samaras it looked to him that the Lindos police office was also drawing a blank in observing Deborah in that respect.

Tom Carpenter meanwhile, no doubt suffering a little still from his Lindos Saturday night hangover, acquiesced meekly to Deborah's response. "Yes, I suppose that's true, Deborah. I saw her do that on a few occasions, say some crazy things to deliberately wind people up when she'd had a few drinks, or more than a few, like you said."

Trying to move things on Deborah added, "There you are then, Inspector, just like I said. But what am I thinking? Let me offer you a drink. I made a fresh pot of coffee just before you arrived, would you like some, and some water maybe? The coffee is very good, it's Italian."

Almost in unison the three men said, "Yes, thanks," with Tom adding, "black, and nice and strong for me, please, and some water too please, if that's ok." Karagoulis couldn't resist one more try though, adding, "So, you are sure you don't have any clue as to what Dawn was talking about on the Russians then?"

"As I just told you, Inspector, none at all," as she replied she was already on her way down the flight of stone steps from the terrace and heading towards her kitchen with her back to the three men. She obviously didn't intend to dwell on the subject.

As soon as she had disappeared down the steps and into her villa below her mobile phone rang. She had inadvertently left it on the terrace table. Tom started to shout to her, but before he got beyond "Deb…" Karagoulis interrupted, telling him, "Wait, leave it," because as the Inspector leaned over to look at the mobile phone on the table the words 'Ivan Radischev calling' were displayed on the screen. He stared at the phone as it soon stopped ringing and the caller rang off, then glanced over at Samaras, who had also seen the screen display, and said quietly, "What the fuck is going on here?" Turning to the still seated Tom Carpenter he quickly told him, "I'd be grateful if you would remain silent for a while when Miss Harris returns with the coffee. I have a few much more direct questions about her Russian caller that I need to ask her now. If we accept that what you told us earlier was correct, and her murdered friend possessed a piece of paper with a release date on it for a man called Radischev, I'd be willing to place a rather large bet the Radischev that just called her is the same man. Although at the moment I have no bloody idea why he should be calling her."

Within a couple of minutes Deborah Harris emerged up the stone steps with the coffee and three bottles of water on a tray. Karagoulis waited for her to pour the coffees and sit down before he told her, "Your phone rang while you were downstairs, but before we could call you the caller rang off."

She looked at him with a quizzical frown across her forehead, concerned about what he might say next.

"According to the display on your phone someone called Ivan Radischev was calling," the Inspector continued." Tom here was only telling us a short time ago at his place about an Ivan Radischev, telling us all about a KGB officer by that name in Prague in 1989. Quite a coincidence someone by that name calling you now don't you think, Miss Harris? His number is obviously in the contacts list in your phone for it to come up on your screen display. Why is that I wonder? Is there something more you want to tell us now, Miss Harris?"

Deborah Harris sat staring straight ahead, past the seated Samaras opposite her at the table and out at Lindos bay that stretched out below the terrace. Initially she said nothing, but instead merely reached out and took a sip of her coffee putting the black cup slowly and deliberately to her lips. Eventually as she placed the cup back on the saucer in front of her on the table she said, "It's good coffee don't you think, Tom. I said it was."

Tom looked across at Karagoulis, stunned by her response, or rather, non-response, but the Inspector wasn't letting her off that easily. He leaned on the table and stared her straight in the face, telling her, "A blank response will not work with us, Miss Harris. You know a lot more about this business, these murders in Lindos, than you have been saying, and now I'm getting a bit pissed off with your games and your lies. Obstructing the police in a murder investigation is a very serious charge here in Greece, so you should think very carefully about what you know and tell us everything, now."

As he told her that last point he banged the table with his fist in order to emphasise his frustration and anger. Deborah looked sideways at him and then glanced over at Tom who was slowly nodding his head in agreement with the Inspector.

"This, this, you lied to us about this didn't you?" Karagoulis produced the forensic bag with the piece of paper from Dawn Parsons' Russian dictionary from his pocket. "It says 'Radischev' doesn't it. Tom translated it for us, but you knew that all along didn't you?" He was raising his voice as he stood up from his chair and threw the bag onto the table in front of her. "It's not some code connected with drugs and Russians, is it? You knew that, but you lied to us. It's Ivan Radischev's release date from a Russian prison on the fourth of May this year. Now why, I ask myself, would Dawn Parsons have that, and how would she get hold of that information? And what's that got to do with her murder and Tony Carpentar's? I think you had better start answering some of these questions, Miss Harris and quickly, because, as you can no doubt see, I'm getting pretty pissed off with all the lies and deceit that has been flying about in this little village over the last three days."

He banged the table with his fist again, this time with even more force from a standing position, and continued, "We can do it here now informally or at the station after I've arrested you for obstructing a murder enquiry. It's your choice, so what's it to be, Miss Harris?"

She got up from the table, walked slowly over to the low ornate wall at the edge of the terrace, and stared out over Lindos bay. She stood there for a full minute as Samaras looked over at Karagoulis, who had returned to his seat, and shrugged his shoulders. Tom Carpenter, meanwhile, look bewildered at what he had just witnessed and was taking regular gulps from his bottle of water trying to rehydrate after his night out.

Eventually, Karagoulis said, "Miss Harris, I asked what's it to be. We can't sit here all day. There are some murderers out there in Lindos and it's our job to catch them. So, can we do this here or at the station?"

She was deliberating over whether to give the Inspector the answers he wanted, or at least as much information as she thought necessary in order to answer to his questions. However, she knew that to do so would almost certainly blow her cover, her new identity, and her new life in the 'paradise of Lindos', as she liked to describe it. If she didn't though she would be charged with obstructing the course of justice and she was by no means certain that her former employers in MI6 would be able to pull enough strings to get her out of that charge, especially if Dawn and Tony Carpentar's murders were seen by them as simply related to a drugs trade. And if she was charged with obstructing the course of justice over the murders she knew that all sorts of rumours would start to circulate in the village over her part in them. She learned that much, at least, from living there over the past four years. Then her new life in her paradise would be destroyed anyway. She quickly went over the options in her trained mind as she continued to stare out at what she loved most about her new life, Lindos bay. Finally, after another minute of silence, she concluded that the first option was best, but she would try to convince Karagoulis to keep the lid on most of what she was going to tell him and stop it from becoming public, as far as possible.

"Okay, Inspector, you're right, and what Tom told you about what is written on the piece of paper is correct," she said, as she headed back over to her seat at the table. "You have to give me an assurance first though that, as far as possible, what I am about to tell you doesn't go any further, unless it is to your superior officer, by which I mean the Chief of the Hellenic Police in Athens, not someone in Rhodes. That goes for Tom and your officer here too."

"I'm tempted to ask just how you know so much about my superior in Athens, Miss Harris, but we'll leave that for now. Okay, you have my word that as far as possible what you tell us doesn't go any further, and I'm sure I can speak for Officer Samaras here, but you'll have to trust Mr. Carpenter I guess."

Tom nodded in agreement, saying, "Don't worry Deborah, I will not be saying anything to anyone."

"It wasn't a coincidence, Inspector, it was the same man. The call just now was from the same man that Tom told you about, Ivan Radischev, and yes he was a high ranking KGB officer in their section in Prague in 1989 and also in Vienna for a few years before that. Dawn and I worked together in the British Embassy in Vienna in the nineteen-eighties, and that's where we met him."

"You worked together, but I thought you never knew each other before you both came to Lindos, and what work" Tom interrupted her.

Before she could reply to him though, Karagoulis turned towards him and said firmly, "I think we'd appreciate it if you just remained silent for the moment, Mr Carpenter, and let her speak, go on, Miss Harris."

"I had an affair with him for around six months in 1986," she continued with a revelation that certainly took Karagoulis by surprise, not least in the very matter of fact way she said it, almost like she was giving a report. "It started as a cover for trading information between the two agencies him and I worked for, and Dawn as well actually, although she wasn't involved and had no idea about that or our affair at the time." She hesitated, and it was clearly apparent that she was thinking very carefully about just what to reveal as she reached for the bottle of water to take a swig. She hadn't completely forgotten the training in her former life.

"It was 1986, the start of Gorbachev's glasnost and perestroika ideas and period in the Soviet Union. There was a clear struggle going on in the Soviet Communist Party, at all levels in the Soviet leadership, political, military and KGB. It was between the reformers supporting Gorbachev and the old Stalinist hard-liners. It was chaos, not least in the so-called Soviet 'satellite states' in East and Central Europe, including Czechoslovakia. No one seemed to have any idea just what was going on in those countries, least of all the Soviets themselves, but also including us and the Americans."

Tom knew that was the case from his academic research and his own experiences in some of those countries at the time. He sat there in silence, as Karagoulis requested, and just nodded his head in agreement as Deborah continued.

"We, MI6, couldn't control the Czech and Slovak dissidents. Havel and other dissidents weren't stupid. They could see that something was stirring and changing, not just in Russia but across other states like Poland, with Solidarnosc, the Solidarity movement. Things had been happening there since 1981 and now with Gorbachev's supposed new policies they could see opportunities opening up all over East and Central Europe. But Havel and the other dissidents didn't trust us or the Americans very much more than they did the Russians. They remembered the crushing of the Prague Spring reforms in August 1968 by the Russians and how we didn't lift a finger to help them then."

As she hesitated and took another swig of water Tom added, "Yes, like the British failed to help them when Hitler invaded in 1938, as my Czech friends are always fond of reminding me. But blimey, Dawn's murder is connected to all this and the 'Cold War'?" He received a stern glare from Karagoulis for his comments, and an even firmer, "Please Mr. Carpenter." The Inspector was determined that now he'd finally got her to tell them the truth he didn't want her to be diverted from telling them everything she knew.

"Go on please, Miss Harris," he told her.

"As I said, we couldn't control the dissidents and the Americans, the CIA, were on our backs. They wanted the fall of the Soviet

Empire of course, but the last thing they, or we, wanted was anarchy breaking out all across East and Central Europe, let alone in Russia, with them possessing nuclear weapons. While the Russians, in the form of the hard-line communists, the old Stalinists in the KGB, were increasingly finding they couldn't control the reform communists in Russia or in the 'satellite states', particularly Czechoslovakia where there was a history of the reform communists going back to 1968. So, it was in both our interests to do a deal with the Soviets, the KGB specifically, on the exchange of information on both of those groups, the dissidents and the reform communists in Czechoslovakia. Of course, we never really trusted those KGB bastards, but it was expedient for us and the Americans, you know."

She glanced across at Karagoulis, who clearly 'didn't know', but was nodding his head in agreement anyway.

"So, contact was set up between Radischev and me at an Austrian Ministry of Culture drinks reception in January 1986. Ironically, it was an event organised to commemorate an anniversary of Mozart's birth, Inspector. Very romantic don't you think? It wasn't unusual for both sides to fraternise at those sorts of events on 'neutral ground, so to speak. So, it was thought to be safe, normal almost. Well, we made contact alright. It was easy, almost comfortable, too comfortable, as it turned out. Dawn was there, although she had no idea what was going on. I was her boss at the time, but she wasn't included 'in the loop', as we referred to it. We agreed with our KGB contacts, through the 'usual channels', that the fewer people who knew about it on both sides the better. Dawn actually warned me a few times throughout the evening that I should be careful and that my body language alone was suggesting I was becoming far too friendly with him, but she hadn't a clue, In fact, I only told her about the whole affair six months or so later, after it ended when he ended up having to spend a lot more time in Prague because of the way the situation was developing there."

"The whole affair, do you mean the contact between your agency and the KGB or between you and Radischev?" Karagoulis asked.

"Our affair, we had an affair, Inspector, as I said earlier. The contact between us was supposed to just be on the level of interaction and exchange of information between our two agencies, but it went much further than that and it very quickly developed into a full blown romantic and sexual affair."

As she confirmed that she got up from the table and walked over to gaze out over Lindos bay once again. With her back turned to the two police officers and Tom sat at the table on the other side of the terrace she continued, "Of course, we had to be extremely careful, especially when we spent nights or weekends away in hotels, usually in a place called Baden just outside Vienna. We figured that no one would know us there, outside the city."

She turned to face them as she said, "Did I fall in love? I'm not sure it was really that, but it was definitely passion, and exciting. Was it bloody stupid? Yes, of course, looking back on it now and what has happened since, it was stupid, mad, in fact, but we never ever got caught. I can't speak for his side and the KGB, but I'm sure that until I told Dawn after it ended no one on our side had any idea. When I told her it was clear she hadn't a clue about what had been going on, and I'm certain she kept it to herself and no one else in the agency ever brought it up to me. Anyway, as I said, it finished when he had to spend most of his time in Prague, and then it all kicked off there and across the rest of East and Central Europe towards the end of 1989, and eventually the Soviet Union itself collapsed a couple of years later. I heard that just after that he had been put on trial by the new regime under Yeltsin and sentenced to fifteen years in a labour camp. A lot of the former high-ranking KGB officers were put on trial then."

Karagoulis and Samaras sat listening, periodically swigging from their bottles of water and now looking completely stunned. The Inspector was quickly coming to the conclusion that the two murders he was investigating were about a lot more than crimes of passion or jealousy.

Deborah Harris returned to her seat at the table as she added, "A few months ago I started to get sporadic emails from him, at least they were in his name, but I had no way of knowing if they were really from him or not. I have no idea how he got my email address or knew my new name. If they were genuinely from him he must have had some contact, or maybe a mole, in MI6 I guess, but as the 'Cold War' was over and I had a new life I wasn't overly concerned.

He wrote that when he was released he wanted to see me, at least meet me, although from his emails he didn't appear to know exactly where I was living now, and I wasn't about to tell him.

Just over four years ago Dawn and I agreed it was time to leave the agency. We had become good friends after we both left Vienna and went back to work for them in the UK. But when you're in the agency you have no anchorage in your life, Inspector, nowhere to go in your private life, nowhere to run to, except inside yourself. And one of the first things you quickly learn in MI6 is never to trust anyone. Everything is a lie, and everyone accomplished liars. It comes with the training and the job, so to speak. Dawn was the nearest person to someone I learned I could trust. Most of the time though you're always pretending to be someone else, using a false name, and as I said, the 'Cold War' was over, things had moved on. Dawn and I were both getting older and the job wasn't the same anymore. We were both saddled with desk jobs and that wasn't us, so we put in for retirement. As I remember saying to Dawn at the time, if we are going to have to live our lives forever in the agency using false names we might as well retire, get some proper false names, and come and live in a much more pleasant place like this, with a new life. For obvious reasons, that I hope you'll accept and understand, I can't tell you much more on that side of it, but we were both given new identities and decided to come to live out here, in this paradise, or at least it was until three days ago."

"So, that explains Jacki Walker and the two passports then?" Karagoulis asked.

"Yes, bloody stupid that. We were supposed to hand over all previous documentation. Dawn obviously kept her previous passport. God knows why. I didn't know she still had it, and we certainly can't ask her now can we?"

"So, why did you say you didn't recognise Radischev's name in Russian on the piece of paper when we asked you before when we came here this morning, Miss Harris?" Samaras decided that now was the time he could intervene and ask a question.

"Because I didn't think it could possibly have anything to do with the murders. Yes, it's true that I knew it had nothing to do with drugs and any drugs dealers, but I obviously wasn't going to give away all that I've just told you about having a new identity if I didn't think it was necessary or of any help to your investigation, was I? That would be a stupid thing to do, wouldn't it. I really thought the murders were something to do with some of the games and affairs that have been going on in the village, particularly Tony's. I have no idea how Dawn knew the date of Radischev's release. I can only think that maybe she got it from someone she kept in contact with at MI6 in London, or maybe she was following the Russian news outlets."

Samaras followed up with, "Why would she want to know that anyway?"

"She killed one of his best KGB operatives in Vienna in 1988. She stabbed him after he broke into her flat and attacked her, she said. I don't think he knew she was in there. She wasn't supposed to be in Vienna that weekend. I guess the KGB found that out through their sources and informants, and the operative was obviously supposed to just search the flat for stuff related to our agency work."

She turned towards Karagoulis, adding, "But no, Inspector, before you ask, according to Dawn it wasn't in the neck. The agency got her out of Vienna immediately and back to the UK that night. They disposed of the body, but when their agent disappeared without trace the Russians obviously knew what had happened, and they would have known it was Dawn, or Jacki as she then was, who killed him. My guess is that she had his release date because she was still worried that he, or one of his comrades, would come after her if he found out where she was, although I can't really believe he would have been able to find that out. Dawn was always paranoid about the slightest thing though, even when she was in the agency. She was a worrier, Inspector. I did hear from one of my contacts in London that there was still a small group around him, Radischev, calling themselves the 'Comrades of '89', based in Moscow and awaiting his release. It seems they are old communists from the KGB who believe in the restoration of the Soviet Union under Putin. However, I think they have slightly bigger things to worry about than tracking down Jacki Walker and getting revenge."

"Maybe, but then again, maybe you're wrong, Miss Harris. Someone did kill her, Jacki or Dawn, or whatever you'd like to call her, that's for sure. Perhaps Radischev and his men did find her after all, and now he's calling you, although we don't actually know that he's here in Lindos, of course." Karagoulis said as he now got out of his chair and took his turn walking across the terrace, getting into his usual pacing back and forth thinking aloud mode.

"Well, he is here, in Lindos, Inspector. I can tell you that for sure because he already called me yesterday afternoon, as well as that missed one today. He wanted to see me, meet me this afternoon."

"Jesus Christ!" Karagoulis stopped his pacing and was now standing over her in an extremely agitated way. "If you knew that then surely at some point it must have crossed your mind, if only briefly, that it was possible that it was him or his men who stabbed and murdered Dawn, as an act of revenge after all? This is a man, a hard-line Stalinist ex-KGB officer, who has lost twelve years or so of his life in a no doubt stinking Russian labour camp. Do you not think he is very angry with some people, Miss Harris?"

Now though it was Karagoulis who was getting very angry.

"You are supposed to be a well-educated woman from what you've told us, and a no doubt highly trained ex-MI6 agent, yet you don't put all the facts you know together and come up with the obvious answer, that he murdered your former colleague and supposed friend in an act of revenge, probably with some help from his former KGB henchmen?"

Deborah Harris sat at the table staring ahead once again while Karagoulis berated her. Her response was not one of a 'shrinking violet' though. Instead it was an almost dismissive one, that of a hardened ex-MI6 officer. "That may well be your theory, Inspector, but I couldn't really see any evidence of that. So, for me, yes it crossed my mind, but I came to the conclusion very quickly that it was just conjecture. As I said before, it seemed much more likely that Dawn's murder had something to do with an affair and sex between people in the village, between the ex-pats, especially after what you told me happened between her and Alan Bryant. That was certainly the impression you gave when you questioned me at Symposio last night. You seemed almost set on that as the motive, so why would I bring up all this conjecture and put my own cover, and my new life, in jeopardy?"

Karagoulis calmed down a bit as he resumed his seat and reached for another drink of water.

"He was here to kill someone though, Inspector. He told me so, though it wasn't Dawn, or Jacki, as I guess he knew her previously."

Karagoulis nearly spat the water straight across the table at Samaras as Deborah dropped another bombshell.

"For fucks sake, Miss Harris, is there anything else you're going to eventually tell us that you think maybe useful? I don't usually swear at people I'm interviewing, especially women, but you are really trying my patience. I repeat what I said earlier to you. If you don't want to be charged with obstruction I suggest you tell us all you know now. My patience is getting very thin." The Inspector rubbed two fingers of his right hand across his forehead displaying his evident exasperation.

Yet again from her training, Deborah Harris knew the best approach was to drip information out carefully, just letting her questioner know precisely what she wanted them to know and when she wanted them to know it.

"I told you, he's been in touch and that he called me yesterday afternoon. I have no idea how he got my number. I didn't ask, but he said he wanted to see me before he leaves at around three this afternoon. That's when he's going back to Moscow."

"Where is he staying?" Karagoulis asked in a tone of voice exhibiting his even greater anger.

"At Lindos Memories hotel, he wanted me to meet him there, not in the village. I suppose if your theory about him being Dawn's murderer is correct there is some possibility that he did see her by chance and recognise her in the village. He did tell me he had come here for revenge, but he never mentioned Jacki, or taking revenge on her though. He said he had a list of people that he wanted retribution over for the twelve years of his life he'd lost in the Russian prison, and he was starting with a man here in Lindos. That was the word he used, retribution. I thought it a bit strange at the time, although his English was always perfect. 'The Queen's English' was the way he described it. Anyway, that also made me think he had nothing to do with Dawn's murder, because he said it was an English man he was here to kill."

"What English man, did he say who, was it Tony Carpentar?" Samaras jumped in with his own conclusion, which drew another glare from Karagoulis.

"He didn't say a name," she replied. "He just said the man was English. He said he was here to get his revenge on the English bastard, as he put it, who was in Prague in November 1989. The one who he knew had obviously disclosed the plans for the KGB plot over a fake death on the demonstration on the seventeenth of November. I knew all about that afterwards through the agency, the plot and the KGB involvement, and subsequently the new Czechoslovak government under Havel held an enquiry. Amongst other things, the fake death of a student was supposed to discredit the dissidents for putting out false media reports, but it all went wrong."

"Yes, Tom told us about all that earlier," Karagoulis interjected.

Deborah glanced sideways at Tom, who was looking somewhat bemused. She assumed it was just his hangover lingering and continued, "Really, well anyway, Radischev believes that after the demonstration there was a leak about the plan to the student part of the dissident movement by one of the Czech Secret Police agents undercover in that group. He believes the agent told his girlfriend about it, who then told an English guy in Prague she knew at the time, and that is how it got out to the dissidents and the western media, and why the aim of the plan didn't work. The changes, and the 'Velvet Revolution', really kicked off after the demonstration that night and the KGB plan that went wrong, and eventually the communist government fell, of course. Radischev was in charge of the whole operation. He was head of KGB operations in Prague at the time, so he was the one who suffered most career-wise in the KGB, and ultimately with imprisonment after the collapse of the Soviet Union."

Scratching the back of his head this time, Karagoulis said, "But how could that have been Tony Carpentar? He wasn't in Prague in November 1989. His bullshit about all that was exposed in Socrates bar with you and Dawn that night. You and Tom both told us about that."

Tom Carpenter looked even more dazed, although this time it wasn't from his hangover, as he sat open-mouthed listening closely to everything Deborah Harris was telling them. Eventually, in response to Karagoulis, he said, "No, but I was, Inspector."

He leaned back on his chair and ran his hand through his thinning hair as the reality dawned on him. "It must have been me he came here to kill. I knew a woman called Jana in Prague then. I told you about her earlier, and I was on that demonstration with her. She had a boyfriend named Jiří Kaluza. I told you about him too. He was quite high up in the student dissident organisation. I was always suspicious of him, and a few times I thought he might be an infiltrator from the Czech Secret Police. It seems I was right all along, Inspector. Remember I said he was always asking people about me, but I never knew about the KGB plot at the time so I couldn't have told anyone about it. However, obviously Radischev doesn't know that."

Before Tom could continue Karagoulis interrupted him exclaiming, "Yes, of course, the similar names, Carpenter and Carpentar! Tony's passport was stolen in Rhodes Town a few weeks ago, but the thief didn't take anything except that, which seemed a little odd to me when my Sargent told me it came up in one of the checks we ran on Tony. It didn't fit with the usual thefts from tourists that we come across in Rhodes. The thieves usually take anything they can lay their hands on in tourists' bags and rucksacks; credit cards, cash, and anything else, not just a passport. What if it was Russians working for Radischev and they got the wrong man? Maybe it was the same Russians who have been popping up all over Lindos over the last couple of days, the two well-built guys we've heard about repeatedly. I bet they were the same two well-built Russian guys who were hassling the guy on the door in Arches on Friday night because they were trying to leave just after Dawn left. They were obviously following her and were pissed off because they couldn't get out of there at the same time as she did, but had to wait a minute or two. So, perhaps they did kill her, as well as Tony. Both murders for revenge, or what was it your friend Radischev called it, Miss Harris, retribution? Tony Carpentar because they got the wrong man and Dawn because she killed one of their agents in Vienna years ago."

Now it was Tom's turn to say, "Jesus," as his face turned white with the shock, any Lindos suntan quickly draining out of it.

Meanwhile, Deborah sat shaking her head at the explanation that Karagoulis was now expertly piecing together.

The Inspector hadn't quite finished completing the puzzle though. "Also, apparently Tony was going on and on about Prague to two guys in Jack's bar the night he was murdered, before Carol Hudson turned up, and before the fight he had with Alan Bryant. Jack Constantino said he thought he overheard the guys say they were from Eastern Europe, and he also said that from their conversation with Tony they seemed to know Prague. Tony probably couldn't resist telling them that bullshit about being there in November 1989, and in doing so he signed his own death warrant."

Karagoulis looked across the table at an increasingly concerned and white faced Tom Carpenter, saying, "So I reckon you're right, it was you they came here to kill. Ironically, the next day, on the Friday morning, they were probably the three Russians sat only a few metres away from you in Giorgos, the ones you told me were arguing and that you said Dawn seemed so interested in when you told her about them later. But they obviously didn't recognise you, even if they saw you. However, now we know why she was so concerned, don't we, Miss Harris."

Deborah Harris didn't respond, but Tom Carpenter gulped visibly at that last comment from Karagoulis, who, as he made it, got up from his chair and began to pace across the terrace once more as he continued, "You said you'd been told a few times in Lindos that you looked like Tony. Perhaps the two well-built guys even checked out his name with Tony in Jack's bar that night? Introduced themselves, no doubt with false names, but they obviously wouldn't have picked up the one letter difference in the spelling between his name and yours, Tom. Why would they even ask? It probably never occurred to them. Even if he went into his line, which he was apparently fond of telling people, that the spelling was one letter different from the usual English name of Carpenter, that probably wouldn't have registered with them. They were looking for a guy named Carpentar, who's passport they had with a photo in it that matched the guy they were now in conversation with in Jack's on that Thursday night. As far as they were concerned they'd found him, the man they'd come to kill and get retribution for their boss, Radischev. The more Tony went on about Prague, and bullshitted about being there in November 1989, no doubt the more convinced they became that they had their man, the right man."

As Karagoulis continued his pacing back and forth across the terrace, in silence this time as he tried to work out the best next course of action, Deborah Harris added, "I can tell you from my experience of him, Inspector, Radischev will definitely not be here operating alone. As I told you earlier, the last I heard there was a small group of the old hard-line Stalinists, many of them ex-KGB operatives from Prague, this 'Comrades of '89' group, and he was their leader. So, the two guys you referred to are almost certainly working with, and for, him."

Karagoulis turned on his heels across the terrace to face her saying, "We know that both murders, Tony's and Dawn's, would have needed two people, so you're probably right about that."

"But it's also very unlikely he would have carried out the murders himself, Inspector. He wouldn't have been involved with the actual killing" Deborah added. "He would have had them do that for him, probably ordered them through some rank thing in the 'Comrades of '89'. From what I knew about the way he operated in Vienna in the nineteen-eighties he never liked to get his hands dirty, if you know what I mean. In the agency we knew he liked to recruit Soviet ex-Afghanistan war veterans known for their proficiency in undercover guerrilla operations to his group and elite squad of operatives. That included their proficiency in the best way to kill someone quickly and silently, usually by stabbing in the right place. We lost an agent in Vienna in 1982, killed by a stabbing in the neck. We were sure at the time that it was one of his agents that did it."

"Right, I think we need to pay a visit to comrade Radischev as soon as possible, before he leaves." Karagoulis had quickly decided on his plan of action. "I doubt if he and his henchmen are booked into Memories hotel under that name, but use any contacts you have there now and give them a call to check, Samaras. If they aren't, ask how many Russian guests they have staying there, and be discreet for Christ's sake."

While Samaras made the call Karagoulis told Deborah Harris, "You are actually the only one of us who knows what he looks like.

Tom told us he doesn't have a clue what he looks like. So, when Samaras has finished calling the hotel, unless he is booked in there under his real name, which I very much doubt, I am going to have to ask you to call him and arrange to meet him there, just as he wanted you to do before."

Before she could answer Samaras finished his call and told Karagoulis, "The Manager said there is no one called Radischev staying there. He must have used a fake passport."

"That wouldn't be unusual from his contacts and previous line of business. He wouldn't have any problem getting hold of one of those," Deborah confirmed.

"Yes, okay Samaras, but how many Russian guests do they have there at the moment?" Karagoulis was growing impatient, and getting a little warm pacing back and forth on the terrace in the hot sun trying to run through a range of scenarios in his mind about the best way to confront and deal with Radischev and his comrades.

"Twenty-two, according to the Manager, sir, apparently there's a Russian wedding party staying in the hotel."

"Well, we can assume our comrade Radischev is not part of the wedding party. You need to call and arrange to meet him there now please, Miss Harris," Karagoulis told her. "It's one-fifteen now. We need to arrange some cover. Samaras will drive you there in a taxi and we'll follow in an unmarked car. So, call and say you'll meet him at two at the hotel, if you wouldn't mind. You said he was leaving at three, so that will be enough time I guess. Samaras, you need to get to your place and change out of your police uniform, and then arrange to borrow a taxi. I'm sure you have some contacts in the village you can arrange that with. I'll call Papadoulis and tell him to bring our unmarked car from the car park at Lindos Reception and meet us in the Main Square in thirty minutes with the two other Lindos officers. I'll also get him to arrange some back-up on the road to Rhodes, just in case they give us the slip. Presumably they'll be heading for the airport."

"What about me, should I come with you, Inspector?" Tom asked.

"I don't think so, Mr. Carpenter, definitely not. It's bad enough that we have to involve Miss Harris here in this, without including anymore civilians and endangering their lives unnecessarily."

Tom took another swig of his water and looked somewhat relieved. He'd had quite enough excitement in his summer long stay so far, and it was only early June.

As Karagoulis was running through his plan, and informing Tom he wasn't included, Deborah Harris sat slumped in her seat going over in her mind again just what her options were. She quickly came to the conclusion that she really had no choice other than to go along with what the Inspector proposed. In any case, the type of situation that she was being asked to put herself in was one which was by no means strange to her. She had been in a similar dangerous confrontational situation a few times before, even with some of Radischev's Soviet agents, although that had been over ten years ago or more, of course. If Karagoulis was right though, Radischev had ordered and arranged the killing of her friend, Dawn. Yes, she had an affair with him eighteen years ago, but that was a long, long time ago and she had no feelings for him whatsoever now. Her life had changed, and as she told Dawn the night before she was murdered, the world was a different place now.

Karagoulis wasn't waiting for her answer however, as he asked Samaras, "Before Miss Harris makes the call, tell me quickly what the layout of this Memories hotel is like. I've never been there."

"It's quite an open sort of hotel, sir. By that I mean that behind the lobby and reception block there is a long open area, almost like a piazza, a courtyard or a small square, and the rooms are on two floors running along either side of it. Then there are some more rooms and suites over a sort of archway facing the swimming pool, beach and the sea."

"What about the road access?" Karagoulis added.

"There is only one road down a slight hill from the main road, Inspector. It's probably about four or five hundred metres long."

"So, just the one way in and out then, good, you drop Miss Harris at the hotel entrance in the taxi, Samaras, and park up like you are waiting for another fare, in case they have someone watching. With the hotel full of guests we really don't want to confront them in there. You need to arrange to meet Radischev in his room, Miss Harris, and try and get them out to the front of the hotel, by the road, somehow. Myself, Sargent Papadoulis, and two other officers will be waiting in an unmarked car at the front of the hotel near Samaras' taxi. We'll make sure we arrive a couple of minutes after you go in."

"When he called yesterday he did say that not only did he want to see me, but that maybe I would consider going away with him for a while to see if we still had feelings for each other?"

"And do you?" Karagoulis was double-checking that he could rely on her to act the way he wanted.

"No, certainly not, Inspector, how could I when he murdered my friend, or at least, had her murdered, if you're right. I just meant that I could play along with him, suggest that I would be prepared to go away with him now for a few days, but that we'd have to come back here on the way to the airport for me to pick up my passport and some clothes. That would get him and his comrades out at the front of the hotel. I'm guessing they've got some sort of hire car, so maybe you'll be able to spot it when you arrive at the hotel. Guests' cars are usually parked out the front at the bottom of the road coming down the hill."

As she finished speaking Karagoulis picked up her mobile from the table and handed it to her saying, "Can you call him now, please?"

As she took the phone she told him, "You know there is an old KGB saying that we picked up in our dealings with them in MI6, Inspector. Hope for the best, expect the worst."

25

A beginning in magical Prague and Vienna, an Amphitheatre ending in Lindos paradise

Ivan Radischev had sounded a little surprised at first to get a call from Deborah Harris. He had all but given up on her getting back to him, especially when he got no answer to his call earlier that morning. After a couple of minutes of general conversation, however, mostly about when he was leaving and for where, she told him, "So, if you still want to meet before you leave I can jump in a taxi and come to your hotel in about thirty minutes, around two o'clock?"

"That would be good," he told her, sounding more enthusiastic. "It will be better if you come to my room, number nine, and we can have a drink."

"What time is your taxi to the airport," she asked. Even though she guessed they would have a hire car, she wanted to get, and check, as much information for Karagoulis as she could.

"We have to leave at three, but not by taxi, we have a hire car."

He confirmed what she thought, but she pushed it a little, again looking for confirmation of what she already guessed she knew.

"We? So you aren't alone then."

"No, just a couple of associates with me, helping me with some business here, see you soon" he told her and immediately rang off.

Karagoulis had been hovering over her right shoulder on the terrace and as the phone went dead she turned to him and sounding circumspect and a bit worried said, "Hmm…I wouldn't say he sounded overly convinced, Inspector. A little colder and more matter of fact than I thought he would be. What if he suspects something?"

"He's probably just being really cautious," Karagoulis tried to reassure her. "He and his comrades have committed two murders over the past two days, so of course he's going to be cautious. I'm really surprised that they are still here though, and hadn't left long ago. Perhaps it can only be because he wanted to see you that they are still here, and then he thought you didn't want to see him. That's what you said you told him yesterday when he called, so maybe he's just a little confused as to why you've suddenly changed your mind, and only an hour before he's leaving. Anyway, Miss Harris, I'm afraid we don't have much choice do we? If we want to catch him and his killer comrades you will have to go and meet him. Don't worry though, we'll make sure we are there to protect you, and I'm sure that you've been in these sort of situations before judging by what you told us about your past."

"Yes, a few times, Inspector, but I'm a little out of practice. I haven't done this type of thing for over ten years. Not sure how much you heard, but he's in room nine at the hotel and he's with 'a couple of associates', as he put it. His henchmen I guess, but I obviously didn't get what room they are in, the next one maybe?"

Just over thirty minutes later Samaras, in his borrowed taxi-driver uniform and taxi dropped Deborah outside the front of Lindos Memories hotel. The hotel was a low rise, only two storey, light sandstone block complex, with an impressive vista out over the swimming pool to Navarone bay, as it had become known. The whole setting was very picturesque and gave off a very relaxing atmosphere, which was more than can be said for how Deborah Harris felt as she walked around the right-hand side of the reception block and checked from the signs where room number nine could be located.

Once she had disappeared out of sight from the front of the hotel, the dark grey Nissan Primera occupied by Karagoulis, his Sargent, Papadoulis, and the two other Lindos based police officers moved slowly down the road from the main road to the front of the hotel, and parked alongside Samaras in the taxi.

Pointing to a car parked to their left on the other side of Samaras' taxi, and about twenty metres away near to the main gates of the hotel, Karagoulis said, "There's a black Jeep Cherokee over there with what looks like a car hire sticker across the back window. I'm guessing that's their car, Sargent."

After Papadoulis and the two other Lindos police officers had picked up the Inspector from Lindos Main Square, he had quickly briefed them about what he and Samaras had learned from Deborah Harris earlier. As they sat in the parked unmarked Nissan waiting for her to hopefully reappear at the front of the hotel with the Russians, Papadoulis asked, "Do you believe her, sir, that she's going to help us, and that she used to be in the British Secret Service?"

"After what we've heard and been told in this place over the past three days I can't say I'm entirely sure, Sargent, although it does seem to make most sense of all this. Why? Don't you?"

"Like you, I'm not completely convinced, sir."

"I guess it's like the story about the Cretan man, Sargent, don't you think?" From working with him over the past few years Papadoulis had quickly learned from experience that Karagoulis liked to tell Greek fables, so he just answered with an accommodating, "What story is that, sir? I don't think I've heard that one," knowing perfectly well that he and the two other officers were about to.

"A Cretan man tells people he meets that he is from Crete, but also that all men from Crete are liars. So, Papadoulis, if he really is from Crete he must be lying, but if he is telling the truth he can't be from Crete, can he?"

Looking confused Papadoulis asked, "And how does that relate to Miss Harris, sir?"

"Well, Sargent, she told us this morning that everyone in MI6 lives a lie, they are all accomplished liars, that is what they are trained to do, and no one trusts anyone there. So, if all MI6 agents are liars, and she is an ex-MI6 agent, she must be lying to us about some of the things she told us. If she's telling the truth, however, she can't be an ex-MI6 agent. You see?"

"I think so, sir," Papadoulis decided the simplest thing to do was to agree, although in his mind he was thinking that he definitely didn't 'see'. Nevertheless, he decided to go along with his Inspector's confusing reasoning, and in trying to understand and extend his logic added, "So, are you saying that she could be making up all that she told you this morning, sir, because she is the murderer, perhaps along with the Russians? And maybe Tony Carpentar found out about her past and was going to expose her in the village, ruining her pleasant new life, so she got her Russian friends and former lover to dispose of him. But what about Dawn Parsons' murder though? How does that fit into that little scenario?"

"Well, she was the only other person in Lindos who knew the truth about Deborah Harris' past, and Miss Harris said herself that she was a worrier. Also, Tom Carpenter told us that when she was very drunk one night Dawn was shouting her mouth off about how her and Deborah could tell him a few stories about Russians. Maybe Deborah heard about that and decided Dawn was saying a little too much. Perhaps she thought there was increasingly a good chance that she would reveal their little secret one night to someone when she was drunk, so she had her bumped off by her Russian friends too."

Even as he described that possible scenario though, Karagoulis didn't sound very convinced of it himself, so he added, "Anyway, we will soon see, depending on what happens in room nine here. I think that I'm still more inclined to believe what she told us this morning was true though, Sargent."

Papadoulis just nodded in agreement.

Meanwhile, Deborah Harris was gently tapping on the door to room nine on the ground floor of the hotel. As Ivan Radischev opened it and invited her in the first impression she got was how much thinner he looked, and considerably greyer all over than the man she knew so intimately in Vienna almost twenty years before. His swept back jet black hair of that time was now very grey and thinning. It wasn't just his hair that was grey though, his whole complexion was pallid and his cheeks drawn, like he was permanently sucking them in. He appeared shorter than she remembered. He stooped a little and his straight-backed stature had gone. Could this man really be such a danger, an organiser of murder and a threat to her now? She quickly, and she hoped discreetly, surveyed the room. There was no sign of his two comrades.

"It's very good to see you after all this time. You look very well, with a nice suntan. I suppose that is living here with all this sunshine. It suits you," he told her, followed by, "I suppose I should call you

Deborah now, Elizabeth, although to be honest I was never even certain that was your real name all those years ago back in Vienna, and Baden of course."

"Deborah will do now," she told him curtly.

"Of course, would you like a glass of wine? White isn't it, if I remember correctly." He was guiding her towards the two maroon armchairs on the far side of the room next to a low wooden table.

"No, just some still water will be fine thanks." She wanted a clear head, not one befuddled by wine in the middle of the day. She came straight to the point as she sat down in the chair while he got a small bottle from the mini-bar and poured some water into a glass for her. "So, you said on the phone yesterday that you came here for retribution, and you have a list of people. Am I on it by any chance?"

A slight grin spread across his face as he sat down in the chair opposite her with a glass of wine. "Why should you be on it? What have I got to exact retribution on you about? Surely there is nothing, especially after what we had in Vienna?"

"That's right, Ivan, there is nothing. What about Jacki though? Why did you find it necessary to kill her, or should I say have her murdered?" His reference to what went on between them before wasn't having any effect of softening her approach. She was drawing on all her recollections of her MI6 training and was determined not to let her barriers down. As soon as she entered the room and saw him she recalled how she spent over twenty years of her life fighting against what he represented. Even a few months of passion eighteen years ago wasn't going to wipe that out, especially after what had happened to her friend two days before.

"That was a bloody mistake, Deborah. Jacki wasn't even on my list. That was an unfortunate occurrence by my two comrades. One of them saw her just after we arrived in Lindos and was sure he recognised her. He said he was sure it was the same woman that killed his brother in Vienna in 1988. I ordered him to leave it, but he ignored that and they killed her. As I told you yesterday, my plan was to come here to deal with the English guy who was here that fucked up our plot in Prague in November 1989. It never involved killing Jacki. So, my aim was to do what I wanted to do, kill the English guy, and then act like tourists in the hotel for a day or two while I tried to get to see you before we left. I got some of my Russian comrades from Prague in 1989 to search while I was in those stinking prisons in Moscow and Mordovia to try and find where you were for when I got out. Purely by chance you happened to be here, in the same little Greek village as that bastard Carpentar. So, we dealt with him, or rather my two comrades here with me did. He got what was coming to him. Payback, retribution, whatever pretty English word you want to use, he got it anyway."

"No, he didn't, Ivan. You killed the wrong guy." She had sat in silence sipping her water while he tried to explain what had happened, but now she moved forward to the edge of the armchair and calmly told him, "You got the wrong Carpentar, spelt with an a and an r at the end. The man you wanted, although I'm not really sure he gave away your little plot in Prague in 1989, was called Carpenter, spelt with an e and an r. I was talking to him about an hour ago at my villa, so he's very much alive, Ivan. You fucked up again, or your goons did." She was a little surprised just how easily she had slipped back into her old aggressive MI6 officer mode.

He looked stunned. Meanwhile, she was rapidly thinking this wasn't exactly the way Karagoulis had suggested it should go. She was meant to be persuasive not aggressive, even to the point of putting on a convincing performance that she was actually willing to go away with him. Having attacked him verbally so forcibly she was hardly going to be able to convince him of that, and thereby get him outside into the car park where Karagoulis and his men were waiting.

"How did we get the wrong guy? That's rubbish, you're making it up. Why should I believe you? My men got his passport in Rhodes a week ago. It was him. I know it was him, even from the photograph. Why are you telling me this bollocks?" Now he was angrily banging his right fist into his open left palm as he stood up from the armchair. This definitely wasn't going as planned, she thought.

"I know you, Elizabeth, or Deborah, or whatever you call yourself now," he continued. You haven't forgotten all your old MI6 techniques have you? Old habits don't just disappear, I know that from my experience, believe me. Lies and more lies, just to confuse your opponent, your enemy, that's what they teach you, isn't it? That's what they taught us too, and how to see through them."

Before she could answer he stepped over and banged once on the wall to the adjoining room. Instantly the door to Radischev's room swung open and his two henchmen appeared through it. He told them, "She says you killed the wrong man. She said it is something to do with the way his name was spelt or something crazy, and you got the wrong man."

"No, it was the same man as in the passport photograph, sir, I'm sure," Dobrovski replied.

"And he was going on and on in that bar before about being in Prague in November 1989, he even said he was on the demonstration on the seventeenth," Sokolov backed up his comrade. "It was definitely him." He turned towards the still seated Deborah saying, "No, you're lying, it was him."

She stood up from the armchair, ignored Sokolov and instead just said very calmly to Radischev, "Think about it, Ivan, think it through carefully, why would I do that, make up a lie like that? What would I have to gain by lying over that? The passport your guys stole did belong to the murdered man, so obviously his photo matched, but it was the wrong man. It wasn't the right Englishman you wanted from Prague in November 1989. The man you had killed was English, and had been to Prague a few times, but he was bullshitting about being in Prague in 1989. He'd done it a few times before in the village, and had even been caught out about it once by the very man you came here to kill, Tom Carpenter, not Tony Carpentar who you did kill. And by the way, Tom Carpenter told me that he never actually did what you blamed him for anyway in Prague in 1989. He never gave away your little KGB plot. In fact, he said the first he knew about it was afterwards, after the whole 'Velvet Revolution' period, from the outcome of the new Czechoslovak government enquiry." She was now standing with her back to the sliding glass doors to the room's patio as she spelt out strongly to the three Russians how they'd fucked up. What was actually going through her mind at that point though, was how the bloody hell was she now going to get out of there alive.

A slight look of doubt and confusion did now begin to creep slowly across Radischev's face as Deborah described his men's mistake. Before he could say anything she decided her best form of defence, and possibly her survival, was to attack and come clean about the real situation in which the Russians now found themselves. She calculated it was her only chance. After their aggressive exchange, especially over Dawn's murder, Radischev was never going to buy the idea now that she would go away with him.

"So, the right Englishman you wanted retribution on is actually here in Lindos, Ivan. As I said, I was talking to him an hour ago, and hearing all about you and Prague in 1989, and your grand KGB plot."

"What, where is he now, where is he staying?" Radischev asked.

She ignored his question and trying to appear as calm and cool as possible added, "He was telling me and the police all about it at my villa."

Radischev glanced over at Dobrovski and Sokolov as he replied, "The police?"

She hesitated, deliberately making him wait for her explanation as she turned to gaze out of the room's sliding glass doors to the patio and over at the rough scrub land alongside the hotel, with its roaming wild goats.. It was another technique learned from her MI6 days, designed to disorientate her opponents while they mentally speculated about her response.

After around a minute she turned to face him and said in as calculating and superior a manner as possible, "Yes, they are outside waiting for you in the car park, so there's no way now you can escape. I suggest you give me your weapons and walk out to meet them without any unpleasantness, Ivan. And before you think otherwise, I can assure you I am not lying to you."

"What the fuck! You've set us up." He was now literally right in her face as he spat out his angry words. The first instinct of his two comrades was to move towards the door, but Radischev stepped away from her and told them, "Wait; there's no point in rushing out there. Let's find out first just what they are expecting."

It was impossible to get any view whatsoever of the front of the hotel and the car park from immediately outside Radischev's room, or from the patio, so he told Sokolov to, "Go and check the front of the hotel, but for God's sake do it discreetly. We don't want them seeing you. Presumably they will not be out there in police cars."

"Ivan, you're on an island, just how the bloody hell do you think you are going to get away? I'm guessing that you don't have a boat handy, and there is only one airport, which the Greek police are certainly not going to let you get anywhere near are they? You'd be far better just giving yourselves up, before anyone else gets hurt." Trying to exude an air of calmness and confidence once more from her past training, and an impression of being in total control of the situation, Deborah Harris sat back down in one of the armchairs almost nonchalantly and took a sip of water.

"I assume you have the number in your mobile of the police officer in charge outside? Call him now," Radischev instructed as he walked across to stand over her in the armchair.

"To tell them that you're coming out to give yourself up?" she asked.

"You just call the officer in charge. Get him on the phone and I will talk to him."

"Inspector Karagoulis, that's his name," she informed him as she removed her phone from her handbag and tapped the number in her speed dial.

"Miss Harris, what is it?" Karagoulis answered still sat in the unmarked car in the hotel car park.

"Ivan Radischev wants to talk to you, Inspector."

"Okay, put him on."

"Inspector, we have a little confrontation here, I believe," Radischev began.

"Not really," Karagoulis told him. "You and your men just need to come out into the car park at the front of the hotel without any weapons, and then there will not be any further unpleasantness will there, Mr Radischev?"

"And then you will let us leave?" the Russian asked, pushing his luck.

"No, of course I can't do that, you and your men have committed two murders, of two members of the British community in Lindos. We can't just overlook that now can we? We will arrest you. Just come out now, without any weapons." Karagoulis knew full well that the Russian was stalling, playing games, so for now he was going along with him.

"The Russian government will not allow that, Inspector. You should be aware that I have very good old friends in high places, including President Putin himself, and they will claim that we have diplomatic immunity," Radischev said down the phone, with an authoritative tone in his voice, but the Karagoulis wasn't having that and wasn't going to be intimidated.

"Nice try, Mr Radischev, but I think even your friend President Putin will find it hard to help you on this, even if he wanted to, which I doubt. You, and your two comrades in there with you, murdered two British citizens, and I have a feeling President Putin will be very reluctant to get involved in an international incident with the British and Greek governments over some sort of revenge killings like this." Karagoulis replied just as forcibly. "There is no diplomatic immunity in this case. For a start, you definitely aren't diplomats. You know that, and I know that, don't you, and I think even President Putin and the Russian government will know that and think better of getting involved."

The phone went dead as Radischev rang off. Deborah Harris had sat calmly in the armchair sipping her water throughout the two men's phone conversation. From Radischev's comments and his angry reaction she assumed that Karagoulis hadn't bought his friends in high places and diplomatic immunity argument.

While their boss was having his phone conversation with Karagoulis Dobrovski and Sokolov stood leaning against the walls by the door to the room. As he ended the call Radischev turned to them and asked, "Whereabouts in the car park did you leave the car?"

"About ten metres to the left of the main gates in front of reception, sir" Sokolov answered.

"Right, call your friend the Inspector again now. I need to talk to him once more," Radischev told Deborah who was starting to look a little confused and somewhat concerned. She was thinking that surely Radischev was not contemplating a shoot-out in the hotel car park? That would be madness, and if nothing else, from her past liaison with him she knew he was a very calculating man who always weighed up every option very carefully.

While she waited briefly for Karagoulis to answer, Radischev walked quickly over to Sokolov and Dobrovski on the other side of the room and whispered something to them in Russian that she was unable to pick up.

As Karagoulis answered once again she handed up the phone from her seated position straight to Radischev, but instead of speaking into it immediately he covered the mouthpiece with his hand, turned away from her and nodded his head at his two comrades. Deborah could vaguely hear Karagoulis' increasingly agitated voice saying "Hello, hello, Deborah," through the phone covered by Radischev's hand when Dobrovski and Sokolov pounced on her in the chair, one from behind and one from the front, almost sitting on her. Even with her previous MI6 training, and even though she tried to struggle, she was powerless against the two well-built men as she was taken by surprise. While one of them held her arms the other wrapped silver coloured duct tape over her mouth and round the back of her head. From the front Dobrovski then quickly pulled her forward and pushed her hands behind her back, while the other man fastened them with a clear nylon plastic cable tie.

Her eyes were wide with alarm as she tried to figure out quickly just what her former lover could possibly have planned in him and his men's precarious, seemingly impossible, situation. She didn't have to wait long to find out.

"Inspector, I think you are forgetting that we have our own insurance for diplomatic immunity with us in here, Miss Harris," the Russian informed Karagoulis. "We intend to bring her out with us in a few minutes, and you and your men will allow us to get into our car with her and drive to the airport, where you will arrange for a plane to fly us to Moscow. If you or your men make any move at all to stop us, here or anywhere between here and the airport, or at the airport, you will have another British citizen's body on your hands. Do I make myself clear?"

There was a silence on the phone for thirty seconds, at which point Radischev said again, "Inspector, do I make myself clear?"

Karagoulis' brain was now racing, desperately trying to think of a way to extricate Deborah Harris alive from the very precarious life threatening situation in which he felt he had placed her. Given her previously admitted affair with Radischev almost twenty years before, the thought did very briefly cross his mind that what if she was, in fact, colluding with him and his two henchmen now in a scheme to get them all out of the country and back to Russia. Was she, indeed, the equivalent of the Cretan man?

He had to quickly dismiss that though as he reckoned he simply couldn't take the chance that she wasn't actually a genuine hostage. Stalling for time he told Radischev, "Okay, yes, but that will take a little while to arrange."

"No, Inspector," the Russian told him. "I will give you twenty minutes. That will be more than enough time, as it will take us thirty minutes or so in addition to that to get to the airport. Call me in twenty minutes on Miss Harris' phone or she will die." With that he hung up.

"So, you're going to be our little insurance policy, Elizabeth, our own little diplomatic immunity package. I'm sure from your experience you know how the game is played, my dear." Radischev taunted her reverting to her previous name and identity as he was busily throwing what few clothes and things he had with him into a bag, and gathering up some papers. Dobrovski and Sokolov had disappeared to the room next door to do the same and reappeared back in Radischev's room after ten minutes.

Deborah sat in the armchair gagged with the duct tape and hands fixed behind her back the whole time. In her mind she was frantically exploring possible options of escape, either in the room or later in the car park, but was rapidly coming to the conclusion that there weren't any.

Exactly on the twenty minutes her phone rang. Radischev picked it up from the low wooden table and answered with a curt, "Yes."

On the other end of the line Karagoulis told him, "It is all arranged. No one will stop you on the way to the airport. Myself and my officers here outside in a dark grey Nissan Primera car will follow you at a discrete distance to ensure that is what happens." The Inspector knew that really wasn't strictly necessary, but it was the only excuse he could come up with for following them while he tried to think of a plan to stop them eventually without putting Deborah Harris' life in danger. He hoped Radischev would buy it.

"Ok, but any tricks, or if you try and get too close in your car, and Miss Harris will die. When we come out I want to see all your officers out of your car with their hands clearly in view and placed on the roof of the car, palms down."

As Karagoulis told him a simple, "Ok," it appeared that Radischev had, indeed, bought it. The Russian immediately pulled Deborah to her feet and ripped off the duct tape from across her mouth, telling her, "Right, we are going for a little walk out in the Rhodes sunshine my dear. Don't try anything, Dobrovski is going to be right behind you with a gun in your back the whole time, and believe me, he will not hesitate to shoot you. He has a very good reason not to like British women ex-MI6 agents."

The three Russians and the English woman left the room straightaway and emerged into the sunlit hotel inner courtyard. It being the middle of a warm June afternoon most of the hotel guests were either by the swimming pool or on the hotel's small beach, so the courtyard was deserted. Sokolov was in the front carrying his small bag, with Dobrovski's rucksack slung over one of his large shoulders. Deborah was close-up behind him, with Dobrovski close behind her holding a gun firmly in the middle of her back with a cotton sweatshirt wrapped around it hiding it from sight. Radischev was at the very back carrying his small bag and briefcase.

They walked around the left side of the reception block and as they reached the hotel gates they could see Karagoulis, his Sargent, Papadoulis, and two other officers from Lindos stood by their car with their hands on the roof, as Radischev had instructed. Samaras though remained sat in his nearby parked borrowed taxi, assuming that the Russians wouldn't recognise him as a police officer in his taxi driver outfit. Despite the obviously tense situation Deborah managed to appear cool and calm, and managed at least to make eye contact with the Inspector, even though he and his men were at least twenty metres away. She gave a very slight, almost unnoticeable shrug of her shoulders and an equally slight shake of her head. Even that was noticed by Dobrovski though and he grabbed her left upper arm and rammed the gun barrel further into the small of her back, followed by an abrupt, "Nyet." That prompted Radischev to add,

"Don't be stupid, Deborah, just keep moving towards that black Jeep Cherokee to the left over there."

Karagoulis fixed his stare on the car, trying to take in every detail and noticing Deborah's hands tied behind her back as Dobrovski bundled the Englishwoman into one of the rear seats and Radischev got in beside her. Sokolov had got straight into the driver's seat and started the large car up with a roar on the accelerator as Dobrovski joined him in passenger seat in the front, still holding the gun, but now without its sweatshirt covering and in full view.

As Sokolov slammed the two-and-a-half litre Jeep Cherokee into reverse and swung it backwards out of the parking space with a with a loud reverse gear whine Karagoulis shouted to his officers, "Quick, get in the car," followed by a shout across to Samaras in the nearby commandeered taxi, "You stay here and check out their rooms."

The Cherokee roared up the bumpy road and towards the main Pefkos to Rhodes road. By the time they had all got in their car Karagoulis and his officers were around a hundred metres behind in their less powerful Nissan Primera. Although it clearly couldn't be a car chase given the hostage situation, the Russian's weren't hanging about. Their car was accelerating rapidly up the slight incline of the road when around halfway up Deborah shouted, "Watch out!" as one of the many stray wild goats so evident on the rough ground and scrubland by the hotel wandered aimlessly into the middle of the road. Sokolov wrenched the steering wheel to the right and the two wheels on the passenger side of the Jeep lurched off the road and on to the rough ground alongside it, hitting a couple of small rocks with accompanying bumps as he struggled to get it back on the road.

Deborah turned her head to look out of the rear window saying, "You clipped it. It's lying in the middle of the road."

"So fucking what, it's a goat," Dobrovski turned from his front seat and told her. "What do you expect us to do? Stop and put it out of its misery, like we did your friend Jacki perhaps? Maybe a knife in the throat would do it. Just like we did with her and she did with my brother? The fucking bitch!"

Deborah decided the best response was no response as she saw no point in angering him further. As he turned back to face the front of the car though his comrade, Sokolov, had his right foot hard down on the accelerator and the car was rapidly approaching the crossroad onto the main road to Rhodes, where around thirty metres to the left the Pefkos to Rhodes public bus was travelling at a somewhat more sedate speed. Sokolov had no intention of giving way however. Instead he hit the accelerator even harder and swung the vehicle out directly in front of the bus causing its driver to slam on the brakes and the bus to veer rapidly with a screech to the left across the road. Eventually the well-worn vehicle shuddered to a halt as the standing passengers in the packed overcrowded bus were all flung forward, many letting out screams of anguish. The black Jeep Cherokee had almost tipped over onto two wheels as Sokolov swung it around the junction corner onto the main road and then it lurched to the right and nearly once again onto the scrubland alongside the road before the Russian yanked the steering wheel to the left and the vehicle re-stabilised on a straight, if rapid, course on the correct side of the road. As the bus driver screamed abuse in Greek at the Russians in the Jeep Cherokee Sokolov hit the accelerator once more and the car sped off up the road.

Above the roar and the howl of the accelerating car's engine, and seeing the rough terrain alongside the road flashing past, Deborah tried once more to calm the situation down, saying, "Why are you in such a bloody hurry. You'll get us all fucking killed driving like that. You know they are not going to chase you. That was the deal wasn't it, Ivan?" She wanted to buy as much time as possible over their journey to Rhodes airport in the hope that Karagoulis would be able to come up with something to stop them and rescue her. The longer it took the better.

Radischev wasn't accepting that though, telling her, "I don't trust them. Why should I? The quicker we get to the airport and off this island the better."

Meanwhile, Papadoulis, driving Karagoulis' car, had been forced to slow down considerably at the end of the road from the hotel, and then carefully manoeuvre the Nissan Primera around the halted bus onto the main road. As their car cleared the bus Karagoulis told him, "Step on it, we don't want to lose sight of them."

The Inspector could feel the power of the car straining under them as Papadoulis carried out his order. Meanwhile he tried to rationalise his decisions. "We had no choice. We had to let them out of the hotel. There were too many people, guests, in there to risk a gunfight. With these bloody maniacs we could have had a real bloodbath on our hands. We have to figure out a way to stop them before they get to the airport though. The last thing we want is them at the airport with guns and desperate. In mid-afternoon it'll be full of tourists."

The Russian's car was just about in sight ahead as the policemen saw it approach the tricky bend by Lindos Reception, with its sharp curve and reverse camber. Sokolov ignored that though and just cut straight across the corner on the opposite side of the road without decreasing speed or having any possible view of what might be approaching down the hill on that side of the road.

"Jesus!" Papadoulis exclaimed. "Is he fucking crazy? They are lucky. He couldn't possibly have seen whether anything was coming around that bend. If he carries on driving like that, Inspector, we will not have to worry about them getting to the airport. He'll get them killed before they get there."

"Well, whatever happens we are not going to let them get there. I told Rhodes I want patrol cars out of sight at regular intervals between here and the airport, but that under no circumstances are they to approach them. Also, we've got three patrol cars and officers on the road three kilometres from the airport. If we can't think of any other way, if necessary that's where we'll stop them as a last resort."

As he swung the Nissan around the Lindos Reception bend Papadoulis responded to his Inspector's comments with, "And the plane they want, sir? What about that?"

"No way, Sargent, under no bloody circumstances are they getting a plane, and as I said, they aren't getting anywhere near the airport anyway."

The tyres of the Russian's Cherokee scorched across the hot sun-baked road as it raced past the Flora supermarket and the main Lindos car park, ignoring another 'Give way' sign and crossroad with the road coming up from the Main Square. As it streaked on up the hill Deborah Harris could see out of the car window to her right the stunning vista below over Lindos Bay, Pallas Beach and the picturesque village and wondered if she would ever see it again.

In pursuit, Papadopulis temporary slowed down at the crossroad before, seeing that it was clear, yanking the car's gear stick through the gears in order to attempt to accelerate once more up the hill on the top road above the village. Although the incline was relatively gentle and steady the hill was long and the Sargent was struggling to get the power out of the older and less powerful Nissan compared to the more powerful Russian's Jeep Cherokee. The clearly older Japanese car's engine was rumbling and howling in protest at its Greek driver as he slammed it down a gear in order to try to get more power of acceleration up the hill.

Consequently, the Russian's more powerful car was now beginning to disappear out of their sight towards the bend by the Amphitheatre Night Club at the top of the hill. Sokolov was lining up the Jeep so as to once again approach the bend in such a way as to cut across it and take it on the wrong side of the road.

Karagoulis shouted at his Sargent, "You're losing them. Put your-" But before he could finish, immediately after they saw the Russian's vehicle disappear from sight at speed around the corner, they heard a loud bang and a piercing, deafening screech reminiscent of a war cry from the Native Americans after whom the Russian's vehicle was named. As they approached the bend seconds later the picture that greeted them was one of a large Mythos Greek beer delivery lorry at right-angles right across the road and the Cherokee rolling over and over, bouncing like a pebble skimmed across the clear blue water of Lindos Bay below, and down the side of the hill into the rough scrubland below the night club.

Karagoulis and Papadoulis leapt out of their car and headed towards the top of the hillside and the Jeep below that had now come to a halt against some larger rocks, while one of the other officers called the emergency services and another went to check on the driver of the lorry. As the Inspector and his Sargent reached the top of the hillside though, the Cherokee burst into flames followed seconds later by an almighty explosion.

Papadoulis started to attempt to scramble down the side of the hill towards the burning Jeep until the Inspector stopped him, saying, "Stop, it's futile. No one will have survived that, Sargent. Stay here. Leave it to the emergency services. There have been enough people killed in Lindos over the past few days without adding a policeman to them for no reason."

Karagoulis was rubbing the back of his neck as he paced a few steps back and forth on the top of the hillside and said, "What a waste, what a bloody futile mess, and in such a wonderful place as this."

As he stopped and stared out over Lindos bay stretched below he added, "So, Sargent, it seems that what started in the magical central European cities of Prague and Vienna ends over a Rhodian cliff by a club named Amphitheatre, meaning in Greek, of course, a central space for the presentation of dramatic or sporting events. Ironic really, I suppose there is not much that is more dramatic than revenge, retribution and murder. Almost a Greek tragedy, given what Deborah Harris and Dawn Parsons, or whatever their real names were, did in their past lives, perhaps they both knew it was always bound to end this way."

"Yes, sir, maybe that's true," Papadoulis agreed, "although I guess Samaras will be relieved, and the bar, restaurant and café owners down there even more so."

As he said it he extended his arm to point to the white village below.

"Yes, despite all the rumours and gossip about affairs and infidelity, which still may or may not be true, Sargent, in the end the little picturesque paradise village of Lindos at least doesn't have any killers living in it," Karagoulis replied, accompanied by a shrug and a wry smile

Printed in Great Britain
by Amazon